GALACTIC KEEGAN

GALACTIC KEEGAN

SCOTT INNES

unbound

First published in 2020

Unbound
6th Floor Mutual House, 70 Conduit Street, London W1S 2GF
www.unbound.com
All rights reserved

Comet illustration © Dan Mogford
Customised images by Mecob from iStockphoto.com and Shutterstock.com

Text design by PDQ Digital Media Solutions Ltd.

A CIP record for this book is available from the British Library

ISBN 978-1-78352-651-2 (paperback)
ISBN 978-1-78352-776-2 (ebook)

Printed and bound in Great Britain by Clays Ltd, Elcograf S.p.A.

1 3 5 7 9 8 6 4 2

For KB, who made it happen
and
for Laura, always.

PROLOGUE

The more things change, the more they stay the same.

I forget who said that – possibly Bryan Robson. I'd ask him, but last I heard he was rounded up and forced to perform hard labour in the phlebonium mines on Gralka IV. He'll be disappointed with that.

But either way, it's true. You go through a great deal in your life and in my seven or so decades I've maybe seen more than most. Some things I'll treasure: my Liverpool days, my time in Germany, taking over at Newcastle. But then there are the things I'd sooner forget: that header at the '82 World Cup, falling off that bloody bike on *Superstars*, giving Paul Ince my phone number (seriously, there are only so many times you can tolerate receiving a breathy phone call at three in the morning as Incey says, 'Gaffer – it's happened again.'). And, of course, the lowest of the low: 1995–96.

Everyone likes to harp on about how my Newcastle lads threw away the league title that season, chucked a twelve-point lead in the bin and allowed Man United to pip us on the final day. But the thing that I've always said – and I absolutely stand by this today – is that if the league season had finished in January rather than May, we'd have won the title. And that's what makes it such a bitter pill to swallow.

But whichever way you look at it, 1995–96 was a gut-punch. I really thought we were going to do it. We had Pete Beardsley and Les Ferdinand up top and Daz Peacock and Warren Barton at the back – and if you think you can name any other defensive pairing with more luxuriant hair than those two then frankly you're lying. And yet it wasn't enough. My one tiny consolation at that time was that I was convinced I'd never be able to feel any worse. I had hit rock bottom and Sir Al Ferguson was riding high. But the more things change the more they stay the same. Now it's not Sir Al Ferguson that I'm up against.

It's the bloody L'zuhl.

Adapting to life on a new planet is a lot like taking the reins at a new club – you don't know your way around, you can't remember anybody's name and you worry constantly about being vaporised by an aggressive alien race. Well, maybe not that last one.

Life on Palangonia hasn't been easy, even a year down the line. When the L'zuhl invaded Earth and laid waste to everything mankind had built over however many thousands of years, I was already gone. Say what you like about politicians, but they had a plan and you have to give credit where it's due. The Alliance Assembly (the big conference of galactic bigwigs) had been fighting the L'zuhl war for generations while we on Earth were blissfully unaware – until the L'zuhl fleet was pretty much on our doorstep. The Assembly helped us to evacuate as much of Earth's population as possible to various distant planets with the intention that we could regroup and then join them in the fight against the L'zuhl – we weren't the first or the last planet to get that kind of treatment. Others sadly fell to the L'zuhl before the Alliance could step in. We were the lucky ones, I guess. Depending on your point of view.

The human Compound here on Palangonia is in many ways like a massive great prison – thick stone walls, machine-gun turrets, a heavy law-enforcement presence. But at the same time it has a library, a cinema and three Costa Coffee shops, so I shouldn't knock it too much. Over six thousand people are housed within the walls and, aside from their occasional attacks on the Compound gates with their spears and their bows and arrows, as well as their repeated claims that we've annexed their sacred land and defiled their heritage, the native Palangonian tribespeople have welcomed us with open arms.

But of course, the best thing about the Compound is also the very reason I'm here. My football club: Palangonia FC – the beating heart of the community. Sure, it's a small operation at the moment, but listen, you've got to start somewhere. And yes, okay, there are some people who believe that funding a football team during a time of galactic war is an appalling frivolity – I won't name names, that's not my style, but General Leigh is one of them. The way I look at it is this: if not for the beautiful game – the unparalleled glory of a last-minute winner, the jaw-dropping splendour of an overhead kick, the agonising outstretched arm of the goalie keeping a well-struck penalty at bay – then what the bloody hell are we even fighting for? How can the displaced people of Earth (the ones who drew the short straw and ended up out here at the rotten arse-end of space, anyway) possibly hope to keep that stiff upper lip in place without the prospect of going to the match on a Saturday afternoon and watching my boys take on a side from a neighbouring nebula? That's why Palangonia FC is here. That's why Kevin Keegan is here. That's why it matters.

It's really all we have left.

PALANGONIA FC

I closed the door to the dressing room, the distant hum of the crowd extinguished with the click of the latch. I stared straight down, puffed out my cheeks and shook my head in dismay.

'Just not good enough, is it?' I said to my shoes. 'Not good enough at all. You've bottled that. You've disappointed me today, boys.'

There were a few awkward coughs and the clacking of boot studs on the floor. I sized up my players in turn, each of them looking anywhere but in my direction (except for Little Dunc, my left-back, though he's severely cross-eyed so it's hard to tell either way). My midfield general, Wiggins, looked terribly out of shape and was blowing out of his arse, to be quite frank. I made a mental note to forbid him from going back for seconds during the next pre-match roast dinner. Gribble, central defender of giraffe-like proportions, was staring sullenly at his boots. My holding midfielder, Aidy Pain, a thorn in my side who stubbornly refused to ever do a damn thing I told him, had let us down badly after I shouted to him to keep the energy up midway through the second half – he had promptly sat down in the centre circle for a rest. It had been a shameful showing – from all of them. They weren't fit to wear the shirt (Wiggins, quite literally).

'We should have had the beating of that shower today,' I huffed. 'This Piscean side are punching well above their weight in this division and yet you let them walk over you and take away all three points. It's disgraceful, actually.'

'Ah, now, Kev, let's be fair,' said a voice beside me. 'The ref gave them the rub of the green.'

I turned to look at my assistant, eyebrows raised in surprise at his interjection. For me, Gerry Francis is one in a million. No, let me dial that back a bit – one in a hundred, let's say. A solid pair of hands. The funny thing is, although we got along fine and occasionally saw one another socially, Gerry and I never worked together at all back on Earth in the years before the L'zuhl invasion. He just so happened to be on the same evacuation shuttle as me when Earth went all to buggery and it's always nice to see a familiar face. It's actually quite a heart-warming story, if you look past the genocidal context.

'Don't forget that handball they got away with at 0–0,' Gerry went on. 'The fourth official told me the ref couldn't give it on account of the Pisceans having flippers rather than hands. That old chestnut.'

There were a few murmurs of assent from the squad.

'Okay, fine,' I conceded the point. 'But what about you, Gilly? You were clean through on goal in that second half and you produced the most timid shot I've ever seen in my life. The keeper didn't even bother to catch it, he just leathered the shot right up the other end of the pitch!'

'But, gaffer,' Andy Gill said nervously, 'I play right-back. That wasn't a shot, it was a passback to our own keeper in our own box and then he cleared it upfield.'

'Aye, well,' I muttered, feeling some of the wind retreating from my sails. Gilly was a top-class player, no question, but the trouble was he knew it. I'd signed him on a tip-off from Glenn Hoddle, who'd seen him play for the team from the human colony on Flaxxu, a desert planet a couple of star systems over. Glenn had spent most of that day telling me about 'Christian Values' but when I couldn't find any player on the Cross-Galaxy Database with that name, Andy Gill proved a decent second choice. And yet, here he was undermining my authority with, to be fair, a well-argued rebuttal.

'The point is,' I went on, determined not to let them off the hook, 'we're disappointing our fans week after week. There were almost thirty-seven people out there tonight and every one of them is going home disappointed.' I sighed despondently and ran a hand through my hair. 'Go on, get ready for your warm-down. I've said my bit. Think on.'

Wordlessly, my players began to peel off their kit, the smell of sweat, grass and that sticky translucent substance that coats the scales of the Piscean players leaving a sharp tang in the air. As the boys began to file out to the showers, I caught sight of Rodway, my star striker. He was yawning like it was going out of fashion, and in that moment my patience with him reached an end.

'Everything okay, gaffer?' he asked brightly on catching my eye. He had one foot out of the changing room door before I yanked him back in by the elbow.

'Don't "everything okay" me, son,' I replied sternly. 'Your performance today was abysmal. You've been out all night at bloody Misogynate again, haven't you?'

He looked sheepish, though not particularly contrite.

'I have, yeah,' he said.

'Don't lie to me,' I said.

'I didn't,' he replied, baffled.

'Oh...' I said. To be honest, I'd expected him to put up a bit more of a fight. 'There's nothing between your ears at all, is there? Kid, I thought we had an understanding.'

'I'm sorry, gaffer,' he mumbled, still not sounding all that sorry. 'It probably won't happen again.'

'You said that last time,' I reprimanded him. 'I just don't get it – you've got everything going for you, the most talented footballer in the Compound, maybe even in this nebula, and yet you spend your nights on the razz in some seedy strip club. Which is especially galling given that the Compound library is right next door.'

'You should give it a try some time,' Gerry chipped in. 'Expand your horizons. There are some cracking books in there.'

This was a bit of a stretch. I borrowed this one book, *Twenty Thousand Leagues Under The Sea* – what rubbish! I've been involved in the game my entire life and I know for a fact that you can't play football under water, let alone implement any kind of league structure. Let's get serious, please.

'I promise it won't affect me on Saturday when we play Groiku IV,' Rodway said. 'I'll be raring to go.'

'No, you won't,' I said. 'I'm putting you on the bench. Now be on your way and think about what you've done. You're on thin bloody ice, son.'

Rodway looked stunned but said nothing as he clomped off down the tunnel.

'Crikey, Kev,' Gerry said after a moment of tense silence. 'Bit harsh on the lad, weren't you?'

It's true that I can be a bit of a disciplinarian as a manager. Back at Fulham, I regularly had the lads in for training *three* times a week. Even so, I know I'm prone to being a little sensitive whenever any manager's methods are questioned. I remember back in '76 I invited John Lennon to come and watch a Liverpool match – after our hard-fought victory I asked him what he thought of the gaffer's game plan and he just said, 'Imagine no possession.' I mean, just woefully naïve tactics. Embarrassing, actually.

'No, I don't think I was harsh at all,' I sniffed defiantly to Gerry. 'Rodway has had it coming for a while – no player is bigger than the team. And I've always believed in tough love. Anyway, let's go. The sooner they finish their warm-down, the sooner I can take them over for pizza and ice cream.'

I watched as Gerry jogged around the John Rudge Memorial Stadium pitch with the lads at the end of the warm-down session. The stadium had been named in honour of the former Port Vale stalwart, who had been the Compound Council's first choice for manager once the settlement on Palangonia had been built. Sadly, poor John was reported killed during the L'zuhl invasion of Earth, and once I got the job I insisted on honouring his memory, one of so many lives we lost during that terrible episode and a fitting tribute to the great man. It later transpired that John was in fact alive and well and coaching an amateur side over on Pesquikta, a planet a couple of thousand light years away, but by then we'd already paid for the steel lettering above the stadium entrance so the name stuck.

I was lost in my thoughts – the match against Groiku IV was a big one; they were one of the real up-and-comers in Galactic League C. I still found it offensive that any human side should have to start off in the third division – we invented football, for heaven's sake! We should have gone straight into the top flight. But nope, apparently alien communities can observe the beautiful game – unquestionably mankind's greatest achievement – through long-distance super-powered telescopes and learn to play it for themselves and that's enough to give them a higher ranking than us. I wrote to the top brass to complain but their reply came back in Besakrtapollian, which is a language I don't speak and have no intention of learning. Probably just an attempt to intimidate me – everyone in the Compound knows that humans are a complete laughing stock within the Alliance because of how timidly we surrendered Earth to the L'zuhl.

I reflected on what Gerry had said. Had I been too harsh on Rodway? He was only twenty-two after all. But then, that was exactly my point – he had a glorious career in football ahead of him but only with the right guidance. I was forever exasperated back in the day by reports of my lads going out on the town and making prats of themselves – I just didn't understand and I still don't. Why would you want to go and get drunk when there are any number of National Trust properties you can visit? At every club I managed, that was always something I arranged on day one: annual passes for every player. It's the gift that keeps on giving.

Gerry has always been more of an arm-round-the-shoulder kind of coach. In many ways, Gerry and I are like John and Paul – two different styles, but together, it just works. Actually, that's a bit strong. He's probably more of a Ringo. I suppose I could compromise and say he was a George but that would be a monumental slap in the face for the actual George.

As the lads filed past me to go and get changed before we headed to Giuseppe's, I approached Gerry, who was trying to explain something to Andy Gill.

'It's all in the arms,' Gerry said. 'You can't just kick it into play like you did during the match today – that's why it's called a "throw-in". Don't worry, you'll get there.'

'But, Gerry, I wasn't taking a throw-in, it was a free kick,' Andy insisted, slightly impatiently.

'Well, we'll have to agree to differ on that,' Gerry said, shoving his hands into his pockets.

'Gerry,' I interrupted. 'Is Gillian in her office?'

His face darkened a little.

'I haven't seen her,' he replied. 'She's been to several meetings of the Compound Council this week so I guess she's been preoccupied.'

I snorted derisively.

'Nice to know where her priorities lie, then,' I said. 'The club's going to pot while she's arsing about in meetings. Honestly, she's the worst chair this club has ever had.'

'Though I suppose she's the only chair this club has ever had,' Gerry replied.

'Which just proves my point,' I agreed. 'I need to speak to her about signing a new striker. I won't give up on Rodway, but the kid's on the road to death and destruction so we need a plan B.'

'Good call,' said Gerry. 'I'll take the lads over to Giuseppe's. See you there after?'

'Wouldn't miss it,' I replied and hurried down the tunnel to take the elevator up to the sixth floor and Gillian's office.

Little did I know that what would happen next would put the very future of Palangonia FC in jeopardy – and change the course of all our lives.

LOGGERHEADS

I've always liked Gillian's office – I find the wood panelling on the walls oddly reassuring. My own office is a more muted affair. I've just got a desk in the corner and a filing cabinet which I've never used. It's full of blank printer paper. Gerry suggested I set up a filing system of transfer targets, scout reports of opposition teams and tactical formations, but I don't need all that stuff, never have. It's all up here, committed to memory. At the end of the day, how hard is it to remember 4-4-2? My only decoration is the calendar Ray Stubbs sent me at Christmas. Every month features a different photo of Ray pointing wistfully at a distant mountain range, apart from July, which features a watercolour painting by Ray of former Premier League referee Uriah Rennie. (Listen, the lad's clearly in a bad place. Good luck to him.)

'Gillian?' I said, knocking and walking in. 'Have you got a sec?'

Gillian is about forty or so – maybe younger. Or maybe older. I've never been good at placing people; I remember I once bought Warren Barton a Happy 30th Birthday card and he said, 'No, I'm actually twenty-nine.' I've never felt so embarrassed! But having said that, Gillian has none of Warren's flair and she'd be the first to admit that. She was appointed chair of the academy by the Compound Council and soon set about putting her own stamp on things and cutting corners financially. Within weeks she'd axed my weekly trip to Flix, the Compound cinema, where I'd take the lads to unwind after a gruelling thirty-minute training session. Other essentials were quickly trimmed away too: Alfonso, the club baker, was shown the door (no more pre-training eclairs, which makes you wonder why you even bother really), my pot of money for necessities like training cones or a bottle of Brut for the man of the match went out of the window, and my Friday night 'Kev & Pals' music extravaganza, in which I and a special musical guest would regale the lads with a performance of a different classic album each month, was actually cancelled mid-show one week when Gillian got up on stage and literally pulled the plug, saying it was 'an appalling misuse of Compound funds'. You should have seen the look Jimmy Nail gave her. In her year as chair, Gillian had systematically eroded everything that made my football club tick – little wonder it was all now going to seed.

As I came in she looked up from her desk, and although she tried to hide it, I spotted the look of tired disdain in her eyes when she saw that it was me. I'd had that same look on my own face countless times when Graeme Le Saux used to come in to see me to complain yet again about the lack of recycling facilities at England's training complex.

'Yes, Kevin,' she sighed, leaning back in her chair. 'What's on your mind?'

I'm not having a pop, that's not my style, but Gillian simply doesn't understand football. She doesn't know a 4-4-2 from a... well, whatever other formations there are. And listen, that's not a sexist thing – I know plenty of blokes who are just as clueless about the game. Steven Taylor, for one – you'd give him simple instructions and his eyes would just glaze over. Mind you, I'm one to talk. I hadn't even heard of the offside rule until 1999. At the end of the day, Gillian's a bureaucrat, a cynical pencil-pusher whose only consideration is about the numbers, the bottom line, the ingoings and outgoings. She doesn't understand that what really matters at a football club is the graft, the passion, putting the ball in the net, the catering facilities. I knew that prising a few quid out of the coffers for a new striker was going to be a big ask, so I decided to play it cool and blindside her.

'Nice sunny day outside,' I said casually.

'Yes, I suppose so,' she agreed.

'Can I have a new striker?'

'No,' she replied wearily. 'We've been through this before, Kevin; we simply can't afford to spend money on player recruitment right now. The budget is stretched thin as it is, you know that.'

'We're getting killed in the league,' I protested. 'We're wallowing in the bottom half of the table.'

'We've only played one match; most other teams haven't played their opening fixture yet,' Gillian argued. I rolled my eyes.

'Yes, but on alphabetical order, Palangonia FC are right down in the doldrums,' I said. Once again Gillian had displayed her woeful lack of knowledge.

'Look, I'm sorry, but it's absolutely out of the question,' she went on. 'I was at a meeting of the Compound Council just last night and General Leigh was making a big stink again about how much money is already set aside for this football club. There's a war on, Kevin – a big one – and it's not going to end any time soon. You know the L'zuhl are making great advances across the galaxy.'

'No, I don't.'

'How can you not know?' Gillian asked patronisingly. 'It's been all over the news – they annihilated the horse-mutants of Teplok in a raid just yesterday. They're really upping the ante. We have to be prepared for the possibility that they'll strike Palangonia next. If they find out about our military presence here... It's no secret that the L'zuhl were furious to discover that some of us managed to escape during the invasion of Earth. It made them look weak and that is one thing they are most certainly not, and if they begin to see our small outpost here as a threat then they will not hesitate. Mankind is high on their list of targets.'

'And a new striker is high on mine,' I argued. 'Anyway, if the bloody L'zuhl come down here and see how half-arsed an operation this football club is, how's that going to make us look? If we're going to win this war, we need a team that's competing for promotion to Galactic League B. That's basic.'

'I sometimes wonder what planet you're on,' Gillian said quietly, shaking her head.

'Palangonia,' I replied defiantly. 'You know, the one with the football club that has no firepower up top.'

'You've got Rodway,' Gillian said. 'He scored hatfuls for us last season. There's no reason he can't do the same again.'

'The kid's cracked,' I snapped irritably. 'Out until all hours, drinking himself silly and then going to seedy clubs. Probably snorting weed too. He's a liability. I can't have it affecting the other lads.'

'I'm sorry, Kevin, that's my final word,' she said, putting her glasses on and looking at her computer screen, which was her way of saying that she wanted me to leave. (Also, she then said aloud that she wanted me to leave.)

'Fine,' I grumbled. 'But remember this conversation when we get our arses handed to us on Saturday. You need to wake up, Gillian – the real war is out there, on the pitch, eleven against eleven. Everything else is window dressing.'

'Oh, and Kevin?' Gillian said as I stood up to leave. 'Have you considered switching to three at the back, perhaps utilising Rooker and Nightingale as attacking wing-backs supporting Rodway and Alex Booth up front? Or perhaps even a move to one striker and drop Rodway into the hole as a creative playmaker? Just something to think about, anyway.'

'Aye, well,' I shrugged. I didn't need strategic advice from anyone, thank you very much. (Though I made a mental note to adopt pretty much everything Gillian had just suggested.)

'Take Barrington12 with you,' Gillian said as I opened the door. 'Maintenance have discharged him; they couldn't see a problem but reckon it may have been a clogged oil filter that caused him to keep saying… what he kept saying.'

I sighed – that was insult to injury. It was bad enough having to marshal a skeleton crew of a squad without having to deal with a walking, talking tin can as part of my coaching setup. I asked them for Sammy Lee and they sent me Barrington12. It just summed everything up.

'HELLO, KEVIN KEEGAN,' he said in his foghorn, mono-tone voice as I stepped into the corridor outside Gillian's office. The robot staggering uncertainly towards me was the absolute bane of my life – a clattering, clanking, insufferable relic that had been ready for the knacker's yard for decades. Now he looked up to me like a father, though he also looked down at me from his height of around eight feet. His limbs were gangly and thin, his legs little more than coils of wire around metal bars that looked like leftovers from a Meccano set. His bulky mid-section was like a household boiler and his head was an upturned metal bucket with an approximation of a face, two small blue dots for eyes and a thin, unmoving slit for his mouth.

'Back so soon?' I asked miserably.

'YES, I AM BACK,' he replied amiably. 'I WAS SUFFERING FROM A CLOGGED OIL FILTER, A COMMON COMPLAINT ASSOCIATED WITH THIS BARRINGTON MODEL. THIS BLOCKAGE HAS BEEN REMOVED SO I WILL NOW FUNCTION AT NORMAL CAPACITY.'

'No more of your filthy talk, then?' I asked, eyebrows raised. In the week or so before he was finally shipped over to maintenance, Barrington12 had been acting peculiarly, ending every sentence, irrespective of the subject matter or the person to whom he was speaking, with the phrase 'I'D LIKE TO ALSO REMIND YOU THAT I AM FREE OF ERECTILE DYSFUNCTION.' It got rather wearying after a while but Gillian didn't seem minded to approve the cost of a once-over from maintenance – not until we had that class of youngsters from the Compound school over for a sports day. I haven't had to apologise so profusely on someone else's behalf since I had dinner in that posh restaurant with Al Hansen and he ordered 'a dry white wine'. I had to hurry after the waiter and say, 'I'm so sorry about that – he means "wet".'

'ALL SUCH PHRASES HAVE NOW BEEN ERADICATED FROM MY VOCABULARY,' Barrington12 reassured me.

'Well, let's hope so,' I said haughtily. 'Come on, let's get down to Giuseppe's. We've probably missed pizza now, but we should make it in time for ice cream.'

Gillian's office door opened and she poked her head out.

'Oh, good, you're still here,' she said. 'I meant to say – the thrice-weekly pizza and ice cream trips have also been cut from the budget.'

KEEP CLEAR
WINGED TERRORS

PIZZA AND ICE CREAM

With the loud buzzing of Barrington12's mechanised legs clattering along behind me, I headed out of the John Rudge Memorial Stadium through the wrought-iron gates and down the paved streets towards the bustling Compound Square, the hub of the human Palangonian community. Given that it'd been barely more than a year since humans had arrived here, it was difficult not to just stop and marvel at all that had been achieved in so small a timeframe.

At the entrance to the square was the imposing Council building. Gillian had one of the five seats on the Council, from where she could undermine me at every turn, as did that oaf, General Leigh. I realise that supposedly there's a war on but the amount of sway the General holds over Compound life is outrageous. Next door to the Council building was a large Tesco and adjacent was Flix, the cinema. There were dozens of restaurants, a library, a leisure centre, a car park (bit of a misjudgement, that – with the exception of the little buggies that big cheeses like Leigh use to ferry themselves about, there are no cars in the Compound), the infirmary and a big TV studio. It was like being back on Earth, except for the twin

20

suns burning in the sky and the frequent sirens going off to warn of an impending attack by Winged Terrors, flying ape-like beasts that swooped over the walls, picking off anyone unfortunate enough to be out in the open. I'd lost three good full-backs to them (well, two good ones and one who worked hard but, with respect, was never going to make the grade).

'Keep up, son,' I scolded Barrington12 as he slowed to stare into the window of the library.

'SORRY, KEVIN KEEGAN,' he replied with a strangely wistful air. 'I JUST LOVE KNOWLEDGE.'

'No harm in that,' I told him, 'but you're a Barrington model – you already have everything there is to know about everything stored in your data banks. You'd never know it to look at you, but you're probably the smartest guy in this Compound. You won't learn anything new in the library.'

'ALL LIFE IS THERE,' he replied sadly.

A robot in the midst of an existential crisis. Just what I bloody needed.

'Come on,' I said, 'we need to stop Gerry going mad with the ice cream; I'm not made of money. If he's given them double scoops, I'm going to absolutely kick off.'

As we hurried towards Giuseppe's, the pleasant Italian restaurant beside the post office, a low rumbling sound could be heard.

'PLEASE BE AWARE – I DETECT A SIZEABLE VEHICLE HEADING IN THIS DIRECTION.'

'A what? There's nothing like that here; the Compound's pedestrianised,' I said. 'Are you quite sure they cleaned all the gunk out of your system?'

'BARRINGTON12 ADVISES IMMEDIATE REMOVAL OF OUR PERSONS FROM THE CENTRE OF THE PATH,' he went on. 'OR IMMINENT DEATH IS PREDICTED WITH AN 83% CHANCE.'

The rumbling got louder and I couldn't deny that it sounded like the engine of a large vehicle. We hurried over to huddle in the doorway of Flix as other Compound residents also scattered, looking equally confused as to what was happening.

I watched in dismay as it came round the corner – a large, black hulking mass on six wheels, each one taller than I was. A member of the Compound Guard was behind the wheel, eyes obscured by his intimidating black visor, and I had no doubt there were other guards packed into the back of the tank-like monstrosity. On the roof was mounted an enormous machine gun with another visored figure sitting behind it, his thick-gloved hands resting keenly by the trigger. I'd heard of the Harbingers before but had never seen one of the behemoths up close – they were the most disturbing sight I had ever seen (and I once rode a tandem bike with Arsène Wenger sitting in front of me while his shorts snagged under the seat and got pulled all the way down). In a small jeep following behind sat the members of the Compound Council, no doubt being provided with a demonstration by Leigh, their fellow Council member, of precisely how their finances were being spent. Bloody show-off. The jeep passed quickly, a glass-eyed guard behind the wheel, but I glimpsed them all huddled in the back, some deep in conversation – miserable Doreen McNab from the education board; Sir Michael Bowes-Davies, the eccentric philanthropist; Dr Andre Pebble-Mill, the Compound chief of medicine; and then Gillian herself, gazing forlornly out of the window – they must have picked her up very shortly after I left her office.

'That's… not good,' I said in a quiet voice as the Harbinger rumbled past. I glanced up and there in the passenger seat on the near side to us, wearing a guard uniform decorated with medals but sans helmet, was the man himself – General Lawrence Leigh, head of the Compound military. He looked deep in thought, a grave expression on his craggy grey face. Our eyes met briefly and I could feel his disdain burning right into me. I gave as good as I got – I'm not scared of that arsehole. If he thinks I'm going to be intimidated by someone driving around with a machine gun attached to his vehicle then he hasn't seen me deal with Steve McManaman after he's swigged nine bottles of Sunny Delight and customised his Mercedes. I'm no pushover.

Moments later the vehicle was beyond us, turning a corner and vanishing from sight.

'THAT WAS UNUSUAL,' said Barrington12. 'SUCH A DISPLAY OF MILITARY MANOEUVRES IS HIGHLY PECULIAR OUTSIDE OF THE EMMELINE MILITARY BASE AT THE NORTH END OF THE COMPOUND.'

'Yes, thanks, I'm aware of that,' I muttered. 'I'm sure it's just General Leigh trying to look like the big I-am. Showing off to the ladies, trying to look like a tough nut. You know how vain he is.'

We hurried on, and the square quickly reverted to its normal bustle as though a terrible war machine had not just roared directly through our midst. I didn't believe a word of what I'd just said, of course. Something was very, very wrong.

*

'There you are!' Gerry greeted me as we hurried into Giuseppe's. My heart sank as I saw Rodway at the table in the corner, tucking into a double-scoop butterscotch sundae. I was too late.

'Sorry,' I said as Gerry shook my hand eagerly like we hadn't just seen each other barely an hour ago. 'Got held up.'

'Did you hear that thunderstorm just now?' Gerry asked. 'Big old rumble right outside here.'

'Yeah,' I replied quietly. 'Seems to have passed now.'

No point in worrying him unnecessarily. Gerry was prone to overreacting – he refused to shop at HMV for years back on Earth in protest at their decision not to shelve *Grease* in the sci-fi section. 'The bloody car flies off at the end, are you blind?' he'd shouted in vain at the young lad behind the till as security ejected him from the premises.

'Anyway, I've ordered you the Enormo-Bloat,' Gerry said proudly. 'Twenty-seven scoops of ice cream with fudge pieces, flakes, strawberries, whipped cream and gherkins. Obviously you can just peel the gherkins off. Everyone does.'

'Oh, bloody hell,' I replied. 'How much is that?'

'Kev, don't worry – the club'll cover it.'

'No, they won't!' I said, exasperated. 'Gillian's cut our funding again. She's killing this club, Gerry. Do you know she turned down my request for a jukebox filled with Motown classics for the dressing room last week? She said it had nothing to do with the game of football. What a slap in the face for Marvin Gaye.'

'Outrageous,' Gerry agreed. 'Everyone knows that *Let's Get It On* is about a referee deciding that a match can go ahead after a pitch inspection. Y'know, Kev, I hate to say this, but... do you think we ought to maybe look elsewhere? I heard that Dave

Moyes is on the verge of the chop from that swamp planet in the Fifka System. Who knows, it might be just the fresh start we need.'

I had to admit, it was tempting. Life at Palangonia FC was slowly but surely falling apart around me. A threadbare squad, inadequate training facilities – I'd even heard Gillian remark in passing at last year's end-of-season party when I did a DJ set consisting of *Rumours* played back to back six times that she preferred early Fleetwood Mac to the Buckingham-Nicks era. I mean, what kind of madness had I involved myself with?

But as all of these thoughts zipped around my mind right there in Giuseppe's, I looked over at the faces of my lads as they innocently stuffed their faces with ice cream and realised there was simply no way I could walk. I'd come to Palangonia with the sole aim of building a club that could compete (as well as to escape the L'zuhl genocide on Earth, obviously) and I couldn't just bail out because the top brass didn't appreciate my maverick ways. These kids relied on King Kev.

'Giuseppe,' I said, a steely note to my voice, 'I'll take the Enormo-Bloat. And please make it payable to Gillian Routledge at Palangonia FC.'

THE IRRESISTIBLE
FORCE

As predicted, the second match of the Galactic League C season against Groiku IV was a disaster of, well, disastrous proportions. With barely enough fit players to field a team, I was left with just young Booth up front on his own – the very idea of playing with only one striker made me feel physically ill but I had no choice. Or at least none that I was prepared to make.

Gerry was vehemently against my decision to leave young Rodway on the bench. The kid was itching to play and had been on his best behaviour in the few days since his dressing down, but listen, people need to understand that actions have consequences. Like the time I sent Joey Barton home from training when he wore a baseball cap that read F**K THE POLICE. I was disgusted. I said to him, 'Sting is Newcastle's favourite son – he deserves better.'

'Kev, our goose is cooked without Rodway up top,' Gerry said when I handed him the team sheet before kickoff. 'He's our star man. We need him.'

'I can't believe you have so little faith in our squad,' I scolded him. 'Little Dunc has come on leaps and bounds in pre-season.

He lobbed the keeper from the halfway line in that practice match last week. That takes a special kind of quality.'

'Yeah, but that was an own goal,' Gerry said doubtfully. 'He was aiming the other way and scuffed it.'

'Look, you can't get bogged down in details,' I insisted. 'We're going with Alex Booth up front, Tilston as an advanced playmaker behind him.'

'Tilston? He's the goalkeeper, Kev.'

'I know, but I want to play a high pressing game against this lot – he's wasted back there in his own box.'

An emphatic 6–0 defeat later and Gerry gave me just the faintest 'I told you so' look as our lads trudged off the pitch dejectedly. The boys from Groiku IV were a good side; their crusty red skin made them fairly impervious to most of our attempts to tackle them – in fact Wiggins, our midfield general, knackered his own knee going in for a crunching tackle on their number nine.

Still, despite everything, I didn't feel too downhearted. No one enjoys a defeat (least of all John Gregory, who once lost a game of Connect 4 to me in the green room before we appeared on *Football Focus* in 2003 and hasn't spoken to me since) but I saw this capitulation as simply a means to an end. Gillian was up there in the stands and she'd have seen just how little I had to work with. And with a record crowd of over forty-one people in attendance, she'd be feeling the pressure even more. In a strange way, this defeat was going to turn into a victory in the long run. I just had to wait for Gillian to call me up to her office – which, an hour or so after the match, she did.

'Shall I come too, Kev?' Gerry asked as he put the boys

through a warm-down after the match. 'Moral support and all that.'

'I'm sure it's fine,' I assured him. 'I can fight my own battles, you know.'

And that was true – like when that Hollywood studio tried to make that film based on my life back in 2003. I was told it was going to be a straight biopic job, my life story from A to B to C and then however the rest of the alphabet goes. I'd insisted ahead of time on being given script approval and input on casting – Jack Lemmon to play me was a deal-breaker, but they kept fobbing me off with 'he looks nothing like you' and 'he died two years ago', and so in the end I had no choice but to pull the plug. Their loss.

Anyway, I made my way up to Gillian's office once again, trying hard to disguise the spring in my step. We certainly hadn't thrown the match – I would never do that – but I'd known going in that we'd more likely than not end up taking an absolute battering. Now the ball was in Gillian's court. Cough up or watch the football club slowly drip away down the plughole.

'There you are,' Gillian said as I came in. I hurriedly wiped the expectant smile off my face as I entered – it was crucial that I look depressed. I tried to focus on sad memories to contain my exuberant mood, like the death of my childhood hamster, or the time Rob Lee told me that he didn't like *Auf Wiedersehen, Pet*.

'Hiya,' I said in a solemn voice. 'I assume you saw what just happened out there. Now, I want to say, we did our best but at the end of the day—'

'Close the door, please,' Gillian said ominously. Slightly perturbed, I did so and took a seat opposite her desk. She looked quite pale. It had been a dismal performance, sure, but she seemed to have taken it quite badly. Well, so much the better. I reached over her desk and extended a hand and, as ever, failed to prepare myself for her iron grip. My eyes were almost watering by the time she released me, entirely oblivious to her own strength. She'd have given that Arthur Schwarzenegger a run for his money, I can tell you that much.

'Now you can see what I'm up against,' I continued. 'But the important news is that it's a problem that can be remedied. There are thirty-six more games and plenty of time to mount a promotion push. I've taken the liberty of drawing up a list of potential signings...'

'No, Kevin, be quiet for a minute,' Gillian said as I unfolded the sheet of paper from my pocket and placed it in front of her.

'I'm not asking for every name on this list,' I explained to reassure her. 'We already have the spine of a good team, we just need to add a few limbs. A good six or seven of these players and we'll be well on the way.'

To my astonishment, Gillian screwed up the piece of paper and tossed it towards her waste paper bin (missing by a fair distance, which just about summed up the day really).

'Oh, I see,' I said, folding my arms across my chest. 'You want to play hardball. You're killing this club, you know.'

'Kevin, there *is* no football club. It's over!' she said, voice cracking with emotion. I was taken aback.

'Bloody hell, Gillian,' I said. 'Steady on. It's only one defeat – you realise we have another match in midweek, yeah? A few of those new signings that you just dismissed out of hand and we'd get some points on the board for sure.'

'Kevin, I'm sorry to be the bearer of bad news, but it's done. The plug has been pulled. Palangonia FC is no more. The Council voted on it this afternoon. I'm... sorry.'

My stomach was in knots – surely it couldn't be true? Had my decision to leave Rodway on the bench and consign us to inevitable defeat really had such devastating repercussions?

'I voted against it,' Gillian went on as I just sat there, frozen, 'of course I did, as did Dr Pebble-Mill, but it was a 3–2 majority. Something has happened and, well, all but the essential Council expenditure is to be redirected to General Leigh.'

'Oh, I might have bloody well known!' I snapped, breaking out of my trance. 'Leigh's been waiting to bring me down all year – you know full well he thinks Palangonia FC is a waste of time and money. And now he's got his wish. Brilliant. Well done! Happy now?'

'Kevin, if you knew what I know, you'd understand—'

'And if you knew what I know, about how important football is to the morale of the people in this Compound, people who've been displaced by a bunch of bad alien sods without so much as a by-your-leave, you'd realise that this is the worst possible decision!'

'Kevin, it's not like that at all – yes, Leigh is opposed to the football club, but we still enjoy broad support on the Council—'

'Do we?' I huffed. 'Funny way of showing it!'

'It's not a personal attack on you or the club,' she insisted, adopting a calmer tone in an attempt to defuse the palpable tension in the room. 'It's a matter of necessity.'

I was flabbergasted.

'What could be more necessary than *this*?' I asked, waving my arms at the room and the wider stadium beyond. The fire had gone out of my voice now. I sounded helpless. An immovable object had met with an irresistible force, and the irresistible force had won. The dream had died.

'So, that's that then?' I asked, getting to my feet and trying not to pout. 'After all you and I have been through?'

'Well,' she said, sounding a little surprised, 'I mean, we've only worked together for a year.'

I gestured to the framed photos on her desk – happy scenes of a man and two young children, taken years ago on Earth. The bloke was, by any estimation, quite the looker. Ordinarily I'd have assumed these were pictures of family or friends but Gillian didn't have any of those. Although she was a confident, gregarious person in her working life I had noticed that she was a solitary, closed-book of a person with few apparent friends beyond her professional capacities – it was entirely likely that the pictures in the frames were the placeholder templates and she hadn't got around to putting anything in them yet. (Pride of place on my own desk at the stadium is a photo of the 2003 Man City youth team squad, signed by Ronan Keating. I forget how that came about.)

'Your family must be so proud of you – I hope you tell them all tonight what you've done today,' I said bitterly, knowing it was a low blow. Gillian looked like she'd been punched in the gut and I instantly regretted what I'd said. She didn't respond and, stubbornly, I pressed on. 'I really did think you were better than this, you know. Gerry said you were a tight-fisted penny-pincher but I always stuck up for you. And yet here we are.'

I reached for the door handle to leave Gillian's office for surely the final time. Maybe Gerry was right – a fresh start was the best way. My hand stopped in mid-air at what Gillian said next.

'There's a L'zuhl spy in the Compound, Kevin. And by hook or by crook, Leigh is going to flush them out. Until that happens … *everyone* on Palangonia is a suspect.'

THE SPY

I stepped into Mr O's Place, feeling tired and dejected. The café owner was the enigmatically named Andy O – he was sitting in his usual spot on a stool by the side of the counter, reading the *Compound Chronicle* and muttering to himself about the recent increase in overheads for businesses in the square. He was always fairly hands-off as an owner, delegating the day-to-day running of the place to a man with an enormous head whose name I'd never managed to catch. I had a lot of time for Andy; he was a regular at our games (well, I'd seen him there once – though thinking about it, it might have been a pile of training cones) and he had even once generously provided emergency catering on a match day after Gerry's sleepwalking flared up again the night before and he wolfed down the contents of four chest freezers before dawn.

'Morning, Pete,' Andy said to me as I approached the counter. I rolled my eyes and sighed heavily.

'Aye, morning, Andy, lad,' I replied. 'Though as I said yesterday, and the day before, and basically every morning for the past year, my name is Kev.'

'Right you are,' Andy said, winking as though I'd just let him in on some elaborate joke. 'What's new with you?'

'Actually, I've got a lot on my mind today. I'm not allowed to say what. Politics, you know.'

'Say no more,' Andy said, holding up both hands agreeably. He rapped on the counter to attract the attention of one of his team, a spotty young lad who looked like he ought to be in school, who sidled over to take my order.

'It'll all come out eventually anyway,' I sighed as I put my wallet away. 'Let's face it, you can't keep news of a spy under wraps for long.'

Andy straightened up in his seat and stared at me intently.

'A spy?' he asked urgently. 'Here, in the Compound?'

Buggeration.

'No, no,' I said, clearly flustered but trying to play it cool. 'I think you misheard me, son. I said… Fry. Stephen Fry. Yeah, apparently he's coming to Palangonia on a book tour or something. It's all very hush-hush.'

Andy looked at me sceptically.

'Stephen Fry,' he said, eyes narrowed. 'Right. But you said the news had left you with a lot on your mind. So how does that work?'

'Well, he uses all those big words, doesn't he?' I explained as though it was the most obvious thing in the world. 'It stresses me out, if I'm honest. Anyway, I'll let you crack on. Have a good one, yeah?'

I took my breakfast and hurried over to a seat by the far window and sat there watching life in the square outside go by. The fried-egg sandwich tasted like ashes in my mouth – and not just because the head chef, Alf, chain-smoked over the pan while he was cooking. A spy in the Compound – could it really be true?

Who would ever want to sell mankind out to the bloody L'zuhl? Oh, sure, there had been some notable defectors – not least the Great Betrayer, Richard Madeley, the popular TV host who had decided, as the horde of alien lizard men laid siege to Earth, that he would be better off joining the winning side. Prat. Last I heard he'd been appointed to the role of L'zuhl propaganda minister. For me, you just don't do that.

Who could it be? Gerry? Surely not – no one would ever hand over state secrets to a man with hair like that. Then my heart stopped – could it be me? Was *I* the spy? I quickly batted the idea away. The only notable thing I'd been able to observe during my time on Palangonia was the complete lack of forward thinking from the club hierarchy. And anyway, I'm not cut out to be a spy. Not a real one. James Bond though? That's a different matter.

In 1994, I'd thrown my hat into the ring to replace Tim Dalton after he unexpectedly quit the role. I was managing Newcastle at the time and things were going great guns, but nevertheless, the role of Bond is not one you pass up when the opportunity presents itself. The producers kindly offered me an audition, after I put together a little video of celebrity testimonials endorsing me for the part, with contributions from footballing heavyweights like Tony Parkes and Howard Wilkinson, all the way up to Hollywood A-listers like Griff Rhys Jones and Chris Tarrant. I decided that Bond needed a fresh approach so I outlined my vision to them during the meeting.

'The way I see it,' I told them, 'the whole MI6 thing is a bit old hat. I propose that, instead of a super spy, Bond is a fully CRB-checked under-11s football coach who leads his team to glory while also defeating corruption within the highest echelons of the junior league structure.'

I could tell they were interested – they said, 'Well, let's get this over with,' which was a clear indicator of how keen they were: the sooner my audition was in the can, the sooner the announcement could be made that Kevin Keegan was the new 007. (Oh – and that was another condition: I asked them if we could change his codename to just '7', in keeping with my old shirt number.)

Anyway, as soon as the audition was in the bag I headed over to St James' Park to break the news to the chairman, Sir John Hall. He was stunned by the revelation, coming as it did in the middle of a league campaign, but he said he would not stand in the way of such an opportunity. Cracking bloke, Sir John. He began to draft a press release and I went downstairs to break the news to my lads. I bumped into Andy Cole, my top man, and – knowing what a huge fan he was of the series – I wanted him to be the first to know.

'Heard who the new James Bond is, Andy?' I said cheerfully.

He nodded. 'Yeah, Pierce Brosnan apparently. Heard it on the radio on the drive in. Should be good.'

Horrified, I dashed down to my car and put on the radio. I had to wait forty minutes for the next news bulletin, which was tedious in the extreme – though that's not a dig at Ken Bruce, who is an absolute master of his craft. Anyhow, when the news bulletin finally came round and they confirmed that Brosnan, whoever the hell he was, had indeed been given the role of Bond, I was utterly crushed. I went back up to see Sir John with my tail between my legs and I haven't watched a Bond film since. Shame.

As I mulled over this bitter memory in Mr O's Place, someone suddenly sat down opposite me. I looked up from my sandwich and was surprised to see Rodway looking back at me.

'Morning, gaffer.'

'Aye, morning, son,' I replied gruffly. He was no doubt here to grouse about being left out of the previous game – how was I to break the news to him that he'd be missing the next one too? And the thirty-four after that?

'You look terrible,' he said, pinching one of the sausages from my plate. 'Even worse than I did during the week.'

I was miserable – it felt like everyone was out to have a pop at me and now here was Rodway sticking the boot in.

'*Et tu*, Rodway?' I asked, sarcastically.

'No, I ate one,' he said, wolfing down the sausage. 'Any road, I'm sure we'll get a result on Wednesday, boss. The team from Blipplip are the whipping boys of this league. I mean, their species is just microscopic bacteria – we'll literally walk all over them. Keep the faith, gaffer. We believe in you.'

It was all I could do not to burst into tears right there. Here was this wayward kid who I'd been quite prepared to dump on the scrapheap and now, with me at my lowest ebb, he was giving *me* a pep talk. I could see from looking at him that he'd made a conscious effort to clean up his act – he looked fresh, healthy and fit. He was back to the Rodway I'd signed almost a year ago, a street urchin who had been orphaned during the L'zuhl invasion and had stowed away on an evacuee shuttle to Palangonia. This kid was the future of football, I'd known it from the moment I clapped eyes on him mugging a defenceless old man to steal his wallet. I'd said to Gerry as

Rodway kicked the ailing man to the ground, 'Hell of a left foot he's got on him.'

'Listen, son,' I said. 'I've got… something to tell you. Something you won't want to hear.'

'If it's about Gerry's naked sleepwalking then don't worry – Gillian warned us all about that months ago.'

'No, not that,' I said, though now I felt depressed all over again. It's worse. Palangonia FC has been canned.'

Rodway frowned, confused.

'What do you mean?' he asked. 'They've kicked us out of Galactic League C? For one defeat? Can they even do that?'

'No, the Compound Council have chucked us in the bin,' I explained. 'There's a… well, there's something going on. Some problem the military top brass have got their knickers in a twist over, so the budget is being redirected to General Leigh, the prat.'

'What kind of situation?' he asked, suddenly concerned. 'Is something happening with the L'zuhl? Are they planning an attack?'

I frowned in annoyance. Here I was, telling him that the club was toast and yet all he was interested in was what the L'zuhl might or might not be doing.

'You need to get your priorities straight,' I said. 'In fact, everyone does. They've never valued what we do. What we bring to Compound life.'

'Um… what *do* we bring?'

I was aghast.

'What do…? Come on, get your head on. We bring what the beautiful game always brings: joy. Excitement. A reason to get up in the morning. Hope, Rodway. We bring hope. And I'll tell you… the galaxy needs that right now, more than ever.'

'So… what can we do? Make them change their minds somehow?'

'Fat chance of that,' I scoffed dismissively. 'Not with Leigh calling the shots.'

'So we just give up?' Rodway asked, sounding genuinely startled. 'That hardly sounds like you. Last year when we lost that cup game in the ninetieth minute, you had us play on for hours after the final whistle until we equalised, even though the other team had gone home.'

'Another couple of hours and I really think we'd have nicked a winner,' I said, cursing the memory. I'd written to the league to have the result officially acknowledged as a draw but I never heard back. Up to them.

'I can't believe this is really the end,' Rodway said, wistfully looking out of the window. I had a horrid realisation that with no football club to occupy his time, Rodway would doubtless slide back into his wayward lifestyle. I couldn't see that happen.

'It doesn't have to be,' I said. 'The end, I mean. Not for us. Gerry and I… we've had another offer.'

'You have?' Rodway replied, intrigued. 'From another team?'

'Yep. Well, no. Not exactly. But Dave Moyes is right on the brink, apparently. They lost 5–0 yesterday. The man's dead on his feet. Once he's gone, they'll fall over themselves to get me and Gerry.'

'So they'll sack their manager for losing 5–0 and then hire a replacement whose team has just lost 6–0?' he asked carefully. I bristled.

'Yeah, well, that was extenuating circumstances,' I said. 'Our striker had let us down badly, so we were demoralised. Shame, that.'

That shut him up.

'The point is,' I went on, after a long pause to let him stew in his own juices, 'we can make a fresh start, a new beginning. Me, Gerry... and you.'

'Me?'

'That's right. You're my Les Ferdinand, and I don't say that lightly.'

'I don't know who that is.'

'I want you to come with us to... wherever the hell it is,' I went on. 'It's Galactic League D, I appreciate that, but I really think we could mount a serious promotion push once I clear out all the dead wood that Moyesie has inevitably signed.'

'I don't know what to say,' Rodway replied, sounding stunned.

'Say yes, son,' I said. 'It's either that or you get left here on Palangonia, the galaxy's rancid arsehole, for the rest of your life. Stuck here with Gillian and General Leigh lording it over everyone, acting like they own the place. And football? Forget it – within a generation it'll be forgotten in this nebula. It's up to you.'

'Yes!' Rodway beamed. 'Let's do it!'

'Attaboy,' I said, shaking his hand. He could be a bit of a one sometimes but the kid had the guts of a damn lion.

'I'd better get home and start packing,' Rodway mumbled excitedly, getting up from the table.

'Mind you don't say anything to the other lads,' I warned him. 'The likelihood is that I won't be able to take most of them with us.'

As I said these words I felt sick. The last thing I wanted to do was abandon these boys, but I was powerless to help them here. By taking Moyesie's job over on... wherever the hell it was, I could build a team around which the galaxy could unite and provide a glimmer of hope to the runts I had to leave behind on Palangonia (which would be the vast majority of the squad, in all honesty – my holding midfielder, Rooker, had arrived at our first training session carrying a tennis racket, and Caines, my left-winger, was, well, a bit of a left-winger who refused to play unless there were guarantees that all players would have an equal share of possession during a match.)

'I won't,' Rodway said, heading for the door. 'You, me and Gerry. The dream team. I'm sorry I let you both down this week. It won't happen ever again.'

I nodded.

'Good on you, son,' I said. 'Remember: you're my Ferdinand.'

'I still don't know who that—'

'Don't spoil it,' I muttered.

I felt a strong pang of guilt at letting Rodway get so carried away by the idea of our moving on to a new club. It was far from in the bag – and I knew that Alan Curbishley was also making noises about being interested in Moyesie's job if he got the chop (but then again, Al was the first on the scene at every vacancy – I remember he put his name forward for the new host of *Blind Date* on Channel 5 when they brought it back, despite his shameful lack of light entertainment experience. Pathetic, really.)

And then, as though like clockwork, General Leigh rode roughshod over my plans once more. His clipped tones came blaring out of the speakers dotted throughout the Compound

Square outside Mr O's Place, which were normally only utilised to indicate an imminent Winged Terror attack or to announce the winner of the Saturday raffle (Gerry won a cracking four-slice toaster a month earlier).

'This is General Lawrence Leigh, commander of the Palangonian Compound,' he said, sounding so far up his own backside that his head was practically coming up through his throat. 'This is an important notice for all residents. A Section Z order has been put in place on an indefinite basis. No one can leave this Compound without my personal written authorisation. As of this moment… we are in total lockdown. Thank you for your compliance.'

Rodway, who was standing in the doorway, ready to leave as the announcement was made, turned to look at me slowly.

'Gaffer?' he asked timidly. 'What does this mean?'

'It means,' I said, standing up with a heavy sigh, 'that we're not going anywhere.'

At least, not immediately. But I knew full well what this was all about. And I knew that the only way to resolve this mess was for Kevin Keegan to get his hands dirty.

No more Mr Nice Guy.

KEEP CLEAR
WINGED TERRORS

LOCKED DOWN

On Monday morning, I was a man on a mission. No more mucking about – we were beyond that point now. If General Leigh wanted to mess with me, well, that was just fine. I'd give it back in spades.

As the first of Palangonia's twin suns climbed beyond the rim of the Compound wall, I entered Emmeline Military Base, known colloquially as Fort Emmeline, via the visitor entrance and explained to the guard on the gate that I wanted to register a formal complaint against the General. The base was enormous, taking up almost a third of the total area of the Compound. To my left was a squadron of soldiers marching to the harsh orders of a drill sergeant, while beyond them I could see a fleet of armoured tanks, and still further away, glinting menacingly in the morning glare, an airfield with fighter jets packed in wing to wing. The guard looked up impatiently from her crossword and directed me towards a nondescript concrete building nearby.

'That's where Leigh is?' I asked, enjoying a moment of delicious smugness as I stared at the drab little building. *These* were Leigh's quarters? It was barely bigger than a large greenhouse!

'What? No, of course not,' the guard replied. 'He's in a

meeting with the Alliance command. You'll find a form on the table to your left. No pens, though – you'll need to bring your own. There's a war on.'

Perplexed, I walked through the gate, which closed with a loud clang behind me, and marched across the muddy, puddled floor towards the small building.

It was a waiting room. There were six or seven other people crammed inside the space, which was almost entirely bare save for the thin, uncomfortable-looking fold-out chairs which, aside from those currently occupied, were stacked untidily against the far wall. At the right-hand side of the room, beside a sleepy-looking guard who was on the verge of nodding off on his feet, was a table upon which stood a black box with the word 'Applications' plastered across the front of it. I grabbed the top piece of paper from the pile by the door, unfolded one of the chairs and sat down, staring irritably at the form before me.

'What the heck is this…?' I mumbled.

FORM 227/B99 – REQUEST TO LEAVE PALANGONIA DURING COMPOUND LOCKDOWN. HIGHEST APPROVAL REQUIRED.

'Highest approval'. General Leigh, in other words. He'd said as much in his la-di-da announcement the day before. I felt suddenly deflated. I'd come to Fort Emmeline ready for a ruck, a chance to tell Leigh that no one messes with Kevin Keegan's football club and gets away with it, but instead I'd been bundled into a room to fill in a form begging for Leigh's blessing to be allowed to go. I knew full well that no matter what I wrote on the form – urgent hospital treatment, work commitments, a friend's christening, reuniting with Sylvain Distin for a reprisal of our

Lighthouse Family tribute act from 2005 – nothing would see Leigh acquiesce and approve my request. He wanted to see me gone from Palangonia forever, sure, but knowing that this was now something that *I* wanted too meant he wouldn't be able to bring himself to grant it. He'd happily see himself suffer if it meant I'd suffer even more.

'I cannot get my head around this bloody thing,' came a voice from opposite where I was sitting. I looked up to see a woman wrapped in a wool coat and scarf, her hair a messy tangle of grey-black curls. She was squinting down through a pair of thick spectacles at her own form perched on her lap and was chewing the end of her pen vigorously.

'I know what you mean,' I nodded wearily. She glanced up at me.

'Oh – I know you, don't I?' the woman said, smiling. 'I'm sure I do.'

Oh, here we go. Earth may have been a distant memory but being a famous face still carried some cachet, it was true.

'Maybe,' I said coyly.

'Didn't you have a meltdown on TV or something?' she asked. 'Sorry, I don't mean to sound rude, but that was you, wasn't it?'

'No,' I said bluntly and returned to my form. 'You must be thinking of someone else. Eamonn Holmes probably. Sounds like the kind of thing he'd do.'

'I'm sure it was you,' she said thoughtfully. 'You said you'd hate it if something happened. "I will hate it if they lose – hate it!" It was definitely something like that …'

'It was "I will love it if we beat them",' I said in a slightly scolding voice. 'And I don't know what you're talking about.'

'Must be getting my wires crossed then,' she said. 'I hope I didn't offend you or anything.'

'Not at all,' I said, waving a dismissive hand. 'No harm done.'

'I'm Caroline, by the way,' she said, holding out her hand. 'I work in the Compound library.'

'Kevin Keegan,' I said. 'I run the football club. Or, at least, I did.'

'Keegan…' she said, chewing over the word much as she had the end of her pen. 'Are you absolutely sure you're not the—'

'Nope,' I said. 'You're definitely thinking of someone else.'

There was a moment of awkward silence as we both stared blankly at our forms. The fact I was even filling one out was humiliating enough – Leigh wasn't going to approve it, so what was the use? Why give him the satisfaction?

'Sod this,' I said, standing up and screwing the paper into a ball.

'What, you're not going to apply?' asked Caroline, shocked.

'Leigh'll never give me permission,' I explained grumpily. 'All he's concerned about is "his military" and the L'zuhl – that's how he likes to tart it up, anyway. But the reality is that his real aim in life is to kill Palangonia FC. And with this stupid spy malarkey, he's finally managed it.'

'Spy malarkey?' Caroline said, sitting up straight. 'Is that what this lockdown is about?'

Bugger.

'What?' I asked absently, trying to think of a way to cover myself. I didn't want to be arrested for revealing military secrets – the Compound Council would have me executed, or worse.

'You said the General was worried about a spy. Is there one in the Compound? Is that why we're not allowed to leave?'

'I didn't say "spy malarkey". I said…' – my mind raced – 'David Starkey. You know, the grumpy historian off the telly. Apparently he's flying in for a special visit and Leigh wants to make sure security is cranked up.'

'That sounds like a lie,' said Caroline dubiously.

'Yeah, it does a bit,' I admitted, sitting back down. Caroline sighed.

'I really need to get out of this Compound,' she said miserably. 'It's life and death for me.'

'Same here,' I agreed. 'What's your situation, if I'm okay to ask?'

'My sister,' Caroline replied heavily. 'She was evacuated to a different planet – Drebloot in the Phoenix Treble delta. She's come down with approxial mylosia. A bad case, apparently.'

Oof. That was a nasty one. Approxial mylosia was better known by its colloquial name, 'infinite malaise'. It afflicted approximately 15% of those who had made the journey from Earth into the various reaches of deep space and among its many gruesome symptoms it resulted in severe lethargy, depression, anxiety, multiple organ failure and exploding limbs – and not always in that order. There was no known cure. Around a third of those who got this dreaded and mysterious ailment made a full recovery within a few months or so, but for the others…. well, let's just say the outlook is pretty bleak. (They die, basically.)

'I'm really sorry to hear that,' I said. 'I lost a lot of good friends to the infinite malaise.'

'You did?' Caroline asked sadly. 'How awful.'

'Yeah… well, no. But I hear it's absolutely horrible.'

'Yes, well,' muttered Caroline, 'I don't like to think about that. I just want to see her. And if it really is the end, I want to be with her when it happens.'

'Entirely understandable,' I said. 'Though sadly I wouldn't hold out much hope for gaining Leigh's sympathy.'

'What's your reason for wanting to get away then?' Caroline asked. 'You said yours was life or death too.'

'Aye, exactly,' I said. 'The life and death of the beautiful game.'

'I'm sorry, the…?'

'Well, you know General Leigh hates my football team here on Palangonia,' I said.

'You mentioned it, yes,' Caroline said with a barely perceptible eye roll. I let it pass.

'Now that he's strangled the team to death, me and Gerry – he's my assistant – have had to look at other options. Apparently Dave Moyes is on the brink over in… wherever he is, so we wanted to jet out there to throw our hats into the ring for the gig. And now, thanks to bloody Leigh, we're stuck here. He's petty and vindictive, he really is.'

'So that's… life and death,' Caroline said in a flat voice.

'Exactly,' I nodded vehemently. 'If *you* can see where I'm coming from, why can't Leigh? And Gillian, for that matter.'

'Gillian Routledge, you mean?' Caroline asked. 'From the Compound Council?'

'You've met her then,' I said.

'Yes, she's wonderful – she had the casting vote on extra funding for the library to fill out our reference collection and she really got behind us. She's been a real champion of the library project.'

'Oh, of all the nerve!' I snapped. 'This is the final straw in the coffin, this really is – she's systematically undermining me and the club at every turn while at the same time frittering money away on – no offence, Caroline – a load of dusty old books that no bugger will ever read!'

'Actually, the Compound library has seen significant footfall,' Caroline said. 'I think a lot of people see it as one of the few tangible links to our past on Earth.'

'Football is our most tangible link to our past,' I countered passionately. 'It was mankind's greatest achievement – I've always said that.'

'Well, let's not get carried away,' Caroline said. 'I think there were plenty of other things humanity achieved prior to the invasion that were of greater significance than a silly sports game.'

'Name one!' I cried.

'God, where to start – landing a man on the moon—'

'A doddle,' I said. 'We played a friendly on a moon six months ago.'

'—the power of flight—'

'Which ultimately led to players diving all over the place; it poisoned the game. Next.'

'—eradicating disease—'

'Bit of deep heat, you're right as rain.'

'—organ transplants—'

'Sell an Andy Cole, get yourself an Al Shearer.'

'—the list is endless really.'

'I think all you've done here is prove my point,' I said. I hadn't felt this fired up since I overheard Mark Viduka saying that Genesis were 'a bit bland, if I'm honest'. (I transfer-listed him on the spot.)

I stood up.

'It was nice to meet you, Caroline,' I said, 'and I hope you get out to see your daughter.'

'My sister,' she said.

'Her too.'

'What are you going to do?' Caroline asked. 'Find another job outside of football? We might have a vacancy ourselves in a month or two, once the new funding from the Council comes through.'

'Not a chance,' I said defiantly. 'It's football or nothing for me. If General Leigh thinks he can palm me off with a poxy form like I'm some riff-raff – not you, I mean – then he's got another thing coming. Oi, you!'

I marched up to the dozy-looking guard. He blinked at me.

'Get Leigh down here – I want a word!' I fumed.

'Fancy seeing you here, Coogan,' came a powerful voice from the doorway behind me. I – and everyone else in the room – froze.

They didn't need to bring me to General Leigh after all.

He had come to me.

GENERAL LEIGH

'We've never seen eye to eye, have we?'

It was all I could do to stop myself losing my breakfast. The Compound wall was a heck of a lot higher when you were standing on top of it.

'No,' I managed breathlessly. 'We haven't.'

Leigh smiled grimly and stared off at the distant horizon towards the long-dormant volcano, Great Strombago, which dominated the landscape. Immediately beyond the Compound on this side there lay a thick growth of forests, eventually giving way to boggy marshland to the east and to the west a tight knot of steamy jungle. Beyond the volcano... well, nobody really knew. Behind me, at the opposite end of the Compound, beyond the woods that bordered us on all sides, there lay an arid yellow desert as far as the eye could see. There were rumours that on clear days you could just about make out a distant grey ocean but as I turned to look in that direction now (carefully, so as not to spew everywhere), I couldn't see anything beyond the shimmering expanse of sand. I gingerly turned back the way Leigh was facing, still staring down into the darkness of the trees.

'They're out there, you know,' Leigh said quietly – for a

moment I thought he may have been talking to himself. Then he looked at me, awaiting some kind of response.

'Who are?' I asked, sighing. He was toying with me and we both knew it. 'The L'zuhl?'

'No,' he replied. 'At least, not yet. Our settlement here is small, that's the only reason this place still stands. They don't know about our increasing military presence, though our mysterious spy may very well rectify that, and soon. No, I'm talking about the Palangonians.'

We didn't see the native tribespeople very often but when they mounted their doomed assaults on the chunky brick walls of the Compound with their elaborate war paint and orange-brown cloth outfits, armed with crudely fashioned spears, swords and bows and arrows, they were always swiftly rebuffed. Their archers occasionally managed to get a shot away at the Compound guards manning the machine-gun turrets but barely enough to pierce their thick armour. I didn't blame them for having a pop at us – no one likes to see someone come strolling in and parking up on their territory as we had. It's like Roy Evans at Liverpool in 1998 when they brought in Gérard Houllier as joint manager alongside him. Though I should stress that at no point did Roy resort to attacking the Shankly gates with any home-made weaponry. I want to go on the record about that.

'Not just the tribesmen,' Leigh continued, waving an arm across the expanse beyond the wall. 'I'm talking about everything. There are multitudes of weird and not-so-wonderful beasts out there on this godforsaken planet. And a great number of those would love to feast on our sweet human flesh. The damned drelkor lizards and the flying falcon spiders for one thing – well, two – and of course, there are the Winged Terrors. They're the hardest to keep at bay, but we're working on our defences.'

'Speaking of,' I said in a slightly alarmed voice as my eyes quickly scanned the cloudy beige skies above our heads, 'are we safe up here like this?'

'Perfectly,' he said. 'We're flanked by heavy artillery in the lookout posts on either side of us. Those bastards wouldn't dare.'

Reassuring.

'Why'd you bring me up here, General?' I asked impatiently. Behind and below me, down in Fort Emmeline at the far north end of the Compound, life continued as normal. Guards patrolled the perimeter, engaged in training exercises; there was the constant rat-tat-tat of the shooting range. Further away within the Compound, beyond the gates of the army base, was the wider community – the square with its bustling shopping areas and restaurants, families out spending the day together – and way over on the far northern end I could see my home, the accommodation blocks, which were really nothing more than glorified high-rises. This was our life now. The L'zuhl had taken our planet from us but they couldn't take everything. My eyes flicked over to the John Rudge Memorial Stadium at the west side of the Compound, squeezed in beside the school, which had class sizes barely in the double figures – not many children had made it out to Palangonia during the evacuation. It wasn't exactly a great platform from which to repopulate the species and, more worryingly, it would have grave implications for the future of football as the few remaining human players began to grow older. Further beyond lay the shuttle bays, which currently looked empty and rather melancholy with the lockdown in place.

'I brought you here, Coogan, because—'

'Come on, you know my name's Keegan,' I snapped irritably. 'Let's have a bit of respect, please. I managed the national side, for goodness' sake.'

Leigh glanced at me and to my surprise actually looked a little chastened. He was a fit man in his early-to-mid fifties, military to his core, supposedly signing up at sixteen and now responsible for the stewardship of one of the hundreds of human colonies trying to establish themselves in the far reaches of space. He had short greying hair under his black beret and even in his Alliance-issue black uniform (which personally I think made them look like the real baddies, not the L'zuhl – what's wrong with a nice yellow or a pleasant mint-green type of thing?), the man looked absolutely ripped. His legs were like tree trunks and his arms were two hulking joints of meat. Fair play to the guy, he had looked after himself even into his later years. I knew of one or two former pros who could've taken a leaf out of his book rather than just letting themselves go – not least Razor Ruddock. Then again, you couldn't expect much common sense from a man who slathered himself in Old Spice because he thought the Liverpool club slogan was 'You Never Wore Cologne.'

'You're right,' Leigh said – probably the first and only time he'd ever say such a thing to me. 'You deserve my respect. Keegan.'

'Aye,' I said suspiciously. 'Fine then. But you still haven't told me what this is about, why you're waffling on about the indigenous Palangonian races and all that. Everyone knows about them – we got handed the crib sheet on the shuttle out here last year. I got 76% on the "Test Your Knowledge" bit at the end. I won a key ring.'

'I'm showing you this,' the General said, 'to emphasise the size of the task facing me here. Facing all of us. There are other dangers on our doorstep each day than merely the threat of L'zuhl annihilation, you know. I appreciate you don't care much for me, Keegan, and – be assured – the feeling is more than mutual, but I have a job to do here and by God, I'm going to carry it out.'

'What job's that then?' I asked defiantly. 'Shutting down my football club? Cheers for that, by the way. Must have made you feel such a big man.'

Talking to the General like that ran the risk of my being shot on the spot but I was so riled by his anti-football agenda that in that moment I simply did not care.

'Your silly little football team is a gross abuse of Council funds,' Leigh said stuffily. 'I've said that from the very beginning and I maintain as much today. But the Council voted in favour of its creation and I've abided by it. I don't agree with it, and I've found your tiresome attempts to influence the Council to invest additional funding in your inconsequential project deeply distasteful, but I accepted it.'

'What attempts?' I asked, wounded. 'I haven't tried to influence the Council at all, I'd never do that.'

'So you're really going to look me in the eye and say that you didn't send gift baskets to all five Council members six months ago, myself included, containing a box of cupcakes with little footballs on them, signed copies of Gary Neville's memoir *Right Back Atcha*, mini bottles of Newcastle Brown Ale and a card signed "With love from an anonymous donor. All the best, Kevin Keegan"?'

'Nowt to do with me,' I shrugged. Though on the inside, I was panicking – if they brought in fingerprint forensics, I was buggered.

'In any event,' Leigh pressed on, 'despite all of that, I've tolerated your football club. I respect the rule of democracy and you had, by that account, as much right to exist as these walls upon which we now stand.'

Pull the other one, I thought. Leigh's sole objective was to see the club fail and by creating a daft spy story, he now had the perfect cover. It was so plainly obvious. Ask anyone. Well, ask Gerry.

'So I hope we can clear the air about that, at least,' he continued. 'We can just agree to dislike each other without there having to be some grand conspiracy to undermine something which, as I hope I've now explained, is quite some way down my list of priorities during an intergalactic war.'

He must have had an even lower opinion of me than I'd previously thought if he expected I'd fall for this. I felt genuinely insulted.

'I must say, however, that I was surprised to see you in such a hurry to leave Palangonia,' Leigh added, his voice suddenly darkening. 'I mean, given your dedication to your club and all.'

'Well, there's no club to dedicate myself to now, is there?' I huffed. 'Thanks to you and your spy flim-flam. It's a competitive marketplace out there, you know. Any of the managers from Earth who survived the L'zuhl genocide are scrabbling about for every job going. If Gerry and I don't get over to… wherever Dave Moyes' team is based, then Big Sam or Brendan Rodgers will steal a march on us. That's basic.'

'I know how committed you've been to your team here,'
Leigh continued. 'You even made a short promo film of yourself
helping out around the stadium, painting walls and making cups
of tea to show how loyal you were to the cause. I must say, I
haven't cringed so hard in years.'

'How do you know about that?' I asked, flushing red in
embarrassment.

'There was a DVD copy in that bribery gift basket.'

Oh yeah.

'Well, anyway,' I said, puffing myself up, 'I *am* loyal. But like I
just said, it's all finished now. Thanks to you.'

'So defeatist,' Leigh said. 'I didn't expect this from you. Why, I
may catch this damned spy tomorrow and then, who knows, the
Council may very well be foolish enough to vote to restore your
funding.'

'Fat chance of that,' I said dismissively.

'I'm disappointed that you're so sceptical of my efforts to weed
out this L'zuhl informer, Keegan,' Leigh said in a tone that I really
did not care for one bit. 'As it turns out, I think this whole affair
might be resolved far more quickly than anyone dared hope.'

Leigh clicked his fingers loudly (which was quite impressive
given that he was wearing leather gloves, you have to hand it
to the man) and I was unceremoniously seized by two visored
guards who had appeared as though from nowhere.

'Hey, hey!' I cried in panic. 'What's this in aid of? I was just
about to get off home!'

'Au contraire,' Leigh said with a relishing grin. 'You're staying
right here where I can see you. I mean, I'd have to be pretty stupid
to catch the L'zuhl spy only to let him go again, now, wouldn't I?'

And, like the day I advised Mike Ashley that Newcastle needed more flair and told him to 'go and get a Brazilian', I felt utterly sick.

LOCKED UP

I paced up and down, my mind working overtime. How had I managed to get myself into this mess?

General Leigh told me he'd make sure I got 'one of the finest suites' in the Mark Aspinall Prison at the far end of the base (named after one of the most fearsome barristers in the Alliance who had famously prosecuted the Great Betrayer himself, Richard Madeley, in absentia the previous summer for crimes against humanity) but it turned out that by this he simply meant the toilet might flush now and then. The running water from the tap was barely more than a trickle and the mattress was stained with… well, I tried not to think about it.

'Hello?' I called through the bars of my cell door, the iron cool against my face. 'Lunch is meant to be at one and it's now twenty past! You're treating me like a prisoner here. It's not on.'

But of course, I *was* a prisoner. Worse than that, in the eyes of Leigh and his soldiers – no doubt by now, four days down the line from my arrest – and to the wider Compound, I was the evil turncoat spy who had been turfing over military secrets to the L'zuhl.

My heart sank at the prospect of my lads seeing the front page of the *Compound Chronicle*. BELOVED FOOTBALL MANAGER

ACCUSED OF SPYING would no doubt be the headline plastered everywhere. The fact that Gerry had not come in to visit was worrying me. Oh, sure, I could well expect it of Gillian – she was no doubt thrilled to discover that someone had taken me out of the equation, putting a stop to my pleas for greater investment in the playing squad. But Gerry? Surely he wouldn't just accept the accusation at face value like that? His support was all I had to cling on to as I spent my days staring hopelessly at the four grey stone walls around me. The only indication that anyone else had ever been held here before me (aside from the stain on the mattress) was a few bits of graffiti on the wall – one read 'Eff Palangonia!' Except it didn't say 'Eff'. I mean, what kind of sick mind writes something like that? What if a kid had seen it? Well, all right, probably unlikely, but still. The idea of my being kept in a ten-foot cell like the sort of dangerous deviant who'd write something so disgusting made my stomach turn. I led my country to an international tournament for goodness' sake! And we'd ultimately finished a respectable third. In Group A. Look, let's not get bogged down in that, it was ages ago. The other bit of graffiti was about the General himself, referring to him as a 'L'zuhl shagger' which at least made me smirk slightly despite my disapproval of the act and, frankly, the language.

'Hey!' I shouted into the empty corridor beyond my cell. 'I'm starving!'

No response. What was this, a bank holiday? I sat down on the bed and rested my chin in my hands. Obviously it wasn't enough for Leigh to destroy my football club, oh no – he also had to ruin me as well.

'Did you think I wouldn't put two and two together?' he had

taunted as his two goons dragged me aggressively down the steps from the top of the Compound walls. 'It was painfully transparent! I put the Compound in lockdown so we can hunt for a spy, and then, suddenly, Kevin Keegan cannot wait to leave! How *very* convenient.'

Certainly didn't feel that convenient to me as I sat there, bored rigid, in my cell for four days, being fed nothing but beans on toast thrice daily (though at least for the evening meal they gave me those beans with the little sausages in). In a way, this was all Gerry's fault. Look, I'm not one to pass the buck, I'll own all my mistakes, but if he hadn't planted the seed of our moving on and taking Moyesie's job, I'd never have ended up in this situation. I'd have probably fought harder for Palangonia FC, too. Thanks a bunch, Gerry.

Suddenly, a wave of despair washed over me. Why *hadn't* I fought harder? I'd mouthed off to Gillian and complained in the loudest terms but I hadn't really *done* anything. I'd just accepted Gerry's suggestion that we might have a better time of it elsewhere. I'd taken the easy way out – and that is not the Kevin Keegan way. Palangonia FC was mine. And I had to stand up for it.

'Oi,' came a voice from outside – I hadn't even heard the masked guard approach.

'Oh, finally,' I grumbled, getting to my feet, arms outstretched. But the guard held no tray of beans.

'Forgotten something, son?' I asked, eyebrow raised.

'Come with me,' he said darkly. 'You're to be interrogated. The General wants answers.'

'So do I,' I said, and waited for the cell door to slide open.

*

The interrogation room was every bit as dingy as my cell – I was baffled as to why, given that Fort Emmeline had only been built little more than a year ago. They had plenty of opportunity to give the place a bit of character, a colourful paint job, a skylight – a conservatory would have been ideal to catch the sunshine from the twin suns setting in the late afternoon. Instead, it was grey brickwork and a cold stone floor, with a wooden table in the middle of the room and a mirror on the wall. I initially assumed, on walking inside, that this was the obligatory two-way thing for people to watch the interrogation but actually, it was more likely to be pure vanity from Leigh. And sure enough, he was already sitting there at the side of the table facing the mirror. Pathetic.

'Keegan,' he said gruffly without getting off his arse. 'Take a seat. You look well.'

'I look how I feel,' I snapped, sitting down opposite the General. Beside him, a young woman in a smart suit was scribbling on a sheet of paper. There was an empty seat next to me.

'Well, you brought this on yourself,' Leigh said.

'You honestly cannot believe that,' I said, shaking my head in exasperation. 'I'm a pure football man, not a secret agent.'

'Perhaps we should hold fire until we begin,' the woman said, looking up. She wasn't wearing a military uniform but looked very officious. I had a bad feeling about this.

'Mr Keegan's lawyer isn't here yet,' she went on. 'This spy business is big, General – we want to make sure we play things by the book.'

'Right you are,' Leigh agreed, sitting back in his seat and

knitting his hands together over his stomach like he was relaxing in a lawn chair. Honestly, I have never felt the urge to slap another human being as much as I did in that moment. He oozed smarm – that's a trait I simply cannot abide. I remember years back there was that Swedish boy, Zlatan Ibrahimović. Hell of a player. But one day I heard him remark during an interview that he was unquestionably 'the greatest living Swede'. I mean, I had to laugh. Did you write 'The Winner Takes It All' then, son? Nope. Next.

Still, though. A lawyer? For me? I didn't even know I had one. Back on Earth, I'd always represented myself whenever I was involved in legal proceedings – like when I took Cineworld to court after I paid full whack for a ticket and yet the film only lasted three minutes. (They won on some weird technicality, claiming it was only a trailer before the main feature. Aye, right.)

'Who's my lawyer?' I asked – and then right on cue, the door opened behind me and a portly man in a Hawaiian shirt and combat shorts bustled in, a sheaf of folders under one hairy arm. He had long hair at the back but was bald at the front – he looked like a sweaty Terry Nutkins. The only good thing I could say about him was that he was brave enough to wear socks and sandals together, a sartorial combo that society had wrongly shunned but for which I remained a proud standard-bearer. No one needs to see your manky toes, thank you very much.

'So sorry I'm late,' the horrendous-looking man said in a thick southern-US accent. He had a whistle in his nose when he exhaled which I could already tell was going to drive me absolutely potty.

'Please don't say you're my—'

'Your lawyer,' the man said, extending his hand to shake mine as he sat beside me, scattering his folders and paperwork all over the floor as he did so. 'Bill Attick.'

With a heavy sigh, I shook his pudgy, clammy hand and glanced across the table at General Leigh. I knew that smirk would be on his face before I even saw it.

'Shall we crack on?' Attick suggested amiably. 'I can't imagine this'll take too long.'

'I never hired you,' I said, trying not to let my distaste at this poor state of affairs show. 'I don't even have a lawyer.'

'I was employed by one...' Attick consulted his notes, squinting, 'Gerald Francis. You know him?'

'Aye,' I grumbled. 'Wish I didn't. He hasn't been in to see me once.'

'Oh, he's tried,' Leigh said. 'Tried to scale the gates to the base at one point. We had to taser him.'

'Christ – is he okay?'

'That's when he contacted me,' Attick explained. 'The General is free to prohibit visitors to his prisoners but cannot rebuff an Alliance-appointed lawyer.'

'Bully for you,' I said miserably.

'Shall we begin?' suggested the woman, who had been sitting quietly all the while. 'As Mr Attick observed, this oughtn't take long.'

'Open and shut case,' Leigh said.

'My name is Helen Brody; I'm the appointed litigator for the Compound command force, of which the General is leader. Mr Keegan, you are here today, a prisoner, on suspicion of espionage. Is there anything you'd like to say?'

'No comment,' Attick muttered in my direction.

'I've plenty I'd like to say,' I blustered. 'First off, can you turn up the air con in here? It's boiling. Secondly, I'm not a spy. I wouldn't even know where to begin. I may hate this toad of a man sitting here with me—'

'I'm doing my best,' Attick said, wounded.

'I mean the General,' I sighed. 'I may detest that oaf with every fibre of my being for what he's done to my beloved football club, but I would never put my hatred for him over my love for my species. For my home planet. For all mankind. I'm a patriot. You ask anyone – ask Brian Laws, ask Les Reed, Robbie Martínez. They'll tell you.'

'That's a very impassioned argument,' Brody said coolly. 'But it doesn't change the fact that no sooner was the General's lockdown announced, you immediately sought to leave the Compound. You, whose loyalty to his football club is known far and wide.'

'Purely circumstantial,' Attick said. 'I really hope that's not the best you've got.'

'It's more than just circumstance,' Brody went on. 'There is no justifiable reason why someone as committed to his role here on Palangonia as Mr Keegan would attempt to flee as soon as the news broke that there was a spy in our midst. And there's also the question of his behaviour. Mr Keegan has been personally abusive in his language to the General on numerous occasions.'

'Have I heck,' I snorted, waving a hand dismissively. 'Give me one example.'

'You referred to him as a toad not one minute ago,' Brody replied.

'That was a one-time thing,' I insisted.

'You then went on to call him an oaf. Again, this was barely a minute ago.'

'Figure of speech,' I mumbled and then fell silent. Best to know when you're beaten.

'This still doesn't add up to enough,' Attick said. 'It'll never stand up in court. You have not a sniff of proof that my client, Mr Coogan, was—'

'It's bloody Keegan, come on,' I said, exasperated.

'—was in any way connected to this spy business. What I'm seeing here is two people with a vendetta against one another and the fact that it's come to this sorry situation should be a cause for embarrassment on both sides.'

I felt suddenly heartened by Attick's defence of my position. Brody seemed momentarily lost for words.

'Do you realise quite how much of a march the L'zuhl have on the Alliance at this moment in time?' Leigh said testily, leaning forward across the table. 'They're one step ahead of us with everything we do at the moment – and it's all thanks to this damned spy.'

He glanced at me. I shrugged. Not my problem.

'At the Battle of Fallak, they knew exactly what numbers we would be bringing and they outmatched us. We were vanquished and had to fall back. Laika was en route to the Alliance headquarters at The Oracle for a meeting of the Assembly and there was a L'zuhl assassin already in wait. Fortunately, she survived with only a grazed paw.'

I hadn't heard about that. Even I knew that the loss of Laika would have been an enormous blow to any prospect of victory against the L'zuhl. She had been the first dog in space back in the 1950s and, after floating away into the vast darkness of the cosmos, had developed super-intelligence and an unnaturally long life. (That old chestnut.) Now, she was one of the most respected figures in the galaxy, a noted academic and decorated politician, and her guidance and leadership at the highest levels of the Alliance was crucial. It's like when Sir Al finally retired after twenty-six years at Manchester United: lightning simply does not strike twice. Unless you're Dave Seaman playing golf – he was struck sixteen times in one afternoon and still bought a round at the club bar afterwards. The man's a diamond, he really is.

'I didn't know that about Laika,' I said, a slightly tremulous note to my voice. 'I'm glad she's okay.'

'Sure you are,' Leigh sneered.

'Let's try to keep this civil,' Brody interjected.

'General, this still does nothing to implicate my client – these are a number of unfortunate incidents at which Mr Coogan was not even present.'

'You want proof?' Leigh said, suddenly looking a little rattled. 'Did you not hear what happened just last night in the Adelphi Six sector? The Alliance moved a fifth of its arsenal there in order to use the Frelf wormhole to transport them over to The Oracle – and as soon as they arrived at Adelphi, they found a L'zuhl battalion awaiting them. Thousands upon thousands of lives were lost in the ensuing dog-fight. Mr Keegan, the spy, fed this information to them. There is no way they would have known about our strategy otherwise. This decision was made by me, at a meeting held within these four walls of the Compound just this Tuesday. By foul means, Keegan evidently infiltrated the room and passed on our plans to his paymasters.'

'Absolute hogwash, that,' I said, shaking my head. 'Nowt to do with me whatsoever. You're better than this, son.'

'How is that proof?' Attick asked again.

'I know it in my bones,' Leigh said. 'Keegan is the spy. And I'm going to keep him rotting in that cell until I find some incontrovertible evidence. And believe me, I will find it.'

'Well, if that's where we're at, that's where we're at,' Attick said, folding his paperwork away and tucking his pen into the top pocket of his ridiculous shirt.

'What, so I can go then?' I asked. 'I mean, he has no proof, after all.'

'Go?' Attick frowned. 'Why, of course not. General Leigh is calling the shots here. Until you're ruled out as a suspect, if indeed you ever are, you're here at his pleasure. I can't do anything about that.'

'This is a travesty!' I cried. 'I've seen some injustices in my time but this takes the bloody cake!'

Leigh gave me a cold look and stood up alongside Brody.

'It won't be so bad, I'm sure,' Attick said, placing a meaty, sympathetic hand on my shoulder. 'You've just got to keep a positive attitude.'

'And in the meantime, you'll try to find proof that I'm not the spy, yeah?' I asked hopefully.

'What?' He seemed genuinely surprised. 'No, of course not. I only do this part time; I'm back at the day job this afternoon. I make birdhouses.'

I deflated like a football after an Al Shearer piledriver.

'All the best, Mr Coogan,' he said. 'Tomorrow's Friday – you've managed almost a working week inside already. The months and... well, yes, most probably years will fly by.'

I felt like crying right there in the interrogation room. Leigh had won. He'd destroyed Palangonia FC and now he'd broken Kevin Keegan too. I couldn't face a fifth day inside. If the L'zuhl really were on the warpath as the General claimed, I didn't want my fate to be sitting in a cell watching mankind crumble to nothing around me. Hearing that many thousands of lives had been lost the night before was horrifying, even without the responsibility being laid at my feet. Christ, what would my lads think of me when I copped the blame for that? I mean, it's not like I could even— *Wait one damn minute!*

'Attick!' I cried, and my idiot lawyer/birdhouse maker paused in the doorway and looked back at me.

'You okay?' he asked, sounding concerned.

'Okay?' I asked. 'I'm better than okay, son. I'm a free man. Get the General back here *right now*!'

THE LIGHT BULB

'Kev! So happy to see you!'

Gerry fired off a party popper right in my face; I winced and pushed him away.

'Let's try to keep some dignity, please,' I scolded him.

Still, it felt absolutely fantastic to walk back into my old flat again. The black-and-white striped Newcastle United wallpaper, the weird damp smell that I couldn't shift. I was home. Gerry had crudely put up some decorations around the walls and had hung a large banner that read GOOD LUCK, KEV! which I'm pretty sure he'd recycled from the time I went on *Celebrity Mastermind* in 2011. That was a catastrophe by the way – no one told me you were allowed to pass on a question, so when I didn't know the answer to the first one I just sat there in silence for two minutes.

'You look pretty good, considering,' Gerry observed in a backhanded-compliment sort of way. 'I thought you'd be all emaciated and have tattoos on your face and all that.'

'I was only in for four days,' I said – though it had felt like a lifetime. I couldn't help wondering how this experience would change me, the psychological damage it might have inflicted on my personality. Would I ever be the same Kevin Keegan again?

'There's a buffet in the kitchen,' Gerry said, leading me through.

'Cracking,' I said. 'I'll tell you, honestly, I will love it if there are those battered prawns on sticks – love it.'

In the kitchen, to my surprise, were many more familiar faces. Alongside Barrington12 stood Rodway, who beamed as I came in. Squeezed in like sardines around the small table were all my lads – Gribble, Little Dunc, Wiggins, Nightingale and several more, including two or three whose names I'd never quite caught and was too embarrassed to ask. I was swelling with pride (and also from being a bit backed up after four stressful days in the clink). Standing in the corner holding a glass of wine was Gillian. I was astonished when she approached and gave me a peck on the cheek.

'It's so good to have you home,' she said, smiling warmly. 'I was horrified when I heard what had happened, I really was. I'd have come to visit you in there immediately, but I've been stuck in endless Council meetings. I repeatedly tried to call a vote to have your arrest rescinded given the flimsy evidence the General had on you, but he carries a lot of sway on the Council and boy, does he know it.'

I had to admit, I was rather surprised by this. The idea that Gillian had pulled out all the stops to try to secure my release… could that really be true? Or was she merely making excuses after the fact for her own inaction, to pretend that she had never doubted me?

'Thank you for trying,' I said eventually, still feeling dazed. 'Hello, everyone.'

'And so say all of us!' said Gerry. Trust him to make me look a tit in front of them all.

'Great to have you back, gaffer,' Rodway said through a mouthful of caramel éclair. (It was a bit rude that they'd all cracked on with the buffet before I'd arrived, but I thought better of saying anything.) 'Hasn't Gillian done you proud with the spread?'

'Gillian made all this?' I asked, astonished. I reflected again on what she had said a few moments earlier. Maybe, just maybe, she really *was* on my side after all.

'Hidden talents I guess!' Rodway said. 'We're all just so glad to see you home.'

'And you,' I said, trying to blink back the tears that I could feel welling behind my eyes. 'All of you. It's fantastic to have your support at a time like this. My name's been dragged through the mud this past week.'

'I'd have loved to have seen the look on old Leigh's face when you broke the news to him,' Gerry said with a delighted cackle.

Leigh had turned a worrying shade of grey when I called him and Brody back in and put the blindingly obvious fact to him: if the attack on the Alliance arsenal the night before had been as a result of someone leaking those plans to the L'zuhl, how on Earth could it have possibly been me? The meeting in which Leigh and the Alliance had made their plans to move ships to Adelphi Six had been on Tuesday night. I'd been in the nick since lunchtime on Monday. I was exonerated. Leigh was completely unapologetic (apart from when he begrudgingly apologised to me as I was released) and looked more worried about the fact that his work in catching the spy would have to continue than about my own welfare. Typical. Always thinking about himself.

'Serves them all right for making up this whole spy nonsense in the first place,' Gerry said.

'No, I've changed my mind on that part at least,' I corrected him. 'I did initially believe it was all a ruse, a plot to undermine the football club, but having heard what I did during my interrogation, I'm sure it's the real deal. I'm just glad they can rule me out.'

'Wow,' said Gribble, my lanky centre-half, so tall that his hair was scraping the ceiling, his neck at an awkward angle. 'Who would want to sell us out to the L'zuhl like that?'

'Not me, that's the main thing,' I reiterated. Still, my realisation that the spy was real had somewhat dampened my mood. I'd been utterly convinced it was a ploy to get at me. Now I had to face up to the reality that my football club had in actuality been chucked on the scrapheap for legitimate reasons.

'That really is it, then,' Gerry said glumly, picking a strawberry from a cheesecake on the table. 'If the spy is legit, we're not getting our funding back.'

Later, as Gerry showed an appalled Gillian his taser battle scars, Rodway came over and spoke in a conspiratorial whisper.

'Gaffer,' he said. 'Are we still on for... for the plan we discussed? About getting out of here to move to that new club? Once the lockdown is lifted, I mean.'

This was something to which I'd been giving a great deal of thought myself during my incarceration – and seeing my lads huddled in the kitchen of my tiny flat to welcome me home had only confirmed and vindicated the decision I had privately made. (A decision which, by the way, was in no way influenced by the fact that Moyesie's team had secured an emphatic midweek win in Galactic League D during my time inside and his job was suddenly less precarious than it had been.)

'Palangonia is our home, Rodway,' I said. 'We can't walk away from what we've built here.'

'But—'

'I'll admit I got carried away and perhaps spoke to you about it when I should have still been weighing up my options. But it's the coward's way out. We have to stay. We have to stand and fight.'

'I do admire your dedication, Kevin, I really do,' Gillian said, wandering over. 'But while this spy is at large, there's no prospect of the club's funding being restored. And, as you've witnessed for yourself first-hand, the guards have nothing to go on. He, or she, is out there somewhere. But they clearly have no idea where to start looking. The bottom line is, short of you going out and finding that spy yourself, Palangonia FC is not coming back any time soon.'

In a flash, a light bulb was suddenly illuminated above my head.

'That still playing up, is it?' Gerry said, squinting at the ceiling. 'Mine does that sometimes. I'll see if I can get someone in to fix that for you.'

'That's it,' I said. 'Gillian, you're a genius.'

'Am I?' she said, bemused. 'That's not exactly the tune you've been singing this past year, I must say.'

'I'm going to save Palangonia FC. And if it helps win this stupid war at the same time, then so much the better.'

'You've lost me,' Gerry said blankly.

'First thing tomorrow,' I said, 'I'm going out into the

Compound. And I'm not coming back home until I catch that bloody spy myself.'

TO THE LIBRARY

At dawn, I rose quickly and, after a handful of stale crisps from the half-eaten buffet in the kitchen (which no bugger had stayed behind to help me clear up, by the way), I headed out. It wasn't the most nutritious breakfast given the big day I had ahead of me, but then again Gary Lineker has been contractually obliged to eat Walkers crisps for every meal since 1995 and look at him. The man's an Adonis.

I went down to the ground floor of Accommodation Block 8-B. The blocks were a proper Upstairs, Downstairs arrangement – the bigger-name celebrities and important public figures were housed in the swanky upper floors and even had a special lift that bypassed the riff-raff on the lower floors. The hierarchical system was disgraceful and I wanted no part of it. Having said that, I was on the twenty-second floor of sixty in Block 8-B and it was my life's quest to get myself moved higher up. No disrespect to people like Jimmy Carr or Michael Portillo, but do they really outrank a genuine public servant like Kevin Keegan? Exactly.

With a spring in my step for the task ahead, I headed to the Compound Square.

*

'Right then,' Gerry said as we sipped the hot chocolates he'd bought from the Costa on the corner. I noticed that he'd added marshmallows to his and not mine. I'd remember that. 'Where do we start?'

'To catch a spy,' I said, trying to sound like I had the first clue what I was talking about, 'you have to think like a spy.'

'Agreed,' Gerry said. 'So how does a spy think?'

'Dunno,' I said eventually.

'Sorry we're late!' came a voice from behind us.

'All right, Rodway?' Gerry said. 'Not often we see you up and about this early.'

My star striker brushed off Gerry's dig and breathed on his hands to warm them up. Behind him stood Barrington12, looking around vacantly, as per.

'Come to join the hunt?' I asked, feeling proud that they had both stepped up to the plate. The other boys were notable by their absence, but then again, we couldn't exactly stake out any suspects with fifteen people in tow.

'WE ARE HERE TO HELP CATCH AND TERMINATE THE SPY FOR HIS CRIMES AGAINST HUMANITY,' Barrington12 announced in his foghorn voice.

'No, no, no, son,' I told him. 'We're not terminating anybody. You're like the killer robot in that film who goes around terminating people; what's it called again, Gerry?'

'*Gorillas in the Mist*, I think,' Gerry said, scratching his chin.

'Listen, Barrington12, we're not here to kill anyone. I can't emphasise that enough. Violence is *never* the answer. I'm on record about that – it once cost me and Nigel Martyn victory at the FA's end-of-season quiz night, but I stand by it.'

'I AM SORRY, KEVIN KEEGAN,' Barrington12 said sadly, lowering his head with a mechanical buzz. 'I WILL ADJUST MY OBJECTIVES ACCORDINGLY.'

'Good lad,' I said. 'Glad to have you both on board.'

'We were just discussing where we should start,' Gerry told them. 'I was thinking of maybe handing out flyers – "Are You the Spy?" – and then seeing if anyone says yes. If they do, I think that's our guy.'

'No, that won't work,' I said. 'This spy is clever – they'll see right through that. We need to think… what does a spy want?'

'Money,' Gerry suggested.

'Well, yeah,' I shrugged. 'That's probably the ultimate objective. But I mean, in order to obtain secrets and learn about their environment, what would they need?'

'Information,' Rodway said. I nodded affirmatively. Gerry looked disappointed.

'That was going to be my next guess,' he muttered dejectedly.

'Correct,' I said. 'Information.'

'So… where do we go?' Gerry asked.

'It's like Graeme Le Saux said in the dressing room after my England boys qualified for Euro 2000 and wanted to celebrate in style. Gentlemen: to the library! Though let's grab an early lunch first. I'm starving.'

As we entered the vast and musty old library building with its high glass-domed roof and stacks of shelving stretching as far as the eye could see, I decided we'd be better off splitting up.

'It's a big old place,' I said, 'and we'll cover more ground that way. Plus, we need to remain inconspicuous. For all we know, the spy could very well be in the library right now.'

'Keep your eyes peeled for anyone acting suspiciously and if you see any books that might be of interest to someone with treachery in mind – anything on the Palangonian Compound itself, or biographies of key figures like Laika or anyone the L'zuhl would be interested in taking down – let me know. If we can find out who borrowed them and cross-reference a few key titles to look for the same name, we might well be on to something.'

'The library won't tell you who's previously borrowed their books though, Kev,' Gerry insisted. 'I took out a book on fly fishing last month and some thug had drawn these doodles in the margins. I asked for the names of all previous readers so I could go and box their ears but they said it was confidential.'

My heart beat a little faster. I was sure I'd erased those doodles (drawn accidentally when I went over the edge of my scrap paper while spending an idle evening trying to list my top 50 Bryan Adams songs. Listen, there's not a lot to do here in deep space).

'Probably just someone with too much time on their hands,' I said accurately. 'I wouldn't worry about it.'

An hour or so later, Rodway and Barrington12 had returned, their arms straining under the weight of the books they'd picked out. I'd stayed in the restaurant area for a coffee but obviously my brain was doing a lot of heavy lifting of its own as I devised a plan.

'Where's Gerry?' I asked.

'Still searching, I think,' Rodway said. I rolled my eyes.

'Fine, we'll start without him,' I said. 'Let's get those names.'

I headed over to the counter to see a familiar face, engrossed in her computer screen.

'Hiya,' I said, rapping my knuckles amiably on the desk. 'Remember me?'

Caroline looked touchingly pleased to see me as she lifted her glasses from her nose and perched them on her forehead.

'I do indeed!' she said. 'Kevin Keegan, who definitely didn't have a bit of a meltdown on TV that time.'

'Bang on,' I said.

'For a while there I didn't think we'd be seeing you again,' she said, lowering her voice. 'There were some ugly headlines in the *Compound Chronicle* this past week.'

'The General stitched me right up,' I said, annoyed by the memory. 'I'm totally innocent, they just took their time realising it.'

'Well, that's a relief,' she said, and it seemed like she really meant it, which in turn meant a lot to me.

'How is your...' I trailed off with a wince.

'Sister?' Caroline suggested. I nodded, relieved that she hadn't left me hanging. 'She's... well, I have no idea. Leigh rejected my application to leave and with the lockdown in place, very little information is coming in or out of the Compound. I'd like to think I'd have heard if... the worst had happened. But for now, I just have to sit here and stew. It's so difficult, it really is. I'm itching to be with her.'

'He's an absolute bin of a man,' I said sadly.

'It's great to see you anyway,' Caroline said, changing the subject. 'Can I help you look for anything in particular?'

'Well, not exactly. I'm here on other business.'

'Oh...? Like what exactly?'

'I can't tell you that,' I whispered, tiptoeing around the

subject, 'but let's just say the reason I was imprisoned… well, I want justice to be done. I really can't elaborate more than that; I'm sorry to be so cryptic.'

'You want to find the real spy,' Caroline said immediately. Christ, was I really that transparent? I thought I was being so enigmatic, when in fact she'd seen right through me like I was Gordon Strachan on a sunny day.

'How did you…?' I trailed off and glanced hurriedly behind me to make sure no one was listening in.

'Hey, believe me, I won't blow your cover,' Caroline said reassuringly. 'I want the spy found too – it's the only way I'm going to see Angela.'

I stared at her blankly.

'Who's Angela?'

'My sister.'

Bugger.

'Oh, right, yeah, of course. Well, good. Because I might need your help. I mean, if that's okay.'

'Count me in,' she replied in a determined voice. 'Let's just catch the bastard.'

'That's exactly the advice I used to give to David James before a match,' I said. She frowned in confusion but I waved a hand to say it didn't matter. 'My associates here have some items we'd like you to look at.'

Rodway and Barrington12 placed the books on the counter and the hunt began.

CLUES

Mustering all my reserves of patience I watched and paced while Caroline scanned the barcode of each book onto the system.

'Right,' said Caroline. 'That's all of Rodway's books done. We're getting there. Now let's cross-check them with… I'm so sorry, I've forgotten your name.'

'HELLO, CAROLINE KELLY. I AM BARRINGTON12. I AM FLUENT IN OVER SIX MILLION FORMS OF FOOTBALL FORMATIONS AS WELL AS—'

'All right, put a cork in it, she doesn't need to know your life story,' I said, a little more grumpily than I'd intended. Barrington12 paused while he processed this request.

'KEVIN KEEGAN, PLEASE REPEAT AND SPECIFY WHERE THE CORK MUST BE INSERTED,' he said quizzically. 'ALSO, BARRINGTON12 DOES NOT OWN A CORK. PLEASE ADVISE.'

'Just be quiet a minute,' I said with a sigh. Immediately, he stood frozen in place staring at the bare wall opposite, as though a switch had been flicked.

'Wow, a 12-series model,' Caroline said, staring at him with great interest. 'I thought they'd been scrapped years ago.'

'They were,' I muttered, 'and he most definitely should've been.' But then I felt bad. Barrington12 had given up his Friday to help us find the spy – I owed him better than that. 'He's just tired,' I said, more sympathetically. 'He's not been charged up all day, so his batteries will be running on air.'

'Actually I saw him using one of the library charge points while we were book-hunting earlier,' Rodway said.

'There's normally a fee for that,' Caroline muttered under her breath. Little wonder she and Gillian got on so well – both such sticklers for the rules. Mind you, I'm one to talk. I once heard a commentator describe a relegation scrap as 'a real six-pointer'. I was disgusted – it's three points for a win; you cannot just go about changing things like that so late in a season. The FA never even replied to my letter about it, which tells you everything you need to know about that shower.

'Right,' Caroline said when she was logged in. 'What's the next title?'

Rodway handed over one of the books Barrington12 had found – *The Unexplored Country* by Bartholomew Modge. I frowned.

'What's this when it's at home?' I asked.

'It *is* at home,' Rodway said. 'It's about our home. Part of it, anyway. It details the geography of several planets in this nebula, including Palangonia. Good call, Barrington12.'

The robot didn't respond as he continued staring into space as instructed.

'Professor Modge's speciality is documenting the more forgotten and overlooked areas of the galaxy,' Caroline explained. 'And prior to the establishment of this human colony, Palangonia was certainly one of those. This might have some important info on escape routes and points of expansion, underground tunnels and caves, that kind of stuff.'

I was distracted – there was still no sign of Gerry. I clicked my fingers at Barrington12 and told him to go and retrieve him. Dutifully, he woke up and clanked away.

Methodically, Gillian worked through the rest of the list – *Weapons of the Alliance* by JB Pilfer, *Camouflage Techniques* by Liz Lassiter, *Hiding in Plain Sight: My Life as an MIS Operative* by Craig Revel Horwood, several others. The names were a blur and Caroline scrolled down too quickly for me to get a handle on anything.

'Well, there are a lot of names who only appear once with no duplication,' she said, jotting the last few down. 'So we can put them right at the bottom of the maybe list. If our spy has indeed been using the library to advance their knowledge, I'd say it's unlikely to be any of those.'

Caroline started crossing out names from the list, people who had borrowed only one of the books from our pile. Her face took on a darker hue as she looked at the remaining name, someone who had borrowed at least three of the books in question.

'What is it?' I asked, finding it near impossible to read her handwriting. She'd clearly missed her true calling as a doctor with penmanship like that.

'It's… well, this is unexpected,' she said. 'I don't know if I should—'

'Go on,' I prompted.

'There's one name that keeps coming up,' she said carefully. 'I mean, it could just be a coincidence, it doesn't mean they're actually the spy…'

'Just tell me,' I said.

She sighed unhappily.

'It's—'

'KEVIN KEEGAN,' came a voice from behind us, startling me to the point that it probably took a decade off my life. We all whipped round in unison and saw Barrington12 waving a metal arm at us frantically from the corner of a row of shelves. 'THERE IS A PROBLEM.'

'What's wrong, son?' I asked, fearing the answer.

'THERE IS A MAN,' he said, bending forward slightly, as though trying to catch his breath – no doubt something he'd seen and copied from watching the lads in training. It was kind of sweet in its own way – almost as though he wanted to be one of us. 'IN BIOGRAPHY AND MEMOIR. HE IS PINNED BEHIND SOME SHELVING.'

'Gerry!' I cried. 'It has to be!'

'I REGRET THAT I MUST ALSO ADD,' Barrington12 said, as gravely as a dispassionate machine can, 'THAT ON FIRST OBSERVATION THERE IS A CHANCE THE MAN MAY HAVE PERISHED.'

GOODBYE,
ENGLAND'S ROSE

With a stitch burning in my side, I tore after Barrington12 as he led the way through the library. Not Gerry, it *couldn't* be. He had so much yet to live for. I mean, there was nothing specific coming to mind, but still. He was my friend. My loyal number two. And Jesus Christ, this would be such a stupid way to die as well. Typical bloody Gerry.

And then I saw him. There, his face contorted in a purple mask of agony, flanked on either side by the cheerful covers of the biographies of Paul O'Grady (cracking bloke) and George Orwell (never heard of him), was my Gerry. I gripped the edge of the shelving but I couldn't budge it even an inch. It was hopeless.

'PLEASE, KEVIN KEEGAN,' said Barrington12, 'ALLOW ME TO TRY.'

Without waiting for approval, he tugged the shelf with what seemed only minimal force and it tumbled forward, scattering its contents onto the carpet at our feet. Now no longer pinned between the shelving and the thick stone wall, Gerry's body flopped onto the floor at an undignified angle like some kind of knackered ragdoll. I noticed his fly was half undone. He'd have been disappointed with that.

'Gerry,' I said, kicking the books from my path and kneeling down beside him. I took one of his hands in mine – it was cold and clammy. Rigor mortis was probably already beginning to set in. Oh, Gerry, why now? When we were so close to finding the spy and getting Palangonia FC back.

'I can't do this without you, Gerry,' I said, and suddenly found that I was crying. I couldn't help myself. It was all finally catching up with me – losing my club, my livelihood, my dignity in Leigh's prison cell, and now my best friend. It had been the worst week I'd had since Mr Al-Fayed quarantined the Fulham training ground after becoming convinced that one of us was a shapeshifter in the employ of the royal family.

'Oh, Kevin,' said a voice, Caroline's, and she squeezed my shoulder.

'He didn't deserve this,' I said, wiping my eyes with the back of my hand. 'He's a good man. A pure football man. Oh, not like this, Gerry! Not like this…'

'We'll all miss him, gaffer,' said Rodway. How awful that he should have had to witness such a scene.

I placed a hand on Gerry's chest, my palm flat. He still felt warm underneath his tight shirt.

'Goodbye, England's rose,' I whispered, leaning forward to kiss him on the forehead.

I stood up and sniffed back my remaining tears. A sombre silence descended for some moments, until Barrington12 raised a hand.

'KEVIN KEEGAN, I FEEL IT IS MY DUTY TO REPORT

THAT MY SENSORS INDICATE FOUR INDIVIDUAL LIFE SIGN READINGS IN THE IMMEDIATE VICINITY.'

'Good for you,' I said absently.

'No, wait, hang on...' Caroline whispered, crouching down beside Gerry's corpse. 'Oh my God – your robot's right. Gerry's still breathing!'

'He is?' I exclaimed happily, kneeling beside her and staring at him. 'How can you tell?'

'Because I can see him breathing,' Caroline replied. 'Look.'

She took out her phone and held it under Gerry's nose – it seemed an odd thing to do at first but then I saw: Gerry's breath was steaming up the blank screen. He was alive!

'Get in there, Gerry, lad!' I cried, patting him on the belly enthusiastically. 'This is just like scoring late doors in a cup final!'

Whether as a result of my manhandling him or pure coincidence, Gerry suddenly opened his bloodshot eyes and sat bolt upright. He looked at each of us in turn, his eyes finally resting on me.

'Kev...' he groaned, rubbing his back and wincing. 'What... happened?'

'You died is what,' I said. 'But luckily it wasn't fatal. You're all right, son. It's going to be okay.'

'Who did this to you?' Caroline asked, standing and offering an outstretched hand. Gerry looked at her a little suspiciously, squinting.

'She's all right,' I explained, remembering that Gerry had gone off gallivanting through the library before I'd got chatting to her. 'This is Caroline, she works in the library. She's helping us out.'

'So what did happen, Gerry?' Rodway pressed.

'I... don't remember,' said Gerry unhelpfully, rubbing the back of his head. 'I was looking for a book on Fleetwood Mac for Kev's birthday. I thought it'd be a nice surprise.'

I welled up with emotion. That was a lovely gesture.

'But... this is a library,' Caroline said, frowning quizzically. 'Even if you'd found a book to give to him, it'd only have had to come back a few weeks later.'

'Then what happened?' I pressed on.

'I was scanning the shelves on my tod in here,' Gerry said, straining to recall. 'Then... I heard a noise behind me, from that room over there.'

He pointed at an unremarkable door in the corner with a small PRIVATE sign on the front.

'What?' said Caroline, looking alarmed. 'Are you absolutely sure it was in there?'

'One hundred percent,' Gerry said. 'I heard it with my own eyes.'

'But that... oh no,' Caroline said, rubbing her forehead. I hadn't seen anyone look that stressed out since I tried to explain the twenty-four-hour clock to Steven Taylor.

'What's the problem?' I said to Caroline. 'What's in that room?'

'That's the server room,' she said in a quiet whisper. 'One of three in the Compound. The others are in the infirmary and in Fort Emmeline. They all contain the same information; they're spread out to avoid overloading any one connection point. They are where all the data is stored. Oh, Christ...'

'What kind of data?' I asked. This was getting dangerously

close to being too technical for me. The first time I tried to use the internet on my home PC, I was following instructions that Gareth Southgate had written up for me. The first direction was: open a window. It was January – I nearly got bloody hypothermia sitting there. Never again.

'Everything,' Caroline said anxiously. 'Every electronic communication, every inventory of personnel or equipment – it all goes through these server banks. They're strictly off limits; that's why we don't put a sign on the door identifying what it is – no one's allowed in. Even I don't have a key.'

'Well, someone does,' Gerry said obstinately. 'Because I definitely heard someone rooting around in there. That's how I ended up in this mess – I walked over to the door, being a bit nosey and all that, and tried the knob. It wouldn't open, but obviously whoever was in there knew I'd rumbled them because next thing you know, the door flies open, hits me in the mush and I go flying back against that wall. All I could see was stars blowing up in front of my eyes, everything was a blur – then whoever it was squeezed me in behind the bookcase and smashed it into me until I stopped moving. I passed out, then next thing I know I'm on the floor with all of you around me.'

'Oh, this is really bad, Kevin,' Caroline said. 'We need to report this immediately.'

'Don't worry, Gerry's fine,' I said reassuringly. 'Look at him, good as new. No harm done.'

'Not that!' she cried. 'The spy got into the server bank – if they know what they're doing, which is pretty likely given how clever they've been in evading detection so far, they'll have managed to access everything they could wish for: documentation of the

General's meetings with the Alliance top brass, tactical decisions he's made, everything! This could be catastrophic.'

'Surely it can't be that easy,' I said doubtfully. 'It can't just be a case of breaking into one of these server rooms and looking at a screen.'

'Well, no,' Caroline said. 'Of course not. Even if someone tried to hack in it would take many dozens of hours. There's a strong firewall.'

I frowned – Mr Al-Fayed had once tried to make us use that illegal tactic to defend free kicks at Fulham but I refused point blank to have any of my players set ablaze just to prevent a goal being scored.

'The only way of accessing the information on the servers is to use a Q7 Keycard,' she went on. 'But there are only five of those in the entire Compound and they cannot be copied or spoofed.'

'Five Keycards,' I repeated. 'Where are they kept then?'

'Nowhere,' Caroline said. 'They're not just lying around – they're issued to each of the five members of the Compound Council. They're the only ones approved by the Alliance to have access.'

My eyes widened.

'So you're saying...' There was a long pause while I desperately hoped for someone to answer my half-finished question. No bugger did, so I sighed and admitted defeat. 'What are you saying?'

'It would appear...' Caroline began in a heavy voice.

'... the spy has their own Keycard,' Rodway finished slowly. 'The spy... is on the Compound Council.'

I felt a horrible weight in the pit of my stomach – like when

I went to Nick Faldo's dinner party and found a golf ball inside my curry that I swallowed whole because I was too polite to say anything. Surely it couldn't be true? One of the five people entrusted to keep us safe in our day-to-day lives in the Compound conspiring against us? Everyone knew who they were – there was the General of course, Gillian too; there was the dour head of the Compound education board, Doreen McNab; the eccentric billionaire philanthropist Sir Michael Bowes-Davies; and then there was Dr Andre Pebble-Mill, chief of medicine at the infirmary. Could Caroline honestly have been suggesting that one of these five was the spy?

We all stood there in a circle, processing this terrible information in silence. I hadn't seen such ashen faces since the day Joey Barton brought that German shepherd in to training one morning. The poor bloke was terrified. He couldn't speak a word of English; he had no idea what the hell was going on.

'It must be a conspiracy,' Rodway said. 'Has to be.'

'Doubt it,' I said, shaking my head. 'Though having said that, I used to be big on conspiracy theories myself – at one point I was going round telling people that Elvis was still alive. Mind you, that was in 1974 and he was.'

'We need to report this,' Caroline said. 'I'll send word to Fort Emmeline immediately requesting General Leigh's attention as a matter of urgency.'

'Hold your horses there,' I cut across her. 'We're not telling the General anything.'

'What?' Caroline said, appalled. 'Kevin, do you not realise how serious—'

'Too bloody right I do,' I said. 'And that's exactly why we can't tell that prat about this. Think about it, everybody! Leigh is one of the five Council members! What if... look, I hate to speak ill of anybody, but what if General Leigh is in fact the spy?'

A hush fell again. Everyone looked mortified by the suggestion (except Gerry, who was still arching his back painfully and didn't appear to be fully paying attention) but none of them could deny that this, however unlikely, was a genuine possibility. And a terrifying one at that. If it was true, the damage a man with his power – a man with the nuclear launch codes – could unleash if his secret was uncovered was simply unfathomable.

'So... what then?' Caroline asked, waving her arms in exasperation. 'We do nothing?'

'Far from it,' I said. 'Like I say, we report it. Just not to Leigh. There's only one person on that Council board whom I know and trust. She may have frittered away potential funding for my football club to fund daft things like the library—' Caroline looked stung '—but she's someone I'd trust implicitly in matters like this. She's a bog-standard chairwoman, yes, but she's a solid, upstanding citizen. I'm going to speak to Gillian.'

The strength of my feeling on the matter surprised even me – sure, Gillian and I had been frequently at loggerheads during our time working together at Palangonia FC, but her organising my coming-home party and laying on the top-drawer buffet the night before (as well as the affectionate peck on the cheek she'd given me) had convinced me that, at the end of the day, her heart was surely in the right place and that she was on our side.

I'd expected Caroline to be pleased with this compromise but she looked troubled.

'What's wrong?' I asked.

'I don't think we can tell Gillian,' she said slowly.

'Why ever not?'

'Just before Barrington12 found Gerry,' Caroline said delicately, 'I'd narrowed down the one name that appeared on the borrower history of all the books you'd identified.'

I didn't want to hear what Caroline said next but I had no choice. I closed my eyes pre-emptively and pinched the bridge of my nose in disbelief.

'It's Gillian. Her name came up again and again. Kevin, it's… it's entirely possible that Gillian is in fact the spy. And has been all along.'

NONE SO ARROGANT

Could it really be true? *Could it?*

I lay there in bed, tossing and turning, unable to switch off. I glanced over at the digital clock on my bedside table – it was gone midnight. I got up and padded into the kitchen to get a glass of water then sat down at the kitchen table among the festering remnants of the welcome home buffet and sighed heavily.

I had to admit, the pieces *did* all seem to fit: not only did her role on the Council give her Keycard access to the computerised what-have-you room, she'd borrowed almost all of the titles from the library that we'd identified as being potential spy bait.

There were also the little things that pointed towards Gillian's culpability. I kept thinking of those photos on her desk, a bloke and two youngsters that no one had ever seen in the flesh. She'd never even mentioned them in conversation; I wouldn't have known they existed if not for those pictures. And that was surely the point – they *didn't* exist. That much was now clear – they were a front, a way to make herself seem more respectable, just a regular non-spying member of the Compound community. Little wonder she kept so few friends – she was ready to leave at the drop of a hat once her cowardly business was concluded. I remembered too how I'd been impressed by

Gillian's unexpectedly strong handshake and had, on occasion, seen her walking home through the Compound Square carrying up to six heavily laden shopping bags without even breaking a sweat; I'd felt a hernia coming on just watching. Had she been secretly beefing up in anticipation of a potential battle to come? Either way, she was more than capable of bundling Gerry behind a bookcase and smashing him to pieces with it, there was no question about that. And, of course, there was also the fact that Gillian had callously and systematically starved my beloved club of funding. It probably didn't tie into her campaign of espionage but was testament to how unsavoury a character she now clearly was. How foolish I'd been in starting to sympathise with her! Clearly I'd been right first time. Gillian was the spy. All the pieces fit. I should never have doubted my gut instinct – it's never done me wrong. It's like when I pulled out all the stops to sign Les Ferdinand at Newcastle – Les wasn't completely sure about the move and kept dithering but I knew in my heart I simply had to have him. I'd heard that Les had a bit of a sweet tooth so I assured him he'd be well catered for if he signed. 'If you like a lot of chocolate on your biscuit,' I told him, 'join our club.'

'But hang on a second though,' Gerry had said as we'd walked home from our day in the library. He was limping a bit but seemed otherwise okay after his brush with death. 'If Gillian is the spy, why did she suggest that you try and uncover their identity?'

This was a valid question and one I had been pondering myself – Gillian had told me at my shindig the night before that the only hope for restoring Palangonia FC to life would be for me to find the culprit myself. She'd been joking of course, but the seed had been planted and now here we were.

'There's none so arrogant,' I said to him, 'as those who think they won't get caught.'

Nevertheless, before calling it a day I decided to split up our little posse of spy-catchers with instructions to spend the rest of the afternoon inconspicuously tailing the other Council members and keeping an eye out for anything fishy or untoward. It wasn't inconceivable, either, that more than one Council member was involved. Doreen McNab looked like a woman who lacked any sort of excitement in her life – was this how she got her kicks? And Sir Michael – well, with the best will in the world, the man was an absolute crank and it wasn't beyond the realms of possibility that he might have stumbled into becoming a spy by mistake. I wasn't genuinely prepared at this point to indulge the idea that Leigh might actually be the spy – as much as I loathed the buffoon, were you to cut him he'd surely bleed Alliance loyalty. Plus, more to the point, we couldn't exactly follow him around inside Fort Emmeline unseen. So, I dispatched Rodway to follow Dr Pebble-Mill and Gerry to Doreen McNab, while Barrington12 was sent to keep tabs on Sir Michael. I went to look for Gillian. We regrouped at dusk to report back.

'If Doreen is the spy,' Gerry sighed as we convened around a picnic table in the quiet square as it wound down for the day, 'then I know nothing about nothing. Seriously, Kev, I haven't been that bored since Graeme Le Saux's birthday party when he gave us that three-hour presentation listing all the historical anachronisms in *Braveheart*.'

Gerry detailed his tedious afternoon browsing the notice boards at the education department as he kept tabs on Doreen – she spent ninety-five minutes counting and re-counting the paperclips in her drawer and then took a long conference call with the head of a school in a neighbouring system.

'Almost two hours blathering non-stop about the optimal size for Post-it notes,' Gerry grumbled in dismay. 'I genuinely thought I might die, Kev. My body felt like it was shutting down to protect itself.'

Rodway's report on Dr Pebble-Mill was a little more dramatic: he had performed complex keyhole surgeries on two patients who had fallen asleep and landed on upturned garden shears (unconnected incidents) and he had spent a good forty minutes gently consoling a bereaved woman whose husband had died (though it later transpired the man had been at the pub all afternoon and that she had jumped to conclusions).

'If Pebble-Mill is the spy, he's the nicest one in the world,' Rodway concluded. 'I followed him around all day pretending I was a junior doctor assigned to shadow him. I was worried he'd see straight through the fake hospital ID badge I showed him but he just nodded and said it was good to see young people taking an interest in medicine and allowed me to tag along during his rounds. Honestly, he seems like a genuinely cracking bloke. I kind of wished he was my dad. That's probably a weird thing to say, isn't it?'

'Yes,' I agreed, then turned to Barrington12.

Barrington12's encounter with Sir Michael Bowes-Davies had been predictably inane. His appointment to the Council had been highly controversial and had been purely a gesture of acknowledgement for his generous contributions to charity down the years back on Earth, particularly the £52m he had donated to Children in Need in the hope of finally fixing Pudsey

Bear's bandaged eye, which had ultimately proved unsuccessful. The man was ninety-three years old, had a loose bag of marbles rolling around up top and people were liable to lose a whole day to his rambling anecdotes if they so much as caught his eye on the street.

'SIR MICHAEL SPOTTED ME FOLLOWING HIM AND WITH A WINK HE INFORMED ME THAT IF HE WERE SIX DECADES YOUNGER, HE'D HAVE CERTAINLY BEEN INTERESTED IN ME. I WAS UNSURE AS TO HIS MEANING SO I ASKED HIM OUTRIGHT WHETHER OR NOT HE WAS THE COMPOUND SPY.'

'Bloody hell, son,' I muttered. 'So much for going incognito! What did he say to that?'

'FOR REASONS THAT REMAIN UNCLEAR TO ME, HE RESPONDED BY ASKING FOR MY VIEW – WITHOUT ALLOWING ME THE SPACE IN THE CONVERSATION TO OFFER IT – OF A CAR INSURANCE CLAIM LODGED AGAINST HIS SON AT A T-JUNCTION IN INVERNESS IN 1996. I EVENTUALLY HAD TO INITIATE LOW-POWER MODE IN ORDER TO CONSERVE MY BATTERY UNTIL HE LOST INTEREST AND WALKED AWAY, OTHERWISE I WOULD NEVER HAVE BEEN ABLE TO COME BACK TO YOU WITH THIS REPORT. I FEEL VERY SECURE IN SAYING THAT THE LIKELIHOOD OF THIS INDIVIDUAL CONDUCTING COVERT OPERATIONS IN THE COMPOUND IS EXTREMELY REMOTE.'

'Well, I guess that just leaves Gillian,' Rodway said quietly.

It did indeed. In truth, I had discerned little from loitering around the empty stadium where she still kept an office, hoping to see her making a covert phone call or skulking around in the corridors. In the end, she had spent the entire time cooped up behind her desk, typing away and completing paperwork, seeing or speaking to nobody whatsoever in all that time. She had still been there when I finally threw in the towel.

I felt confident now in ruling out the others, and anyway, the facts seemed indisputable. Caroline couldn't enter the server room in the library, but she was able to access the swipe panel on the door and there it was on the user history, clear as day, no room for ambiguity: G. Routledge. She'd accessed the room that very afternoon. There was really no question, as much as I hated having to face up to it.

As I sat there stewing in my kitchen with only the distant screech of a flock of Winged Terrors on the prowl somewhere out there in the darkness far beyond the walls of the Compound, I decided there was only one thing for it. I was going to have to return to the stadium in the morning to confront Gillian. She and I needed to have it out and, once she had admitted to her crimes against humanity, I could hand her over to General Leigh who – feeling chuffed at my saving his bacon – would then reinstate Palangonia FC with extra funding and install a chair sympathetic to the needs of my club. No more 'You have twelve strikers on the books already' fob-offs, no more 'Are you sure the offside rule is just optional?' training-ground interventions. It was perfect. All I had to do was get her to confess, because there was no way Leigh was going to believe me otherwise. I could present all the evidence I liked but he'd never believe it if it came from me.

I went back to bed and tried to sleep but my mind was racing, knowing what I had to do the following day. I lay there wide awake for at least forty seconds before I finally drifted off into an uneasy ten-hour sleep.

With a heavy knot in my heart, I approached the stadium gates. Gerry had implored me to speak to Gillian peaceably, even handing me a bottle of wine to give to her to demonstrate there would be no hard feelings if she owned up.

'No chance,' I told him. 'And anyway, Gerry, this isn't wine, it's vegetable oil.'

'Is it? It's not.'

'It is. Says right there on the label – Crisp 'n Dry.'

'Oh. I thought that was just a brand name.'

'It is,' I sighed. 'For vegetable oil.'

No, there was not a chance I was going in all smiles. If she really was the spy, there could be no mercy. I strode into the John Rudge Memorial Stadium with its Palangonia FC mural on the brickwork outside. It had been designed by me: a falcon swooping down and fighting a badger. I don't exactly remember what my thinking was, but I had been eating an industrial amount of Laughing Cow cheese triangles at the time and had started to hallucinate. I suppose I do have a bit of an addictive personality sometimes – I remember as a younger man how I once passed out at a New Year party, absolutely off my face on Lilt. Mind you, I was in a bad place back then. Doncaster, specifically.

To my surprise, I bumped into Rodway on my way in – he had an empty kit bag under one arm.

'All right, gaffer?' he said brightly. 'Didn't expect to see you here. I'm just heading in to clear out my locker before they close us down for good.'

'Aye,' I said sombrely. 'You do that, son.'

Trying to keep my eyes on the prize, I trotted nimbly up the stairs to the sixth floor and Gillian's office. I glanced out of the windows in the stairwell at the empty pitch below and the lonely-looking stands. The place was like a ghost town. I hadn't seen a football stadium so deserted since I agreed to let Graeme Le Saux use Wembley for his nineteenth-century Russian literature book club.

I heaved open the door to the fifth-floor staircase and walked right into Barrington12, who was wearing a kind of weird pinafore and brandishing a mop. He looked at me as I regained my balance and, despite being a robot with a head made of metal, his face seemed to soften slightly on recognising me.

'HELLO, KEVIN KEEGAN,' he said cheerfully. 'WHAT A PLEASANT SURPRISE TO SEE YOU HERE.'

'Aye, well,' I muttered. 'Until those gates clang shut for the final time, I'm still the gaffer round here.'

His eyes blanked for a second, a sure sign that he was scanning his memory banks for something.

'ACCORDING TO CURRENT EMPLOYMENT STATUS RECORDS, YOUR POSITION WAS OFFICIALLY TERMINATED TWO DAYS AGO. THE CLUB REMAINS OPEN FOR THE NEXT FEW DAYS WHILE ADMINISTRATIVE PROCEDURES ARE CONCLUDED. FURTHERMORE—'

'I don't give a buggery what the records say,' I told him loftily. 'Palangonia FC *is* Kevin Keegan. And I'll be here until the day this club dies, make no mistake about that.'

'THAT WILL BE TUESDAY,' Barrington12 confirmed unhelpfully.

'Any road, what have they got you doing?' I asked. 'You were brought in as a member of my coaching staff, not some kind of dogsbody. They'll have you cleaning the bloody toilets next.'

'ALL LAVATORIES ON THIS FLOOR HAVE BEEN CLEANED BY BARRINGTON12 AS OF 11:28AM,' he announced. 'IF YOU HAVE ANY COMPLAINTS AS TO THE QUALITY OF THE WORK, PLEASE DO—'

'This is poor, it really is,' I said sadly. 'I'm going to have stern words with Gillian about this.'

The words froze on my lips as I remembered that I had other far more stern words to fire Gillian's way.

'BARRINGTON12 IS HAPPY TO ASSIST THE CLUB IN ALL MATTERS,' he said, nodding his head enthusiastically. 'I AM—'

He stopped as something clattered onto the stairwell behind him. I rolled my eyes and reached down to pick up the memory card which had jolted itself loose from its compartment in the small of his back in the course of his chores. The cards were effectively the brains of a Barrington model; there were five in there, between them storing everything from speech patterns to data logs, and Barrington12 was relentlessly careless with his. He could get by for a day or two without the full complement but it would eventually drain his battery at a greater speed than normal. I was guaranteed to find at least one of the cards dotted about the pitch at the end of every training session.

'THANK YOU, KEVIN KEEGAN,' he said gratefully. 'FORGIVE MY CLUMSINESS. I HOPE IT WON'T REFLECT POORLY ON MY PERFORMANCE AS A CLEANER.'

'Well, if all goes as planned today, we might well have you back on the touchline where you belong very soon,' I assured him. It was funny – I'd always resented Barrington12's presence, foisted on to me and Gerry against our will, not only because he was, frankly, a bit annoying, but also because it was symptomatic of the club's corner-cutting approach. If we absolutely had to have a robot on the coaching staff, could we at least have bought one that had been designed this century? But suddenly, with things being as they were, I almost felt a burgeoning sort of affection for him. His unsolicited assistance on the spy hunt the day before had really touched me.

'BARRINGTON12 IS AWARE OF NO PLAN,' he said, sounding almost a little hurt by the idea of having been left out.

'I promise I'll fill you in on everything afterwards,' I said, reaching up on tiptoes to put a comforting hand on his shoulder. Then I hurried up the final flight of stairs to the sixth floor and pushed open the door at the top of the stairwell just as Barrington12's voice floated up to me from below.

'PLEASE, KEVIN KEEGAN,' he said mournfully. 'DON'T DO ANYTHING YOU WILL REGRET.'

I paused just for a moment. Sometimes that soft-headed robot would come out with things which sounded almost… I shook my head. The last thing I needed was a machine that had started to think it was flesh and blood. I wondered whether the whole spy saga had started to adversely affect my thinking – it was exhausting enough having to contend with the idea that my boss might be a spy, I didn't have the energy to consider whether or not a robot might start to become human.

'Don't you worry about me, son,' I assured him breezily. 'I will continue to have the best time – hope you do the same.'

I pushed on through the door and found myself staring down a long, dimly lit carpeted corridor. At the far end was a nondescript door with the words GILLIAN ROUTLEDGE – CHAIR written on a small clear plastic sign.

This was it. Time to expose the worst act of treachery I had experienced since Shay Given referred to Status Quo as 'just some old granddad music'.

No turning back now.

SOME KIND OF
BAD DREAM

The sound of my footsteps padding on the carpet seemed to reverberate all along the eerily silent corridor. I suddenly felt oddly exposed – if Gillian came at me with a knife or tried to pistol-whip me, there'd be no one around to hear my cries for help. I mean, it might have sounded a bit unlikely, but she did have a handshake like a bloody vice; she probably wouldn't even need a weapon to take me out. I opened the door to Gillian's office and walked in – but there was no sign of her at her desk. For a moment I thought I'd missed her but then I saw her through the French windows out on the balcony overlooking the stadium. She turned round in fright at the sound of me coming in.

'Jesus Christ,' she called across the room to me, placing a hand on her chest to regain her composure. 'Kevin, can you not knock?'

I felt mortified. Even given the circumstances, it was horrifically rude of me to just barge into the room uninvited. I was better than that.

'I'm so sorry, Gillian,' I said, backing hurriedly out of the room.

I stepped back into the corridor and closed the door. I waited five seconds or so, and then knocked gently. I heard Gillian sigh wearily from within.

'Yes?'

'Gillian? It's Kevin. Kevin Keegan.'

'Yeah, I know it's— look, just come in, for heaven's sake.'

I pushed the door open and stepped back inside. I walked across the room to the balcony and paused, hands in pockets. How exactly was I meant to broach this? I've never been good at accusing people of treason. It's always been a real weak spot for me.

'I wasn't expecting to see you here today,' Gillian said.

'Enough small talk, Gillian,' I said in what I hoped was a tough, no-nonsense voice. I didn't tend to go stern very often, but when I did, people knew I meant business. Like when I rollocked Geoff Horsfield for ruining that *Sixth Sense* film for me with his obnoxious spoilers. Mind you, I was still surprised by the ending. Who would've thought that Bruce Willis was the lad's social worker all along?

'You look like you have something on your mind,' Gillian said perceptively. 'I'm all ears. But please, Kevin, don't ask me to do anything to resurrect the club because that's beyond my power. While the spy is at large, everything stops. And there are certainly no guarantees it'll come back after the fact, either. Leigh has indirectly found a way to shut us down – he won't rescind that readily.'

'I don't know how you can stand there with a straight face and say all this,' I muttered darkly, staring at her through my eyebrows. 'Of all the bloody nerve.'

She looked perplexed – I had her full attention now.

'I'm sorry?' she said, a little sharply. 'I'm not entirely sure I care for your tone. If you've got a bee in your bonnet about something, then come on, out with it.'

'I'll tell you what,' I said, trying to keep the emotion from my voice, 'I've met some arrogant so-and-sos in my time, but this takes the biscuit.'

'Kevin, where are you going with this?'

'I'll tell you where I'm going with this,' I said, stepping out to join her on the balcony and pointing an accusatory finger in her face. 'You're going to jail!'

It didn't come out quite as articulately as I'd hoped, to be fair.

'What? Why? You're not making any sense.'

'Gillian, stop pretending. I know. We *all* know.'

'Know what?!' she snapped. I had never seen her this irate, not even when I spent a fifth of my annual budget on Panini football stickers.

'It's you,' I said in as calm a voice as I could muster. 'You are the Compound spy.'

Gillian turned white.

'You cannot seriously believe—'

'I didn't want to,' I said. 'But the evidence is overwhelming.'

'Come on then,' she said, turning to face me. 'Let's hear it.'

'I've spent a bit of time at our friendly local library,' I said, walking back into her office. She followed and raised a dubious eyebrow as I explained my theory about the spy using the library for research and how Gillian's name had appeared in the charge history of several red-flagged titles.

'Oh, for heaven's sake,' she said. 'Is that it? Talk about clutching at straws. Any court in the galaxy would throw you out for presenting that. And, for the record, I haven't borrowed *anything* from the library. I've been far too busy for that, sadly.'

My arse.

'It's not just that,' I went on. 'We know the spy is a member of the Council.'

This wiped the smirk from Gillian's face. I'd got her.

'Are you serious?' she asked, grasping my arm firmly. 'If this is a joke or a trick, tell me now.'

'No trick,' I said, slightly shaken by her haunted reaction. 'Gerry saw someone in one of the server data room things at the library – you can only get in there with—'

'A Q7 Keycard,' Gillian finished. 'Good God. Oh no, this cannot be happening, this cannot…'

She looked completely traumatised by this revelation – surely a ploy to throw me off the scent.

'A traitor on the Council… this is beyond even my worst fears,' she said, her eyes darting about anxiously as she processed this information. 'You think it's *me*? That I'd do something this heinous?'

'Well,' I said ominously, 'that's the thing – the Keycard was yours. It was used just yesterday; it was right there on the user history panel, clear as day. I don't know how you managed to overpower Gerry when he rumbled you, but nevertheless…'

'This is just…' she shook her head and trailed off. I was done mucking around. I grabbed the receiver of the phone on Gillian's desk. Her eyes widened in horror.

'I'm sorry, Gillian, but enough's enough,' I said.

'No! Please!' She grabbed my arm but I shook her loose and

dialled the number for the Compound Guard emergency station inside Fort Emmeline.

'Hello?' came a tinny voice.

'This is Kevin Keegan,' I said as Gillian watched me with imploring eyes. 'I'm in the office of Gillian Routledge at the John Rudge Memorial Stadium... What do you mean, "who"? He was Port Vale manager for nigh on two decades – let's have a bit of respect, please. Listen, never mind all that – I need you to send over a couple of armed guards pronto. There's an emergency situation here. I have something the General is going to be *very* interested in.'

'I'm sorry, sir, this is Flix, the Compound cinema – would you like to book a ticket for a screening?'

With the wind taken out of my sails a little, I slammed the phone down, dialled the correct number and repeated my message.

'I'll dispatch a unit from Sentry Point D,' the operator said. 'They'll be with you in three minutes.'

I put the phone down and stared at Gillian defiantly. She looked hollowed-out, crushed.

'You can't do this to me,' she said, tears welling in her eyes. 'I've done nothing wrong!'

'That's just what Robbie Elliott said to me once when I subbed him at half-time,' I replied. 'It didn't work then, it won't work now. You're bang to rights, Gillian. It's over.'

'I believe in this Compound,' she insisted, trying to compose herself. 'It has to be a success. The sacrifices were too great to make it a reality and now it just feels like it's all... slipping away. Kevin, I know what the L'zuhl are capable of. The things they can do. They won't just raze this Compound to the ground. They'll obliterate this entire planet and everything on it. Any survivors will be rounded up, tortured to within an inch of their lives and then, if they have breath left in their bodies, they'll be doomed to a lifetime mining for phlebonium to keep the L'zuhl weapons and spacecraft fully stocked for millennia. That is what they do. Anything they can use, they take. Anything they can't, they destroy. This place, Kevin, this Compound... it's all we have left. I'd die before I saw it fall apart. You really have no idea. After all I've been through to get here, to still breathe air, to have survived when so many others...'

She trailed off, clamping a pale hand over her mouth to silence herself. My eyes followed hers to her desk, to the photographs, the smiling teenagers and the man who, again, was a bit of a dish. I shook my head – I couldn't allow her to throw me off this easily. It all just made too much sense; little wonder she had stood idly by while my football club had been tossed in the bin! I'd been so naïve. Of course that was the first thing the L'zuhl were going to target – it was clearly the greatest asset the Compound had; just ask one of the thirty-odd fans who turned out every week to watch us (though understandably that figure would usually drop to single digits if there were extenuating circumstances, such as rain). Gillian, the L'zuhl master spy, had murdered Palangonia FC. Spying for a foreign power was one thing, but this, by any estimation, was beyond the pale. As for why she would do such a thing? Outside of her work she had few friends or connections within the Compound. She was ripe for radicalisation. A quiet life with the L'zuhl probably suited her down to the ground.

'I wish I could believe you,' I shook my head. 'I really do.'

'Right!' Gillian said, wiping angrily at her eyes. 'You want proof? Fine. I can scan my Keycard on my computer here and show you the list of all its previous uses – you'll see there's been no access to the library server room on there, then you'll see… What the hell…?'

Gillian had produced a ring of keys and fobs from inside her jacket pocket and was sorting through them frantically.

'Oh, come on, no…' she muttered to herself. 'Don't do this to me.'

'Problem?'

'Oh god,' she said, slamming the keys down onto the table. 'This is like some kind of bad dream.'

'Listen, Gillian,' I said, 'let's not make this more difficult than it has to be. You made a mistake, got yourself mixed up with a bad element. I'm sure the General will be merciful – maybe they'll just exile you to one of the Quxan colonies for the rest of your life. Manual labour probably isn't as bad as they always make out.'

'You don't understand – my Keycard should be here,' she said, as much to herself as to me. 'I'd never take it off this ring, not ever. Someone's stolen it.'

'More like you dropped it when you were out on one of your espionage missions,' I said, refusing to crack.

'You have to listen to me,' she said, walking up to me and looking me right in the eye. 'I am *not* your spy. I don't know why the library computer thinks I've borrowed those books, but I can assure you I haven't. Whoever the actual spy is, they have got my Keycard. Even if they find the spy eventually, they'll crucify me for this. I'll be exiled from this nebula, I'll be finished.'

Gillian stared at me, ashen-faced. I met her gaze but said nothing. Could it really be … ?

'Kevin,' she said in a choked voice. 'I need your help. I'm not the traitor, but whoever it is has my credentials. They'll pin this on me and get away with it and someday soon the Compound will fall to the L'zuhl. We have to stop this. And we can, if you'll just trust me.'

There was a commotion at the door behind me – there stood two Compound guards brandishing rifles, their black visors down over their eyes.

'You Coogan?' one of them barked, stepping forward.

'Yes,' I said. 'Well, no. It's Keegan. But I'm the one who…' I looked at the terrified Gillian and hesitated. 'The one who called you in.'

The other guard cocked his gun and approached.

'Dispatch said you had an emergency situation here,' he said in an urgent voice. 'Something the General would want to know about.'

I looked from the emotionless blank of their visors to Gillian. She cut an almost timid figure now, powerless and effectively at my mercy, a far cry from the Council bigwig who had overseen the demise of my beautiful football team. So long my adversary in the financial management of the club, she now seemed so small, so alone. So human.

'Please,' Gillian whispered, squeezing my arm urgently. 'This is my life we're talking about. I'm telling you, Kevin: it's not me. It isn't.'

I was torn. There was every chance that this was an act to buy her own survival, a cornered animal doing everything it could to escape from harm. But as I looked at her, I realised I couldn't go through with it. It wasn't necessarily that I believed her – it was that I wanted to.

'Well?' snapped the first guard. 'What is it?'

I turned to face them. 'What do you think of the décor in here?'

'The... what? What are you talking about?'

'The wood panelling aesthetic – what do you make of it? I was never all that keen before but I've started to come round to it. I think it has quite a calming, soothing effect.'

'What in God's name are you blathering about?' asked the second guard, lowering his gun. 'You said there was an emergency.'

'There is,' I nodded. 'Fort Emmeline is so drab, you guys must have noticed that. Grey walls, no atmosphere. I think the General needs to seriously consider a redecoration job. Something like this might be just the ticket.'

The first guard flipped open his visor and looked at me with venomous eyes.

'You're a real piece of work, Coogan,' he said. 'The General will hear about this. Wasting Compound Guard time is a criminal offence.'

He pointed his rifle at us both threateningly and then the two of them marched out of the office and stomped away down the corridor, muttering to one another in annoyance.

'Kevin,' Gillian said, hanging her head and taking a deep breath before looking at me. 'Thank you. I... don't know what to say.'

'Don't say anything,' I replied. 'Not yet. Because I still haven't made up my mind about you. But I will. Like Iain Dowie with a league table, I'm going to get to the bottom of this.'

'We both will,' she said determinedly. 'The spy, whoever it is, has crossed a line. And with access to a Keycard, we'll all be in grave—'

She stopped suddenly and we both stared fearfully through the open balcony doors as an ear-piercing scream filled the air... along with the dreaded sound of flapping wings.

DEATH FROM ABOVE

I stood there on the balcony, helplessly watching as a pack of Winged Terrors, six of them at least, swarmed down. The two guards were under attack, one of them completely incapacitated and already in the process of being torn limb from limb. The other was injured, a bloody gash across one forearm, his armour easily pierced as he fired indiscriminately into the air with the gun in his free hand.

I'd never seen the foul creatures this closely before – they were muscular and strong, chests like those of a gorilla, covered in a mat of dirty black fur. The claws on their hands and feet were razor-sharp and their faces were something from a nightmare; the menacing grins on their hideous goblin-like features sent a chill down my spine and their wingspan was like some kind of enormous hang-glider. I could barely see either of the guards now as the group tore and swiped at them while they pleaded in vain for help. The day before, I'd assumed that being smooshed behind a big bookcase was the worst way to die but now I knew better. Suddenly, my heart skipped a beat as another figure appeared on the scene, watching in horrified fascination.

'Rodway!' I shouted down from the balcony. 'Get back inside and out of sight, you damn fool!'

My star striker looked up at me, his face pallid with shock – and then within seconds, two of the Terrors broke free from the main throng and set upon him. With a muffled cry he fell to his knees.

'What do we do?' Gillian asked in distress, clutching the balcony rail with white knuckles. 'The guard outposts are too far away – we're on our own!'

'Oh, Jesus and Mary!' I cried as two of the Terrors flew away, one carrying the first guard's legs, the other hoisting guard number two's upper torso. The remaining two beasts gathered up Rodway, thankfully still in one piece – but barely.

'Stop right there!' I bellowed angrily at them. 'He's my top target man!'

The Terrors looked up at us on the balcony and one of them, the leader going by his size, barked a harsh, guttural laugh. Then, carrying my poor number nine between them as he struggled to break free, they flew up and over the Compound walls and vanished from sight.

I looked at Gillian who stared back at me in utter horror.

'What now?'

'What do you mean, "what now"?!' I said, incredulous, as I swung a leg over the balcony railing. 'I've got to rescue him – he was still alive when those flapping wazzocks grabbed him, there's no time to waste!'

'Jesus Christ, Kevin, this is the sixth floor!' Gillian said, grabbing my arm and pulling me back onto the balcony. 'Take the lift down to the ground level at least.'

It was a smart call. I'd always had a terrible fear of heights – Steve Bruce once quipped that this was probably why my Newcastle side choked the league title in 1996. Prat.

'Kevin, stop,' Gillian said as I tore back inside her office. I turned impatiently in the doorway and looked back at her.

'I have to move fast,' I said in frustration. 'There'll be no Fergie time here, the clock is ticking!'

'What are you going to do?' she asked in a 'don't you get it?' kind of tone. 'The Compound is in lockdown – there's no way they'll open the gates for you. And if you try to sneak past the guard posts, you'll be shot. I'm on the Council, remember. I know how seriously they're taking matters of security at the moment.'

She faltered slightly as she said this last part – we both knew we had unfinished business in that arena to discuss.

'Well, I'm not just going to stand here and do nothing,' I said eventually. 'That kid out there was a complete waster until I talked some sense into him. Now he's turning his life around – I'm not going to sit on my hands and watch it end like this. If I have to die in a hail of bullets, then so be it.'

'It doesn't have to be that way,' said Gillian in a thoughtful voice – I could see she was running something through her head. Finally, she said, 'I'll help you. I know a way. And maybe I can prove to you for certain that I'm not the spy after all.'

I listened stoically as she outlined her plan. When she finished, I nodded.

'That'll do.'

At dusk, I stood with Gerry and Barrington12 behind the bins at the back of the Compound infirmary. Every little sound had me on edge – if anyone got wind of our plan, we were buggered. It was a chilly evening and I wished I hadn't left my thick gloves at the bottom of my backpack. Gerry had brought an enormous cricket bag, packed with clothes, four bottles of Irn-Bru, a six-pack of Vimto, twelve tins of baked beans, nine tins of spaghetti hoops, seven tins of mulligatawny soup and a Toblerone.

'I told you to pack some bottled water,' I told him when he showed me the contents. I was irritable, distracted. I felt the weight of the world upon my shoulders ahead of our expedition and longed for the days on Earth when I could have just called up any of the other ex-England managers for advice. A lot of people don't realise the special bond we all share. It's unlike anything else in football – no one else has experienced life in that goldfish bowl as we select few have done. I haven't seen the old gang as much as I used to since the invasion of Earth, but back in the pre-L'zuhl days we'd regularly meet up to set the world to rights. I got along famously with all of them, despite some of their eccentricities. Let's face it, Glenn Hoddle can be a difficult man – I remember years back, the FA came really close to introducing a rugby-style sin bin system in football, only for the scheme to collapse after Glenn insisted that it also include sins from former lives. He travels the galaxy now with the disembodied living head of his faith healer Eileen Drewery in a jar, dispensing their New Age wisdom. Good luck to them.

Sadly, I fell out with most of them in 2016 – and it was over one of my proposals too. It was for an ITV Sunday night drama series called *King & Country*. The concept was simple but ingenious – we would all play ourselves in the show, driving round provincial English towns in a van and getting into scrapes with the locals and solving some kind of mystery in each episode. Everyone was well up for it, though Roy Hodgson took some persuading. He kept saying, 'I only watch BBC Four,' which to me sounded like a lie. There's no such channel. Anyway, eventually they all signed on: me, Terry Venables, Glenn Hoddle, Sven, Steve McClaren, Fabio Capello and Roy. We had Joanna Lumley signed up to play a kind of mastermind figure to our gang who would listen to police-band radio and tell us where any strange unsolved crimes had taken place, and I'd even had an approach from Danny Boyle to direct the pilot episode. I was only too happy – I said to him, 'I'm not a fan of your silly druggie films if I'm being brutally frank, but your sister, Susan, has the voice of an angel.'

Sitting down with the boys in the writers' room was where the trouble began. I had a basic outline for the opening episode: there's a spate of weird big cat sightings in a Cornish village, so we all pile into the van and drive down – we stop off at a pet shop on the way to buy some toys and treats to lure the big cat out of hiding.

Then, Sven asked if there could be a woman working in the pet shop.

'Okay, sure,' I said, scribbling it down. 'The pet shop is owned by a woman called Sarah.'

'And then Sven seduces her,' Sven said, nodding.

'No, of course not,' I replied, appalled. 'This is going out at 7 p.m. on a Sunday night. Get a grip, please.'

Well, I've never seen a man go from aroused to angry so quickly – Sven stood up and kicked over his chair, calling me all sorts of filth before storming out. Then Steve Mac and Venables said they were nipping out for a coffee and never came back; Glenn and Fabio fell asleep. It was a disaster. ITV passed on my rejigged proposal (just me riding around in a van solving mysteries alone, with a title card at the start explaining that the others had all been killed by an unexploded World War II bomb beneath Wembley) and *King & Country* was no more. I'm not sure I'll ever be able to forgive them.

As we stood there behind the Compound infirmary, a figure turned the corner and hurried towards us. Gillian was wearing a thick waterproof coat and was carrying a rucksack over one shoulder – Millets, so she definitely wasn't mucking about.

'Sorry I'm late,' she said. 'This afternoon's Council meeting ran late – there's been a spate of zero-gravity hotspots appearing around the Compound, small pockets where the laws of physics have ceased to apply; not uncommon in this nebula apparently. Anyway, yesterday we lost an entire Pizza Express and every diner and staff member within it, just floating off into space. Terrible business.'

The zero-gravity problem had been a real irritation, so I was pleased to hear that something was finally being done about it. We had lost a pre-season friendly against the hobgoblins of Raskus Fortuna when Rodway's last-minute penalty happened to pass into one of the hotspots and the ball had floated up into space barely a foot from the goal line. I'll tell you what, I never once had that problem in the Premier League, so credit to them where it's due.

'Let's get going,' Gillian went on, speaking quickly, and, I felt, a little nervously. She sounded the way we all felt. 'I told the Council I wasn't feeling well by the end of the meeting, that I'd eaten something that didn't agree with me – that ought to buy me a few days of peace, but if I'm gone for longer than that then people are going start to start asking after me. Right: according to biological assessments of the planet, Winged Terrors are believed to eat a full meal once every one to two days. They took away two Compound guards, so if we're lucky, they won't get round to Rodway until tomorrow night or even the morning after. But just remember your end of the bargain too, Kevin – if I assist you with this, you must help me find my Keycard before anyone else does. My career depends on it. Possibly my life.'

'Hey,' I said, 'let's not have any more of that kind of talk. We four are a team now, as much as any I've ever played for or managed. There's a kid somewhere out there in the dark, scared out of his wits and maybe not long for this world. But I happen to know that there's something those Winged Terrors didn't count on: us. Let's bring our boy home, alive and in one piece.'

ETCHINGS

It was pitch black in the tunnel. I couldn't even see my own hand if it was outstretched in front of me – and when I tried it just ended up caught in a filthy mass of cobwebs that turned out to be Gerry's hair.

'Watch where you're going!' Gillian snapped as I clipped her heel for the fiftieth time.

'I can't, can I?' I whispered back. 'It's darker than that book of poetry Martin Keown self-published!'

'I can't believe not one of you thought to bring a torch,' she sighed.

'That's fine, we can just use one of those that you brought with you,' I replied bitingly.

'I was packing in a hurry,' she said, sounding a little hurt. I felt bad for losing my rag slightly, so made a mental note to send Gillian a WHSmith voucher when we got back.

'KEVIN KEEGAN!' Barrington12 exclaimed from behind me. I rolled my eyes.

'What is it this time?' I asked impatiently. 'Bearing in mind that I've already explained to you three times today how indirect free kicks work. The answer is: nobody really knows.'

'I WAS GOING TO OFFER MY SERVICES,' he went on.

'I CANNOT HELP BUT NOTICE THAT THE THREE OF YOU ARE STUMBLING ABOUT AHEAD OF ME AS THOUGH YOUR VISUAL ACUITY HAS BEEN SIGNIFICANTLY IMPAIRED. PERHAPS IF I ACTIVATED MY NIGHT MODE IT WOULD IMPROVE MATTERS FOR ALL CONCERNED.'

There was a loud click and suddenly the tunnel path ahead of us was wreathed in light – I had to shield my eyes from the initial glare. I looked behind me at Barrington12, who had had to hunch over in order to fit into the tunnel in the first place – a large light bulb was now protruding from each of his clunky shoulder panels and I could now see clearly for a good ten yards ahead of us.

'Ah, that's better!' Gerry said, and then bent to look at the sole of his shoe. 'Oh, I knew it, Kev – stepped in dog muck.'

'It won't be dog muck,' said Gillian ominously. I found myself feeling grateful that she didn't elaborate. I was still stunned by the fact this network of tunnels existed beneath the Compound – and also by Gillian's apparent knowledge of them.

'Well, you found a book in the library that should give you a few clues,' she had explained as she led us to the tunnel entrance. 'I haven't read it myself, despite what the library computer may say, but I know that the Modge book has a wealth of writing about these subterranean routes – though even he didn't know who originally built them. They've been here for centuries and whoever constructed them has long since departed. It can't be the native tribespeople; these designs are too advanced. But once we humans arrived and built this Compound here, it made sense to retain access to them in the event of a L'zuhl strike.'

'Or a promising young striker being kidnapped by bad alien bats,' I added.

'That too.'

The tunnel entrance, one of several hidden away around the Compound – which had been strategically built on this location in order to take advantage of them – was located beneath a tangle of weeds and shrubbery on the wasteland at the far end of the infirmary premises. It had become a bit of a dumping ground; there was litter and a few white goods left in pieces all around, which only added to the surprise when Gillian pushed her way through the grass and heaved open the heavy grille entrance with relative ease – once again I was quietly impressed by her physical prowess. Inspired, I made a mental note to make sure I went out for a jog at least once a month once life returned to normal – if indeed it ever did.

That had been almost an hour ago as I looked at my watch, bathed in the glow of Barrington12's shoulder lights. There was still no sign of the tunnel reaching its end. Inside there was no human litter, understandably, but the walls were smeared with unpleasant-smelling goo of which I really didn't care to know the origin. The soil beneath us was split by a tiny trickling stream, the dirty-looking water the only sound we could hear other than our own footsteps.

'Look at these,' Gerry said, scrunching his nose at a crudely drawn painting scratched into the stone wall to our left.

'My goodness,' Gillian said, hurrying over for a closer look. 'These must have been made by whoever built these tunnels – the alien race who once lived on Palangonia! These are extraordinary! Barrington12, more light please!'

I peered at them, but they didn't look all that impressive to me. I mean, I'm not having a go but I think I could have drawn better than that, and in the dark too. They seemed to depict several kneeling stick men around a large platform with runes and other symbols that I didn't recognise. One did look a little bit like the Blackburn Rovers club crest but I decided that was more than likely just a coincidence. Atop the platform was another stick figure, this one with long flowing hair at its back; he was ascending to the heavens as beams of light shone down.

'Kids' stuff,' I sniffed. 'They wouldn't even bother showing that on *Blue Peter* if someone sent it in.'

'Oh no, Kevin, far from it,' Gillian said, scrutinising the art closely. 'This is one of the most incredible things I've ever been privileged to see!'

'PRELIMINARY SCANS OF THESE ENGRAVINGS SHOW THAT THEIR SOURCE IS NOT FOUND ANYWHERE IN BARRINGTON12'S DATA BANKS. THESE ARE HITHERTO UNKNOWN TO WIDER GALACTIC CIVILISATION.'

'So was Shaka Hislop until I signed him from Reading,' I muttered. 'Look, I'm sorry to have to break up this little Sister Wendy thing you've got going on here, but there's a young man's life at stake somewhere above ground, you know.'

Gillian straightened up and looked at me; she nodded.

'You're right, Kevin, I'm sorry. We have a job to do and no time to waste. I hope we'll be able to come back this way, with Rodway in tow, and examine these amazing discoveries further.'

What a treat, I thought miserably.

We walked on in near silence, each of us lost in our own

thoughts. At one point I could have sworn I saw something scuttling along the ceiling right above us, but if I did, it moved too quickly. Most likely just my imagination – they say your eyes can play tricks on you sometimes. Certainly that's the excuse I always used after paying £6 million for a crocked Robbie Fowler. Then, just when I began to wonder whether the tunnel might not have any kind of exit at all and that we'd be forced to trek all the way back the way we'd come with our collective tails between our legs, Gillian spotted something.

'There, look,' she pointed to the wall on our right just ahead. It was a grille, identical to the one we'd squeezed through to enter the tunnel (some of us with more dignity than others – seeing the arse of Gerry's trousers begin to split right in front of my face as we shuffled our way in head-first had not been on my to-do list for the day). The tunnel continued on into the black up ahead, suggesting that there must have been at least one other exit along the way.

'I think this is about right,' Gillian said, scratching the back of her head. 'I don't remember every detail of the tunnel maps but given how long we've been walking and the direction we've been travelling, this should be the place. Barrington12, could you do the honours, please?'

Without any hesitation, he stretched out an arm and plucked the grille free as though it was a ripened apple on a tree. One by one – Gerry first as, with respect, he was probably the most expendable and he'd be the first to admit that – Barrington12 gave us a leg-up through the grille, where we wriggled our way out.

Finally, there was a waft of fresh air as Gerry forced open the hatch at ground level and spilled out into the coolness of the night. I was close behind (his trousers had now split to all bloody hell ahead of me) and once outside, I reached a hand back in to tug Gillian out to freedom. With a scraping, clattering effort, Barrington12 soon joined us.

'Wow,' I said, looking around us in wonder. 'I've been on this planet for a year and I've never seen anything beyond the four walls of the Compound. And now... this.'

By a combination of Barrington12's lights and the pale glow of Palangonia's three large moons, we looked around to find ourselves in a wide forest clearing. Tightly packed trees circled us on all sides, their boughs reaching high into the sky, taller than any I had ever seen back on Earth. The grass underfoot was spongy and damp; it had evidently rained not long before. I pointed at a flattened trail ahead of us, which suggested someone had walked through the meadow relatively recently.

'The tribespeople,' Gillian said darkly. 'We must all be on our guard. They don't trust us and with good reason. They're unlikely to hesitate if they see us out here.'

I glanced back over my shoulder and gasped. The others followed my gaze and looked on in silent awe. Through a gap in the trees, way off towards the horizon, we could faintly make out the thick grey outline of the Compound, small lights twinkling on the machine-gun turrets positioned across the breadth of the wall. It had a strange kind of beauty when viewed from afar, out in the wilds of an alien planet like this.

'It's not much,' I said, 'but it's our home. Come on – let's find Rodway sharpish and get ourselves back to it.'

'This way,' said Gillian, pointing. 'There was an intel report from General Leigh's team at a Council meeting a few months ago which said that most of the Winged Terrors seemed to originate from nests on the lower slopes of Great Strombago. If we're going to find him anywhere, it'll be there. Though Christ knows how the hell we're going to get up to retrieve him.'

I swallowed hard – I hadn't realised *that* was going to be our destination. It would've been just our luck for the long-dormant volcano, one of the great Palangonian landmarks that had spewed its last over ten thousand years prior, to choose today to wake up.

'We'll deal with that problem when we have to,' I said, pressing on across the clearing.

Little did we realise we'd have several others to deal with first.

INTO THE WILD

We hiked through dense forest for a couple of hours before Gillian suggested we make camp for the night. Aside from being pestered by mosquitoes the size of 50p coins, we were entirely alone. I was only too happy to stop – my legs were aching something rotten and Gerry looked half-dead. It was probably the most exercise he'd had since he bought that treadmill which got stuck on the fastest setting. He ran full pelt for a day and a half before a power cut finally rescued him.

'Let's try to be as quiet as we can,' Gillian suggested as she set down her pack beside a thick black tree. 'We've been lucky so far, but there are many strange and foul things out here in the forests of Palangonia and we'd be well advised not to draw attention to ourselves.'

This was clearly a dig at me. I'd brought my guitar so that I could regale everyone with my own interpretations of the songs on *Rumours* (though my interpretations were absolutely identical to the album versions – why would you want to tamper with perfection?). In truth, what I felt most was embarrassment – Gillian seemed to have taken to this adventure with gusto and with little outward fear or anxiety for what may lie ahead. Me, I still felt like a tourist, ready to complain to one of the guides because bad weather had obscured the best view of some local landmark.

We began to unpack our sleeping bags and blankets. Gerry hadn't brought any – no room amongst the junk food in his bag – and he was looking at my quilted one enviously. I was astonished to see Gillian produce one of those snazzy pop-up tents from her pack – why hadn't I thought of that? Right on cue, heavy rain began to fall between the leaves of the trees above, spattering us with fat drops which soaked me to the skin within thirty seconds.

'Crikey,' Gillian said, clambering into her tent quickly, 'not a moment too soon! Goodnight, all. Tomorrow, if our luck holds, we may reach the foot of Great Strombago by late afternoon. Sleep well.'

She waved and then zipped up the tent door. I glanced at Gerry, who was leaning back against a petrified tree trunk, pulling his knees up to his chest and looking thoroughly miserable. Barrington12 just stood there doing nothing.

'You *are* waterproof, aren't you?' I asked. It had never come up before.

'Nope,' Gerry sniffed. 'I'll probably wake up dead from pneumonia in the morning.'

'Not you,' I rolled my eyes.

'BARRINGTON12 IS BUILT TO WITHSTAND EXTERNAL LIQUID INTERFERENCE,' he confirmed. 'IF YOU WISH, I CAN STAND GUARD TONIGHT AND WATCH FOR ANY INTRUDERS BROACHING THE BORDERS OF OUR CAMPSITE.'

'That'd be cracking,' I said. 'Thanks.' And actually, I did feel reassured. He may have been a complete liability as a football coach (once suggesting that I play with only one striker in favour of a tighter midfield – the very idea!) but the kid could handle himself. I snuggled down in my sleeping bag beneath a large overhanging luminous blue leaf to keep the water off my head. I've never been a fan of camping, really. As far as I'm concerned, it's like sleeping indoors, only nowhere near as good.

'Kev?' Gerry whispered from close by. 'You awake?'

I frowned.

'Well, yeah,' I said. 'I only climbed into my sleeping bag twenty seconds ago. What's up?'

'Do you think we'll find Rodway?'

'One way or another,' I said grimly. There was silence for a few moments before Gerry spoke again.

'What do you make of Gillian?' he asked. 'Do you still think she could be the spy?'

I glanced over at Gillian's tent and considered this for a few moments.

'No,' I said finally. 'I don't. She wouldn't be out here if she was.' But then, I'd been wrong before. I mean, I used to think 'dreadlocks' was a fear of keys.

'I hope you're right,' Gerry said. 'If anything happened to us out here, nobody would ever know.'

This was certainly a good point. If Gillian was the spy, and had come so close to being exposed, what better way to deal with those who had discovered her secret than to offer to take them beyond the Compound walls and out into the great Palangonian nowhere before quietly bumping them off? If Gillian tried anything during the night, would Barrington12 intervene?

His loyalties would be divided between her and me and he'd probably just stand there doing naff all.

With these unwelcome thoughts swirling in my mind, I floated off into a dreamless sleep.

I awoke with a start. What was that sound? I poked my head up slowly from the warm depths of my sleeping bag and looked around. The light through the trees was dim but it was clearly close to dawn. The rain had stopped, and it felt pleasingly cool. There it was again! A heavy rustling sound, like something large moving through the undergrowth in the distance. All the hairs on the back of my neck stood on end. I glanced over at Gillian's tent and sat up with a jolt. It was unzipped and the flap was open – there was no one inside. I stumbled to my feet and, wearing just my pants, socks and the T-shirt with my own face printed on it (I'd had a box of them made to hand out to my England lads as a souvenir when I resigned – there were no takers, so I kept them for myself. Waste not, want not). I padded quickly over to the tent and peered inside. It seemed a bit of an invasion of privacy, but then, if she was indeed the spy and had legged it during the night, she'd already invaded the privacy of everyone in the Compound. Inside, her sleeping bag was empty.

'Gerry!' I cried, pulling on my trousers and jacket and whirling round to the dead tree beside which he'd been sleeping. 'Gillian's gone – she slipped away in the night!'

My jaw dropped. Like Gillian, Gerry was gone. I looked up ahead to where Barrington12 had stationed himself, but there were just the indentations of his heavy feet on the muddy forest trail. I was completely and utterly alone.

Except I wasn't. Something was making that dreadful sound. And it was coming closer.

'Pssst!'

I glanced up, and to my alarm saw three figures perched quite high above me in the boughs of an enormous tree.

'Quickly, Kevin!' Gillian said, waving frantically to me to join the three of them in their lofty sanctuary. 'It'll be here any moment!'

'What will?' I asked, still slightly dazed with sleep and half-wondering whether this was all some strange dream elicited by sharing a full bottle of Irn-Bru with Gerry during the journey the evening before.

'That!' cried Gerry in horror, pointing through the trees behind me. And then I saw it.

Worse – it saw me.

Fear is something to which, in football, you cannot succumb. The roar of a hostile away crowd, the anxiety of a hopeless relegation scrap, the bowel churn before taking the decisive spot kick in a penalty shootout – these are things you must not be afraid of, otherwise you're setting yourself up for failure. And as I stood there in the great Palangonian nowhere, I realised that 'coming face to face with a monstrous space bear' was most definitely another one for the list.

'Kev!' Gerry screamed again, and I knew from the unabashed terror in his voice that I was in big trouble. That, and the fact that a giant space bear was heading right for me. I leapt into the air but the branch around which Gerry had wrapped himself was far too high.

'I can't... get it...!' I grunted, hopping on the spot in complete futility. Each time I landed, I felt the ground beneath my feet vibrate – but not from me. An ear-splitting growl filled the air, reverberating off the thick black trunks of the trees circling our clearing. A flock of small birds took flight immediately and were gone – I'd never felt more jealous in my entire life.

'Wait!' Gillian said.

'I don't have time for that!' I snapped, allowing myself a glance over my shoulder – the bear was breaking through the trees at a rate of knots and in less than a minute would be upon me, tearing me limb from limb.

'Hang on...' Gillian said, and I looked on from ground level, baffled and annoyed at the lack of any assistance from my companions. She scuttled agilely along the same branch that Gerry was impotently clinging on to and then she turned back and gestured frantically to the motionless Barrington12, who was sitting in the boughs of the tree, watching the terrible scene unfold impassively. 'Barrington12, I need you!'

Instantly, he stood up and, with the posture and balance of a high-wire walker, followed Gillian onto the branch. I heard it begin to groan ominously above me, before the sound was drowned out by another roar from the bear.

'I'm going to die!' I cried, almost laughing as a strange hysteria began to take hold. This really was the end. To my bemusement, I realised that my final thought was going to be one of disappointment – not at my demise (though that was going to be a pain in the arse, quite frankly) but at the fact that I'd never uncover the identity of the spy after all. I could only trust that Gerry would continue to fight for the truth after I was gone. I closed my eyes and exhaled slowly. We all had to go sometime.

'Kevin!' Gillian shouted down. 'I think this could work, but you need to buy us some time!'

I opened one eye and then the other, then immediately closed them again – the bear was standing at the edge of the clearing, reared up on its hind legs and pummelling its chest, roaring so loudly that I thought my ears might bleed.

'How am I meant to do that?' I shouted back as the bear started scraping the ground in front of it with both feet in succession, like a bull preparing to charge, its razor-sharp claws cutting great thick clumps out of the soil.

'Try to give it the runaround!' Gillian suggested urgently.

'Oh, simple as that, is it?!' I said in exasperation. 'Right… okay…' I took deep breaths and shook my head to clear the fear and doubt. I'd once read that to survive in a situation like this you needed to make a wild animal respect you, so I took a few steps forward on legs made of jelly and stared straight into the burning yellow eyes of this killing machine the size of a double-decker bus.

I stood there, rooted to the spot like Kieron Dyer defending the far post during a corner, as the horrifying beast bore down on me. Its thick fur was matted and dirty and badly afflicted with mange. Its paws were each twice the size of my head and its mouth was big enough to swallow me if not whole then certainly with a couple of big chews. The thing that differentiated it from a bear on Earth, aside from its luminous yellow eyes and its incredible size, was the enormous swishing tail that whipped around behind it as it ran, trailing like a loose shoelace. The forest floor beneath my feet seemed to tremble as I awaited my inevitably grisly fate. Somehow I'd always known I'd cop it by being ripped to shreds by some kind of giant space bear. Bloody typical.

'Almost there,' Gillian grunted from above me but I couldn't look – my eyes could not tear themselves away from my impending doom. Then, just as the bear was upon me, it stopped and turned its back. All I could hear was my heart beating to break free of my chest as, with a low growl, it flicked its tail out and towards me. Instinctively, I jumped backwards and the thin, barbed tip of its tail swept through the air right in front of my midriff, ripping a gash right across my Newcastle Brown Ale jacket. I blinked, stunned. Had I had my usual waistband-expanding jumbo breakfast at Mr O's that morning, I would surely have been scrabbling about collecting my innards at that very moment.

'It's toying with you!' Gillian said from somewhere close by. 'You're just sport!'

'Reassuring,' I muttered.

'It's a chance,' she said – and she was right. The bear looked at me with cold disdain but also, just maybe, a grudging respect. Clearly, it had expected to finish me with one move but they didn't call me Cool Hand Kev for nothing. (To be fair, they've never called me that.)

The bear flipped its tail out towards me but again I dodged it, this time with more room to manoeuvre. My confidence began to grow and I felt on top of the world, like Lee Dixon must have done that time he won Crufts (before the subsequent investigation and career-ending scandal that revealed he had been wearing a dog costume all along).

'Almost,' Gillian said in a strained voice, but I only had eyes for the monster. It turned back to face me, realising that its tail trick was not going to get the job done. Even from thirty yards away I could smell its foul breath. Fat globules of drool flew from its maw as it studied me, a more challenging foe than it had expected to face. My eyes darted about for something, anything I could use to keep the thing at arm's length for just a little longer. It was circling me, evaluating me, but it wouldn't wait long to make its move. Then my foot crunched on something. I allowed myself the briefest glance to the ground and saw I was standing in a small cluster of large cones, at least double the size of your average pine cone back on Earth. Before I even had time to think about it, my feet seized the initiative.

'Come on then,' I cried, fire in my eyes. 'Have a bit of this!'

The bear snarled and made its move – and so did I. With the deft moves of a man who had scored over two hundred career goals, I flicked one of the heavy cones into the air with my left foot and with my right I leathered it on the volley, grinning with satisfaction as it thwacked painfully against the creature's snout. It yelped in pain and surprise, curtailing its run and retreating back a few steps.

'You want some more?' I asked, giddy as the adrenaline coursed through my veins. 'Here we go!'

Unfortunately my second volley went way off target – I was only wearing socks; I must stress that it absolutely wasn't an issue of technique – and instantly the bear sensed weakness. Before I could line up a third cone, it was running at me, jaws wide, tired of playing games.

'Gerry,' I said, closing my eyes. 'Tell my lads I'll never forget—'

I never got the chance to finish that thought. Mere moments before it reached the spot upon which I was standing, I found myself hoisted painfully into the air. My arm was almost ripped from its socket, but then that was the least I could've expected had the space bear got to me first. I opened one eye and looked up – hanging from the mercifully sturdy bough above was Barrington12, one strong metal hand clasped firmly around the branch. Hanging from his other was Gerry and gripping Gerry's other hand (painfully tightly, if her strained pink face was anything to go by) was Gillian, who had hooked her free arm around mine and plucked me from the ground. We now swung in the air, a human-robot daisy chain, tantalisingly out of reach of the space bear as it spat and hissed in fury below us, occasionally swiping one of its great paws at my feet – and coming perilously close, too.

'Barrington12!' Gillian groaned. 'Pull us up!'

With remarkably little effort on his part, Barrington12 clambered back up onto the widest expanse of the branch and pulled us all up as though removing the plug from a bath. We flopped onto the flat of the bough and clung on for dear life to steady ourselves. Once I'd got my breath back, and with the beast still mithering several feet below, circling the trunk of the tree purposefully, I flopped over onto my back and stared up at the whitening sky through the green expanse of leaves above.

'I thought I was a dead man,' I whispered.

'You almost were!' Gerry gasped, swinging his arm in his socket uncomfortably. 'It was Gillian's quick thinking that saved the day.'

I looked over at her, sitting almost in Barrington12's lap, her brow shining with sweat.

'Thank you, Gillian,' I said. 'Man alive, I don't know where you got muscles like that but I'm bloody glad you have.'

'Two hours' boxing in the training ground after you softies have gone home, five nights a week,' she said nonchalantly. 'We all need our hobbies.'

I was quietly impressed – I didn't even realise our training ground had a gym. Mind you, I'm not the most observant of people. I once phoned up 5 Live to give my views on the chaos in Italian football only to be told, eventually, that the discussion was about Syria, not Serie A.

'You saved my life,' I said, still not entirely sure how I was still drawing breath.

'Don't make me regret it,' she replied, putting her head between her knees to gather herself.

Once we felt like ourselves again, we realised our new predicament. We were out of the frying pan and into the fire – there was simply no way to climb down to ground level without the space bear gobbling us up. Gerry suggested we leap from tree to tree, but realising that the nearest outstretched branch was about twenty feet away soon put the skids on that idea.

'There's really no way,' he said miserably. 'We're stuck.'

'Until the creature leaves, I fear you're right,' Gillian agreed with a sigh. 'Our best hope is that it gets bored and wanders off. I suggest we sit here and wait.'

'Rodway can't wait,' I replied in a quiet voice. If the digestive habits of Winged Terrors had been estimated correctly, he had until first thing tomorrow morning before those flapping prats got peckish – and that was if we were being optimistic. There was every chance they'd get stuck in by nightfall.

'We have no choice,' Gillian said, and although she annoyed me by saying it, I knew that she was right.

I looked down at the space bear below and its yellow eyes looked right back. That bugger was going nowhere.

Five hours later, so it proved. The four of us were sitting cramped together, leaning against the thick tree with nowhere to go. It was like that scene in that film where the dinosaurs escape in that theme park and the man has to take refuge in a tree with the two kids – I forget what it was called. *Notting Hill*, I think. The infernal bear was now sitting back on its haunches, looking up at us with its black tongue lolling out like a hungry dog waiting for scraps from the dinner table. It had already completely decimated our small campsite and had ripped my guitar to pieces. This was a painful blow – it had been a birthday gift from Nick Knowles.

Gerry was asleep, his head resting against Barrington12's upper arm, using his sweater as a balled-up pillow. The robot was in low-power mode to save his remaining battery life. He'd had a full charge before we left so should've been fine to last the duration of our expedition, but it was best not to push our luck. If the sodding bear didn't sling its hook soon, we'd never make it to the foot of Great Strombago by nightfall and Rodway would be doomed.

'He's dead to the world,' Gillian observed in a tired voice, looking over at Gerry.

'Yeah,' I nodded. 'He never was cut out for life on the road. He used to hate travelling to away games – Spurs had to hire a lookalike for some of their matches because he couldn't be bothered with the aggro of making the trip. And imagine how hard it is to find someone else with hair like that.'

'Little wonder he's nodded off; he was tossing and turning for much of the night. I think he was having night terrors at one point – I could hear him even from inside my tent.'

'Yeah, he'll do that,' I said. Personally I hadn't heard a thing from the comfort of my sleeping bag. I'd slept like a log – which is, coincidentally, what Gerry had ended up using as a pillow. There was quiet for a few moments. I munched one of the Toblerone triangles I'd been rationed – it was the only part of Gerry's food that was usable. I was just grateful he'd had wits enough to lug his bag up into the tree with him before the bear attacked. His tins of soup, beans and spaghetti hoops were rendered mostly useless by him buying the cheaper old-style ones without a ring-pull lid, coupled with his failure to bring a tin-opener.

Far off in the distance, I heard a faint screeching sound, the ghastly echoes floating through the trees.

'Winged Terrors,' Gillian muttered. 'They're stirring. Probably not the same group that took Rodway; those should be satiated for a little while longer.'

'This planet really is a waste of time,' I said impatiently. 'We never had this kind of aggro on Earth. I used to gripe about stuff all the time back then, but now… Christ alive, I really miss it.'

'Me too,' Gillian said. 'Every day.'

'It's the little things, mostly,' I went on. 'A quiet pint in a country pub. Pottering around in the garden and listening to 5 Live. Driving out to a National Trust property on a Sunday afternoon. Most of all, I miss watching the seasons change.'

'I know what you mean,' Gillian agreed sombrely. 'I'm the same; I used to love seeing the leaves turn brown and fall and then return again in the spring.'

'Oh – I was talking about football seasons, but yeah,' I said. I looked over at her – she looked incredibly sad.

'You're not the spy, are you, Gillian?' I asked hopefully. 'You wouldn't do something like that.'

'Absolutely I wouldn't,' she agreed. 'And I'd be lying if I said I wasn't slightly disappointed that you'd assume I was.'

I felt a little stung by that but said nothing.

'But I don't blame you really,' she continued. 'This traitor, whoever they are, has turned friends and family alike against one another. What better way to assess your enemies' strengths and weaknesses than when they're in complete disarray?'

Something did still trouble me though, and I decided I had to ask.

'Gillian... who are the people in the photos on your desk? When I'd decided that you were the spy, I assumed they were spooks created to support your make-believe backstory. But if you're the real deal, then... who are they?'

For a long time she said nothing and I almost began to wonder whether she'd heard a word I'd just said, very much like my England lads while I was giving my pre-match team talk.

'They're not fake,' she said at last, in such a small voice that I had to lean in a little to hear. She was staring straight down at her feet as she sat opposite me on the bough. 'They're my family.'

I could already tell I'd put my foot right in it. I remembered with a wince how I'd sarcastically remarked that Gillian's family would be so proud of her after Palangonia FC got the chop and the look on her face as the words left my lips had been like a punch in the gut.

'It's just that... I've never seen them around,' I said delicately. 'I know I mostly see you within the work environment but I've caught you out and about around the Compound from time to time and you're always… very much alone.'

'I *am* alone,' she said. 'Quite alone, much of the time.'

'What happened to them?' I asked. 'I'd understand if you told me to keep my beak out.'

'They never made it,' she said, looking up at me for the first time. There was a faint sheen of tears around her eyes. 'They never got out. It was just me.'

I reflected on my doubts about the photographs on Gillian's desk, of my assumption that they couldn't have been her family. My thinking had clearly been affected by the disagreement we had been having at that time, by my frustrations with the closure of the football club. Perhaps a part of me didn't want to accept that she was a survivor just like everyone else, that she, too, had lost people she loved. The L'zuhl invasion of Earth had claimed a catastrophic number of lives – around 80% of all humans were believed to have perished as their warships laid waste to the planet. It was only my having been the former manager of our national team that saw me given priority access to the evacuation shuttles, to be escorted by the Alliance into various pockets of deep space to rebuild and start again. On signing my contract with the FA in 1999, they'd made it clear in a number of clauses that I would be guaranteed preferential treatment in the event of any hostile encounter between mankind and an extra-terrestrial race and, to be fair to them, those guys were absolutely true to their word – the ones that weren't incinerated in the first wave of attacks, that is. I'd been given the chance to begin again. As had Gillian – but at what cost?

'We got separated early on,' she said. 'David and the girls,

Jessica and Amelia – it's painful even saying those names, but not doing so is somehow even worse.'

I nodded but kept quiet. I never know what to say in these kinds of situations. I almost chipped in to empathise by saying I'd lost almost all of my Beach Boys vinyl records during the evacuation but I decided it probably wouldn't help.

'That's why I took up the boxing. Silly, really. I guess I just… I needed somewhere to put all that energy. That anger, that pure rage. God, I miss them, every day I miss them. Now they're gone and I'm still here. Trying to carry on living in a universe that seems to have a one-way ticket to oblivion.'

'You can't think like that, Gillian,' I said. 'They may be gone but at the end of the day, there's still everything to play for and we have to fancy our chances against the L'zuhl.'

I realised I'd slipped into football-speak cliché but that was instinct more than anything.

'If this spy gets their way, it'll all have been for nothing,' she said, dabbing her eyes defiantly with the back of her hand. 'The L'zuhl will find us and will raze the Compound to the ground. I may as well have died on Earth with my family.'

'Then we'll make sure that doesn't happen,' I said firmly. 'Once we have Rodway home and recovering, we'll find that Keycard and the arsehole who nicked it. And they'll rue the day they tried to sell out the human race. We survived the L'zuhl invasion, Gillian, we can bloody well survive this.'

She smiled then – not a full beamer, but enough. It was enough.

I sighed and looked down at the space bear; it snarled up at me as our eyes met.

'No sign of this mangy old brute getting the hump and going home,' I said in dismay. 'As far as this rescue mission goes, our goose may well be cooked.'

'Rodway's will be, that's for sure,' Gillian added.

'Even if... the worst has happened,' I said. 'This trip cannot have been in vain. We bring back whatever is left of that boy. He deserves a proper burial, not being left out here in the wilderness, forgotten about for all eternity. It's not right.'

'I agree, Kevin,' Gillian said. 'One way or another—'

There was a piercing whistle from somewhere below us and I whirled back around and stared down. The space bear was no longer sitting there looking up at us. It couldn't, even if it wanted to. It only had one eye. The other had been entirely obliterated by an enormous wooden spear which now protruded from its socket as the creature flailed wildly about in a mad panic.

SLASABO-TIK

'Who *are* they?' Gerry asked in a hushed voice, now sitting bolt upright and awake, as we watched the startling scene play out far below us. We were looking down as though we were up in the posh boxes at the Royal Variety Performance (only without Darren Anderton having one too many bottles of Sunny Delight on the drive in and shouting across to the Queen that she was 'a right sort').

The space bear was stumbling around half-blind and making a cacophonous racket, the thick green wooden spear wedged right into its skull. It swiped its enormous claws at thin air, as though suspecting its assailant had the power of invisibility. And, in a way, it would have been right – I didn't even spot them until they slowly closed in around the ailing creature, by now limping heavily from the arrows sprayed across its legs and belly. The native tribespeople surrounded the bear and for just a moment, with its one good eye, it glanced up at the four of us with an almost pleading expression. I had to fight the urge to feel sorry for the damn thing. And then, with a final volley of spears and arrows, it was defeated, tumbling over with a gurgling growl and falling still.

'Flipping heck,' I whispered. They knew how to take care of themselves and no mistake. I hadn't seen such a ruthless finish since Les Ferdinand in his prime. They barked at each other in guttural voices, speaking a language I didn't understand (mainly because it wasn't English or very, very basic German). They were grey-skinned and humanoid, with massive eyes and tiny antennae-like nubs poking out from just above each brow. They wore only a loincloth, or in some cases a kind of swimsuit-style fur. Their ears were FA Cup handles in proportion and their arms and legs were thin and puny in appearance, which belied just how expertly they had dispatched of the monstrous bear, which they were now in the stomach-churning process of skinning. The sound and smell of it all was completely nauseating.

Gillian put her index finger to her lips and looked at me. I nodded warily. We'd outlasted the bear. Now we just needed to let these lads and lasses do their thing and then we could be on our way, back on the path to Great Strombago. I put my finger to my own lips in kind and looked at Gerry. He too nodded (eventually – it took him a solid thirty seconds to twig exactly the message I was trying to communicate to him) and he turned to Barrington12 and gave the same gesture.

'DON'T WORRY, GERRY FRANCIS,' he said in a voice that seemed to blare out even more loudly than usual in the stillness of the forest, 'BARRINGTON12 CAN CONFIRM THAT THERE ARE NO CRUMBS ON YOUR LIPS, NOR ANY OTHER TRACES OF FOOD-RELATED DETRITUS.'

'Shhh!' implored Gillian, Gerry and I in unison.

'I AM SORRY,' Barrington12 said, looking crestfallen and confused. 'I SOUGHT ONLY TO REASSURE YOU.'

'For Christ's sake, son!' I hissed angrily. Then I sighed. Barrington12 could undoubtedly be a bit of a liability but at the same time, I found myself feeling oddly affected in some intangible way. The idea that a supposedly emotionless machine would have any inclination to want to comfort others in a time of strife… it was behaviour which, for me, was only to be encouraged. The galaxy was a bleak enough place already; we surely had to take kindness and compassion wherever we could find it.

There was a strangled cry from the ground below as one of the tribespeople turned and saw Gillian and me peeking over the edge of our little cubbyhole. The others whirled round and immediately drew back their bows, nocking arrows ready to fly. We ducked back quickly.

'Stay here,' I hissed to Gerry and Barrington12, who were far enough back to be out of sight from the ground. 'I'll handle this.'

'I'm coming with you,' Gillian insisted.

'There's really no need,' I replied.

'Of course there is,' she said. 'No disrespect, Kevin, but you'll almost certainly say the wrong thing and get us all killed.'

It was a fair cop.

Tentatively, I extended my arms out in front of me to show that I was not armed and wanted to negotiate a peaceful descent.

'Look, no knives, no guns!' I called down in a loud, slow voice. The one who'd spotted us shouted something again.

'Didn't catch that, son,' I said, shrugging theatrically so they'd realise that I didn't understand. 'Hu-mans. From Earth. But we're not the same ones who sit up on the machine-gun turrets and take pot shots at you lot, I promise you that.'

'Probably best not to remind them of that,' Gillian said in annoyance.

'Down,' I said, pointing from me and Gillian to the ground. 'Coming down! Don't hurt us. We are no threat.'

One, who was a few inches taller than the others and whom I took to be the leader (I'd often hand the club captaincy to the tallest player, where possible), said something else, more quietly to his associates. They didn't lower their bows or spears but they also didn't loose anything sharp at us. So that was something.

Slowly, painfully slowly, I inched down the tree, Gillian just above me. Fortunately the branch spacing was bang on and it was a relatively easy journey – sometimes you just have to give Mother Nature credit where it's due; she designed that tree faultlessly, I really mean that.

Once back on the ground – and desperately resisting the urge to put my jacket sleeve over my nose in an attempt to stifle the odious stench from the half-skinned space bear – I raised my arms above my head in the internationally recognised symbol for 'I'm not armed, please don't attack me' and turned round to face them. They looked even uglier close up and I was dismayed to see that the leader's meat and veg were poking out slightly from beneath his tiny loincloth. That was poor from him, frankly. There's never any call for that. Gillian joined me – I could only hope she wouldn't spot it too.

'Greetings—' I began, before Gillian elbowed me in the ribs to silence me.

'My name is Gillian,' she said in a firm voice. 'I hail from Earth. We mean you no harm. We seek only our friend, taken from us by Winged Terrors.'

'*Klakktu smesheebe la?*' the leader asked, squinting dubiously at the pair of us.

'Exactly,' I agreed, hoping that would be that. Instead, he clicked his fingers and one of his underlings (who was a bit cross-eyed, bless him) handed him a particularly large spear. Its tip glistened with a wet purple substance as he pointed it in our direction testily.

'Poison,' Gillian whispered to me from the corner of her mouth. 'That's how they took down the bear creature so quickly.'

It seemed to me that stabbing something in the eye with a massive pointed stick would do plenty of damage on its own, but I said nothing.

'*Skrash!*' the chief snarled, and his companions quickly began closing in, glowering menacingly.

'Please,' Gillian said, arching back to try to evade the spear tip. 'We come in peace.'

'Aye,' I agreed, nodding vigorously. I did feel that I probably wasn't bringing much to the table.

'*Tak-bak slano baffka!*' the leader said, cocking his head and smirking, showing off a row of ugly black teeth. I know they were living off the land but really, a little dental hygiene was surely not much to ask in this day and age. Dreadful.

'Well, we did our best,' I said, closing my eyes as I'd done hours earlier with the bear advancing on me. 'But we've bollocksed this right up.'

'I implore you to reconsider!' Gillian said desperately but it was no use. The leader's spear was pointed right at her head. He pulled back his bony arm to thrust it into her skull when suddenly there was a cry from above.

'Stop! Please! Violence solves nothing!'

In the drama of being sentenced to death by a strange alien

race, I'd completely forgotten about Gerry and Barrington12 still cowering in the boughs of the tree. Now my assistant came scuttling down to ground level, with the robot clunking heavily after him, both hurrying to stand beside us.

'Great plan, Gerry,' I sighed. 'Now he'll have four of us to impale, rather than two.'

I looked over at the tribe leader, feeling resigned to my fate despite this momentary stay of execution. But rather than his smug grin, I beheld a different expression altogether – one shared uniformly by all of his followers.

It was awe.

'Slasabo-tik!' he cried in a hoarse, disbelieving voice. 'Slasabo-tik!'

'Slasabo-tik!' they all said in chorus, dropping to their knees and bowing their heads. They were grovelling even more than I did to BBC bosses after my episode of *Desert Island Discs* got pulled by Radio 4 because I'd insisted on performing all of the chosen songs myself, with Steve Coppell on bongos. The leader fell to the ground, prostrating himself in front of us. Well, no, that wasn't exactly accurate.

He was prostrating himself in front of Gerry.

'What did I do…?' Gerry asked me, dumbfounded.

'I haven't the first idea,' I replied quietly. It was really quite astonishing – they were all crouched double, heads pressed against the soil, eyes closed, muttering 'Slasabo-tik' over and over again. The low droning of their voices was like a swarm of bees.

'What are they so fascinated by?' I asked, stepping back to give Gerry a closer look. There was nothing remarkable about his clothing – he was wearing a plain grey woollen sweater (a gift, negotiated as part of his contract at QPR), brown cords with the arse still ripped open after his mishap in the tunnel and a rather knackered pair of mud-stained trainers. In short, he looked exactly as he always looked. And yet the tribespeople were entranced.

'Maybe we should just… go?' Gillian suggested, jerking her thumb over her shoulder to the path leading on through the forest towards Great Strombago on the horizon. 'Quite apart from anything else, time's really a factor for Rodway now. That bear-thing set us back by quite a way.'

'Good shout,' I agreed, beginning to tiptoe away. 'But let's just take things slowly as we… extricate ourselves… No sudden movements…'

Gillian mimicked my gait and Barrington12 attempted to but was so heavy-footed that he looked like some abortive attempt to create a robot ballerina. Gerry, still looking at the reverential tribespeople bowing before him, brought up the rear – quite literally given the hole in his trousers. Far from being repulsed by this unedifying spectacle, the tribespeople seemed doubly thrilled by the sight of it, one or two of them even looking close to passing out with joy as though it was some kind of bizarre symbol of virility. I mean, to each their own, but come on.

Just as we reached the path to leave that area of the forest behind us, a great, anguished wail went up from the group and I glanced back over my shoulder with a wince – I'd expected them to be tearing after us, whatever strange spell that had come over them evidently now lifted, but it wasn't so. Instead, I beheld the really quite ridiculous sight of the tribespeople still in their bowed poses but scurrying after us like strange little spiders.

'What in the name of bloody hell...?' I shook my head in exasperation. Don't get me wrong, I was delighted that they no longer seemed intent on killing us, I was absolutely made up about that in fact, but I did not have the time and certainly not the patience to indulge whatever peculiar ritual they were now performing.

'Hold it right where you are,' I said, putting my hands up and pushing the air like a steward trying forlornly to ward off a rapturous crowd. 'Gerry's a smashing bloke and I'm chuffed that you're so taken with him, but we have a lot on today and we need to get off. I'm sure you understand.'

Alas, they did not. Or, if they did, they didn't care. All they were interested in was Gerry; they huddled at his feet whispering that nonsensical phrase over and over again.

'What is their game? I mean, honestly,' I said in annoyance.

'Gerry, can you really not think of anything about you that might have attracted them?' Gillian asked.

Gerry looked small and afraid.

'Don't think so,' he said.

'Well, there must be something,' I said. 'With respect, Gerry, nobody is going to start worshipping you without a bloody good reason.'

'I wish we could understand what they were saying,' Gillian said, looking at them in exasperation.

'Maybe after we've got Rodway they'll follow us all the way back to the Compound and we can get someone to translate,' I suggested.

'Unlikely,' she replied, shaking her head. 'There are numerous indigenous tribes on Palangonia and the Alliance knows next to nothing about their language and customs. No one's ever really got close enough to them to do any kind of study. Believe me, what we're witnessing right now is beyond extraordinary.'

'Slasabo-tik!' cried the tribe leader, looking up at Gerry before quickly averting his eyes again.

'We don't know what you're blathering on about!' I said in a patronising tone. 'I mean, you can say it as much as you like…'

'KEVIN KEEGAN?'

Barrington12 had been unusually quiet, having said nothing at all since he and Gerry had climbed down from the tree. You'd think that if any one of us was going to garner the curious attentions of a group of people who'd been detached from society for aeons, it would have been our ridiculous robot.

'Aye, what is it, son?' I replied wearily.

'PERHAPS I MAY BE OF SOME ASSISTANCE.'

'Thanks,' I said to Barrington12, 'but I don't think now's the right time for one of your relaxing shoulder massages. Maybe later.'

'I MEANT IN REGARDS TO OUR PRESENT PREDICAMENT,' he explained. 'MY DATABANKS CONTAIN INFORMATION ON MANY BILLIONS OF LANGUAGES AND DIALECTS AND THIS APPEARS TO BE ONE OF THEM.'

'Wow, really?' Gillian said, sounding genuinely impressed. 'But how?'

'IT'S ENTIRELY POSSIBLE THAT THIS TRIBE ARRIVED HERE FROM ANOTHER CIVILISATION

MANY THOUSANDS OF YEARS AGO, A CIVILISATION CURRENTLY ON GALACTIC RECORD, AND THAT IS WHY THE LANGUAGE IS STORED IN MY MEMORY. SOME OF THE WORDS THEY HAVE USED ARE NEW TO ME, NO DOUBT DUE TO THE NATURAL EVOLUTION OF THEIR SPEECH, BUT MUCH IS TRANSLATABLE. INCLUDING THE PHRASE THEY HAVE BEEN REPEATING REGULARLY.'

'You know what it means?' I asked, stepping towards him. 'You understand what "Slasabo-tik" is?'

'YES,' Barrington12 said – then paused for a second for what seemed like dramatic emphasis. Poor from a robot, that. 'IN OUR TONGUE, SLASABO-TIK WOULD TRANSLATE LITERALLY AS... MULLET GOD.'

I turned and stared at Gerry and the brittle, outdated mop of hair at the back of his head.

'But... but what does that mean?' Gerry asked me in a tremulous voice.

'It means,' I said, not quite believing these words were actually coming out of my mouth, 'that you are a god to these people. Gerry... you're the Mullet God.'

THE PROPHECY

I stared at the tribespeople in astonishment. Gerry Francis? A god? I mean, had they not seen his record at Tottenham?

'I don't like this,' Gerry said, anxiously. 'They've obviously got me mixed up with somebody else.'

'Well, of course they have,' I said. 'I've known you for forty-odd years, Gerry, and believe me, you are not a god.'

'Wait, hang on,' Gillian said. 'Barrington12, if you can understand much of what they say, can you speak to them on our behalf, translate what we're saying?'

'OF COURSE,' he replied. 'PLEASE INDICATE WHAT YOU WOULD LIKE ME TO SAY.'

'Ask them who Slasabo-tik is,' Gillian said.

'*SPRAKK BUKBAKTA SHON SLASABO-TIK?*' Barrington12 said to the tribe leader. He raised his head slowly, clearly surprised that these peculiar visitors should speak their language. The leader didn't say anything – he just extended a stick-thin arm and pointed at Gerry, all the while averting his eyes.

'We already knew that,' I sighed. 'Ask them about the god, what makes him such a big cheese and all that.'

Barrington12 did and the leader slowly climbed to his feet, still not looking fully at Gerry. He began to babble excitedly, gesticulating and becoming more and more fired up. His people continued to crouch down, murmuring 'Slasabo-tik' rhythmically.

'Well?' I asked, once the leader's verbal diarrhoea slowed to a trickle.

'HE IS THE LIGHT AND THE WAY,' Barrington12 replied dispassionately. 'HE GAVE LIFE TO THE GALAXY AND HAS THE POWER TO TAKE IT BACK AGAIN. SLASABO-TIK IS KINDNESS, HOPE, POSITIVITY; ALL THE FINEST ATTRIBUTES THE DENIZENS OF THIS GALAXY CAN STRIVE FOR. HE IS THE BEST OF ALL OF US. HE EMBODIES THAT WHICH WE SHOULD BE.'

'Aye, right,' I said, rolling my eyes. Listen, I'm not having a pop at religion, let people crack on and believe what they like. But it did make me laugh back on Earth when people used to describe the Bible as 'the greatest story ever told'. I mean, had they not seen *Brassed Off*?

'What else?' Gillian asked.

'HE SAYS THAT THE MULLET GOD HAS NOT BEEN SEEN FOR MANY HUNDREDS OF THOUSANDS OF YEARS, BUT THAT A PROPHECY FORETELLS THAT HE SHALL ONE DAY RETURN TO THIS GALAXY TO SAVE IT FROM DESTRUCTION, GIVING HIS OWN LIFE TO ENSURE OUR OWN. HE WILL THEN ASCEND TO THE HEAVENS AND ALL WILL BE AT PEACE.'

'Sounds a bit unrealistic,' I observed. I was itching to get moving and this seemed an unhelpful distraction. It definitely wasn't that I was jealous of Gerry being hailed as a lord and saviour rather than me. I wasn't bothered about that. Listen, it's beneath me.

'Oh my goodness,' Gillian said, her eyes suddenly widening. 'Of course! The tunnel!'

'You've lost me,' I said, scratching my head.

'In the tunnel from the Compound – we spotted those archaic scratchings, those drawings on the walls. Don't you remember what they were?'

I shrugged.

'Dunno. Stick men or some such.'

Then suddenly I did remember. There was an etching of a group of people kneeling before a platform covered in strange runes while a man standing above them floated up into the starry sky. A man with long hair at the back.

The Mullet God.

'Oh, this has to be some kind of daft prank!' I exclaimed, my tolerance of this madness now at an end. 'There is no way Gerry is some kind of galactic deity. I mean, look at him! His backside is hanging out all over the shop!'

'It doesn't matter that we don't believe it,' Gillian said. '*They* do. I mean, they really, *really* do.'

'Yeah, well,' I said. 'David James firmly believes, even now, that the world will end in the year 2000. People can be stupid.'

'It's just so fascinating,' Gillian said in wonder. 'I feel privileged to have witnessed this.'

'Listen,' I said, 'the only thing we need to be fascinated about right now is a young kid who's very special to me. Means the bloody world to me, in fact. And his name is Rodway... er...'

I glanced at Gerry.

'What's Rodway's surname?'

Gerry shrugged. 'Bit above my pay grade, that, Kev.'

'Right,' I said, returning to my train of thought. 'Well, anyway, he's the only thing I'm focusing on right now. If he's not already dead, he soon will be.'

The tribe leader then said something else, something which made the others look to Gerry with hopeful anticipation.

'HE INVITES SLASABO-TIK TO SAY A FEW WORDS TO HIS LOYAL SUBJECTS,' Barrington12 said.

This was not going to be pretty.

'Do I have to, Kev?' Gerry looked over at me, whispering under his breath.

'Just… speak from the heart,' I said. 'Tell them how proud you are to be their Mullet God and that you won't let them down, that sort of guff.'

'But I don't want to encourage them!'

'Listen, just keep them onside so we can head off to find Rodway,' I told him.

Apparently somewhat reassured, Gerry turned back nervously to face his adoring fans.

'I, er… hello,' he said uncertainly.

'Slasabo-tik!' screamed one particularly emotional man who then promptly fainted. No one went to his aid – they all continued to watch Gerry, transfixed. As he spoke, Barrington12 translated for the tribe.

'My name is… I am Gerry. Apparently I am your Mullet God. Which, er, is very nice of you. I really appreciate that. I'm going to knuckle down and do my best and, um… well, at the end of the day, the ambition has to be for us to win a league title. No, sorry – not that…'

He trailed off and looked back at us for help. I put my hand over my face in embarrassment.

'Jesus wept,' Gillian muttered, turning away.

Gerry, panic in his eyes, turned back to face their expectant stares.

'So… yeah. It's great to be back, like the prophecy said – or whatever. Look, shall we just leave it there? All the best.'

A roar of approving hoots and whoops went up from Gerry's adoring crowd. I sighed and shook my head. Life must be so much less stressful when you're that easily pleased.

'Listen, we have a job to do: find Rodway, bring him home, then get back to hunting for that spy. Explain that to this lot, please,' I said to Barrington12. 'Just the basics, I mean, you don't have to tell them about the spy stuff – let's keep it simple.'

'You're right, Kevin,' Gillian said. 'Quite apart from anything else, the longer we're out here, the stronger the likelihood of someone back in the Compound noticing we're gone. If General Leigh finds out we snuck away during his lockdown, he'll never let us back in again – it won't matter whether I'm on the Council or not.'

'*Akkkk!*' screamed the tribe leader animatedly as Barrington12 passed this on. The others were now standing up and looking on in slightly discomfiting silence.

'Sounds like that news went down well, then,' I said wearily. Though the one benefit of their believing Gerry to be some kind of weird god was that the likelihood of them resorting to any more threats of violence against us was now practically nil.

'AKPLATAK HAS AN OFFER HE WISHES TO MAKE,' Barrington12 said, turning to us.

I raised an eyebrow.

'Who the chuff is Akplatak?'

'THE LEADER OF THE WATLAQ PEOPLE,' Barrington12 replied.

'Who the chuff are the—'

'Clearly these are the Watlaq and Akplatak is the… chap whose meat and veg keeps flapping out from under his cloth,' Gillian cut in.

She had clocked it then. Shame.

'What offer?' Gillian asked. 'What is he talking about?'

'AS DIRECTED, BARRINGTON12 EXPLAINED OUR SITUATION AND OUR QUEST FOR THE NEST OF WINGED TERRORS ON THE LOWER SLOPES OF GREAT STROMBAGO. IT WAS MADE PLAIN THAT THIS WAS OUR JOURNEY AND THAT SLASABO-TIK COULD NOT STAY HERE.'

Bang on. He'd done us proud there; couldn't have put it better myself.

'AKPLATAK WAS AGHAST AT THE IDEA OF SLASABO-TIK WALKING INTO ALMOST CERTAIN DEATH WITH SUCH DISMAL AND ILL-PREPARED COMPANY.'

Rude.

'Get to the point,' I muttered irritably.

'AKPLATAK SAID THAT SLASABO-TIK MUST BE PROTECTED AT ALL COSTS. AND SO THE WARRIORS OF THE WATLAQ WILL ACCOMPANY US TO THE MOUNTAIN AND WILL GLADLY GIVE OVER THEIR LIVES SO THAT SLASABO-TIK MIGHT LIVE. NOT ONLY THAT, BUT THEY SAY OUR CURRENT ROUTE IS

ILL-SUITED AND KNOW OF A PATH THAT WILL HALVE THE DISTANCE AND TIME. WE CAN AVOID THE DANGEROUS JUNGLE AHEAD AND TRAVEL VIA THE MARSHLAND TO THE EAST.'

'Okay, tell him we agree,' Gillian said immediately.

'Well, hang on just a second,' I interjected. 'Do we not even discuss it then?'

'Okay,' Gillian said. 'Our options are to continue on what is apparently a dangerous and circuitous route to Great Strombago alone, or we take a shortcut with a host of skilled and well-armed fighters who will, apparently, stop at nothing to save the life of one of our number. Which is it going to be?'

'Obviously the second one,' I said quietly. She'd made me look a right prat there. And in front of the Watlaq, too.

Akplatak responded enthusiastically.

'HE IS DELIGHTED,' Barrington12 explained unnecessarily. 'HOWEVER HE INSISTS THAT WE MAKE FOR THE MOUNTAIN AS SOON AS POSSIBLE. HE IS FEARFUL OF THE NIGHT AND WHAT IT WILL BRING.'

'That makes two of us,' I agreed and turned to Akplatak. 'Akkie – lead the way.'

Akplatak stared at me blankly. I sighed.

'Barrington12, tell him to lead on.'

THE MARSHES

We followed the Watlaq along numerous winding forest paths, heading further and further into the wilds of this strange alien planet, our home about which we knew so little, towards the boggy marshland that would take us over many a weary mile to the foot of Great Strombago. My stomach was really grumbling but we couldn't stop. Not yet.

Akplatak walked ahead of his fellow tribespeople, who surrounded us on all sides to escort us through the forest. I felt twitchy at every sound, expecting another one of those space bears (or something even worse) to come bursting forth from the trees. But then, I reassured myself, if they did then at least they'd go for the tribespeople first, as they were walking on the flanks of our travelling party. The black-trunked trees made the day seem darker than it was and the flat green and blue leaves formed a canopy above our heads that was strangely calming. I wondered whether this was the secret to the Watlaq's survival out here – any Winged Terrors flying overhead would have a heck of a time trying to spot them through the thick sprawl of foliage.

At the centre of it all was Gerry. He walked a little ahead of the rest of us – it happened organically but the Watlaq seemed most at ease when he was slightly separate from me, Gillian and

Barrington12. Gerry seemed very unsettled by the whole thing and kept glancing anxiously over his shoulder at us.

'How's he doing?' Gillian asked me in a hushed voice. I frowned.

'What do you mean? Who wouldn't want to be thought of as the lord and saviour of the galaxy?'

'It's a lot of pressure to put on someone just out of the blue like that,' she said cautiously. 'I don't think he's ready for it. And when the time comes to return to the Compound, I'm not sure how happy they're going to be to let him go.'

'What do you mean?' I asked.

'Think about it,' Gillian said. 'If your whole life was built around worshipping a god and then one day he actually marches into your village, would you be happy waving him off as he leaves with a group of strangers?'

This was, admittedly, a worry. I knew how frustrating it was as a manager to know that someone else coveted your best players and this would have been precisely the same thing.

'Let's just cross that bridge when we come to it,' I advised. 'These guys are pretty tasty in a combat situation so let's try not to get on their bad side until after our job is done.'

We pressed on, our feet aching but our spirits undimmed. Every time I felt myself flagging or wishing I was back at home, tucked up in bed with a Puzzler and an Ovaltine, I'd think of poor Rodway and the hell he was no doubt going through and my resolve would be renewed tenfold.

In the end, it was the Watlaq who rang the dinner bell as we reached the outer rim of the great forest. Before us, sprawling to the haze of the horizon and the faint outline of our mountainous destination, was a stinking marshland, spindly tree branches poking out from the bubbling depths, green and orange weeds splayed over the narrow paths that criss-crossed the treacherous ground, and the smell – my god, the smell. It was as though a public toilet had exploded.

Akplatak raised one bony arm into the air, pointing with his spear to the grey skies above our heads, and the Watlaq halted. They turned to face their leader, standing proudly beside Gerry, and made their way towards him, huddling together in a group.

'*Smepka*,' Akplatak said to me. I just shrugged. '*Smepka!*' he said again insistently, this time pressing his thumb and forefinger to his thin blue-painted lips.

'Ah,' I said, the penny dropping. 'I'd love a bit of *smepka*, good call.' I turned to Gillian behind me and said, 'That means it's time to eat— oh.'

Gillian was already sitting down on a slimy rock on the edge of the bog and was eating a triangle of the Toblerone Gerry had brought with him.

'Save me a bit,' I said. 'Not that I'll be able to keep anything down with that bloody stench. What a great choice for a picnic spot. Amateur hour, this.'

I sat down beside her and watched as several of the Watlaq began to unfold a large animal skin which two of their number had been carrying. Inside I could see rotten chunks of meat swimming with maggots and other strange insects and lice that I didn't recognise and had no desire to see up close. Poor Gerry was being offered first dibs and he looked over at me imploringly. I nodded to him to have some – it wouldn't do to upset our guests, after all.

'*Traspla?*' one of the warriors nearest to us said, offering a handful of the rank grey meat to Gillian and me.

'Not a chance in hell!' I blurted, and then, on realising from the wounded look on his face that my disgust had transcended the language barrier, smiled gratefully and pointed to my chocolate.

'I'll be back in a sec,' Gillian said, standing up and walking towards a patch of dying brush nearby.

'Where are you going?' I asked. She looked at me with faint irritation.

'Call of nature,' she said. 'If that's okay with you.'

'Aye, on you go,' I said, blushing and turning away. There was very little of the disgusting meat left and Gerry looked quite green for having ingested some. The Watlaq appeared thrilled to have shared a meal with him.

'So then,' I asked Akplatak, pointing at Barrington12 to translate for me. 'How do we get across this swamp? I don't like the look of it, I have to be honest. Are there any particular hidden dangers we should keep an eye out for?'

Akplatak nodded attentively as Barrington12 relayed this and then spoke back in a loud voice so that everyone could hear, like an actor projecting on stage to an enormous theatre.

'THE PROPHECY OF SLASABO-TIK SPOKE OF HIS GLORIOUS RETURN WHEN THE GALAXY WAS AT ITS LOWEST EBB,' Barrington12 translated. 'HE WILL SAVE THOSE WHO BELIEVE IN THE PATH OF THE RIGHTEOUS, WHO REJECT EVIL. NOW THAT HE HAS RETURNED TO US, THIS IS A DAY OF BOTH JOY AND OF CAUTION. DARK DAYS ARE UPON US NOW AND MANY WILL NOT SURVIVE.'

'Right, okay,' I said, 'but that's not really what I asked.'

'WHEN SLASABO-TIK VANISHED ALL THOSE MANY THOUSANDS OF YEARS AGO, OUR PEOPLE FELL INTO DESPAIR. WHY HAD HE FORSAKEN US? HOW WOULD WE CONTINUE WITHOUT HIS GUIDING EYE? WHERE HAD HE GONE? THOSE QUESTIONS ARE NO LONGER IMPORTANT, FOR HE IS HERE, WATCHING OVER THE WATLAQ AS IN TIMES OF OLD, AND WE WILL PROTECT HIM WITH OUR LIVES. FOR HE IS THE LIGHT AND THE WAY, PRAISE HIM!'

'Again,' I said impatiently, 'you're giving me a lot of extraneous information here.'

Akplatak began speaking again but was cut off by the sound of a loud splash and a grunting cry from behind me. Gillian.

I shot to my feet and ran towards the bushes, hoping for her sake and mine that whatever had happened had been either before or after she'd commenced her what-have-you. Fortunately, it was after. Unfortunately, there was something far worse to deal with.

'Help!' I cried, hopping helplessly on the spot and looking back at the group. 'Help, it's got her! Something's grabbed Gillian!'

It was hard to know what it actually was – a thick, brown, slimy tentacle had wrapped itself around her ankle and was pulling her on her front towards the grim depths of the bog. Gillian's arms were scrabbling about, her fingers desperate to find some purchase, but there was only damp soil and tiny weeds. Before the first tribesman had arrived on the scene, Gillian had been pulled into the bog and the only trace of her was a small circle of bubbles dancing on the grimy surface.

'No!' I shouted. 'Do something!'

The Watlaq stood on the path, spears raised, and aimed at the water. There was a splash of movement and one immediately threw his weapon into the depths, where it vanished forever.

'That's no good, Kev,' Gerry said, arriving beside me out of breath. 'They could hit Gillian!'

I immediately waved at the group to put down their weapons.

'It must have a head,' I said desperately. 'If we could find it and get it in the eye, maybe it'll release her!'

'*Grek-tapp-slenzho*,' Akplatak said grimly and shook his head.

'IT IS NOT ONE BEAST,' Barrington12 explained, 'BUT MANY. THEY ARE WATER WYRMS; THEY PREY UPON SMALL ANIMALS ON THE SHORES OF THE MARSHES.'

Right on cue, several more of what I had assumed to be the limbs of some undersea monstrosity flapped out of the water – they were like giant, bloated earthworms with no eyes but nightmarish gnashing teeth. They each headed for the person in closest proximity and the Watlaq fought them off as best they could, stabbing at them with their spears, cutting with their knives. One advanced towards me, its large mouth click-clicking as it slithered quickly closer, a knot of weeds wrapped around its middle. I stumbled back in disgust but found only the large rock on which I'd been sitting. I spluttered in fear but the Watlaq were all either consumed by their own battles or else forming a protective ring around Gerry. I kicked out at it with my feet and, just as it made to bite into my shin, it was crushed, splattered and severed into halves by the giant heavy foot of Barrington12.

'I owe you one, son,' I said breathlessly. He looked at me and to my surprise he raised one squeaking arm and gave me a slightly wonky thumbs-up before clumping away across the mud. There was still no sign of Gillian re-emerging and, counting on the hope that most of the water wyrms would have come up for their feast, I ran towards the water's edge. Without another thought – for I knew I'd only talk myself out of it – I took a great gulping breath and dived into the horrid, ice-cold darkness, pushing through the plants and algae. I opened my eyes, blinking away the painful stinging of that foul water, and cast about for Gillian. It was so dark; the light from the suns in the sky seemed incapable of penetrating below the surface but then, just as I was about to kick back up and onto the bank, I saw a flailing movement to my right. I recognised Gillian's top-quality hiking boot and, more importantly, Gillian herself attached to it. The water wyrm was taking chunks out of the shoe but Gillian herself, though unable to shake the damn thing off, appeared not to have been bitten. The foul creatures were deceptively powerful but two humans against one earthworm on steroids was no competition. My chest burning for oxygen, I hooked my hands beneath Gillian's arms and, kicking for all I was worth, I pulled us both up to the surface and dragged her onto the bank. Incredibly she was still conscious, having had wits enough about her to have taken a breath before being pulled under. Her face, like mine no doubt, was a pink-blue mess and the whites of her eyes had red streaks of lightning right across them, but she was alive. She coughed, great hacking sounds, and tried to speak, but I shook my head. She reached out and grasped my hand instead, and that was enough.

Once again, Barrington12 obliged in squashing the persistent wyrm that had taken such a shine to Gillian's footwear and I turned to see the rest of the Watlaq had also bested their own foes while I'd been under, though the tribe now appeared to be one or two fewer in number.

Akplatak called over to us, waving his spear.

'WE MUST GO ON,' Barrington12 said. 'THEY WILL RETURN, IN TIME.'

'No arguments from me, son,' I said, taking a deep breath and hauling myself and Gillian back onto our feet.

GREAT STROMBAGO

As we trekked across the treacherous swampland, with the oppressive sight of Great Strombago growing ever closer, I began to experience a peculiar sensation of contentment. It wasn't just the Vimto I'd swigged along the way – no, it was more than that. I felt like I was doing something worthwhile. Since losing my club I'd been without a purpose. Now, I had something to fight for. And I felt heartened looking around at my friends – Gillian, Barrington12 and Gerry. This trip and its death-defying challenges had undoubtedly bonded us, brought us all much closer than we had been before.

Gerry, at the insistence of the Watlaq, walked several steps ahead of us with old Akplatak never leaving his side (the man was a bit clingy, if I'm honest – no one's a fan of that). The other warriors had spread out, ever watchful for dangers. Most were watching the cloudy skies above – that was where the most likely threat would come from. We were approaching Winged Terror territory now, and they did not welcome guests.

The Watlaq were cutting a very specific path through the marsh. On every side of the unstable paths on which we stepped, there were pools and bogs, overhung with spindly wet trees that looked long dead. The stench was overwhelming, like that Easter weekend when I had Steve Bruce over to stay and I came down on the Sunday to find him washing his pants in the kitchen sink. On Jesus' special day as well. Poor.

An hour into our journey, one young warrior had lost her footing and stepped into a puddle – she vanished with a sticky popping sound and never emerged. The others looked on impassively. They all knew the dangers. So, too, did we.

Another hour further along, and with Great Strombago now tantalisingly close – we could make out the cracks and crevices on the lower slopes that housed the nests of the Winged Terrors, our grim destination – the heavens suddenly opened in a mighty downpour. Thunder rumbled dramatically overhead and lightning forked across the darkening sky.

'Oh, cheers,' I muttered grumpily.

'Or perhaps this is a good thing,' Gillian offered. 'It may provide us with some cover as we approach the mountain.'

I pulled the collar of my Newcastle Brown Ale jacket more tightly about my neck to keep the rainwater at bay. Gerry, the jammy sod, suddenly found himself walking under a canopy propped up by four tribespeople holding wooden posts over which had been stretched the yellow skin of some unfortunate animal. Fair play, these Watlaq knew how to treat their gods.

I nearly jumped out of my skin at a flash of lightning which struck one of the brittle trees not a hundred yards away. Its smoking remains sank forlornly into a nearby pool, gone forever. I took deep, measured breaths to slow my spiking heart rate. I was a bit twitchy about lightning and had been ever since I saw Al Shearer get struck by lightning on TV. (It was a graphic on a Sky Sports Super Sunday advert, but still.) We were close now. It was late in the afternoon, evening really, and if Gillian's estimates were correct, the Winged Terrors that had snatched him would more than likely be just starting to get peckish.

The paths on which the Watlaq led us became even more unsteady as the ground grew increasingly sodden. Another warrior stepped into a puddle and disappeared but still we pressed on. We had to. Our original route through the jungles to the west would no doubt have proved even more deadly. Even Barrington12 found the terrain difficult to negotiate – at one point, true to form, he dropped one of his internal memory cards onto the muddy bank behind him. I wiped it off but he'd already walked on some way ahead, blissfully unaware, so I pocketed it to return to him later.

After trudging on, heads bowed against the chill stinging rain, all of us silent (except for the occasional reprise of 'Slasabo-tik!' chants among small pockets of our escort), the ground gradually grew firmer underfoot. Minutes later I looked back over my shoulder and realised that, at last, we were through. It was over. It had been, without doubt, the worst trip since I took my England boys to Dignitas, thinking it was a Swiss ski resort.

'Finally!' I said, unable to hide my relief.

'We still have to make our way back, mind you,' Gillian observed.

'Don't spoil it,' I muttered.

'Now what?' Gerry asked, turning to look at me. His acolytes did the same in unison.

'I dunno,' I said, craning my neck to look up at the towering volcano beside us. 'We need to get up there somehow.'

'But where?' Gerry asked. 'We don't know where to look.'

'There,' I said, pointing, as, right on cue, something flew from an alcove about two hundred feet above. Something which was heading right for us.

'*Prakbarkk!*' shouted Akplatak and I was astonished by what happened next. The Winged Terror, its eyes full of grim malice, its teeth bared in a hideous grin, was almost upon us but in seconds, the Watlaq had arranged themselves into battle formation, a square block of people with Gerry tucked almost out of sight in the centre. Gillian, Barrington12 and I were left standing exposed to one side. Gerry threw me a slightly apologetic glance but what could he really do? Fortunately for us, the Winged Terror only had eyes for the main group and swooped towards them – where its life was brought to a sudden and painful end by a merciless barrage of arrows. It fell, lifeless and heavy, to the ground right in front of me, its face contorted in agony.

'At least we now know where to go,' I said. 'We just need to find a foothold somewhere.'

Already way ahead of me, the Watlaq were climbing expertly up the side of the volcano, nimbly finding small outcrops and ridges to enable their ascent. One particularly beefy Watlaq warrior (I'd been mentally calling him Gary Barlow during our journey whenever I'd caught sight of him) knelt down and gestured to Gerry to clamber onto him so that he could give him a piggyback up to the nest, from which we could hear an ominous fluttering sound, like a large butterfly trapped under a glass. They were waking up and would soon realise we'd killed one of their boys. Or girls. Listen, I didn't get a good look at its particulars to know for sure. Why would I?

Gerry looked back at us anxiously as Gary Barlow began to climb. Gerry had his arms around his neck, his wrists white from how tightly he was holding on. I would never tell him this, but Gerry looked badly out of shape. I remembered how a few years ago he'd absolutely packed the weight on, to the point that I even recommended he consider looking into gastric bands. He'd waved me away, saying that he 'didn't like that type of music'.

'Well, all well and good for Gerry, but what are we supposed to do?' Gillian asked, putting her hands on her hips. 'I've never been rock-climbing in my life.'

'PLEASE, ALLOW BARRINGTON12 TO BE OF ASSISTANCE IN THIS MATTER.'

Without waiting for a response, Barrington12 grabbed hold of the scruff of my jacket in one mighty metal hand and Gillian's in the other, and hoisted us up onto either shoulder.

'KEEP A TIGHT GRIP,' he advised as he began his climb. 'FALLING FROM A HEIGHT SUCH AS THIS WOULD CARRY A HIGH PROBABILITY OF DEATH.'

'You don't say,' I whispered breathlessly, too afraid to look down. Barrington12 soon overtook the Watlaq warriors to the rear (a small group of them had remained at ground level to keep watch) and promptly drew level with Gerry and Gary Barlow, the latter of whom looked very miffed about it.

'Meet you at the top, I guess!' I called over to Gerry, who had his head buried in the back of Gary Barlow's neck, fighting the urge to spew.

My stomach was doing somersaults but I forced myself to keep looking up. Beyond the Watlaq vanguard, of which Akplatak was the most advanced, there was a deep black ridge cut into the side of Great Strombago. Sticks and vines poked out into the outside world – there was no doubt that this was the nest. We just had to hope it would be the right one. I did not fancy climbing up every side of the volcano hoping for the best, I was shattered enough as it was.

As we climbed and as my stomach began to settle, I chanced a look around us. We were high above ground level now and the sprawling majesty of Palangonia stretched all around us. The trees of the forest beyond the marsh, which had towered so unfathomably high above us while we trekked through it, now looked like mere weeds. The bog itself seemed almost beautiful from up there, the surface glittering in the dull sunlight, with no indication of the water wyrm horrors that lurked below. I tilted my head up higher and beyond the forest I fancied I could just about make out a concrete speck on the horizon: the Compound. Our home. Here, scaling the side of a volcano, it seemed impossibly far away.

The nearer we got to the dark gash in the side of the mountain, the louder the fluttering sound became. I quickly shouted into Barrington12's ear to slow down a little – there was no way I wanted us to be the first to poke our heads in if they were in there primed and waiting for us. It was far more advisable to let one of the Watlaq go first – no disrespect to them, but I had a spy to catch and a football club to save. Whichever way you looked at it, I was not as expendable.

Barrington12 did as he was told and slowed to a halt just below the rim. Akplatak had no such inhibitions, and no sooner had we overtaken him during the climb than he and his first responders were past us again, clambering in through the slit with not a moment's hesitation. Almost immediately, there was a gut-wrenching squeal followed by the noise from what sounded like a ferocious skirmish. The Watlaq screamed battle cries and several more of them shot past us and into the nest to join the fray. Only Gary Barlow hung back, wisely deciding not to take their beloved god into harm's way.

'We need to see what's going on in there,' I said. 'Barrington12, subtly does it, but creep up a bit so we can peek in.' He obliged without a word.

It was carnage. Utter chaos. There were mangled bodies of the Watlaq strewn all over the dank cave. It was surprisingly wide inside, high ceilings covered in a strange moss-like substance, and the ground looked squelchy and gooey under the Watlaq's bare feet. In the dim light afforded by the quickly darkening sky outside, I could discern six Winged Terrors, swarming about the heads of the warriors, clawing at them and, in the case of one poor fellow, flying straight at him and knocking him flying back past us, plummeting to his death far below. I had eyes for only one thing – but I couldn't see him anywhere.

'Damn,' Gillian muttered, clinging to Barrington12's other shoulder and straining to see inside the nest. 'Kevin, I don't see him.'

'Nor me,' I said, bashing Barrington12 in frustration. 'This could all be for nothing.'

But soon, the tide of the battle began to turn in the Watlaq's favour. Two of them brought down the fiercest-looking of the Winged Terror pack, stabbing him savagely with their spears, and this seemed to send the remaining five into disarray and panic. They were picked off one by one, Akplatak himself striking the finishing blow to one of them as it bobbed about just above the floor of the nest with one of its wings already shredded by arrows. He picked up a large boulder and dropped it on the creature's head, squishing it with a sickly crunching sound. Bit unnecessary, actually.

Soon, the fight was over. If anything, it had seemed almost too easy. The Watlaq had sustained a number of casualties, many fatal, but they had won the day. This had been a victory that their Mullet God could be proud of, though I could see from the pained look on Gerry's face that he felt queasy about such acts of violence, no matter their cause, being performed in his name. As the victory cheers went up, I urged Barrington12 to carry us inside; Gary Barlow and Gerry followed just behind.

'*Kwaff!*' Akplatak announced, looking extremely fired up. '*Sewi trik tok slamami!*'

'Absolutely,' I agreed, hurrying past him. I had no time to celebrate – I had to search every corner of that cave for Rodway. This simply could not have all been for nothing.

'I'll help,' Gillian said, starting from the opposite end. There were piles of bracken and bones strewn all over the shop.

'I'll check over here,' Gerry said, but was instantly surrounded by the Watlaq, who looked to him for some kind of victory speech. He looked hopelessly lost but tried to improvise something, as Barrington12 translated for him. 'Erm… we have won a great battle here today. Many lives were lost but in the serving of a great cause. Um… and may the… the spirit of White Hart Lane live on inside us all, forever.'

They looked a little nonplussed but after a moment's hesitation, cheered him like he'd just won the match ball. Once again, they were so very easily pleased. Gerry could have said anything and they'd have held him aloft over their shoulders.

'Any joy?' I asked Gillian, scooping up debris with both hands, desperately hoping to lift some to find Rodway underneath, preferably still breathing.

'Nothing,' she said grimly – and then, 'Oh.'

She held something up and I hurried over to her. It was a Compound-issue ID badge. Not Rodway, but one of the guards who had been killed before Rodway was captured. I felt a twinge of guilt – had I not called them over to the stadium, they'd never have suffered so terrible a fate. If I hadn't deluded myself into believing that Gillian had been the spy... Well, it wasn't the time for stewing over my own regrets. That would have to come later. However, finding this accreditation here in the nest at least meant that we were in the right place. Now the only question was whether Rodway had survived this long.

'Keep looking,' I told Gillian urgently. 'He's here, I know it.'

We resumed our search while Gerry stood by the nest entrance, still surrounded by the adoring Watlaq, who seemed content now just to stare at him for no reason.

We had scoured pretty much every corner of the nest-cave with no signs of life. It was clear – we had been too late. Rodway was gone. I had failed him.

'Damn it!' I cried in anguished fury, leaning back against the wall in despair. 'Damn it all to bloody hell!' I tugged angrily on a grass-like covering on the wall, stuck there like some kind of tapestry. It pulled loose in my hand and, frowning, I heaved it free of the wall and tossed it aside, my eyes bulging in astonishment. Behind it was a large nook, chock-full of trinkets and other souvenirs that the Winged Terrors had clearly pilfered during their years of scavenging – there were gold coins and jewels, broken weapons not dissimilar to those wielded by the Watlaq (no doubt seized during previous attacks on the tribe), and there were even some modern gadgets and treasures that must have come from those they had snatched from within the Compound walls during the past year, another condemnation of General Leigh's failed scheme to machine gun them out of the sky whenever they approached.

And there, lying sprawled on top of it all, was our Rodway. He was battered, beaten and barely conscious – but he was alive. I almost wept at the sight of him. I hurried inside and dropped down beside him (sitting right on top of a broken sword handle – that could have been nasty) and gently tapped his cheeks to rouse him. He had a big crusty cut down the left side of his face and one of his eyes was black and bruised. I noticed to my dismay that one leg was sticking out at an unnatural angle and that the bone was poking through his trousers. It was all I could do to keep myself from being sick. Having said that, if we did indeed get the club back, he wasn't going to be playing anytime soon – meaning there would be no way Gillian could refuse to release funds for a new striker now. I glanced over at her; she had followed me into the alcove and was now resting Rodway's head in her lap. She nodded – she knew what I was thinking.

'I'm glad he's alive too,' she smiled.

Oh.

'Well, obviously,' I agreed.

'Rodway? Is that him, Kev? Is he alive?'

It was Gerry, calling over to us. He was unable to get over to the alcove himself (or at least, not without barrelling his worshippers to the ground) but was craning his neck for a glimpse.

'He's alive, Gerry!' I cried. 'We got him, son!'

I waved to Barrington12 frantically; he stomped over.

'We'll need you to carry him,' I told the robot solemnly. 'He can't walk and even if he could, he's had one hell of an ordeal. Christ, haven't we all…'

I trailed off; I felt suddenly exhausted, like all the energy had been sapped from me. It had been a monumental effort to rescue Rodway and now all I craved was the comfort of my own bed. The sooner we began heading back, the better.

'Actually, hang on a sec. Gerry!' I said, as Gillian and I delicately carried Rodway out of the nook. 'Shout down to the lads on lookout below, tell them we're coming down! Barrington12, go with him, he'll need you to translate.'

'Will do, Kev!' said Gerry, turning and peering over the edge of the cave entrance with Barrington12 in tow.

The message delivered, Gillian and I gently placed Rodway's fragile frame into Barrington12's arms.

'Take him down to ground level first,' I told him, 'then come back up to fetch me and Gillian. Then we're going home. It's over.'

'I AM SO PLEASED,' said Barrington12 – and despite his monotone voice, he did sound it.

I looked at Rodway's sleeping face. He seemed so at peace, entirely at odds with the cave around us, which was decaying with death and misery. I squeezed Rodway's hand gently, and his eyes fluttered open.

'G… gaffer?' he asked, unable to believe what he was seeing. Now, I did weep.

'That's right, son,' I said in a thick voice, completely choked up. 'It's me. We're all here. We've come to take you home. You're one heck of a fighter, I'll tell you that.'

He smiled in delirious happiness and then groaned – the pain was already coming back to him. Aside from Gerry's hay fever medication, we had nothing by way of medical supplies. He was going to have to tough it out until Dr Pebble-Mill was able to work his magic.

'Let's get out of here,' I said, looking to the cave entrance. Gerry was still peering down at the foot of the volcano, a perplexed look on his face. 'All okay, Gerry?'

He turned to me, scratching his head in bafflement.

'It's the lads on watch down below,' he said. 'They look like... Kev, I think they're all dead.'

These words had barely left his lips before everything went completely to hell. What happened next is something I still cannot fully explain.

But it did happen.

IT IS NOT TODAY

Like Ryan Giggs in his prime, it was so damn fast. One minute I was standing there in the cave trying to take in what Gerry had said – how could the Watlaq on the ground all suddenly be dead? – the next, it was chaos.

Gerry was a silhouette in the diminishing light, looking at me with his back to the world beyond. Suddenly, the light was all but extinguished by three enormous shapes hovering in the air directly behind him. Akplatak shrieked in dismay and threw himself into Gerry's path as a shield as the Winged Terror floating in the centre lunged for my best friend. The three beasts were larger than any of those the Watlaq had already vanquished. Akplatak was left with a deep gash in his shoulder as he sank to his knees beside Gerry, who had been knocked backwards as the Winged Terror swiped at the tribe leader.

'Get away from the edge!' I roared as the other two Winged Terrors knocked a couple of the Watlaq out of the cave entrance to the ground far below. Thankfully they didn't require Barrington12's translation of this instruction, they backed away quickly enough on their own. I ordered the robot to go and stand at the far end of the cave to protect Rodway from further harm – the lad had fainted in shock at the return of the foul creatures. I was about to tell Gillian to get back too, but she collected a spear from the cave floor, dropped by one of the fallen warriors, and threw it at the Winged Terror on the right. It struck right above the heart, a deep, piercing wound. It squawked in pain and fury and fluttered backwards away from the cave mouth, trying to grip the spear with its enormous claws to yank it free.

'Heck of an arm you've got there!' I cried, genuinely impressed. 'I'll take care of the bugger on the opposite side!'

I looked around for a discarded spear of my own but there were none to hand. I looked up at poor Akplatak, bleeding badly on the ground beside Gerry, who was just sitting pressed back against the wall of the cave, staring intently at the two remaining Winged Terrors (the third still ailing in the background) as they laid siege to the Watlaq. The tribespeople had won a famous victory first time around, but with this surprise attack they looked hideously unprepared and horrifically disorganised.

'Gerry!' I cried. 'Throw me your man's spear!'

He didn't respond. Surely he hadn't fallen asleep? That'd be just like him as well. Mind you, I'm hardly one to talk. I often used to nod off on the touchline during matches and on being startled awake, with the game still in progress, I'd have to ask the fourth official what the score was.

'Gerry!' I shouted, harsher in tone this time. 'Akplatak's out for the count, son, throw me his spear!'

Slowly, as though hypnotised, Gerry turned and looked at me and I was disturbed to see a completely vacant expression in his eyes. They weren't even his eyes at all – they were milky white and glazed over and there was no recognition at all as he stared in my direction. I shuddered and forced myself to look away.

I didn't have time to worry about Gerry having some kind of fit – the Winged Terrors were rapidly overpowering the depleted Watlaq warriors. Gillian had managed to give the middle Terror a bastard of a shiner by lobbing a rock at his head. She was really quite handy, it had to be said.

'KEVIN KEEGAN,' came Barrington12's almost mournful voice, echoing from the back of the cave, 'STATISTICALLY, THIS DOES NOT LOOK GOOD. I FEAR THIS BATTLE IS LOST. WE ARE UNLIKELY TO WIN AGAINST THESE CREATURES.'

'Thanks for that, you ray of sunshine,' I said bitterly. 'And anyway, that's what they said about my Man City side when we were 3–0 down at Spurs in the Cup. I've got two words for you, my friend: Jon Macken.'

Feeling fired up, I extended my arm to Akplatak at the other side of the cave.

'Akkie!' I roared. 'Throw me your spear!'

His face creased up in agony, he looked at me with a complete lack of understanding – but when I pointed to his spear on the ground beside him and then to myself, he leaned forward with a grimace and rolled it across the cave floor towards me. I seized it and looked at the central Winged Terror, the one that had gone for my Gerry and banjaxed poor Akplatak, and I smiled grimly.

'Hey, ugly,' I cried. 'Eat this!'

Not wishing to be outdone by Gillian, I threw the spear with all my might and it pierced right through the chest with a sickening crunch. The only downside was that it was, in fact, Akplatak's chest.

The tribe leader screamed the place down in agony – honestly,

I felt terrible. The only small mercy was that, in the melee, none of the other Watlaq seemed to have noticed it was me who had impaled their leader. Adrenaline pumping, Akkie grabbed hold of the spear handle and heaved the thing from his body. I was rooted to the spot in fear – was he going to lob it back at me as retribution?

Akplatak bellowed with righteous anger as he clutched the spear – I was crossing my fingers that it wouldn't turn out to be one of the poison-tipped ones. I looked on in astonishment as, instead of throwing it back at me and flattening me against the wall, he aimed straight for the Winged Terror that had injured him and, with incredible power and distance given his slumped position on the floor, stuck the spear right into the centre of its skull. It fell dead from the sky before it even realised what had happened.

'Great shot, Akkie!' I shouted in encouragement – he glanced over at me with utter disdain before crumpling back down, his breathing ragged. Look, I know I'd just wounded him, perhaps mortally so, but I actually thought he was a bit out of order looking at me like that. I mean, how was that supposed to make *me* feel?

Enraged at seeing their comrade struck down in such a fashion, the remaining two Terrors renewed their attacks on the dwindling Watlaq forces with increased vigour. Before they were able to lose their arrows or lob their spears they were being struck down or toppled from the cave mouth to the distant ground below. I looked on desperately as the last fighter, Gary Barlow, though able to cut a gashing blow to one of the Terrors' legs, was decapitated right there where he stood. Listen, I don't care where you're from, that's a horrible way to go. I've always said that.

The two Terrors landed on the floor of the cave, the battle – and their revenge for their own losses – almost complete. There was only me, Gillian, Barrington12, a broken Akplatak and Gerry, still sitting there in his weird daze, the prat. And, of course, there was poor Rodway, who had suffered more than enough already at the hands of these awful creatures. We were here to take away their dinner and that simply would not stand. I briefly considered trying to reason with them, to point out that there were several dead Watlaq all around us that would make for a nutritious, if stringy meal that would last them for weeks. But, like trying to reason with Joey Barton when he insisted the JFK assassination was an inside job despite the footage of the incident clearly taking place outside, I knew it would be pointless.

'Well,' I said, deflated, 'we came so close. It's even more of a sickener this way. But I'm proud of what we did here. You should all be too.'

I looked at Gillian, but she didn't respond; she was still casting about looking for some kind of escape route. But short of flinging ourselves to our deaths, there was to be no getting away from these winged monstrosities. I glanced at Rodway, still out for the count, his mangled body lying limp in Barrington12's arms.

'I'm sorry, son,' I said. 'At least you won't have to die here on your own.'

I sighed and stared at the two Winged Terrors now advancing into the cave. One (the guy Gillian had stabbed with the spear) advanced towards us, the other closed in on the now barely conscious Akplatak and the off-his-tits-on-something Gerry. I never even had the chance to say a proper goodbye to him, which was heartbreaking. Still. This would all be over very soon.

I closed my eyes, took a deep breath and waited for the end. It came mere moments later – but not in a way any of us could have anticipated.

Even with my eyes firmly shut, I could feel the cave being filled with a brilliant white light – it was a pleasantly warm sensation, like a summer's day in the shade, or my seat in the dugout after my old assistant, Terry Mac, had dutifully sat in it for ten minutes pre-kickoff to heat it up for me. I inched my eyes open, with a hand in front of my face to shield myself from the blinding glow. Where on earth was it coming from? But then I realised.

It was coming from Gerry.

He was standing rigid as though he'd been stuffed – he had excellent posture, which was unusual for Gerry. He was staring at the Winged Terror, who had already shrunk back in fear. Akplatak was watching Gerry with adoration, his mouth wide open. From Gerry's eyes, mouth, fingertips and the ends of each mulleted hair shone beams of pure white light, illuminating the entire cave. There was a peculiar ethereal hum which seemed to come both from Gerry and from the very air around us all at once. The other Winged Terror, which had been coming for me and Gillian, was now backing away against the wall. Both of them seemed too astonished to even take flight.

'SOMETHING STRANGE IS HAPPENING HERE,' Barrington12 remarked from behind me.

'Maybe it's just his hay fever playing up,' I whispered, though of course I didn't believe it.

This was… what *was* this? The hum grew louder; Gillian had her hands over her ears. I was pleased that whatever David Blaine-esque trick Gerry was doing had so far succeeded in putting the frighteners up the Winged Terrors but he was going to hurt somebody if he wasn't careful. As usual, I'd have to step in.

'Gerry, lad…' I said calmly, stepping over to him. 'That's enough now.' I put a hand on his shoulder and flew back against the wall like I'd been given an electric shock. I shook my head to try and clear the fug – for a moment I feared I'd gone blind but a few heavy blinks brought everything back into sharp focus. Gillian was beside me, her palm on my forehead.

'You're boiling hot,' she said in a worried voice. 'What is happening here?'

'God knows,' I said over the ever-increasing buzz. 'It's like it's not even Gerry standing there. It's like it's—'

'Slasabo-tik,' Gerry said in a bizarre, deep booming voice nothing like his own. 'I have returned. The prophecy must be fulfilled as the Heavens have willed it. Stand and be true.'

'Who's that meant to be an impression of?' I asked Gillian, frowning. 'Brian Blessed or something?'

'The day approaches fast,' Gerry said, and then he paused. 'But it is not today.'

With a loud smacking sound, a surge of powerful light emanated from Gerry. Gillian and I were thrown back against the wall, winding us both. Nearby, I heard a clanking sound as Barrington12 too was forced back, toppling over and no doubt spilling the unfortunate Rodway to the floor. Then, like a blown light bulb, the cave fell back into the natural semi-darkness of before. I staggered to my feet and helped Gillian rise.

'Oh my god,' she said, which just about summed it up. The Winged Terrors were no more – their silhouettes were burned into the walls of the cave, a two-dimensional black-scarred memorial to their existence, frozen for all time in fearful poses, their clawed hands covering their frightened faces. Gerry stood there where he'd been before, but he was now looking around in bemusement, scratching his head like he'd just woken up from a vivid dream. Most astonishingly of all, Akplatak stood up slowly and touched his shoulder and chest, where a combination of a Winged Terror's talon and my own dodgy throwing arm had combined to damn near end his life. Now his skin was smooth and undamaged; there was no scar tissue or even any blood. It was as though nothing had happened. Those who had fallen in battle sadly remained that way, but Akplatak, the sole survivor, had been completely healed. By Gerry bloody Francis.

'Gerry,' I said eventually. 'What in blazes did you just do?'

'What do you mean?' he asked fearfully. 'I didn't do anything!'

'Slasabo-tik!' cried Akplatak, falling to his knees and bowing over and over again to Gerry.

'You vaporised those Winged Terrors,' Gillian said in a thin voice.

'What are you both on about?' Gerry asked, his face flushing red. 'That's not true. I just… I guess I nodded off for a second or something, I don't know, and then I woke up and everything was fine. I didn't do a thing.'

Whether he was trying to convince us or himself was up for debate.

'Gaffer…?' came a voice from behind me. I whipped round – I'd forgotten all about poor Rodway and his horrific injuries.

But to my amazement, these too had been miraculously cured: his scars and wounds had vanished and his sickeningly broken leg looked as good as new. Aside from his soiled and damaged clothes, he looked the picture of health.

'My word...' I whispered. 'This cannot be...'

'Can we go home now, gaffer?' Rodway asked. 'I don't want to stay here a moment longer.'

I smiled a tired smile.

'That might just be the best idea I've ever heard,' I said.

And I really meant it.

VICTORIOUS DEFEAT

The walk home from Great Strombago was a sombre one. I hadn't experienced an atmosphere like it since the collapse of my campaign to change the national anthem when I was England manager. I remember when I got my OBE in 1982, I was absolutely made up. I said to Liz, 'I hate to gush but honestly, "Bohemian Rhapsody" changed my life. It's your masterpiece.' She didn't reply, which is testament to her humility.

Anyway, despite my enthusiasm for the Royals, I find the national anthem an absolute dirge. It just drones on and leaves you feeling completely cold by the end. With England, I used to encourage my lads to sing whatever they liked when we lined up before a match. I'd often belt out 'Total Eclipse of the Heart' by Bonnie Tyler just to get the blood pumping. In any case, before Euro 2000 I lobbied the FA to pull some strings and sort out a replacement. Personally, I advocated 'Summer of '69' by Bryan Adams but I was flexible. To help speed up the process, I drew up a whole list of potential tunes with the intention of holding some kind of national public vote – and it wasn't just personal favourites of mine, like 'Deeply Dippy' or 'Pipes of Peace', I also threw in a few modern numbers for the youngsters out there so that they wouldn't feel they were being dictated to by old fogeys like me. There was stuff like 'Ooh Aah... Just a Little Bit' by Gina G, 'Scatman' by Scatman John and 'Mambo No. 5' by Lou Bega (which, I don't care how old you are, is just an absolute treat for the ears). And to placate the posher crowd, the old-school Radio 3 demographic for whom I have the utmost respect, I threw in a few classical options too, like 'Orinoco Flow' and the theme music from the ITV series *Sharpe*. The FA were having none of it but my boys were supportive and some of them even helped me make a case in the boardroom.

'God won't save the Queen,' Martin Keown told them darkly. 'She'll die one day, just like everybody else.'

I said, 'All right, son, let's dial it back a bit.' I do like Martin, but he's a bit of an odd bod. He has the unsettling gaze of a man whose Sky box is chock-full of documentaries about serial killers and nothing else.

In the end, the FA told me that I ought to be focusing on matters on the pitch and not being distracted by 'trivial nonsense' before a major international tournament. I felt sickened at hearing the importance of our national song downplayed and belittled by a load of out-of-touch grey-faced men in suits but, at the end of the day, they were calling the shots. With regret, I abandoned my campaign and concentrated just on the football, and we went on to have a fantastic tournament. But the frustration I felt at such short-sighted, pig-headed leadership left me at a low ebb.

That had been nothing compared to the walk back through the marshland after the massacre at Great Strombago. We all felt battered, exhausted and, in a peculiar way, defeated. The mission had, on the face of things, been a complete success: we had navigated the wilds of Palangonia, perhaps further than any outsider had for centuries and certainly more extensively than any human beings in history. We had retrieved Rodway and were bringing him home. And yet… there was no elation. No feeling of achievement, of a job well done. The Watlaq had endured horrendous losses, much like Billy Davies' Derby County side when they were in the Premier League. Akplatak was a shell of a man, his spirit and verve all gone as he trudged silently through the bog alongside Gerry. He had taken his soldiers, brave men and women all, into battle to protect their Mullet God, and in the end he was the only one to make it out alive, returning to break the awful news to those of his people who had remained at home.

But the way that Akplatak stuck close to Gerry on the walk back confirmed for me that, despite it all, he wouldn't ultimately see this as a terrible or ill-judged decision. The casualties had been enormous and unexpected, yes, but the cause was true and the sole objective – keeping Slasabo-tik alive – had been fulfilled. And Gerry's display of… whatever the hell that was, would only serve to confirm for him the power which his god truly held.

That part was a source of enormous unease to me. I had no explanation for what had happened back there and Gerry himself refused to talk about it. It was clear that he had no memory whatsoever of the event and, by extension, no way of explaining it. But it *had* happened – it had been no trick, no illusion. Before our very eyes, Gerry had gone into a trance, begun speaking of the prophecy and had destroyed the Winged Terrors and healed the sick in a burst of blinding light. I'm sorry, but that's not the Gerry Francis I know – a man who believes that *Hamlet* is about a pig that thinks it's a sheepdog.

And as for Gerry… I hadn't seen him look so grey-faced and depressed since he finished reading David James' self-published Robinson Crusoe erotic novel, *Friday, I'm In Love*. It was hardly surprising that he should look such a state after what he'd just been through, but nevertheless, I was privately a little worried. He was quiet, withdrawn, not like himself at all. I was going to have to keep a close eye on him.

'We need to talk about what happened back there,' Gillian said to me in a low voice as we left the marshes behind and headed back into the forest. It was pitch black and gone midnight, but none of us wanted to make camp for the night. We were weary but somehow, collectively, felt we had to carry on. We were relying on the distant pale glow of Palangonia's triple moons – Barrington12, having not been charged since we left the Compound, had been forced to close down all non-essential processes one by one as we walked, and this included his 'night mode' shoulder bulbs. His walking became more measured and he spoke little. It was a bonus that Rodway had been completely healed, because I doubted then that Barrington12 would have been able to carry him all the way back without his battery running flat. And I certainly couldn't carry the lad – not with my back.

'What is there to say?' I asked. 'Gerry doesn't want to talk about it. He was sulking all the way back down Great Strombago; as far as he's concerned, it didn't even happen.'

I sighed and picked at a dead twig from one of the trees as we passed.

'It's daft, this,' I said, shaking my head. 'Are we really meant to… I mean, I intend no disrespect to Gerry, but… can he really, actually be some kind of supernatural being? Him, of all people?

What does Gerry have – apart from a mullet, obviously – that makes him the Mullet God?'

Gillian looked away into the distance as she considered this.

'I don't know,' she said. 'You know him best. You tell me.'

I'd never really thought about it before. Was he so special? Gerry was loyal, kind, entirely free of cynicism, an optimist. Then suddenly I recalled Barrington12's translation of the Watlaq as they explained the prophecy to us: *'SLASABO-TIK IS KINDNESS, HOPE, POSITIVITY; ALL THE FINEST ATTRIBUTES THE DENIZENS OF THIS GALAXY CAN STRIVE FOR. HE IS THE BEST OF ALL OF US. HE EMBODIES THAT WHICH WE SHOULD BE.'*

That was certainly Gerry. I just hadn't realised it could also be so much more than that. That it could actually be a god with the ability to save the galaxy from complete annihilation. I mean, I'd heard people talk about 'the power of positive thinking' but this was in a different league altogether.

'I'd be just as dubious myself,' I agreed. 'Except we saw it, Gillian. Something very, very strange is afoot here. I honestly don't know what happens next.'

'According to what Akplatak told us of the prophecy,' Gillian went on, 'Slasabo-tik would return when the galaxy was at its darkest moment and save us all. If that's true…'

I said nothing, walking on into the night in silence. It wasn't that part of the stupid prophecy that was bothering me. It was the last part. Akplatak said that, in order to save the galaxy, the Mullet God would eventually have to sacrifice his own life.

That was not going to happen. Not on my watch.

*

Early the following morning, after a restless night's sleep under the eaves of the forest, we packed up our belongings and prepared for the home stretch. Akplatak approached me – he looked old and so very tired in the white dawn light. Despite the healing effects of the Mullet God, the expedition to Great Strombago looked to have added years to him. He spoke to us, Gerry standing solemnly by his side. Barrington12, whose voice was slower and more deliberate in its delivery now, translated.

'HE WISHES TO ACCOMPANY US AS FAR AS THE TUNNEL ENTRANCE,' he explained. 'HE WOULD SEE SLASABO-TIK SAFELY ESCORTED TO HIS NEXT DESTINATION AS HE JOURNEYS ON TO PROPHECY'S END.'

'Right you are then,' I said. I felt oddly comforted having Akkie come with us – and, selfishly, the more we put off the parting of the ways, the further away the crippling guilt of what we had done to his people would remain.

Rodway, who was more energised than all of us after being healed by Gerry, heaved open the grille leading back into the tunnel. It felt like an eternity since we had clambered out of there into the fresh air of the Palangonian wilderness. Now, at last, we were going home.

'Who knows, maybe they'll have caught the spy while we were out here,' Gerry suggested optimistically. 'We could have the club back up and running within a week. Think of that, Kev.'

I couldn't. Not then. All I could think of was saying goodbye to Akkie, a man who had given literally everything he had in his life to help us. Or to help his Mullet God, anyway. I put a hand on his shoulder before we descended into the darkness of the tunnel and took him to one side. Had I tried this the day before, I had little doubt that he would have tried to stab me in the neck but now he obliged without complaint. I signalled to Barrington12 to join us.

'I want you to tell the lad what I'm saying,' I told him. 'This is important.'

'O... KAY... KEV... IN... KEEEEEEEGAN...' Barrington12 replied. His batteries were really running on air now – I didn't have time to faff about. But, to my surprise, Akplatak spoke first. Infuriatingly slowly, the robot relayed his words to me.

'SLASABO-TIK IS THE MOST PRECIOUS THING IN THE GALAXY,' he said in a grave voice, far removed from his animated and enthusiastic relaying of the prophecy when we had first arrived. 'I ENTRUST HIM TO YOU FOR NOW, BUT YOU MUST DO ALL YOU CAN TO KEEP HIM SAFE.'

I was stunned – I'd agreed with Gillian when she'd observed that the Watlaq would not countenance letting Gerry go. And yet here stood their leader, doing just that, for the greater good. I looked at Akkie with a level of respect beyond any I had felt for any human (save perhaps Al Shearer, but then that kid is just on another level). I wasn't at all convinced that I could do what Akkie was now doing had our roles been reversed.

'WITHOUT HIM, THE STARS WILL FALL AND DARKNESS WILL REIGN FOR ALL THE TIME LEFT TO COME. IF SLASABO-TIK IS LOST, SO ARE WE ALL. HE WILL DIE TO COMPLETE THE PROPHECY. HE MUST. IT IS TOLD AND YOU CANNOT STAND IN HIS WAY.

A DAY WILL COME, AND SOON, WHEN YOU MUST CHOOSE BETWEEN YOUR FRIEND'S LIFE… AND THE ENTIRE GALAXY.'

His words chilled me to my bones. Plus it threw me off what I was going to say to him, so I needed an extra few moments to regroup.

'Listen,' I said, gesturing to Barrington12 to pay attention and translate for Akplatak. I needed him to hear these words, or I'd be haunted by what we had done forever. 'I'm going to do all I can, son, once I'm back home and after this spy stuff is sorted out, to make sure the people in my Compound do more for you and your kin. We can help you rebuild, to get yourselves back on track. It's the least we can do. I'll pull every string. Akkie, I'm just… I'm so bloody sorry. About everything. Please know… that I'm sorry.'

Akplatak stared at me solemnly. I glanced at Barrington12, who had said nothing.

'Barrington12,' I said, trying to keep myself from getting choked up. 'Tell him what I said. I need him to hear this. It's important.'

'POWER DANGEROUSLY LOW. VOICEBOX NOW DEACTIVATING TO PRESERVE REMAINING BATTERY LIFE.'

He fell silent and said no more. Akplatak glanced from me to Barrington12, then took one final look at his Mullet God standing by the tunnel entrance, who was picking his nose absently, and then the tribe leader turned without a word and walked away. He vanished into the trees and was gone. I was sure that I would never see him again.

'What a mess,' I said under my breath. 'What a damnable mess.'

I walked back over to my friends. Gillian squeezed my arm.

'Are you okay, Kevin?' she asked, concerned. 'You look like you've seen a ghost.'

I thought of Akkie's pallid face moments earlier.

'I think I did,' I replied. Thankfully, Gillian was intuitive enough not to press me any further.

'Well,' she said, slapping her thighs. 'Let's get home. I could murder a hot bath, I'll tell you that much…'

She trailed off and cocked her head. We could all hear it, clear as a bell: footsteps in the tunnel below. Someone was heading our way – and at a brisk pace, too.

'Quick,' I hissed. 'Get down over here. You said it yourself, Gillian: if anyone from back home spots us out here, we're finished – your Council credentials will count for nowt if they pin this spy stuff on us.'

Hurriedly, Rodway replaced the grille – extricating his fingers delicately to avoid clanging it shut – and we all ducked down behind a large boulder to one side of the tunnel entrance. Barrington12 joined us at a painfully slow clip and was only just out of sight by the time the grille was pushed open from within. We all peered round from both sides of the rock and watched as a figure pulled themselves athletically up to ground level and dusted themselves down.

'Please tell me I'm seeing things,' I whispered in horror.

'If *you* are,' Gillian replied, 'then we all are.'

We watched with a growing feeling of dread as the figure hurried over to a large patch of shrubbery to the far left of the meadow and pulled it to one side like a curtain. My jaw dropped as I glimpsed the metallic sheen of a small one-pilot space shuttle concealed behind it. The figure clambered inside and, moments later, with a deafening roar, took off, propelled into the air, soon nothing more than a tiny speck skating across the blue morning sky. Once we could no longer see it with the naked eye, we emerged from behind the boulder and looked at one another, shell-shocked.

'We need to get back to the Compound,' I said. 'Right now.'

I had no idea whatsoever what we were going to do once we got back there. Who was ever going to believe the five of us when we told them that we had just witnessed General Leigh, the head of the Compound military and protector of all the citizens living within those four walls, covertly leaving to pilot a secret shuttle away from Palangonia?

Akkie had warned that dark days were coming. It felt to me in that moment that they had already arrived.

INFINITE MALAISE

Two days passed and I was getting twitchy. Who knew what havoc Leigh was currently wreaking behind our backs? I remembered grimly the coarse spot of graffiti I'd noticed during my spell in prison, referring to him as a 'L'zuhl shagger', and suddenly it seemed less a taunt than a warning. Well, all right, maybe it wasn't literally true (though listen, if it's between consenting adults then just crack on, I say) but it now clearly indicated where the man's true loyalties lay. I'd wanted to summon an emergency meeting of the other members of the Compound Council to announce the General's treachery but Gillian urged caution.

'It would be disastrous for this Compound if we accuse Leigh of such a heinous crime and turn out to be wrong,' she said as we emerged from the tunnel behind the infirmary. 'We have to wait and bide our time, we can't go in all guns blazing.'

I was very unhappy with this but, deep down, I knew that she was probably right. I was still reeling from the fact that Leigh was the spy. Oh, sure, I'd entertained the idea and pictured myself exposing him as a fraud to the citizens of the Compound, with me then being lifted aloft by the crowd and hailed as a hero, followed by Stevie Nicks sending me a pre-recorded message of congratulations while I collected my Medal of Galactic Valour from Laika in front of a packed hall of dignitaries. But I'd never seriously considered it a possibility. He was an odious turd, no question, but I never had him pegged as a lover of the L'zuhl.

But at the end of the day, Leigh was a soldier and – like a pure football man such as myself – soldiers always want to be on the winning side. Leigh was a key figure in the human resistance, working closely with Alliance top brass to try to turn about the fortunes of a seemingly unwinnable war. My own experience out beyond the Compound walls had, whether I liked to admit it or not, affected me in some intangible way. I had seen true horror on that mountainside and had faced the very real possibility of an imminent and violent death. Leigh had no doubt been in just such a position many times in his career on the frontline. Had he seen things that had changed him, convinced him that there could be no victory? Was he working with the L'zuhl purely in the interests of self-preservation? He didn't have to like it – perhaps he even felt shame. But if it was a choice between his victory and his life or his species… well, was it really so far-fetched? Why else would he be sneaking off down the old Palangonian escape tunnels to a hidden shuttle and then jet-setting off into space? Once his leaked intel brought the might of the L'zuhl armada down upon us, he had a handy little escape route mapped out for himself. The more I thought about the butter-wouldn't-melt look on his face as he climbed up from the tunnel and into his concealed craft, the more I wanted to grass him up to see how he'd try to weasel his way out of it.

Gillian raised another vital objection to this, however. If we revealed what we'd seen, then questions would immediately be asked as to why we ourselves were out there during the lockdown. With my reputation already tarnished by my false arrest and with Gillian a member of the Council herself (and one who had lost her security card), Leigh could very easily turn the situation to his own advantage. 'I was in the tunnel searching for them,' he'd say. 'Imagine my surprise at seeing the whole gang loitering outside. I took an emergency shuttle out of there because I feared for my own life after stumbling across their plan; I had no choice…' Damn it all, he'd have us over a barrel.

I cannot abide deception; it makes me sick. I remember when I was at Newcastle in 2008, I got a call from some slimy agent promising me a big-name German international. As you might expect, I was thrilled and invited him up to see us. Well, it soon became clear that something wasn't right. The kid was bang-average at best – and his German accent sounded suspiciously Scottish. Soon, the penny dropped. I marched over to the agent and grabbed him by the collar – I said, 'What are you trying to pull? That's just Hutton dressed as Lahm!' I sent the pair of them packing.

I had no choice but to stew. In the meantime, General Leigh, who had already returned by that evening, was strutting about the place like nothing had happened.

'He thinks he's cock of the walk,' Gerry remarked as we sat by the window in Mr O's Place and saw Leigh cruising by in one of the Harbinger vehicles.

'Don't be vulgar, Gerry,' I said, sipping my hot chocolate. 'You're better than that.'

I had been pleased to see an improvement in Gerry since we returned home. The topic of what had happened to him was given a wide berth and we were both happy with that arrangement.

But the more time passed, the more colour returned to his cheeks and the bags under his eyes – so pronounced during our sad trek back from Great Strombago – had begun to fade. I was still deeply troubled by what had happened up there and I had a whole stack of questions I wanted to ask, but the truth was, nobody would have been in a position to answer even a single one of them. Whatever had taken place might very well happen again and the most difficult part was that I honestly had no clue what I would do if it did.

The other nugget of good news – from our perspective, at least – was that Gillian's Keycard had not been found. On the face of it, that might sound like a bad thing, but I didn't feel that way. Had her lost card been found while we were out on our expedition to Great Strombago, it would have been catastrophic. A lost card and its owner gone AWOL was a disastrous combination. Wherever the card was, it was still out there. Or was it?

My own theory, which I hadn't yet put to Gillian for fear of making her feel even more anxious, was that Leigh himself had it, probably swiping it from her pocket at the end of a Council meeting. He was no doubt keeping it in reserve for when he was in danger of being caught, ready to leave it lying around in order to incriminate her. Or perhaps he was using it to leave a trail of breadcrumbs leading to poor Gillian? Was he perhaps becoming concerned that with her level head and clear thinking she might pose a growing threat to the sway he already held over the Council's decisions? Perhaps he'd used the card to borrow those library books under her name; after all, she had been adamant she hadn't taken any of them out herself. Christ, it was all just too perfect. I'd almost admire the bugger if I didn't detest him so much. How could he do this? I couldn't wait to see him cop for it eventually. And he would. If it took me to my dying breath, I'd see it done. No one messes Kevin Keegan about and gets away with it.

Gerry looked at his watch.

'Visiting hours have just started, Kev,' he said. 'Shall we head over?'

'Aye,' I said, scoffing the last of my doughnut. 'Hopefully they'll let him out today. Kid's right as rain; it's stupid, this.'

As we had emerged, shattered and dirty, from the tunnel behind the infirmary a few days prior, we were stopped in our tracks by the unexpected sight of Dr Pebble-Mill indulging in a cheeky cigarette beside the bins. I hastily tried to act casual, whistling to myself and looking around like I'd lost my bearings slightly, the others behind me doing the same. To absolutely nobody's surprise, the ruse fell instantly flat. He stubbed out his fag and strolled towards us, hands stuffed into the cavernous pockets of his white coat. Dr Pebble-Mill was, as Rodway had observed in his report on the Council members during our earlier spy-hunt reconnaissance, a decent man, having treated me with supreme kindness and dignity after I'd been hospitalised with a suspected severe stroke nine months earlier (eventually diagnosed as an allergy to Nice 'N' Spicy Nik-Naks). He was a handsome chap in his mid-to-late fifties, with a thick mane of hair and a salt-and-pepper beard.

'Morning, doc,' I said. 'Listen, I know how this looks, but if you'll just give me two minutes to come up with something, I'm sure I can explain—'

'Come off it, Kevin,' he said. 'You've been rumbled. Accept it.

And Gillian – your dicky tummy has cleared up, I take it?'

'Please, Andre,' Gillian said, pushing to the front. She knew the doctor well from their time together serving on the Council. 'Just allow us to explain what happened. It's not what it seems, I assure you.'

'You were using the hidden tunnel back there to exit the Compound,' he said, with a sort of shrug. He must have registered our stunned faces then because he grinned. 'What, you think I don't know it's there?'

'So you've used the tunnel yourself?' I asked. He shook his head.

'No. To be honest, I thought the entrance had been sealed permanently shut when we built this place. Very industrious of you; I would never have thought of that.'

'We're not the spies,' Gillian said. 'Any of us. It's nothing to do with that. Or, at least, not directly.'

He held up his hands.

'You don't need to persuade me. You're one of the few with any real compassion and heart on that Council, Gillian. You're the last person I'd believe to be capable of such a thing. Don't worry.'

Gillian flushed bright red and smiled. She was absolutely made up with that. I myself felt happy for her, though also a little embarrassed. I had failed to see so much within Gillian for so long. That I had finally done so now was something, yes, but not enough. Not for my own sense of regret. I had doubted her, publicly, and yet she apparently bore me no ill will. That alone said everything about this woman. I was lucky to be able to call her my friend and I knew it, even if I didn't say it.

'I'm not the spy either,' I said to Dr Pebble-Mill, fishing slightly.

'I should imagine not,' he agreed. 'No offence intended, Kevin, but I think they'd recruit someone a bit more…' he trailed off. Probably for the best.

'So you won't report us then?' Gerry asked, very brazenly.

'No,' he said. 'But I'd advise a little more caution in future if you plan any further jaunts out into the wilderness. Leigh will see you all hanged, I have no doubt. Tensions are running very high at the moment. I don't wish to tell tales out of school, but I hear that the Alliance top brass at The Oracle are having serious qualms about Leigh's handling of this whole spy business. They're getting itchy feet and I fear he might be prone to lashing out at anyone who crosses him. Give him a wide berth, that's my doctorly advice.'

'I'll tell you why he's so highly strung,' I said. 'Guess what we saw this morning while we were—'

Gillian elbowed me painfully in the ribs and shushed me.

'Not until we're sure,' she muttered.

Dr Pebble-Mill clocked all of this of course, but didn't press for more. The man's a class act.

'What on earth were you doing out there anyway?' he asked, scratching his beard. 'Even with the turncoat running amok in the Compound, it's a far safer place than anything you'll find beyond these walls.'

I gestured to Rodway to step forward. He was radiating health, though his clothes were tattered and muddy.

'Hi,' Rodway said, with an awkward wave.

'This is Rodway,' I explained. 'My star striker. A flock of

Winged Terrors swooped down and snatched him, right in front of our eyes.'

'Ah yes,' Dr Pebble-Mill said knowingly. 'My new junior doctor. How are you finding it so far?'

There was a hollow pause and Rodway glanced at me with faint panic in his eyes.

'Oh, come now,' Dr Pebble-Mill said with a small smile. 'Did you honestly think you'd fooled me with that whole act? That fake ID badge you showed me was a bit of a giveaway – it was just your name and a drawing of a stick man on a Post-it note.'

Rodway looked sheepishly at his feet.

'I was just pleased to see you taking an interest in a new career,' Dr Pebble-Mill went on. 'I knew you were from the football team – I'm a season ticket holder; I never miss a game.'

I was bursting with pride at this. I'd had no idea.

'Surviving a run-in with those Winged Terrors, though,' Dr Pebble-Mill puffed out his cheeks. 'There aren't many who can lay claim to something like that.'

'It was awful,' Gillian said.

'Those things are a pestilence on this planet, they really are,' Dr Pebble-Mill agreed.

'Anyway, they took him alive,' I said, 'and… well, I couldn't just leave the lad to die like that. It wouldn't have been right. So we used the tunnel, slipped out of the Compound and retrieved him from right inside their nest. He was at death's door; we weren't a moment too soon.'

Dr Pebble-Mill raised his eyebrows, looking genuinely impressed.

'My goodness me,' he said in awe. 'I'm no expert on those dreadful things but I thought their nests were predominantly found over on Great Strombago.' He paused – we looked back at him until he put two and two together. 'You're not serious? You're telling me you all schlepped over to the volcano and pulled him alive from inside one of their nests?'

'That about sums it up, yeah,' I said with mock-bashfulness. 'All in a day's work, really.'

'That was a brave and selfless thing for you to do. I… scarcely know what to say. It's incredible that you're all standing here in one piece.'

'Listen, if you can survive being England boss, you can survive anything,' I said. 'There's no weight of expectation anywhere in the galaxy greater than that. I mean, they were so disappointed in my tenure that they bulldozed the entire stadium as soon as I left. Rude, actually.'

Dr Pebble-Mill stepped towards Rodway and squinted at him. He unhooked his stethoscope from around his neck.

'Death's door, you say?' Dr Pebble-Mill said, almost to himself. 'But I see barely a scratch on him…'

I glanced at Gillian, who glanced at Gerry, who glanced at his fingernails. The subject was still off-limits for him.

'Long story,' I said eventually, as Dr Pebble-Mill proceeded to listen to an obliging Rodway's heart and lungs and give him a superficial examination of the limbs, ears and eyes. 'We met some tribespeople out in the wilderness there. They knew of a… er… a kind of miracle cure.'

'Miraculous would be the word for it,' Dr Pebble-Mill said in wonder. 'This is most extraordinary, I have to say. I remember

Mr Jones coming in for a minor knee operation earlier this year and yet as I look at him now… there's no scar.'

'Who's Mr Jones?' I asked, baffled.

'That's me, gaffer,' Rodway said. 'Rodway Jones.'

Damn.

'Yeah, of course,' I said. 'Just messing and that.'

'Anyway,' Gillian said, trying to sound as casual as possible, 'I guess we'd better get going, Andre. You've probably got a lot on your plate.'

'I think this supersedes anything else I currently have on my roster,' he said. 'I'd like to admit Rodway immediately for observation. This is all most irregular and I'd like to study him to learn how this could be so.'

'Ah, no,' I said, 'I don't think that's really necessary. Look at him – he's fit and strong, raring to go. We don't need to trouble you with this. It's not important.'

'On the contrary,' Dr Pebble-Mill said, barely able to take his eyes off Rodway, 'this could be of the utmost importance. I'd like to know more about this miracle cure you mentioned – it could have innumerable implications for healthcare here on Palangonia.'

'Well, I mean…' I began.

'The Compound would be indebted to you all,' Dr Pebble-Mill said. 'And it'd be awful if they found out you'd been off honeymooning beyond the walls during the lockdown.'

I gasped.

'You wouldn't!' I cried. He smiled.

'Well, okay, of course not,' he said. 'But still: Rodway, would you consent to coming in? Just for a few days? If we could examine you, perhaps take a few blood samples, we could potentially learn so much.'

Rodway looked at me. I shrugged – it was beyond my purview now.

'Sure,' he said. 'If you think it'd help.'

'Great!' Dr Pebble-Mill said. 'Come on, I'll get you signed in and find you a bed.'

He led Rodway enthusiastically by the arm. Then suddenly he paused and looked Barrington12 up and down, an expression of childlike fascination on his face.

'Good heavens, I've not seen a 12-series in years!' Dr Pebble-Mill said. 'You know, I used to absolutely love putting these things together when I was a younger man. I'd often stay up all night – I even built my own Barrington50 once. It's actually quite soothing work.'

'Aye, well,' I said, not the least bit interested. 'We'd better let you get on. Cheers.'

Dr Pebble-Mill waved in a non-committal way and then vanished inside.

'Well, if his tests determine that Rodway was healed by Gerry's godlike powers then the doc deserves the Nobel prize,' I said. I saw Gerry flinch in my peripheral vision.

'Sorry,' I said awkwardly. 'But, Gerry… we do have to talk about—'

'I'm going home,' he said huffily.

Gerry stalked off, Barrington12 clunking painfully slowly after him.

'Get him charged up before you turn in, Gerry,' I said to his back.

'Goodnight, Kevin,' Gillian said. 'And please, keep this Leigh business under your hat for now. We have to know for definite before we make our move. Anything less and we'll blow it. Trust me.'

I nodded and, satisfied, she walked away. I exhaled deeply, puffing out my cheeks. A chilly midday breeze rattled my aching bones.

'Hell of a damn adventure,' I said to no one in particular.

A WAY OUT

'It really is great of you to come and visit so often,' Rodway said as we sat down a week later in the uncomfortable plastic chairs on opposite sides of his bed. He was wearing a gown and eating from a bowl of grapes. Outside his room, there was the usual bustle of a hospital ward: nurses and clerks at the desk, doctors doing rounds, a cleaner who had taken to calling me 'Big Dog' during each visit and always had his fly open. There had been a bit of hubbub when I'd popped by the previous evening as a patient came in with a swollen green head, spewing pus all over the place, and had been diagnosed with a severe, advanced case of approxial mylosia.

It was the first time I'd ever witnessed the disease up close and it was not pretty. It typically affected those who had recently undertaken deep space travel for the first time but there had been an increasing number of cases in patients who had been healthy for months, even for more than a year after arriving on Palangonia. I had lingered in the doorway of the poor man's room as the medics dashed about trying to save him but once his legs exploded I decided to take my leave. To add insult to injury, I went to the vending machine for a Twirl after experiencing a strong sugar craving only to find it was out of order. I glanced back towards the patient's room, the door now closed, and I felt a certain kinship – we were both having a rotten old evening and no mistake.

Now, the morning after, the hospital seemed mercifully quiet. I unfolded a newspaper and began to scan through it.

'I assume they're still no closer to finding out what happened to you, then?' I asked Rodway – but Dr Pebble-Mill, who had suddenly appeared in the doorway, answered for him.

'Not even close, I'm afraid,' he said, scrutinising his clipboard and frowning. I hadn't seen anyone look that confused since I watched *Inception* with Steven Taylor. 'This really is a genuine mystery. I've been working overtime to try to get to the bottom of it all and I do have one or two theories I'm testing out but… well, as with anything of any importance, it requires time and patience. Neither of which are often abundant in a hospital environment, but I'll keep plugging away.'

'Oh well,' I said. 'You win some, you lose some. A lot like football, actually.'

'Although sometimes you draw, Kev,' Gerry chipped in.

'Good point,' I agreed.

'Well,' Dr Pebble-Mill said with equanimity, 'at the end of it all, the most important thing is your own health. Rodway, you're free to go. I'll sign your discharge papers.'

I clapped my hands. 'Excellent stuff.'

'The tests we ran all came back completely normal, nothing out of the ordinary whatsoever. The strangest thing. The injuries he must have sustained… it's utterly remarkable. As though God himself came down and touched you, healing your wounds.'

I shot a glance at Gerry, who looked panicked. I hastily forced a laugh.

'Haha, imagine!' I said, a little too exuberantly.

'It really was a remarkably brave thing you did, Kevin,' the doctor said, watching me thoughtfully. 'Going out there to retrieve Rodway. I've rarely seen such valour.'

'Oh, well,' I said, feeling a little embarrassed, but also absolutely chuffed. 'At the end of the day it was a group effort.'

'The way Gillian tells it, she practically had to restrain you from leaping off her sixth-floor balcony when they took Rodway,' Pebble-Mill went on.

'Aw, cheers, gaffer,' Rodway said, looking up from pulling his trousers on. 'That's lovely to hear. I'd do the same for you.'

'I've got to head off shortly,' Dr Pebble-Mill said. 'Laika flew in from The Oracle first thing this morning – she's convening an urgent Council meeting to discuss the spy problem. As I say, the Alliance are not at all happy with the way it's being handled.'

Wow. That was huge – the equivalent of Man United bringing Sir Al out of retirement to weather a rocky spell. Leigh would be extremely embarrassed by it too, which was a bonus.

'If you'll bear with me for a moment,' Dr Pebble-Mill said, 'I just need to make a phone call.'

'Aye, on you go, Doc,' I said. 'We'll be out of your hair as soon as Rodway's got his shoes on.'

'Actually if you could just hang around,' the doctor said mysteriously, 'that'd be great.'

He left the room and his footsteps faded down the corridor.

'What was that all about?' Gerry asked.

We waited around for a few minutes but Pebble-Mill did not return, so I tucked my newspaper under my arm and stood up.

'Let's get off,' I said. 'I want to keep an eye on Leigh – I don't feel comfortable with him out there, unmonitored.'

I'd been trying, in the days since we had returned, to keep an inconspicuous eye on the General. Obviously it was near impossible when he was within the walls of Fort Emmeline, but while he was out and about in the Compound – and he'd made a concerted effort to be a more visible preference during the current faffery, apparently vain enough to think residents might be reassured by the sight of him – I wanted to keep tabs as much as possible.

As we made our way down the hospital corridor, Dr Pebble-Mill appeared from a side room. He looked slightly disappointed that we'd headed off without waiting for him.

'Oh… sorry,' I mumbled. 'I was just… looking for the loo.'

'What, all of you?' he asked, surprised.

'We just drank loads of Ribena – it goes right through you,' Gerry offered.

'Look, the reason I wanted you to hang about a second is this,' Dr Pebble-Mill said. He produced a crisp sheet of paper and passed it to me. 'I had Laika's approval to stamp it; I've just spoken to her now and she faxed it over. I didn't tell her the details of your trip beyond the Compound walls of course, but just enough to emphasise your bravery. Even as a Council member, I couldn't override Leigh's order – but she could.'

I took the piece of paper and stared at the heading. *DEPARTURE REQUEST 227/B99* and beneath that, the 'APPROVED' box had been stamped, with Laika's signature (a single paw print) underneath.

'What does it mean?' I asked, utterly dumbfounded.

'It means,' Dr Pebble-Mill smiled, 'that you can go. There's a

+1 on it if you want to take Gerry. I heard whispers that, after your football team was shut down, you had your eyes on another post elsewhere. David Moyes' team or something like that.'

For a moment I wondered how he could possibly have known that, but then I remembered my arrest being reported in the *Chronicle* and how my defence (or 'excuse', as they'd labelled it) had also been included in the story. I was rather touched that the doctor had remembered.

'It's… very kind of you,' I said. 'Really it is. But unfortunately I read the other day that Moyesie got a win in midweek, so his job's safe for a while longer.'

'They played again yesterday,' Dr Pebble-Mill said, tapping the paper still tucked under my arm. I pulled it out and flipped straight to the back page.

FIFKA WANDERERS IN TURMOIL – MOYES AXED AFTER 10–0 HAMMERING, CURBISHLEY AND KEEGAN IN FRAME.

'Bloody hell,' Gerry said. 'With a decent shuttle, we could get to that nebula within a day, Kev. Maybe sooner.'

'Why?' I asked Dr Pebble-Mill. 'Why me?'

'Because you're one of the good ones, Kevin,' he said. 'A brave man to whom this Compound should be indebted. You've proved that by saving this young man's life.' He clapped Rodway firmly on the shoulder. 'The greatest reward I could imagine for your efforts would be for you to get off this sinking ship while you still can.'

I looked from the newspaper to the departure request form and felt utterly overwhelmed. It was there if I wanted it: an escape from Palangonia, with Gerry, to start afresh. To leave the Compound and General Leigh and the whole spy nonsense behind forever and to nip this Mullet God situation firmly in the bud. I could focus on more important things. On the one important thing: football.

'It's turning bad here, can't you feel it?' Dr Pebble-Mill said wistfully. 'Take my advice. Go and never look back. And I'll be cheering on your new team from afar.'

He left us alone then, turning to speak to one of the nurses at the reception desk about another patient. I looked at Gerry and Rodway, who watched me hopefully. A no-questions-asked way to leave the Compound, with Leigh powerless to do anything about it. Any number of people would give their right arm to obtain the piece of paper I was clutching tightly in my trembling hand. And thinking of precisely that, I made up my mind.

'You're going to use the form, aren't you, Kev?' Gerry asked hopefully. 'I mean, you'd have to be crazy not to.'

I smiled sadly.

'I guess I'm crazy, Gerry,' I said and walked away.

A GOOD MAN

'Right, keep them closed.'

'Okay...'

'Are they closed?'

'Yes, I said they were, didn't I?'

'You're peeking, aren't you?!'

'No! Kevin, what is this?'

I took my hands off Caroline's shoulders and stepped back.

'Right then... and... open!'

She blinked and stared around at the near-deserted shuttle bay. Ordinarily this place would have been a bustling hub of activity, people dashing to and fro, hurrying to either board or disembark from all manner of spacecraft – from small one-seater shuttles (like the one Leigh had concealed near the tunnel entrance) to hulking great Stargazers, enormous monstrosities that were predominantly used to ferry weapons and other large pieces of equipment around Alliance-occupied space. That evening, there was almost nothing. There was a skeleton crew of staff pottering around – one man in a high-vis jacket was just staring intently at the floor by his feet, away in a dream – and no incoming or outgoing air traffic. There were several grounded shuttles of varying size and class but all were sat there, lights off and motionless, like relics from an aviation museum. Caroline was nonplussed.

'Why have you brought me here?' she asked. 'Wait – has the lockdown been lifted?'

'Has it heck,' I sniffed. 'They couldn't catch that spy if he was walking around in a mac taking photos of the General's office. Clueless, the lot of them.'

'So then, why…?'

I grinned.

'Because I have something special,' I said. I reached into my shirt pocket and produced a piece of folded paper, handing it to her. 'Have a read of that,' I said.

Clearly intrigued, Caroline unfolded the document and I watched with pride as her eyes scanned over the page. I could only imagine what she must have been thinking as the realisation set in.

'Darcey Bussell, Richard Branson, Anne Robinson, Anneka Rice, Kriss Akabusi, Nelson Mandela, Roland Rat, Dame Diana Rigg and Eddie the Eagle. Kevin, what—'

'Damn, sorry!' I said in dismay, snatching the sheet of paper from her and stuffing it into my pocket. 'That was just something I was working on this morning over breakfast – dream dinner party guests. No, it's this – here you go…'

I handed Caroline another sheet of paper and this time I got the desired response. Her eyes lit up and she beamed at me.

'Oh, Kevin,' she said. 'This is wonderful – however did you manage this? I could never have imagined General Leigh agreeing to this in a month of Sundays!'

'He doesn't know anything about it,' I said gleefully. 'And if he did, there'd be Jack Sprat he could do about it. This departure approval form has come from way over his head – look at the signature there at the bottom.'

'Laika!' said Caroline in astonishment. 'My goodness! I'd heard whispers that she was in the Compound for some big meeting – you mean you've actually met her?'

'Yep,' I said, then thought about it some more. 'Well, "no" is probably more accurate. But Dr Pebble-Mill put in a good word for me and she agreed to override Leigh's order on my behalf. She's an absolute corker, that one.'

'This is fantastic,' Caroline said, handing the paper back to me. 'I really am so pleased. I think this could be a brilliant opportunity for you and Gerry to make a fresh start and continue your football careers. What can I say? I wish you only the best – I hope you'll keep in touch.'

I frowned.

'No, do you not...? Caroline – this is for *you*.'

I handed the form back to her; she took it reluctantly, looking completely bemused.

'For me? What does that mean?'

'It means I don't want it,' I replied. 'Or, at least, I can't take it. Not now, not with so much still up in the air. We're close to finding the spy. Gerry, Gillian and me, we... have an idea who it might be. I can't say anything,' I added hurriedly as Caroline tried to interject, 'but I think it's only a matter of time. Whether we'll be fast enough to stop the spy bringing the L'zuhl down on our heads is another matter altogether.'

'Kevin, no,' Caroline said, 'you cannot forfeit an opportunity like this. And certainly not on my account – this your golden ticket, you must take it. You'd be insane not to.'

'So they keep telling me,' I said. 'But my mind's made up. I've already had a word with the shuttle bay supervisor on shift tonight; he was a regular at Palangonia FC and a Newcastle fan back in the day. It has a +1 but technically the form is strictly in my name; however, he's agreed to turn a blind eye this once, purely out of the goodness of his heart, plus a cash bribe. Caroline, my place is here, for now. And… I dare say there are others who have a more just reason for wanting to get off Palangonia. I'm looking at one of them right now.'

Caroline looked dumbstruck. I smiled.

'Go,' I said. 'Be with your sister.'

It *was* her sister, wasn't it?

'I don't know what to say,' she said, fighting back tears. 'This is a monumentally kind gesture. You're a good man.'

'It's only what any right-thinking person would do,' I insisted selflessly.

'Thank you, Kevin,' Caroline said, leaning in and giving me a firm peck on the cheek. I felt myself blushing. 'And Angela thanks you too.'

'Who's Angela?' I asked, baffled.

'My sister,' she replied and laughed.

'Right, yeah. Well, time waits for no one,' I said, and nodded towards the shuttle bay.

'I honestly cannot thank you enough for this gesture, Kevin. The galaxy is a dark and frightening place these days, but you've proved that there's light out there. Hope for a brighter tomorrow.'

'Nice one,' I agreed, unable to quite replicate Caroline's poetic way with words. I gave a small wave and walked away – turning away from an opportunity to escape this madness forever. I could only hope that I wouldn't regret it.

Suddenly, I clocked Caroline walking out from the shuttle bay entrance. I was stunned – had she had a change of heart already? I doubled back hurriedly.

'Caroline?' I said. She was surprised to see me.

She laughed, putting a hand on my shoulder. 'It was lovely of you to bring me here, eyes closed, a big surprise and all of that. But it does mean I haven't packed a bag or anything.'

'Oh,' I said stupidly, the penny dropping. 'I didn't think of that.'

'You've thought of enough,' she reassured me. 'Now go on and catch that spy.'

With a spring in my step, I walked away again – and right into the endgame at last.

I peered into the window of McGivern's, the Compound bakery. It was the end of the day and they were closing up but, buzzing from giving Caroline her send-off, I had my eye on that final caramel éclair. I licked my lips in anticipation, when suddenly the door to the bakery flew open and out came Gerry. Behind him, clanking heavily onto the cobblestones, was Barrington12.

'Kev!' Gerry cried, red-faced and husky. 'Kev, thank God – it's urgent! You need to come with us!'

Offering no immediate explanation, Gerry trotted hastily to the corner of the street and peeked around the corner, down towards the infirmary in the distance. I overtook the slow-moving Barrington12 and joined Gerry against the wall, peering out at whatever had so transfixed him.

'Gerry, what...?' I asked – and then I saw. Keeping to the shadows of the quiet Compound streets was the man of the moment.

'What's Leigh doing?' I asked in a hushed voice.

'Barrington12 and I have just been to Flix,' Gerry said, gesturing to the brightly lit Compound cinema across the way. 'They were showing an afternoon of sport-themed films – *Cool Runnings, Field of Dreams*, that one with the fast cars – *Rush*, I think it was called.'

I knew the one he meant. I didn't like the film one bit – a complete hatchet job, actually. Yes, Ian's an erratic driver, but would it have killed them to include a little bit of his football career? He deserves better.

'Anyway,' Gerry went on, 'as we came out, we bumped right into the General as he walked down the street. He had his head bowed and his beret pulled down low – almost like he was trying not to be noticed. It was well dodgy as far as I was concerned.'

'Just a bit,' I agreed. 'Go on.'

'He gave us a right rollocking, told us to watch where we were going and that we didn't know who we were messing with. And then, get this, Kev: he said, "I've got important business to attend to tonight, get out of my damn way." And then he hurried on, head down. That's when I decided I needed to find you immediately.'

As we looked on, the General vanished around a corner, heading into the grounds of the infirmary. I gasped as I realised.

'Oh heck,' I said, putting my hand to my forehead. 'You know where he's going, don't you?'

Gerry looked at me blankly.

'Think about it!' I said. 'What do we know is behind the infirmary building?'

Gerry considered this thoughtfully, then his eyes widened.

'That stash of mucky magazines in the hedge!' he cried. 'Of course!'

'No,' I said, rolling my eyes. 'The tunnel! Leigh is heading back out of the Compound again to his secret little shuttle so he can jet off and deliver an update to the bloody L'zuhl!'

'Oh God!' Gerry said in dismay. 'I should've known. What do we do?'

'There's only one thing we can do,' I said darkly. 'We take our own shuttle and we tail him. Wherever he's going, we're going too. It's high time our dear General was exposed for the treacherous vermin that he is.'

'But, Kev,' Gerry said, 'how are we meant to do that? The Compound's in lockdown.'

'Precisely – they've got a skeleton crew at the bays as a result; I've just been down there. We just nab ourselves a shuttle – Barrington12 can fly the damn thing.'

I started to head in that direction – and then stopped.

'But hang on though,' I said, thinking. 'What if we lose track of Leigh? If he gets into the air before we do, we'll have no idea where he is. Damn it.'

'I didn't think of that,' Gerry said, crestfallen. 'If we hurry, we could follow him down the tunnel maybe? Stow away in the back of his shuttle somehow.'

'Get real,' I muttered. 'It was a tiny one-seater job he had out there. What are we going to do, tape ourselves to the wings and hope we don't fall off?'

'IF I MAY CONTRIBUTE TO THIS DISCUSSION,' Barrington12 said suddenly, 'I BELIEVE I MAY BE ABLE TO OFFER A SOLUTION TO OUR CURRENT PREDICAMENT.'

'I'm open to anything at this point,' I said, turning to him. 'Go on.'

'WHEN GERRY AND I ENCOUNTERED THE GENERAL THIS EVENING, MY SENSORS REGISTERED HOW SUSPICIOUSLY HE WAS BEHAVING. AS HE REPRIMANDED GERRY FOR BUMPING INTO HIM, I TOOK THE LIBERTY OF GENTLY AFFIXING A D-86 TRACKER DISC TO THE BACK OF HIS BERET. BASED ON THIS, I CAN APPROXIMATE HIS CURRENT LOCATION WITH EXTREME ACCURACY. FOR EXAMPLE, I CAN SEE THAT HE IS NOW INSIDE THE TUNNEL BEHIND THE INFIRMARY, THUS CONFIRMING KEVIN KEEGAN'S SUSPICIONS AS TO HIS INTENDED ROUTE.'

My eyes lit up – Barrington12 had saved the day! Each Barrington model had a built-in Tracker Mode, even a creaky old relic like the 12-series, I just rarely ever had cause to deploy it – I'd only used it for vitally important matters, like attaching them to the training cones to find out who kept stealing them (it had turned out to be Gerry, sleepwalking) or to find out who kept taking my Tunnock's Teacakes from the mini-fridge in the changing room (Gerry, sleepwalking). Now, Barrington12 had deployed this technique for something equally important.

'Oh, Barrington12, I could kiss you!' I said in delight.

'I MUST STRONGLY ADVISE AGAINST SUCH A COURSE OF ACTION,' he replied tonelessly. 'RELATIONS

BETWEEN HUMANS AND BARRINGTON MODELS ARE EXPRESSLY FORBIDDEN. IN ADDITION, ANY ATTEMPTS AT INTIMACY WOULD POSE INNUMERABLE PRACTICAL AND LOGISTICAL ISSUES.'

'Duly noted,' I muttered, but smiling in spite of myself. Despite those moments when Barrington12 had been almost uncomfortably close to sounding human, clearly he still had some way to go. 'We've got him now, Gerry,' I said triumphantly. 'Right, you stay here – Barrington12 and I can handle this.'

'Hang about, what?' Gerry said, horrified. 'You're joking, aren't you, Kev? We're a team! We're in this together.'

'Gerry,' I said, trying to pick my words delicately. 'You're… I can't risk another incidence of the… what-have-you that we saw on Great Strombago. I'm sorry.'

'Oh, come off it,' he said sourly. 'That was just some weird thing that happened – I'm hardly going to do it again, am I?'

'That's the problem in a nutshell – we have no idea, do we?' I replied. 'I'm sorry, but I'm not going to take any chances with something I don't understand – that's why I've never paid any attention to the away goals rule. And, quite apart from anything else, I saw the state of you after it happened last time. It damn near broke you. You were a shell of a man for days.'

'Look at me – I'm fit as a fiddle!' he insisted. 'You can't go without me. Please, Kev.'

I sighed. I knew I was going to regret this.

'All right, fine,' I said begrudgingly. 'But you're on your best behaviour. Strictly no God stuff. I'm serious.'

I took a step forward then paused. I frowned.

'Hang about,' I said, scratching my chin. 'You two were

coming out of the bakery when you told me all this – surely you didn't stop in for cream cakes before coming to find me?'

Gerry looked down at his feet awkwardly.

'Well, I mean… when you're hungry, you're hungry.'

'Bloody hell, Gerry,' I sighed.

I found myself grateful for the first time for the lockdown being in place. Without it, there was no way we would have gained access to the shuttle bays without being spotted. As it was, the crew didn't clock us until we were right on the landing platforms next to one of the empty vessels – behind the pilot and co-pilot it was a roomy three-seater, which was ideal given how much space Barrington12 would take up, and Gerry for that matter, no disrespect to him. It was a beautiful thing, fresh off the production line, its blue-black metal glinting in the moonlight, not a scratch or blemish on it. It had two robust-looking engines under the hook-shaped wings, absolutely perfect for our needs. I decided there and then to christen it *Sir Les* in honour of Les Ferdinand, who had left me with the same sense of dumbstruck awe when I'd first clapped eyes on him.

With some assistance from Barrington12, who plugged his sub-5 connection port into the release button on the door to force it open, we clambered aboard the vessel and I hurried to the cockpit. Then I remembered that I couldn't actually fly and made way for Barrington12.

At the back of the passenger seats was a small kitchen area with a coffee machine and two tubes of Pringles, which I thought was a nice touch. They were just the ready salted ones sadly, but listen: there was a war on.

'Oh heck, Kev,' Gerry said, strapping himself in next to me and glancing through the window. 'We've been rumbled.'

I leaned across him and saw several of the shuttle bay staff legging it in our direction. It was now or never.

'Get us out of here!' I bellowed as Barrington12 ignited the engines.

'KEVIN KEEGAN,' Barrington12 said. 'TRACKER MODE HAS IDENTIFIED THAT GENERAL LEIGH HAS ALREADY REACHED HIS OWN SHUTTLE AND IS NOW LEAVING PALANGONIAN AIR SPACE AT SPEED.'

'Well, then,' I said, 'let's get after him. It's time to bring an end to this spy nonsense once and for all. Like Ashley Young in the penalty box, the guy is going down.'

With a roar, the shuttle took off at pace, hurtling up towards the sparkling blanket of stars above, and for one brief, blissful moment it felt as though nothing else really mattered any more, only the infinite beauty of that great expanse spreading as far as the eye could see.

But it passed. As Barrington12 hooked himself up to the console display, I watched a tiny speck of blue-white light flicker faintly on the screen.

Leigh's shuttle. No turning back now.

ACBAELION
OUTPOST XXI

We crept along the eerily silent corridors of Acbaelion Outpost XXI, every footstep seeming inordinately loud in our ears.

'Which way?' Gerry asked in an urgent whisper as we paused at a T-junction. The carpeted floor was thick with dust and the walls were completely bare. It was like the *Mary Celeste*. Or was it the *Marie Antoinette*? Look, the place was deserted, basically.

We had tailed Leigh's shuttle diligently across the Antioc Nebula in which Palangonia was located, all the way into the Acbaelion Quad and into the shuttle dock of the outpost. This was a maligned and largely ignored area of space and, as we soon discovered, even the outposts positioned equidistantly around the fringes (for some purpose since lost to the annals of time) were crumbling souvenirs, space stations which had been all but forgotten by the Alliance. It wasn't difficult to see why – there were no inhabited planets left anywhere within the Quad, the last having contained the snail folk of Drikk, who had died of a terrible plague centuries earlier. No one's a fan of that.

On arrival at the outpost, we hovered in the distance to

consider our next move, or to wait for Leigh to leave if it turned out to merely be a flying visit (for all I knew, there might have been a Tesco Express on board the space station from which he was picking up a coffee and some wine gums for the journey). After forty-five minutes with no sign of a departure, and with Barrington12's tracker showing Leigh still aboard the abandoned station, we carefully, quietly landed *Sir Les* on the loading dock beside Leigh's tiny shuttle.

'Well?' I asked Barrington12 as we stood there in the deserted corridor on the basement level of the station, unsure of our next move. 'Where is he?'

'UNFORTUNATELY, I NOTED AS WE DISEMBARKED *SIR LES* THAT THE GENERAL HAD REMOVED HIS BERET AND THE AFFIXED TRACKER AND HAS LEFT IT ON THE SEAT OF HIS CRAFT. I AM THEREFORE UNABLE TO NARROW DOWN HIS LOCATION OTHER THAN TO CONFIRM THAT HE IS SOMEWHERE ON ACBAELION OUTPOST XXI.'

'Buggeration,' I muttered. 'We'll just have to keep our eyes open. Come on – we need to stay together. If we split up, he'll just pick us off one by one, like Tino Asprilla with his air rifle on the roof of Asda when they refused to sell him any more scratch cards.'

We skulked down the corridors of the outpost, a floating tube the size of a small shopping centre hovering there in the middle of the great galactic nowhere. It was running on a backup power system that, in its low energy mode, would last for perhaps a century or two before finally dying forever. Systematically, we moved from door to door on each corridor of the station, moving up a floor at a time (there was insufficient power to operate the lifts, so we had to take the stairs – I was well out of puff after a couple of minutes).

As each door opened, I leapt inside, finger outstretched in an accusing pose, shouting 'Stop right there!' but on every occasion, it was to an empty room. The offices, meeting rooms, personnel quarters and retail spaces that had once been a hive of Alliance activity were neglected and alone, untouched for God knows how many years until we and Leigh had arrived. If we elected to stay there, the strong likelihood was that we would never see another living being ever again. It was a chilling thought and only reinforced my desire to apprehend Leigh and get on our way.

Finally, we found him. And typically it was all the way up on the top floor; I was knackered by the time we stumbled into the main observation deck with its sweeping, panoramic views of the galaxy through the enormous windows on every side. Oddly, there were tables and chairs dotted around the large room that looked brand new, with colourful ribbons tied to each one and name cards on the table before each seat.

But I didn't have time to worry about what that meant – I had eyes only for the General and, fortunately for us, his own were facing in the opposite direction to the door as we burst into the room. He was standing on a footstool and fiddling with what looked like a roll of Sellotape.

'Well, well,' I said in my grittiest Clint Eastwood voice. 'Fancy seeing you here, General.'

His head jerked round quickly and his jaw dropped.

'Keegan?' he said in disgust. 'What in the name of blazes are you doing here?'

'I might ask you the same question,' I said confidently, walking across the (recently hoovered for some reason) carpet. 'It's not a good look, you know – stowing a secret shuttle out beyond the Compound walls so that you can come and go as you please, away from prying eyes. Now why would that be, I wonder?'

He flushed bright red and tugged at the tight collar of his shirt uncomfortably.

'This is none of your concern,' he blustered – I'd clearly struck a nerve. I won't lie, I was absolutely loving it. 'You followed me then? I should have expected little else from a weasel like you, Keegan. Take my advice: turn around, get back on your shuttle and return to Palangonia. You're in way over your heads here.'

'Why'd you do it, General?' I asked with theatrical dismay. I tried to perch casually on the edge of one of the tables, arms folded like a detective on TV, but it tipped over under my weight and sent the place cards and cutlery spilling onto the floor.

Leigh grabbed the footstool, threw the roll of tape down and walked towards me, his barrel chest puffed out ahead of him.

'Er, Kev...' Gerry said from behind me.

'Not now, Gerry,' I said, waving him away without looking. Leigh stopped right in front of me, throwing his footstool to the ground in a fit of pique, and stared down at me from his towering height of six-foot-whatnot, his stubbly jaw set and his blue-grey eyes burning into mine. Like an efficient referee, he was absolutely ready to kick off.

'You're making a terrible mistake here,' he said in a low voice. 'You're going to spoil *everything*.'

'Oh,' I said haughtily, practically standing on tiptoe to get into his face, 'how awful that would be – to ruin your plans to hand the Compound over to the L'zuhl!'

Leigh looked slightly taken aback and withdrew a little.

'What's that supposed to mean?' he asked.

'Kev, if I could just—' began Gerry quietly.

'Shush a minute,' I told him absently as I stared at Leigh. He was trying to obfuscate and worm his way out of things but I wasn't going to let him off the hook that easily. 'The gig's up, General!' I announced. 'You had us all running in circles trying to find out who the spy was and all along it was you. You're a disgrace, kid.'

'What in God's name are you blathering on about?' Leigh snarled. 'I'm not the spy; I've spent the past several weeks trying to find the bastard!'

'Spare me the feeble excuses,' I said, relishing the sight of the pompous oaf on the back foot at last. 'We've got you bang to rights. Just come quietly – I'll ask Laika to be lenient. Fifty years in the slammer should be about right for selling out your entire species to a reptilian alien race, what do you reckon, Gerry?'

'Kev, I really think you should—'

'This is preposterous, it really is,' the General said, sounding more irritated than angry. 'It's completely false. You've got the wrong end of the stick in a big way and you're only going to embarrass yourself.'

'Oh, so I suppose you're going to claim that there's nothing suspicious about you sneaking off through the underground tunnel system to a secret shuttle so you can swan off to this abandoned tin can to feed your intel reports to the L'zuhl then?' I countered.

'It's not what you— Hang on, how do you know about my shuttle anyway? You're not saying that you used the hidden tunnel network yourself, are you? In direct contravention of my lockdown order and all?'

Bugger.

'Don't try to change the subject,' I said, a little rattled myself. 'It doesn't matter how I found out. The point is, you've been rumbled. Just hand yourself over and we can make this as painless as possible. You may as well just confess, it'll save time later on.'

'I'll do no such thing,' Leigh snapped. 'You're going to wreck everything – I'm so behind as it is!'

'The L'zuhl have tight deadlines, do they?' I said in a teasing, sing-song voice. Suddenly, there was a ringing sound from close by – I followed Leigh's gaze to the long table at the front of the room, littered with wrapping paper, tape and bows for some mad reason. Perched there on the edge, vibrating noisily, was Leigh's phone. Before he could move, I grabbed it and read the name on the display – Janice, whose ID display featured a photo of Leigh posing cheerfully at what looked like a barbecue with his arms around a large woman with frizzy blonde hair.

'Give me that phone, you snake,' Leigh said, pawing at it. I held my arm away and smiled triumphantly.

'Let's just see what your wife makes of all this then, shall we?' I said. 'Imagine how crushed she'll be to find out her husband is the greatest enemy of mankind since the day Richard Madeley, the Great Betrayer himself, defected to the L'zuhl!'

'Kev, seriously, you need to—' Gerry said, but I had eyes only for the General.

'No!' he screamed, lunging at me; he whacked his shins hard against the footstool and clattered clumsily over it, falling flat on his front with his legs lolling back over the top of it. I answered the call and adopted a breezy, cheerful voice, despite the blood pumping in my ears.

'Mrs Leigh? No, sorry, the General can't come to the phone right now. No, I'm afraid not. He's very busy at the moment. I'm his good friend, Kevin Keegan... No, not the guy he has pinned up on his dartboard at home in the kitchen. No, must be a different one. Listen, I've actually just bumped into the General all the way out here at Acbaelion Outpost XXI as it happens... Yes, I know there's a lockdown. See, the thing is, it turns out that your beloved husband has in fact been sneaking out of the Compound and has been jetting out here in secret to feed information to his L'zuhl paymasters. Yes, that's right – your husband is the spy!'

That was as far as I got before Leigh shoved me forcefully over; I fell smack on my backside as he snatched the phone from my hand. The impact knocked the wind out of me and hurt like hell, but I didn't care. I'd done what needed to be done. Leigh had been exposed for the cowardly traitor that he was to the one person who would be most hurt by it. It was, for sure, a terrible way for poor Janice to find out but at the end of the day, she was going to hear about it at some point.

'I will never forgive you for this,' Leigh growled at me, holding his hand over the phone. 'You have destroyed *everything*. All I've worked for these past few months in tatters, thanks to your arrogance and your pig-headed determination to undermine me.'

'Truth hurts, son,' I said, clambering unsteadily to my feet.

Gerry hurried over and I leaned on him, wincing in pain.

'We got him, Gerry,' I said, giving a tired thumbs-up. 'Mission accomplished.'

The General had walked over to one side of the room and was talking urgently to his wife in a muted voice. I was sure he'd have his excuses ready but it would surely now be too late for him. Something caught my eye then – above the long table behind which Leigh had been perching on his stool, I saw a large canvas banner pinned along the top of the wall. I recognised the person from the photo in the middle of it: Janice again, whose smiling visage I had seen on Leigh's phone screen not a minute earlier. Either side of her beaming face on the banner were the words *Happy 50th Jan! From Your Loving Husband.* That was… odd. There was other similarly themed signage dotted about the room, now that I stopped to have a proper look around – including a large photo collage of Janice and the General and a roll call of what I could only assume were their family and friends. I looked at the carefully arranged tables and chairs that I'd walked past to confront Leigh and the named place cards for each one. Something was not right here.

'Kev,' Gerry said fretfully, 'I was trying to tell you. Look, I found a stack of these by the door.'

He held out a laminated sheet of paper with another picture of Janice at the top followed by a list of musical performers (including Mark Knopfler – quite a coup, that) and a really rather delicious-sounding menu. At the bottom was a suggested donation to Earth Aid – the charity set up by Bob Gandalf of Live Aid fame for displaced humans struggling to adapt to post-invasion life – for guests to make in lieu of birthday gifts. I felt a sudden lead weight in the pit of my stomach. This was not good.

Moments later, with the call ended, Leigh stormed over to us with a face like thunder.

'Right, before you say anything,' I said, raising my hands, 'you have to bear in mind how this looked. I was only—'

'Four months!' Leigh cried, apoplectic with rage. 'Four months' planning, all the arrangements I had to make to covertly lift the lockdown to allow our guests to attend – down the drain! And all because you couldn't keep your nose out of other people's business!'

'I take that all on board,' I said. 'And listen, I'm sure that one day we'll look back on this and laugh—'

'It was *this Saturday*! Three days from now – everything was prepared! And thanks to Kevin bloody Keegan, I've had to explain to my wife – who was in floods of tears, by the way! – that her husband is not in fact the spy and that the reason I've violated my own lockdown order to leave Palangonia on a secret shuttle is because I've rented out an abandoned space station from the Alliance in order to host a massive fiftieth birthday bash for her!'

'Look, all cards on the table,' I said diplomatically. 'I've cocked up good and proper here. I mean, we really did think you were the spy. Sneaking off in a hidden spacecraft like that, anyone would assume the same thing.'

Leigh's eyes bored into mine.

'I will never, ever forgive you for this. You are dead to me.'

'No change there then,' I muttered unhelpfully.

'Does that apply to me as well, or just Kev?' Gerry asked.

'ALL OF YOU!' Leigh bellowed, his voice bouncing off the

walls of the deserted station. He turned away and pressed his hands against the edge of the table, hanging his head in despair.

'It'll still be a great bash, I'm sure,' I offered, trying to comfort him. 'I mean, I'd love to come along myself, if there's any...'

I trailed off as I realised that any chance of an invitation for me was probably fairly remote.

'Maybe we should just go,' Gerry said after a minute's awkward silence.

'Aye,' I agreed. 'Let's head home.'

I winced as I remembered the manner of our departure, effectively hijacking a shuttle and jetting off with the shuttle bay crew in pursuit. Had we returned with Leigh, unmasked as the traitor, they'd probably have turned a blind eye to our antics. But coming home empty-handed... well, this was going to take some explaining.

As we headed for the door, Leigh's phone bleeped again. I quickened my pace, not wanting to be in earshot while Janice gave him another earful, but in fact, this time it was a message rather than a call. Leigh glanced miserably over at the device on the table beside him and then suddenly stiffened. He grabbed the phone and stared intently at it. More bad news. There seemed to be a lot of it going around these days.

'Well, now,' he said in a thick voice. 'There's a turn up for the books.'

'What is it?' I ventured, almost afraid to ask. Perhaps it was a message from the Compound shuttle bay team.

Leigh strode towards us purposefully and I froze, waiting for him to seize me by the jacket and whack a pair of cuffs on me for stealing *Sir Les*. In fact, he walked straight past us and out into the corridor. Then he turned and looked back at us.

'I don't know why you're all just standing there,' he said officiously. 'There's still a lockdown in place and I want all three of you back on Palangonia with me. That's an order.'

'I'm so sick of this lockdown,' I said bitterly.

'Just as well,' Leigh said. 'Because it's about to be lifted.'

'You reckon?' Gerry asked. 'Why?'

Leigh reappeared and held up his phone.

'That was a high-level alert from Laika back at the Compound. This situation is very nearly at an end: the spy has been identified at last.'

'Wow,' I said, stunned. 'So… who is it?'

The General rolled his eyes. 'They're not going to communicate that over an insecure line, are they?' he replied witheringly. Bit rude. I looked back over my shoulder at Barrington12, standing by one of the large windows.

'Lickety-split, son, let's get off,' I said, snapping my fingers. He turned to look at me.

'KEVIN KEEGAN, I MUST ADVISE THAT ANOTHER SHIP IS CURRENTLY APPROACHING THIS STATION AT SPEED.'

'You what?' I asked, baffled. 'What ship?'

'JUDGING BY ITS VAST SIZE, ITS DESIGN AND ITS FIREPOWER, I BELIEVE THIS TO BE THE *MAKAZKA*.'

Leigh made a noise like he was choking and dashed over to the window. 'Please, no,' he said with something I'd never heard in the General's voice before: fear.

'What's the *Makazka*?' I asked quietly, suddenly feeling the urge to go to the loo.

Leigh followed Barrington12's gaze and then hung his head.

'The *Makazka* is the most deadly warship in the L'zuhl fleet,' Leigh said. 'And it's right on our doorstep.'

THE MAKAZKA

I stopped and leaned heavily on the railings alongside the stairs to catch my breath. I'll tell you, nothing hammers home how out of shape you've become more than having to leg it down thirty flights to escape the clutches of an evil alien race.

'Keegan, come on!' cried General Leigh, looking back up at me from the stairwell below, his own face flushed and his chest heaving. 'We don't have the luxury of time!'

'All right, all right,' I said and heaved myself up. We pressed on, praying that we'd make it back to the shuttle bays in the outpost basement before the *Makazka* docked.

Five minutes earlier, upstairs in Leigh's party room, I had joined the General and Barrington12 by the window, staring open-mouthed at the sight of the hulking brute of a ship approaching the station, blocking out almost all of the stars that speckled the sky around us. The thing was almost unfathomable in its size – like a skyscraper lying on its side, metallic and black with multitudinous lights peppered along all sides of it which, I quickly realised, were tiny windows. The *Makazka* could have ploughed straight through the outpost without even noticing. The number of L'zuhl soldiers housed within would be enough to overrun the Compound a hundred times over. The front of the *Makazka*, only just in view from our angle on the upper floor, was like some kind of dread rictus grin of a face, twisted metal coils that seemed to serve no practical purpose other than to terrify any spacecraft unfortunate enough to end up in its path. Beneath the cylindrical body of the warship were several missiles, primed and ready for action.

It was Gerry of all people who had snapped us out of our trance and told us we had to do something (though typical of the man that he didn't proffer any suggestions himself). The General went into military mode and ushered us out of the observation deck and down to the end of the corridor. With the lifts out of action we headed back to the stairwell; he kicked the door open, which was a bit unnecessary given that it was unlocked, but listen, that's up to him. Now we were hotfooting it as quickly as we could down to our shuttles in the hope that we might somehow fly away in the opposite direction from the approaching warship unseen. It was a big ask, but short of sitting on our hands and awaiting death – or worse, capture – at the hands of the L'zuhl, what choice was there?

'How did they even know we were here?' the General grunted from up ahead. By my estimation, we had seven more floors to go and, thus far, there was no indication that the *Makazka* had yet docked. 'I didn't see anything on my radar when I flew in here, no scout beacons or shuttles or anything. Did you lot?'

I thought back to our journey and realised with a grimace that we'd all been snoozing for most of it – we'd never have had a clue what was on our radar whatsoever unless it flew into our path, in which case Barrington12 would have exited autopilot mode instantly.

'No, we didn't see anything,' I said evasively. 'Definitely not. Anyway, no use worrying about that now.'

'This is grave news,' the General muttered. 'The L'zuhl shouldn't be out this far; they shouldn't have been anywhere *close* to this nebula. Our blasted spy friend will have told them all about our expanding military force out here of course, but to make their move and strike us so soon? Damn it all, we got complacent.'

But still, we retained hope that we might yet slip away on the sly. That was until we reached the second floor, so near to our destination, and the ground beneath our feet shook violently, an earthquake without the earth. I had still been holding onto the handrail for support and was thus able to keep myself on my feet, as did Barrington12 with his powerful legs, but Gerry and Leigh went sprawling painfully down the metal steps, landing together in a messy heap.

'They'll be upon us any moment,' the General said, grimacing in pain and getting to his feet. My heart sank at the sight of his pronounced limp. 'You, Clunkbucket – what's their status?'

'He has a name you know,' I muttered, even while knowing that I had cursed Barrington12 with equally rude nicknames during our time working together. Barrington12 made a bleeping sound as his processors scanned the station.

'THE *MAKAZKA* HAS SUCCESSFULLY DOCKED WITH ACBAELION OUTPOST XXI,' he said. 'I ANTICIPATE THEY WILL BE AIRLOCKED AND SAFELY ABLE TO BOARD WITHIN TWO MINUTES.'

'Two minutes,' Leigh said. 'Two minutes… fine. We can do this. We can still bloody do this!'

And he was off, roaring in agony as he put weight on his bad ankle and, as Barrington12 helped a dazed Gerry to his feet, we followed down the last few flights and out into the shuttle bay.

The bay could house around fifty small shuttles at any one time, each with a designated parking space. The ceilings were high, criss-crossed with metal beams, and the walls were bare, thick black steel. We had landed *Sir Les* next to the General's tiddler and as we pushed open the double doors from the stairwell corridor into the echoing expanse of the bay, hope filled our hearts. Clearly the *Makazka* couldn't fly in through the automated retractable panel at the far end of the bay as we had done, it was far too big; instead it had to sync outside the outpost with what was the equivalent of an airport boarding bridge taking passengers from the terminal onto the plane. We knew from the quake moments earlier and Barrington12's confirmation that they had done so – now it was a matter of hoping we could get into our shuttles and out through the panel before the bridge doors opened.

The General clambered awkwardly onto his shuttle wing, dragging his ailing leg behind him while Barrington12 reached for the door release on the flank of *Sir Les*. No sooner had his sub-5 port connected with it than the whoosh of the shuttle unlocking was drowned out by the zip and clank of the boarding bridge doors.

The L'zuhl had arrived.

I realised, as I whipped round to face them, that I had never seen one of the bastards in the flesh. I had been evacuated from Earth very early in the invasion and had looked back in hollow dread as their attack ships blocked out the skies and all but obliterated the planet I had called home for nigh on seven decades. I'd heard tell of their fearsome appearance but nothing had prepared me for the heart-stopping horror of being in the same room as these cruel destroyers of worlds.

Of the battalion of thirty or so footsoldiers now pouring through the doors into the bay – mere pocket change from the populous ship they had arrived on – the shortest was of Peter Crouch proportions, but most were well over seven feet tall. They were clad top-to-toe in strexan armour, thus far impenetrable to all the weaponry at the Alliance's disposal and the secret to its creation known only to the L'zuhl. The skin that was visible – rough, black-green scales, dried and cracked – was around their mouths, reptilian snarls where their helmets ended, and on their four fingers, poking through the holes in the gauntlets they wore. They wore a reflective visor not unlike the Compound guards back home and I was pleased beyond measure to see my own worried eyes staring back at me rather than having to stare into their own. In their clawed hands, each one clutched a MZ-4 laser rifle – they were not mucking around here. Their leader, a showboat in a purple velvet cloak affixed to the shoulders of his armour, stepped forward and let out a harsh growl. We stepped away from our shuttles and raised our hands. Death would have been preferable to enslavement but, like a relegation scrap, the instinct to stay alive can be tough to shake.

'*Krzk akr kirrt trki!*' he said in a harsh, rasping, sandpapery voice. It was the most bone-chillingly awful sound I had heard since Mark Hughes released that album of reggae-tinged S Club 7 covers.

'What are they saying?' I asked Barrington12 in a small voice, although I wasn't sure I wanted to know.

'THE L'ZUHL COMMANDER SPRAX MAMBO ORDERS US TO SURRENDER OR DIE,' Barrington12 replied. It wasn't surprising but still a bit of a downer.

'Will they negotiate?' I asked.

'Of course they won't,' Leigh remarked from behind me as Barrington12 replied in the L'zuhl tongue. It sounded horrible to hear him speaking that vile language. I realised in that moment quite how fond I had grown of the kid during the tribulations of the past few weeks. He was no longer the clumsy, lumbering machine whose constant barrage of questions – 'How is "ungentlemanly conduct" defined?' 'How is stoppage time calculated?' 'Why are players so afraid of a small piece of red card that they would immediately leave the field when one appears in front of them?' – had so frustrated me. Now I considered him a dear and valued friend – though, admittedly, still a bit of a pain in the arse. But then so was Gerry. And, I was quite sure, so was I.

Sprax Mambo laughed on hearing my request, a sound that seemed to make the room grow colder. He clicked his laser rifle into life and pointed it at us, prompting the assembled squadron standing behind him to do the same.

'That's a no, then,' I said before Barrington12 could reply. Sprax Mambo spoke again, for longer this time.

'SPRAX MAMBO OFFERS US THE OPTION TO DIE HERE OR ELSE BOARD THE *MAKAZKA* IN CHAINS. WE WOULD BE PUBLICLY DISMEMBERED AS AN EXAMPLE TO OTHERS OF WHERE DEFIANCE OF THE L'ZUHL WILL LEAD. THEY WILL THEN PROCEED DIRECTLY

TO OUR NEW HOMEWORLD, WHERE IT WILL BE DESTROYED WITHOUT MERCY.'

'Lovely,' I said darkly. 'He must be a big hit at parties.'

I looked to my left at Gerry; he was trembling as he fought the urge to cry, the sheer hopelessness of our situation getting the better of him.

'I know I said I wasn't a fan, but if you wanted to engage your Mullet God powers like you did back at Great Strombago, Gerry,' I muttered from the corner of my mouth, 'now would be the time.'

He looked at me startled and then hurt.

'I don't… I don't want to talk about that!' he blurted out. 'It's not real, it didn't happen!'

Fat lot of good godlike powers turned out to be when you awarded them to someone who didn't want or comprehend them. Then, with a heavy sigh, I made a decision. I stepped forward and held my arms out wide.

'Take me,' I said flatly. 'Take me on board your daft ship – let this lot go.'

'Kev, no!' Gerry wailed.

'This won't work, Keegan,' said the General. 'Don't be so bloody stupid.'

'I volunteer myself as a hostage,' I persevered as Barrington12 translated. 'But only on the condition that my friends are allowed to go. Let them put their affairs in order before you annihilate our home.'

I was barely thinking about what I was doing. All I knew was that, when push came to shove, I was the expendable one in the room, like my agent was when I told Newcastle back in '92 that

I'd be happy to manage them for free. The General was required to lead the war against our enemies. Gerry, if the Watlaq were to be believed, had an even bigger role to play in the conflict to come. And, on a more practical level, Barrington12 was needed to fly Gerry home. But Kevin Keegan? Perhaps my time had come. Maybe this was my destiny all along. To die so that others may live to fight another day.

Sprax Mambo stared at me with an expression unreadable behind his visor. Then suddenly he smiled, exposing three rows of thin, yellowed, razor-sharp teeth.

'*Skral tik treuk sak sala!*' he cried, and the squadron behind him cackled gleefully. I glanced at Barrington12, who looked at me with what might have been pity, were he capable of expressing such a thing.

'THIS LITTLE MAN HAS VOLUNTEERED TO DIE FIRST,' Barrington12 said, and as my eyes widened and I began to protest that this was absolutely not the deal I was offering to them, I felt a searing hot pain in my abdomen which – as it turned out – was caused by the beam of Sprax Mambo's laser rifle ripping my belly clean open. There was a peculiar smell of burning in my nostrils, which I promptly realised, as I sank to my knees, was a result of my innards being barbecued.

Distantly, Gerry was screaming in dismay, the General was turning the air blue with insults and the L'zuhl were laughing themselves silly. I looked down, all my movements in treacly slow-motion, and saw red and pink gloop cupped in my hands as I cradled my midriff. *Humans look a right state on the inside,* I thought, and then almost giggled at the absurdity of that ending up as my final conscious thought. I felt no real pain, save for a thudding in my head and a piercing ringing in one ear. With great effort I turned to Barrington12, who was looking down at me.

'I just want to say,' I whispered, blood bubbling and foaming on my lips, 'it's been an absolute pleasure fighting the good fight with you all. I… wouldn't have had it… any other way.'

I held out my right hand to Barrington12, ignoring the horrible splatter of the guts I'd let fall to the floor. He stared at me quizzically for a moment and then raised one of his awkward pincer-like hands and gripped mine. General Leigh hobbled forward and placed a hand on one of my shoulders. I extended my left arm towards Gerry, back over my shoulder. He didn't reciprocate.

'Gerry,' I said, turning to look back, my vision swimming. 'I'm trying to say… goodbye.'

But Gerry was staring blankly ahead, his eyes a milky white. He stood there completely rigid, barely breathing. As I squinted at him, with the sound of Sprax Mambo ordering – judging by the sound of thirty laser rifles revving – to open fire on my friends, Gerry suddenly gasped as though in great pain.

'Oh Christ,' I whispered in a thick voice as I began to fade once and for all, slumping down onto the cool floor on my side.

There was a blinding burst of white light and Gerry was consumed in a ball of heat, throwing Barrington12 and the General to the floor beside me. The light pulsated and quickly permeated the walls of the station, which became suddenly translucent, spreading far out into the black sprawl of space. Faintly, I heard Leigh's voice asking what on earth was happening but I could open my eyes no more than the faintest slit. Artificial stars exploded before me and I lay there at peace. Dimly, I saw

Sprax Mambo's squadron turning tail and legging it back towards the bridge doors – but it was far too late. The L'zuhl had not reckoned with the Slasabo-tik prophecy and it was to be their undoing. No more than thirty seconds after Gerry's spectacular light show had begun, the *Makazka* was no more. With a faint *thworp* it burst like a balloon and it was as though it had never been there at all. The fleeing L'zuhl soldiers were, like the Winged Terrors before them, silhouettes burned into the wall of a forgotten space station. Then everything went dark, the Gerry-light was extinguished and he stumbled backwards with a yelp. I slowly inched open first one eye and then the other. My heart was pounding in my chest and my hair stood wildly on end; I felt like I'd been given a severe electric shock. My hands trembled and my breathing was uncertain.

'Gerry…' I whispered. 'How did you…?'

'Need to sleep,' he mumbled and immediately clambered aboard *Sir Les*, where he curled up into a ball like a cat and passed out.

I sat up and looked at my hands. The dark red blood that had caked them a moment ago was gone. More importantly, my insides were no longer on the outside. Tentatively I rubbed my stomach and felt no pain, no lacerations, no nothing. I was absolutely fine. Feeling quite shaken by my brush with certain death, I stood up gingerly and looked at the General – he would have questions. That much was certain. He was stamping his foot on the metal floor of the bay and frowning.

'The damnedest thing,' he said in bemusement. 'My ankle's no longer broken.' He looked up at me. 'Keegan, what in the world just happened here?'

'That's… a long story, General,' I said eventually. 'And one I still don't entirely understand myself. If I ever will.'

There was a brief respite as we took everything in. Twice now, Gerry had been possessed by this altered state and had obliterated our enemies at a stroke when all hope seemed lost. I had cut things fine – I knew from the incident on Great Strombago that his powers could heal the sick but not resurrect the dead and I had come within seconds of going over the precipice. While my prompting him to engage his powers had been fruitless, the sight of me gutted and dying had stirred them into life.

Finally, I felt that I understood how whatever lay within Gerry was triggered. Slasabo-tik, the Mullet God, this beacon of galactic hope, would come forth when that hope was lost. By relenting and allowing Gerry to tag along on this trip, I had put him in harm's way once more and had only myself to blame for the return of those strange powers which slept inside him. Of course, without them I'd have been toast, but nevertheless, I was disappointed in myself. As a manager, I had a duty of care to my players but that surely also had to extend to any members of my coaching staff affected by arcane intergalactic prophecies.

Looking at him now, Gerry seemed sallow, something I had begun to notice since our return from Great Strombago. I had put this weary disposition down to the rigours of what we had been through on our great Palangonian adventure, but now I wasn't so sure. Gerry looked… old. And after each apparently involuntary deployment of his, for want of a less ridiculous term, Mullet God powers, he seemed depleted. Less there. How many times could he do this and survive? And if he couldn't control it or indeed even really remember it happening, as was the case the first time, what could be done to save him wasting away to nothing?

'Whatever it was – and I want a full debrief on our return, I assure you – that was a… brave thing you did back there, Keegan,' the General said magnanimously.

'Look, we're all in this together,' I replied firmly. 'And at the end of the day, you and I are on the same side.'

'The L'zuhl will be back this way,' the General warned us. 'The *Makazka* was only the first. They will not take kindly to losing one of the jewels of their armada – they have rarely experienced such a defeat as this. This is the beginning of a dark new chapter, arriving far sooner than the Alliance had anticipated, and we must all be ready.'

I didn't respond to this. I was simply too exhausted to consider the ramifications of what had just happened.

'Come on,' I said to Barrington12 as we clambered back aboard *Sir Les* as Gerry slept on, the General's shuttle already departing ahead of us. 'Let's get out of here.'

I pushed the lever in front of me to fire up the thrusters and I flew backwards violently. I panicked – had one of the L'zuhl soldiers survived and opened fire?

'KEVIN KEEGAN, THAT LEVER IS YOUR SEAT RECLINER,' said Barrington12.

And so, we headed for home. Our flight back turned out to be a rather sombre affair, perhaps surprisingly given the massive and unexpected victory we had just been a part of. Although I've never been one for lording it over the opposition anyway – that's the reason Freddie Mercury and I fell out. 'No time for losers, because we are the champions'? Come off it, son. A handshake costs nothing.

In the space of just a couple of minutes, we all realised that everything had changed irrevocably. There was still so much left unsaid about what had happened, but for me, there was only one question to which I needed an answer. We would soon know who had betrayed mankind and brought the L'zuhl into the Antioc Nebula for the first – and almost certainly not the last – time. I wasn't sure I'd be able to cope with the heartbreak if it did indeed turn out to be somebody that I knew.

AN ENEMY UNMASKED

I was relieved to have the General with us when we arrived home – a small group of guards were waiting to arrest us for stealing *Sir Les* but at a word from him they dispersed, though not without throwing suspicious glances in our direction. No doubt they had questions as to the General's own absence during the lockdown but they wisely kept their counsel.

As we made our way across the platform towards the exit into the Compound, a throng of people could be seen heading our way. I felt mildly alarmed for a moment, then realised they were not there for us. Walking ahead of them, flanked by her personal bodyguards, was a genuine VIP. Padding along the tarmac was a small dog, its fur a muddy mixture of brown and white with a distinctive stripe down its snout, ears pointing up keenly, eyes sparkling in the glow of the artificial lights that illuminated the Compound.

'Laika,' I said, bowing my head respectfully. 'An honour.'

Laika nodded back and sat on her haunches, regarding us all with a steely gaze that had turned greater men to jelly in the war rooms of The Oracle. The gathering crowd of Compound citizens had not seen a celebrity of her calibre among us before – certainly it put the weekend when cricket legend Ian 'Meaty' Botham came to visit firmly in the shade. Laika was the greatest asset the Alliance had, a decorated leader with a strategic mind most could only dream of. No one, Laika included, knew how her time floating through space after the Russians sent Sputnik 2 into orbit in 1957 had gifted her with this super-intelligence and the ability to speak, not to mention her unnaturally long life, but as a key figure on the Alliance Assembly she had guided the galaxy through many decades of tumult and uncertainty. I felt truly privileged to be in her company – very much like I did on the day I signed Al Shearer. You really do have to treasure those moments.

'I'm delighted to see you return in one piece, Kevin,' she said – and I was bowled over that she even knew my name. Though of course, Dr Pebble-Mill persuading her to sign my departure form would account for that.

'Aye, well,' I said bashfully, my face flushing pink, 'it was a group effort. It was pretty hairy out there for a while, but we got through.'

'The news of the L'zuhl incursion is dire indeed,' Laika said. 'Yes – I've heard all about that. The *Makazka* itself was spotted in this nebula this very day. Though I gather it is no more.'

'It's a long story, ma'am,' General Leigh said. 'I have much to impart, though not all of it can I explain.' He glanced at Gerry.

'We knew a day would arrive when the L'zuhl would come for us here, but not so soon. Had this dratted spy been apprehended sooner...' She threw a dark glance in Leigh's direction and he turned his face away. His failure to find the culprit quickly had played a major part in how things had panned out. Laika suddenly looked up at Gerry, who met her eyes only briefly and looked away.

'You've seen such things,' Laika said suddenly in a strange, wistful voice. 'Things we would never believe or understand. I see it in your eyes. You... have a part to play in all of this when the darkness comes, don't you? I can feel it.'

I shivered at Laika's perception but said nothing.

'So... who *was* the spy, Laika?' I asked, feeling a little emboldened. 'I assume you've got the sad sod locked up in Fort Emmeline by now. I don't usually advocate torture but the guy wants his head felt, he really does. He's bollocksed things right up these past few weeks, I don't mind telling you.'

'We don't have the spy locked up,' Laika said matter-of-factly. 'Though you're right, it's high time we did. That is why I came here to meet you all this evening.'

Laika barked at one of the guards who nodded and unhooked a pair of cuffs that were really more like medieval manacles. I watched in growing horror as he walked over and placed them around the wrists of the spy, who stood there without protestation or complaint, head bowed low.

'No...' I said in a strangled voice. 'No, it can't be...'

'It is,' Laika said. 'The evidence is incontrovertible. I appreciate that this may be difficult to accept.'

I turned to look at the culprit, blinking away tears.

'But... but why? How *could* you?'

'I AM SORRY, KEVIN KEEGAN,' Barrington12 replied plaintively. 'I NEVER WANTED TO DISAPPOINT YOU. I LOVE THIS COMPOUND AND ALL OF THE PEOPLE WITHIN IT.'

'Perhaps you should have thought of that before you began feeding information to our enemies,' Laika said brusquely. 'Your actions have threatened to destroy everything that the Alliance has built here. Mankind's existence in this galaxy hung by a thread following the invasion of Earth – my home planet too, remember – and you have helped them take a great step towards total extinction.'

'I DID NOT MEAN TO,' Barrington12 replied, lowering his head again.

The crowd turned on Barrington12 immediately and as he was led away, docile and broken, they booed him and threw insults and one or two even chucked missiles as he passed – shoes, coins, a banana. They thudded dully off the robot's steel exterior. He did not react. He was bundled into the back of a Harbinger vehicle, Laika hopping in beside him, speeding off towards Fort Emmeline. I had a horrible feeling then that I would never see my friend again.

It was as though I'd been punched in the gut. I met Leigh's gaze for just a moment but his expression was impossible to read. It was closer to disappointment than anything else. He strode away without a word. Gillian suddenly appeared from the crowd and hurried over to us, her face ashen.

'Kevin,' she said. 'I… I'm so sorry. This is…' she trailed off, lost for words.

'It can't be,' Gerry said, looking at me frantically. 'Kev, this must be a joke! Mustn't it?'

My mind was racing; I couldn't begin to compute what had just happened. How could he have done this? *Why?* I stuffed my hands in my jacket pockets dejectedly and shook my head in disbelief. My fingers wrapped around something in my left pocket then, a smooth, flat chunk of metal. I retrieved it and looked at the small internal memory card that Barrington12 had dropped in the mud during our trek to Great Strombago – it already seemed a lifetime ago. I'd picked it up when he'd unwittingly dropped it and had intended to return it to him later on but had forgotten all about it – little wonder his battery had run down so quickly during our journey home and my farewell to Akkie. And now it was too late. It would remain a grisly souvenir.

'Oh!' Gillian said, looking at it in the palm of my hand in horror. 'My Q7 Keycard! Good God, Kevin, where did you find this?'

'I… your what? Barrington12 dropped this. Last week, I… meant to return it to him. I thought it was just a bit of his what-have-you falling off.'

My face fell as the realisation set in. Damn it all.

'He had my Keycard all along,' Gillian said, taking it from my outstretched hand. She sighed. 'It is true, then. He is what they say he is. Who am I kidding? He just admitted as much himself.'

I looked at Gerry, tears now streaming freely down my cheeks.

'Oh, Gerry,' I said, and buried my sobbing face in his shoulder.

THE WEAPON

It had been, without question, one of the worst weeks of my life. Far from returning home as glorious heroes, lauded for our defeat of the *Makazka* and for striking at the heart of the L'zuhl, we had been rent apart, physically and emotionally. Barrington12 was in chains, sitting in a dingy cell in Fort Emmeline awaiting a trial hearing in front of the Compound Council. Gerry was, frankly, a mess – and I'm not just talking about his dress sense or the way he can't eat beans on toast without ruining his shirt and, in many cases, his trousers too. Much like the first time it had happened, he had grown increasingly distant, quiet, withdrawn and really not like the Gerry I knew and loved at all. Now, whenever I sang a quick burst of Charles & Eddie's 'Would I Lie To You?' I was met with silence from my number two, whereas previously he'd have been there, right on cue, ready to interject with an 'oh yeah!' It was heartbreaking – and it wasn't difficult to understand why.

I'll lay my cards on the table and admit that I've never been the subject of an ancient intergalactic prophecy and hence found myself burdened with strange and devastating powers, the full extent of which I couldn't possibly comprehend. I'll cop to that straight away. So there's no way I could ever claim to know how Gerry must have been feeling, the confusion and fear that must have been coursing through his veins every moment of every day since our return from the wilds of Palangonia. That said, would it kill the guy to crack a smile every once in a while? I hadn't seen anyone so depressed since Nicky Weaver got cornered by Stuart Pearce at the Man City Christmas party in 2001 and had to listen to half an hour of Stu telling him about his diabetic dog.

Four days after Barrington12's arrest (a revelation which I was still trying and failing to come to terms with), I arranged to meet Gerry in the Compound Square. My hope was that if we could have a mooch about for an idle afternoon, maybe buy some of those Gryzelphian chocolate truffles he liked, the ones with surprise fillings ranging from strawberry crème to sulphuric acid, it might help to lift his spirits – and that, in turn, we might repair our faltering friendship. I wasn't sure whether he blamed me for getting him into this mess or whether he just wanted to be left alone, but either way I felt like I was losing him – and I couldn't have that.

What I saw on arrival in the square filled me with horror and a sickly dread in the pit of my stomach: Gerry was sitting on the bench outside Flix, as arranged, but he was not alone. Beside him, speaking in a low voice that I couldn't quite hear, was the General.

'What's going on?' I asked, trying to keep the worry from my voice as I trotted over to them.

'Nothing,' Leigh replied darkly. 'And actually, this is a private conversation, so if you don't mind…'

'Well, I do mind,' I said. I looked at Gerry, who had his hands stuffed in his pockets and was staring away across the square. 'What's he been saying to you?'

Gerry shrugged. 'Nothing I want to talk about,' he replied. 'I already told him I wasn't interested. I'm a football coach, not a soldier.'

Leigh slammed a hand down on his own thigh and sat forward, leaning in to speak to Gerry in urgent, hushed tones.

'I'm not talking about conscription or about sending you off to fight in some damned skirmish against L'zuhl sympathisers in the Hran System! I'm talking about *you*, Gerry. I've seen what you can do, the skills you have at your disposal. Do you want the Alliance to win this war? Because I do. And I think we'd have one heck of a better chance of doing that with your help.'

Gerry pulled away, looking angrier than I'd ever seen him – and I'd watched him absolutely lose it in a Sainsbury's once when they'd run out of bagels.

'You think this is easy for me?' he cried. He glanced at me. 'Either of you? You think I like having this… *thing* foisted on me? I didn't ask for this, I didn't choose to be anyone's stupid "Mullet God". I just want to get on with my life and forget any of this has even happened! I'm just Gerry Francis and that's all I want to be.'

'I think you have your answer, General,' I said. 'I think that concludes things for today.'

Leigh had a face like a slapped arse and grabbed my elbow, pulling me to one side.

'This might all seem like a game to you two boneheads, but some of us have real responsibilities. My job is to ensure this Compound survives and thrives in the face of the most hideous threat any of us have ever known and if you think I'm going to forget what I saw up there on Acbaelion Outpost XXI then I'm sorry, but you're deluded.'

'General,' I said, shaking my head, refusing to be cowed, 'he's just a man. He's not a weapon. You can't hook him up to any of your fancy-dan machines or strap him to some enormous warhead. I know hardly anything about what he can do and poor Gerry hasn't got the first clue either. We're all out of our depth. I think... you've just got to let this one go.'

I was fully expecting Leigh to fly into a rage at this and maybe even have me arrested again but instead he just looked profoundly sad. His shoulders sagged slightly and he kicked idly at a small pebble on the ground.

'I want to win this war, Keegan,' he said, finally meeting my eyes. 'I *need* to. The Alliance is hanging on by the tiniest thread, do you know that? Nothing we have tried to repel the L'zuhl's advances has worked. Nothing. Oh, we'll win a battle here, destroy the odd spy shuttle there, but it's small potatoes. They're sweeping us aside. I didn't think they could be stopped, if you want the truth. I thought it was only a matter of time until the Alliance's last defences fell and everything would be lost. Until four days ago when I witnessed something I could hitherto only dream of. A man with the power to vaporise the L'zuhl in the blink of an eye, to eliminate at a stroke the greatest single warship this galaxy has ever known.'

I looked at Gerry, picking distractedly at a bit of loose skin on his thumb; this entirely unremarkable man, suddenly so coveted by so many.

'Not only that,' Leigh continued, 'but this man's powers can also heal the sick, as well as the mortally wounded like yourself –

they can repair the terrible damage wrought by those genocidal maniacs. You say you don't understand his abilities and that's true, neither do I. All I know is that when the chips were down, when all seemed lost, something awoke inside your friend and saved our lives. Imagine that on a galactic scale, Keegan! Or worse, imagine a tool like that falling into the wrong hands. Into L'zuhl hands. Do you want that?'

A tool! I was disgusted – what a way to speak about a fellow human being. Plus, as evidenced by the broken tiles and crumbling holes in the wall of my bathroom from the time he'd volunteered to help me with some DIY, Gerry didn't even know how to use tools, let alone become one.

'Of course I don't,' I muttered numbly. I couldn't deny it, Leigh's words had crawled under my skin. He and I weren't friends, could never be that, but I did feel that we were no longer strictly enemies. Once upon a time I'd have had no time for a single thing that came out of the man's mouth, but our experience together on the outpost had changed all that. I'd held my own innards in my hands and felt myself slipping away into the great whatever-comes-next before Gerry's intervention. Listen, that kind of thing changes a man. I wasn't the same Kevin Keegan as I'd been even a few weeks ago. I'd seen death, stared it right in the eyes and come out the other side. And yet, this was such an ask. *Such* an ask. 'I... General, you can't request this of him. Be reasonable, please. He's suffered enough.'

'The human race has suffered enough,' Leigh countered. 'Families, friends, colleagues... so many of us have lost so much. I don't know if you really know how that feels. Look, I'm not going to send a squadron of guards out to kidnap Gerry in the middle of the night. I'm not going to force anyone to do anything against their will. That's not the kind of ship I want to run. This has to be his own choice. Yours too, if your word is what it takes to ultimately persuade him. But I think the day is coming when you have to choose between your pal… and the rest of us.'

Leigh turned and strode away across the square, leaving me standing there, rooted to the spot. The eerie echo of Akkie's warning to me when we had parted, of how the prophecy dictated that Slasabo-tik would have to give his life for the galaxy, left me feeling quite ill. I'd tried to brush off those words back then. Now, I wasn't so sure. Things were coming to a head, and fast. Time was getting away from all of us.

I turned back to the bench to join Gerry, but he was gone. At the far west side of the square I spotted him, head down and hurrying home, the weight of the world apparently upon his shoulders.

The weight of the galaxy.

RUMOURS

Two days later, on the morning of the hearing that would determine Barrington12's fate, I committed a terrible error of judgement that could have threatened everything.

I was still trying to get my head around the case that was being made against him. The way they told it, it had begun a little over a month ago. The robot had been acting peculiarly for some time before his fondness for inexplicably telling people he was free of erectile dysfunction saw him bundled off to maintenance for repairs. They had, however, either failed to spot or had completely ignored a glaring and ultimately devastating flaw in the creaky old Barrington model. Newer editions, like the sleek 800-series, were built with near-impenetrable firewalls but regrettably, no such safeguards existed for the older models like the 12-series. Most of them had long since been retired to the scrapheap, but such were Gillian's (with respect) penny-pinching tendencies, she had purchased a refurbished 12-series model to assist Gerry and me with team affairs rather than forking out for a snazzier one – and this was to set in motion the terrible events that had followed.

Unbeknownst to any of us, the L'zuhl had been – from afar – prodding and testing the Alliance's networks for weaknesses for some time and had released a kind of 'Trojan Horse' bug into the system – I wasn't entirely sure what that meant but had always found horses slightly unsettling, with their dead eyes and their powerful limbs, and so I felt quietly pleased to have finally been vindicated in my lifelong mistrust. And so, when Barrington12 plugged himself in to a network socket every day or two to recharge his battery, he was handing over everything in his database to the L'zuhl while also having his own system hacked into to carry out their dirty work. He had been feeding them tidbits for weeks; each time he recharged, he'd slip under their control for a short period. I remembered that day at the library how he had stopped to give himself a short recharge – Rodway himself remarked on having seen him. This had allowed the L'zuhl to access his CPU once again and they had forced him to infiltrate the library's server room right there and then – and, if not for Gerry's nosiness in noticing that someone was in there, who knows what information Barrington12 may have handed over. As it was, he had burst out of the room and pinned Gerry behind the shelving, leaving him to die. Once Barrington12's internal memory banks re-synchronised and enabled him to regain control of his system, he was none the wiser. He hadn't the faintest idea that he had just attempted to assassinate one of his best friends. And just thinking about that broke my damn heart.

However, it was the prosecution's contention that Barrington12's actions had not been so accidental or unwitting – they claimed he had behaved with forethought and deliberation. I just could not believe that. I *would* not. It simply wasn't the Barrington12 I had grown to know. I thought about how distressed he had been on discovering Gerry's body trapped behind the library bookcase that day. Could a machine really fake something like that? No – I had to speak up for him even if nobody else would.

I was on the list of names summoned to appear at the hearing, in my case to speak in Barrington12's defence. I had been up half the night preparing what I would say and as I heaved myself out of bed, exhausted and frazzled, I decided to pep myself up by walking over to the stereo system and putting on the Greatest Album Ever Made.

I've seen people submit all kinds of contenders for that crown down the years and have dismissed each and every one of them. *Sgt. Pepper's Lonely Hearts Club Band*? The title's too long so I've never bothered listening to it. *Pet Sounds*? Not half bad, but frankly I can't hear many animals on there. *Blonde on Blonde*? Goes on for ages and the title sounds like a dirty film. *Crocodile Shoes*? It's Jimmy Nail's masterpiece and comes close to the top spot, but not quite. There can be only one.

As the belting first track on Fleetwood Mac's *Rumours* filled the silence of my flat, I hopped in the shower and then had a shave. As I trudged back into my bedroom to the sound of 'Go Your Own Way' and dressed in my best shirt and tie (the latter strategically placed to cover up the mustard stains on the former), I picked up my watch and gasped in dismay. I looked at the clock on my bedside table and realised that the batteries had all but given up the ghost overnight and it was over three hours too slow, the second hand ticking along only very intermittently. It was 11.40 a.m. – Barrington12's hearing had begun at half past.

Given that, at a brisk pace, my flat was only a fifteen-minute walk from the Compound Council building where the hearing would take place, I might have just about made it in time for the start of the prosecution case if I'd thrown my outfit on and dashed out of the door. Under normal circumstances, it would have been doable.

But these were not normal circumstances.

It has been scientifically proven that it is literally impossible to turn off *Rumours* once it has started. I don't just mean that it would be the height of disrespect and a woeful slap in the face to the greatest five-piece in soft-rock history, though of course it would very much be that. I mean that it would be *physically impossible* for someone's fingers to press a button that would stop the music on that particular album. It simply cannot be done, and if anyone claims otherwise, then in all honesty I wouldn't want to meet them because they're almost certainly a serial killer. That's how strongly I feel. You ask Andy Cole, whom I sold to Man United the day after I overheard him refer to the band as 'Fleetwood Cack'. I'm sorry, but what kind of manager would I have been – what kind of *man* – had I let that slide?

I sat there on the side of my bed, feeling dejected and sick, while also simultaneously uplifted by those soulful grooves. I knew I was letting Barrington12 down badly – I'm sure he'd have understood my position, but that wasn't the point. I was trapped, stuck in my flat as time ticked away, waiting for the last seconds of 'Gold Dust Woman' to fade out before I could depart. It was torture. Beautiful, peerless torture.

When I finally arrived at the Council building, bashing into the heavy wooden doors with my shoulder and asking a startled security guard where I could find the Alpha Courtroom, I was sweating, haggard and in no fit state to be anybody's character witness. Outside the chamber stood two Compound guards, their black visors down over their eyes, rifles gripped tightly in their gloved hands. One stepped in front of me as I tried to enter.

'The hearing is in session,' she said coldly. 'No admittance. Please move along, sir.'

'But I'm meant to be in there!' I said, conscious of how small I felt and how pathetic I sounded. 'Please, it's really very important!'

'If it was that important,' the other guard weighed in, 'you'd have been here on time. The hearing started almost an hour ago.'

'That wasn't my fault,' I insisted. 'I'd just put *Rumours* on and then I realised what the time was.' To my disgust, this self-evident explanation seemed to make no difference to either of them.

'Listen, just stand aside,' I said. 'My friend is in there and he needs me.'

'Oh, hang on, I know you,' the first guard said. I couldn't see her face but I could hear her lip curling into a smirk beneath the helmet. 'Yeah, you're the idiot whose robot was spying for the L'zuhl.'

'Oh yeah, I know the one you mean,' joined in Guard Two, openly chuckling. 'God, how embarrassing. I'm not sure I'd ever show my face in polite society ever again after that if it was me. Go on, clear off.'

Without a moment's hesitation – for if I had, I'd never have dared – I threw myself to the polished marble floor à la Jürgen Klinsmann celebrating a goal and slid on my front between the pair of them, into the doors of the courtroom. Had they been locked while in session I'd have probably broken my neck, but fortunately for me, they flew wide open and I clambered ungraciously to my feet, hastily straightening my tie to cover up the rogue stain.

The courtroom was a vast space with a high ceiling, from which hung numerous light fixtures. On the right side of the room was an enormous window through which could be glimpsed, distantly, the thrum of life in the square outside. The walls were painted blue and green, the colours of Earth, and two columns of black metal seating, eight rows deep and currently filled to capacity, were installed either side of a pathway that led towards the imposing benches against the far wall. Behind them, dressed in purple satin robes, sat the five members of the Compound Council: Gillian, General Leigh, Dr Pebble-Mill, Doreen McNab and Sir Michael Bowes-Davies. Seated in the middle of the five, presiding over the hearing, was Laika, a gavel clutched in her tiny paws. To the right of them, standing behind a podium and looking desperately miserable, was Barrington12. I beheld genuine sorrow on his face, and in that moment, he became truly human to me. He raised his eyes as I burst into the room. Every head turned to look in my direction. I hadn't seen a room fall so deathly silent since the hotel bar before an England match when Graeme Le Saux brought along Fiscal Responsibility: The Board Game and asked whether anyone fancied playing.

'Hey!' cried the two guards in unison, stepping into the courtroom and grabbing me painfully by both shoulders and trying to hoist me back out into the corridor. I wrestled free and ran towards the Council benches. The guards pursued angrily and soon grabbed me once more.

'Please!' I beseeched the Council. 'I know I'm late and that's poor form – bang out of order, in fact – but I beg you, let me speak up on behalf of… of my friend.'

'Come on, you!' cried Guard One, whacking me painfully across the back of both knees with a truncheon. I sagged to the ground with a shriek of pain.

'Stop!' came a voice I knew. 'Stop hurting him! Let him go.'

I looked up at Gillian gratefully – she was on her feet behind the bench, looking at the guards with fury in her eyes. They didn't release me immediately – they glanced up at General Leigh, who met Gillian's gaze for a moment and then nodded wearily. Instantly, the guards stepped away from me and marched from the room, closing the door with an echoing boom behind them. Grimacing, and with stars exploding before my eyes, I hauled myself to my feet (and hastily straightened my tie yet again to conceal the shirt stain).

'You have to hear me out,' I said. 'He deserves someone on his side when the whole Compound is against him.'

'Mr Keegan,' Laika said, 'I'm sorry to say that you're too late. We've heard all the statements and listened to all the evidence. Sadly, it did not take long, such was the weight of it. The matter is settled. When you burst in so… enthusiastically just now, you interrupted the Council in the process of delivering its verdict. Please take a seat so that we may continue with our vital business.'

'But…' I tried, but I could see it was no use. I looked across at Barrington12, who lowered his head and said nothing. I had failed him when he had needed me the most. Now, I could only hope against hope that the Council might show clemency.

'I will now ask each of the five Council members to announce their decision in turn,' Laika said as I took a seat on the front row of the public gallery, squeezing in next to an elderly couple who were sitting with a picnic hamper on the seat beside them, tucking into egg salad sandwiches and apparently having a lovely day out. 'Once the verdict has been recorded, I will then pass sentence. Barrington12, will you please stand?'

'THANK YOU, LAIKA, BUT I AM ALREADY IN A STANDING POSITION AND HAVE BEEN FOR THE DURATION OF THIS TRIAL,' Barrington12 replied, lifting his head, his small blue LED eyes twinkling slowly and sadly.

'Oh,' Laika said. 'We did provide a seat for you.'

'I ACKNOWLEDGE THE PROVISION OF A SEAT,' he said, 'BUT MY OWN SHAME IS SUCH THAT I FEEL ANY SMALL, SELF-APPLIED DISCOMFORT IS THE VERY LEAST I DESERVE.'

I felt a mixture of emotions – that Barrington12 could feel and express a sense of shame was, frankly, extraordinary, but at the same time he was doing himself no favours at all by copping to his own guilt before a verdict had even been announced. It was true that he had already all-but-admitted to the charge, but as per Alliance procedure in the event of a crime committed by any non-sentient (where a defendant's own judgement and culpability could not be relied upon), a five-way verdict had still to be delivered and a suitable punishment imposed. Any hope of a reprieve felt remote now. I dabbed at my eyes with the back of my hand as I felt the sudden prickle of tears.

'Council member McNab, may the court have your verdict?' Laika asked, staring straight ahead impassively.

'We must protect the futures of the children in this

Compound,' Doreen said, even slamming a fist down onto the bench in front of her for good measure. 'Guilty. 100%.'

Not a great start.

'Council member Routledge, may the court have your verdict?'

I met Gillian's eyes and she seemed almost to wipe away a tear of her own. She cleared her throat to compose herself and then made me feel proud once again to know her.

'I do not deny that technically speaking, what happened did happen. But if this court had seen what I'd seen…' Gillian said. 'Not guilty, my lady.'

A murmured throb went around the court at this unexpected lifeline, which Laika soon silenced with an angry bark and a whack of the gavel. My heart was racing and not just because the old man next to me had slopped some scalding hot tea from his flask onto my upper thigh.

'Council member Pebble-Mill, may the court have your verdict?'

The doctor leaned forward in his seat and rubbed his forehead.

'As much as it pains me, not least because there aren't many 12-series models like this one still functioning, I can only speak to the facts presented in this case. Guilty, my lady.'

A bloody shame, but I couldn't really fault the doc. He didn't know any better. How was he to know that this machine had somehow discovered things within himself that his manufacturers could scarcely have imagined possible?

'Council member Bowes-Davies,' Laika said, 'may the court have your verdict?'

Sir Michael leaned forward in his red velvet suit beneath his robes and adjusted the carnation in his front pocket. His greased, silver hair flopped forward foppishly over his forehead.

'I've never known of a crime so despicable as this in all my long years,' he said in his rich, oaky voice. 'The accused has brought shame upon this Compound. This man, Khan, has caused nothing but trouble for the Federation, slaughtering innocents and using vile mind-control techniques – for shame!'

Another wave of whispers in the court, this time mingled with bafflement. Again, Laika silenced them all.

'Sir Michael, that is the plot of *Star Trek II: The Wrath of Khan*,' she explained patiently. The other Council members were variously shaking their heads or rolling their eyes in disdain. 'Today we are dealing with the case of a robot accused of spying for the L'zuhl.'

'Ah!' Sir Michael said animatedly. 'Of course! Yes, well, that sounds a fairly trivial matter all things considered, so let's say not guilty and get some lunch, shall we?'

It was all I could do not to leap up and punch the air – the doddery old fool had no clue where he was or what was going on but if it helped see justice served (or at least my own preferred outcome, which is essentially the same thing) then it was all well and good. With only slight hesitation, Laika noted his verdict in her ledger. Just as I began to wonder, to dream, to hope, I remembered who the final Council member was and sank back in my seat.

'Council member Leigh, may the court have your verdict?'

The General watched the shabby figure of Barrington12 intently and then, whether through accident or design, looked briefly in my direction. I implored him with my eyes for the split-second I held him. Would it be enough? He had seen Barrington12 fight alongside us on the outpost; he knew, surely, that there was more to this story than a good robot gone bad. Didn't he?

He didn't.

'Guilty,' Leigh said. 'I find the machine guilty, my lady.'

That was that. Perhaps it was the injustice being served or the impersonal way Leigh had referred to Barrington12 but suddenly I found myself on my feet and approaching the bench again.

'It's not right,' I insisted, my eyes only on Laika. 'It's not fair! Look at him – the poor sod had no idea what he was doing. He didn't mean for any of this; to all intents and purposes he'd been brainwashed – you can't blame him for what happened!'

'Sit down, Kevin,' Laika said, firmly though not angrily. 'This court has made its decision. I respect the passion of your view and I understand your loyalty to your robot, but I'm afraid—'

'See, you did it as well,' I interrupted, exasperated. '"My robot" you called him. And technically that's true. But he's more than that. He's my friend.'

'Yes, well, your friend has just been found guilty of crimes against mankind, so sit down and stop embarrassing yourself,' Leigh snapped from the end bench. I didn't give him the satisfaction of looking in his direction.

'Crimes against mankind,' I repeated, looking down at the tiled floor and shaking my head. 'A guy has to know when he's beaten. So with that in mind, while I strongly disagree with the decision made here today, I will accept it. But let me just say this one last thing. You talk about this situation like it's them and us. It's not. That boy over there, that "robot"... he's shown more humanity than any bugger in this room. He has displayed loyalty. Friendship. Guilt, shame, humility, you name it. The kid's been accused of something he had no control over and yet not once has he tried to duck responsibility for it. That *has* to mean something. It certainly does to me. It's a terrible thing you've done today. I hope you'll remember that.'

The room was completely silent as I returned to my seat. The old man next to me offered me a sausage roll from their hamper, which to be honest I accepted as my blood sugar was through the floor.

'In spite of Mr Keegan's committed intervention,' Laika said formally, 'for a crime of this magnitude I have no choice but to abide by the statutes of the Alliance. Barrington12, for the crime of espionage, I sentence you to be dismantled and scrapped. So be it.'

She barked to order the court to its feet but I stayed seated. Laika stared at me but I saw no reproach in her wide brown eyes. She looked genuinely saddened by the decision she had been forced to make. The sentence had been inevitable since the verdict came in, I'd known that. But looking at the poor sod standing alone, head bowed, was more than I could bear. I briefly entertained a mental image of vaulting over the bench, punching Leigh's lights out, smashing a chair through the window and then fleeing to the shuttle bays with Barrington12's clanking metal hand in mine to make our escape but I knew it was nothing more than the dream of a fool – especially with my back.

It was as I was sitting there glumly, with Laika making her closing remarks, that I realised how dark it had suddenly become in the courtroom. I glanced at my watch – it may have felt like an eternity but it was still only the early afternoon. Outside, it looked more like dusk. I barely had time to process this fact when there came a mechanical, rumbling roar from outside in the square, a bowel-quakingly ominous sound.

'What on earth is that?' Gillian asked, craning to get a view out of the window from her seat behind the bench.

'It's nothing,' Leigh muttered irritably. 'It's only thunder.'

This seemed to calm some of the disquiet in the room but I was far from convinced. I still had the sage words of Stevie Nicks from earlier that day rolling around in my head and so I knew better. I stood up.

'It can't be,' I said. 'Thunder only happens when it's raining. This… is something else.'

No sooner had these words left my lips than the window exploded and the screams began.

THE BATTLE OF PALANGONIA

It was chaos unlike anything I had ever witnessed – and I very much include my disastrous final match in charge of England in that, by the way. The Compound was under attack – a heavy, sustained, violent assault – and not one of us had been prepared for it. After the destruction of the *Makazka* at Acbaelion Outpost XXI we should have all been ready and waiting for the inevitable retribution to follow. And who knows, perhaps Leigh's forces within Fort Emmeline had been rehearsing and training each day since our return for just such an eventuality. If so, it wasn't enough. Not nearly enough. We were overrun – and quickly.

Inside the courtroom, I stood rooted to the spot. Around me, panic reigned – people in the public gallery fled their seats, clamouring for the closed doors, desperately trying to push them open even though they only gave way inwards. Outside, above the din from the square coming through the blasted window, I could hear the two guards frantically urging the escaping horde to stand back and allow the two of them to push open the door from outside but it was all for naught – no one thinks rationally in a moment of extreme stress. You ask Eric Cantona –

I remember the time he suddenly remembered he'd left his oven on during a match and immediately lost the plot, kung-fu kicking some bloke in the crowd. Look, it happens.

I hurried over to Barrington12 who had stepped away from his podium and was ambling over to the window curiously.

'Not that way, son!' I said, dashing after him and grabbing his thin, cold arm. 'We need to get to safety. If it even exists.'

I took the opportunity to steal a glance through the battered window frame and glimpsed complete carnage beyond. The blood-red sky was pitted with L'zuhl warships and shuttles, some small enough to look like distant birds, others hulking great monstrosities blocking the light from Palangonia's twin suns. On the ground, L'zuhl soldiers swarmed, pouring into the streets like water from an overflowing drain, shooting dirty green blasts from their laser rifles at anything that moved. There were bodies scattered in the streets. *Our* streets. Our home.

'Kevin!'

I whirled around in a dazed circle at the sound of the urgent whisper behind me and then realised it was coming from the now-empty judge's bench. Gillian was crouched down behind it, peeking around the corner and gesturing to me frantically. With Barrington12 in tow, I hurried to join her.

'What are we going to do?' I asked. 'We're done for if we stay in here!'

At that moment, the mass of people clamouring at the entrance finally worked out the puzzle and fanned out, allowing the heavy doors to be swung open. The group then promptly poured from the room like sand from an egg timer.

'Come on,' I urged Gillian, 'let's get gone!'

'No!' she pulled me back by my collar. 'Not that way. The Council building faces directly out onto the courtyard. We'd be slaughtered. There's another way.'

'If that's the case then what about everyone else—' I turned to the doors leading into the near-empty and eerily silent courtroom but there was no one left, save the two pensioners with their picnic. They were leaning over the basket and embracing each other as though preparing for the impending crash of a tidal wave. A choking sound erupted from my throat at the sight of them.

'There's no time,' Gillian insisted. 'They're all toast and we will be too if we don't get out of here. Come – there's a tunnel.'

My legs trembling, I followed her through a small doorway that had been opened in the wall behind the bench; Barrington12 had to stoop low to squeeze through. Inside was an antechamber with a large square hole cut in the floor. Beside it was an upturned marble tile. I just glimpsed Doreen McNab drop down into the darkness and Sir Michael readying himself to follow. He stopped before he vanished and looked at the grave faces around him – General Leigh, Dr Pebble-Mill, Laika, Gillian, Barrington12 and me.

'Rum old business,' Sir Michael said, shaking his head sadly. Then he was gone.

'You next, doc,' Leigh said. 'Time's against us.'

'Are we really going to do this?' Dr Pebble-Mill asked, his face a contortion of indecision. 'Flee, I mean? I have… I've a duty of care. To all the citizens of this Compound.'

Leigh grabbed him by both shoulders and forced him down towards the hole until he was sitting with his legs dangling into the black. Below, I could hear the patter of footsteps as Doreen and Sir Michael hurried away.

'Sod your Hippocratic oath, man!' Leigh hissed. 'It's World War III out there!'

I briefly considered suggesting that the invasion of Earth would technically have been World War III and that this, if it even qualified, would be World War IV, but I bit my tongue. Leigh would only go off on one at me, as per.

Dr Pebble-Mill went reluctantly, then Laika and Gillian.

'Friends in high places, Keegan, letting you use this escape route,' Leigh said, but there was no bitterness in his voice this time. Only a tired, weary regret. He regarded Barrington12 coldly. 'This tunnel leads directly to the shuttle bays. Assuming the L'zuhl haven't destroyed them as their first move, which they will have if they're smart, you can all make a break for it. Go to the Alliance headquarters at The Oracle, try to regroup. Laika will see to it that your friend here is scrapped either way, even if you manage to get out of here alive, so don't get your hopes up. Justice must be served. He brought all of this down upon our heads.'

'Oh, that's nonsense and you know it!' I said. 'They're here because of what happened on the outpost. We destroyed the greatest ship in their fleet and killed their greatest warrior. Well… Gerry did, anyway.'

Leigh looked away. He knew it was true.

'There'll be plenty of time to argue later,' I added, readying myself to drop. 'God, what a mess. Such a bloody shame.'

I sensed movement from the corner of my eye and hesitated before sliding into the tunnel. Leigh was at the doorway that led into the courtroom from whence we had come. He looked back at me for a second and then adjusted the beret atop his head.

'For Earth,' he said, and was gone.

As promised, the tunnel emerged directly beneath the shuttle bays, beside one of the control towers. The journey took barely five minutes but with little room to manoeuvre in the dank darkness, it felt far longer. Even crouching low, Barrington12's head scraped against the rough stone ceiling the whole way, the brittle sound harsh enough to make my eyes water.

When I clambered up to ground level, breathing in great gulps of fresh air (albeit scented with dust and what might have been the stench of burning flesh), Doreen and Sir Michael were nowhere to be seen, doubtless having already made their own bids for freedom. I hoped they would make it. Gillian was nearby, standing beside a small shuttle, Laika already in the cockpit.

'Kevin, come on! It's our only chance!'

I looked around. Smoke rose from beyond the shuttle bay and the air was filled with anguished cries, small explosions and a few larger ones as well as the guttural snarl of the L'zuhl as they laid merciless waste to all before them. Dr Pebble-Mill was a distant figure, running away from the shuttle bays back towards the carnage at full pelt, unable in the end to turn his back on those in need. I loved the man in that moment. Perhaps it was this that made up my mind, coupled with having already witnessed Leigh's own display of loyalty to the Compound he served, but I knew then what I had to do. I couldn't leave them behind – not Gerry, not my players. I would never have been able to face myself in the mirror ever again.

'Kevin, please!' Gillian cried from her position halfway up the lowered docking platform of the shuttle as Laika fired up the thrusters. 'It's now or never!'

'It's never then,' I replied. 'Whatever happens next, Gillian, remember what happened here today. Someone needs to tell the story of how the Palangonian Compound refused to go down without a fight. Look after Barrington12, will you? Someone needs to clear his name.' I turned back towards the madness.

'Don't do this!' I heard her cry distantly. 'We're so close!'

'I can't do it, Gillian,' I said, with a final wave. 'I can't be like the kid, Nero, fiddling with myself while Rome burns. I have to stay. Until the bitter end.'

'You're mad,' she called from far away.

'I already died once,' I replied. 'If I have to do it again, then so be it.'

I left the bay and was startled to hear a clanking sound immediately behind me. I whirled round, expecting to see a L'zuhl war machine preparing to open fire, but instead I saw my friend.

'I told you to go with Gillian,' I said to Barrington12 sternly. 'You're no use here; the L'zuhl will have you for breakfast. You need to leave on that shuttle – you have to prove your innocence.'

'I WILL NOT GO, KEVIN KEEGAN,' he replied. 'MY PLACE IS HERE. WITH MY FRIENDS. AT MY HOME. I BELIEVE THE TRUE WAY TO PROVE THE COURT WAS WRONG IN THEIR JUDGEMENT TODAY IS TO STAND AND FIGHT FOR HUMANKIND. PLEASE ALLOW ME TO DO THIS.'

I considered this for just a moment and knew that I could not forbid my friend, my oh-so-human friend, from making his own sacrifice.

'Come on then, big man.' I stood on my tiptoes to reach up and pat him warmly on the shoulder. 'We'll go down with this ship together.'

'BARRINGTON12 MUST POINT OUT THAT THIS IS NOT A SHIP, IT IS A WALLED COMPOUND. THE TWO ARE QUITE DISTINCT.'

Well, maybe not *quite* human.

I jogged to the fringes of the Compound Square, my lungs choking on the acrid smoke. It was impossible to believe that a mere half hour previously, this had been a thriving metropolis: people out shopping, running errands, dining out. Now, it was a rubble-strewn wasteland. The L'zuhl were rounding up survivors and frog-marching them onto their ships, no doubt destined to live out their limited days in the phlebonium mines on one of the L'zuhl moons, the materials from which were used to power their laser rifles to devastating effect, a nut the Alliance had never been able to crack. Several wheeled vehicles armed with enormous Gatling gun-style weaponry were shooting at random buildings as well as people. I was witnessing first-hand the cruelty, the mindlessness, the pure evil that had seen them annex almost half of the galaxy. We were but a tiny community, a speck in the soup; we might even have been ignored had they sailed into our airspace under normal circumstances. But we had angered them. We had wounded them. And that would not stand.

'Psst! Kev!' came a voice from my right. With a sensation of overwhelming relief such as I had not felt since I finished watching *Das Boot* at Owen Coyle's house (I'd been bursting for the loo but Owen refused to let me leave, constantly saying, 'This is a good bit!'), I saw Gerry waving to me through the fug. Crouching, I dashed over to join him behind a partially demolished wall close to Flix with Barrington12 hot on my heels. Gerry looked exhausted and afraid. I knew the feeling.

'Gerry, thank God,' I said breathlessly. 'They're so quick. Such destruction in so little time. They're a bad lot, these L'zuhl. I've always said that.'

'What are we going to do?' Gerry asked. 'I heard there might be some escape shuttles at the bay but I don't know.'

'Nah,' I replied evasively. 'They'll be long gone by now. We're here for the long haul. Lord knows how long we've got left, mind. Where is our own military? I can't see any – oh, speak of the devil.'

The L'zuhl soldiers fell back as six Harbingers, the giant tank-like beasts I had first witnessed that day – so many years ago, it seemed – when Leigh had been patrolling the Compound while rumours of a spy were first doing the rounds. Here again was the man himself, leaning from the passenger-side door of one of them, rifle in hand. Whatever I thought of the man, I could not doubt his courage. He had had a chance to escape and yet he turned his back on it, preferring to lead his men on one final and surely futile last charge.

The L'zuhl did seem to have been caught entirely by surprise, however, and Leigh got my hopes up by blasting several of them into oblivion. None of the Alliance weaponry could pierce that strexan armour but in a display of strategical inventiveness that even Sir Al Ferguson would have been proud of, he ordered his men to fire on the ground immediately before their feet and on the damaged buildings above, throwing them high into the air or crushing them beneath falling masonry. It was then that I spotted something which made my blood run cold.

SMELLS LIKE
TEAM SPIRIT

In the shattered doorway of the café, Mr O's Place, were several familiar faces who had evidently been waiting for any opportunity to make their escape. Led by Rodway, I watched several members of my squad – who had apparently been out for their lunch together, a heart-warming display of companionship from a football club that no longer existed – trying to make a dash for it. There was Gribble, Andy Gill, Little Dunc, Caines and Nightingale, as well as Alex Booth and Aidy Pain. Wiggins, my midfield lynchpin, was still horrifically out of shape and had in fact ballooned in size since the club had shut down.

'Boys!' I shouted. 'This way!'

In the carnage and confusion, they seemed unsure what to do – Rodway, Little Dunc, Nightingale and Alex Booth immediately headed in our direction but, true to contrary form, Aidy Pain decided that it would be safer to head back the way they had just come and Gribble and Wiggins followed, even though it was clear from my vantage point that they were heading straight into the danger zone.

'That pig-headed idiot,' I muttered as I watched them hurry away to their inevitable deaths. Then suddenly I had a brainwave.

'Painy!' I cried, my voice almost cracking with the strain of drowning out the sounds of battle. 'Don't come and hide over here!'

Aidy skidded to a halt, the others almost clattering into him. He looked over at me and narrowed his eyes.

'Sod that!' he replied and immediately ran in my direction, taking the rest of his teammates with him. I grinned – my ingenious double-bluff had worked. The boy would never do a damn thing I wanted him to so I knew he'd enact the opposite of any instruction I gave out. Wiggins was breathless and sweating, trailing some way behind the others – but in actual fact, his increased girth was a real boon as he provided excellent cover for the other lads, shielding them from the L'zuhl line of sight as they reached relative safety. The L'zuhl themselves were too preoccupied with the onslaught from our forces from Fort Emmeline to really notice, so I stood up and whistled to my boys, barely making myself heard through the thick fog of war. Andy Gill grabbed Rodway's shoulder, pointing in our direction. As they hurried to join us, I noticed Little Dunc inadvertently kick something that went skitting along the ground and stopped close to our hiding spot. Dunc was terribly cross-eyed at the best of times and his coordination was all over the shop – he was into double figures for own goals already after shooting at what he thought was the opposition net.

'Gaffer!' Rodway said breathlessly. 'Are we glad to see you. We thought we were dead meat.'

'We may well be yet,' I warned him. 'Unless we find a way to defeat these buggers, we're none of us going home to a hot meal and a bath tonight.'

As Leigh's soldiers continued to engage the L'zuhl in close combat, I cast about to find something, anything with which we could help them.

'Gaffer,' Rodway said, leaning in so that the other players wouldn't hear him. 'What about Gerry? I mean, you and I both know what he can do... what he's capable of. He might be our only hope.'

'No,' I said firmly, raising a finger to silence him. 'That is not an option. If Gerry goes nuclear, it could finish him. This may well be the moment that stupid prophecy spoke of and I'll be damned if I sit here and let the man kill himself.'

If the Mullet God wanted to obliterate the L'zuhl that was fine by me – but he was not taking my best friend along with him.

'What's that one doing?' whispered Gribble, my centre-half. He was the tallest man in the squad and physically incapable of ducking his head down below the rim of the wall, which – while it left him slightly exposed – allowed me to utilise him as a sort of periscope to observe what was happening out in the square. I could have asked Barrington12 but I was too concerned that he might then make himself a target – for soldiers on both sides. Not only that, but Barrington12 had taken it upon himself to clumsily pat each of the lads on the back once they had made it over to our hiding spot and to tell them that everything would be okay, an act of compassion that I could see had brought some small reassurance to some very anxious faces. He was already more than doing his part for our cause. Gribble explained that one of the L'zuhl soldiers had wandered close by, limping badly and apparently frantically scanning the rubble in search of something. I risked a quick look. Then I realised: the soldier was unarmed – that's why he was panicking. He must have been parted from his gun during the battle. Suddenly, I remembered the object Dunc had kicked while scurrying over to our hiding place and I quickly reached an arm over the wall to retrieve it, hand flapping against the stone floor until finally I grasped it. Dunc's knackered eyes may have been a liability on a match day but now they had given us the equivalent of a last-gasp penalty against the odds: it was a L'zuhl laser rifle. I was quite sure that where our own side's weaponry came up short in terms of getting through their thick armour, this one would do the job just fine. I held it in both hands, surprised by its weight but quietly impressed by its sleek silver design. There were all manner of strange symbols etched into the surface – instinctively, I pressed the button that looked exactly like the England Three Lions crest (if you tilted your head to the left and squinted until you were almost blind, I mean) and it illuminated in a cool orange light. I slipped a finger over the trigger and aimed it at the flailing soldier. Then, I hesitated.

'Go on, boss,' Rodway urged. 'He's a sitting duck!'

I sighed and shook my head.

'I can't shoot an unarmed man, boys,' I said. 'I'm not Paul Ince when that pensioner gatecrashed his barbecue. It's just not on, I don't care how evil they are. We have to be better than them. It's the only way to—'

Annoyingly, my finger then accidentally grazed against the trigger and I ended up blowing the lone soldier to smithereens after all, to a roar of approval from my lads. Look, these things happen.

'Well, my point still stands,' I said begrudgingly. Then Rodway pointed – four more soldiers were running in our direction: our cover had been blown. This time I didn't hesitate – these were fully armed and ready to kill. I had to protect my lads at all costs. Nothing else mattered in that moment. I opened fire and the beam of the laser sliced each of them clean in half; they toppled sickeningly to the floor.

'Great shot, Kev!' Gerry said approvingly.

'I'll tell you what, anyone could conquer the galaxy if they had one of these,' I said. 'Right: that's four more of these rifles out there needing new ownership. Come on, boys! Let's get at this shower – it's still 0–0!'

Rodway, Andy Gill and Little Dunc scooped up the guns of three of the fallen L'zuhl soldiers as more approached, peeling away from the main conflict with Leigh's men to tackle us. I tossed the fourth rifle to Barrington12 who looked at it with great curiosity and then did nothing.

'Get stuck in!' I cried.

'WHERE WOULD YOU LIKE ME TO STICK IT, KEVIN KEEGAN?' he asked innocently.

'Don't tempt me, son,' I muttered, but didn't have time to explain so dispatched him to guard Gerry behind the wall, with orders to shoot anyone who approached.

'Except if it's me,' I added, remembering how relentlessly literal his interpretations were. 'Or any of the boys. Or anyone on our side. Look, just shoot the L'zuhl if they come after Gerry, yeah?'

I hurried back into the fray and noted with dismay that three of our Harbingers had already been reduced to cinders. Leigh himself was nowhere to be seen in the mayhem.

'Right!' I cried. 'Two banks of three, high-pressing game!' I looked at Caines and Nightingale and remembered the tactical advice Gillian had given me in her office that day I'd been angling for some new players. 'You two – I want you to attack from the back down the flanks, supporting those at the front. Booth, I want you in the hole as a playmaker, do your thing and take out as many of them as you can. Gribble, protect the defence! Painy – don't protect the defence!'

Painy immediately set about protecting the defence.

It all happened so fast – it was clear that the L'zuhl were rattled to be facing such unexpected resistance. Gerry tried to follow me as we drove them back but I signalled to him to get down behind the crumbling wall. I waved to him to turn around and face away from the field of conflict – he looked confused and unwilling, but he must have seen something in my eyes because he did as he was told. I didn't want him to see. I couldn't risk his being activated again.

We took down the advancing posse; their own shooting was wayward and unfocused, like the time Shaka Hislop pleaded with me to let him play up front for the opening match of the season. If not for the invasion, there would still be lost footballs on top of the St James' Park roof today.

At one point, Caines stumbled and lost his rifle with a L'zuhl footsoldier bearing down on him. I tossed my weapon to Andy Gill – who was closer to his stricken teammate – and he then threw it with expert accuracy to Caines, who caught it and took the soldier down in the nick of time.

'Well done, Gilly!' I shouted. 'Gerry told me you'd been struggling to understand how to take a throw-in but you've just proved him wrong, kid!'

'I *can* take throw-ins,' he grumbled irritably, 'Gerry just gets them mixed up with free kicks.'

Our own small victory was at hand – however, as the last soldier fell, his rifle butt struck the pavement and a beam of hot blue light burst forth and cleanly took off Little Dunc's leg below the knee. The stench of simmering flesh was stomach-churning. He didn't even scream – the shock of it saw him tumble to the ground, all the colour draining from his young face. The real sickener was that it was his left leg – the boy was useless on his right and he'd be the first to admit that. I hooked my hands under his arms and dragged him back over to the wall.

'You'll be all right, lad,' I reassured him unconvincingly. 'You can run it off. Maybe.'

'KEVIN KEEGAN,' Barrington12 said from behind me. 'IF YOU WOULD DIRECT YOUR ATTENTION BRIEFLY TO YOUR RIGHT, YOU WILL SEE SOMEONE WHO MAY BE ABLE TO ASSIST IN OUR CURRENT QUANDARY.'

I looked up as directed and Barrington12 had played an absolute blinder. He had caught sight of Dr Pebble-Mill carrying a Gladstone bag and flitting from one wounded figure to another, miraculously evading any fire, friendly or otherwise.

'Doc!' I roared. 'Over here! Man down!'

A flicker of relief seemed to pass over his sweating, dirt-streaked face as he hurried across.

'What are you doing here, Keegan?' he asked as he knelt beside poor Dunc. He sounded exhausted and little wonder. 'Not that I'm not pleased to see a familiar face, you understand. You had the chance to get on a shuttle and get a hundred light years away from this nebula, why didn't you take it?'

I could feel the eyes of my lads, and of Gerry, turn to me at this revelation but I had no time to bask in their quiet respect (though if we somehow survived, I made a mental note to bring it up in future whenever anyone had a pop at me about something).

'Same as you, Doc,' I said. 'Same as the General. I couldn't leave people behind to die while I went off on some jolly. We're in this together. That's the only way mankind sees this through.'

'You're lucky, actually,' Dr Pebble-Mill said to Dunc, who was hyperventilating with his head in the doctor's lap.

'Am I?' Little Dunc asked, glancing down at what remained of his left leg.

'Well, no, I suppose not,' Dr Pebble-Mill said, 'but the heat from the laser instantly cauterised the wound, otherwise you might have bled out. So... every cloud and all that. However, there might be something I can... do I have your permission to try an experiment?'

'Of course, anything!' I cried.

'I was talking to the patient,' Dr Pebble-Mill replied, but Little Dunc was now close to passing out from the pain. The doctor produced an alarmingly large hypodermic needle and filled it with a clear liquid. 'We have young Rodway to thank for this,' he said, and with a deep breath, he jabbed it into the skin above Dunc's knee. After only a few moments some colour returned to his cheeks and his whimpered, nonsensical mutterings ceased.

'Am I... cured?' he croaked.

'Of a severed leg?' Dr Pebble-Mill replied. 'Alas not. But that should go some way to stemming the pain and keeping you alive.'

'What does it have to do with me?' Rodway asked.

'Well, when we brought you in for testing after your jaunt to the volcano,' Dr Pebble-Mill explained, 'I took away blood samples for some extra experimental testing. Out of hours, off my own back – a little frowned upon, but sod it. Anyway, whatever happened out there to heal you, there was something strange and, well, *alien* in the cells I tested. I've been playing around with a serum and finally prepared something last night – I just needed a test subject. I guess a warzone will provide one eventually.'

I glanced at Gerry who quickly looked away. Whatever the doc had extracted from Rodway's system was evidently not on the same level as Slasabo-tik's undiluted abilities, otherwise Dunc's leg would have grown back right there and then. But nevertheless—

'The possibilities are extraordinary,' Dr Pebble-Mill said, finishing my thought for me. Dunc was sitting up and, despite being down one limb, he looked perky, awake and pain-free. I was stunned – but I didn't have time to dwell on it. The clouds above the Compound parted as a dozen more L'zuhl warships entered Palangonia's atmosphere.

'They just keep coming!' the doctor cried weakly. 'They can't be stopped.'

'Don't be so defeatist!' I replied, though I had difficulty disagreeing with his assessment.

'They're like machines,' he went on. 'They must have coordinated this so well. It's almost as though every ship in their fleet, every soldier on the ground, is somehow electronically linked to one another. It'd be impressive if it wasn't so damn terrifying.'

Just like that, it hit me.

'Doc,' I said. 'Give me your Keycard.'

'My what?' he asked, his hand reaching automatically for his pocket. 'Why?'

'I don't have time to explain!' I urged, and begrudgingly he handed it over. 'You lot – stay in cover and don't do anything rash. I want every one of us to come through this completely unscathed.' I looked down at Dunc on the ground, who was staring at me with disdain. 'Sorry,' I muttered.

I pointed to Barrington12 and ordered him to come with me. Then I did the same to Gerry – I couldn't afford to let him out of my sight.

'Where are you going?' Rodway asked me desperately.

'Just stay put,' I repeated as I began to hurry away. 'You have your rifles if they make a move. If we play our cards right, we can win this and the L'zuhl won't have a leg to stand on. Sorry,' I added quickly to Dunc and then left.

THE LAST STAND

'What's the big plan, Kev?' Gerry asked as we arrived outside the glass-panelled entrance to the Compound library. It had so far evaded much of the structural damage of some of the surrounding buildings.

'We use their own snide trickery against them,' I explained. 'Come on, let's get in before they see us.'

Once inside, the place was empty as far as I could tell – Caroline manned the operation more or less alone and had closed the place during her absence. I led Gerry and Barrington12 to the autobiography section. Gerry shivered, clearly remembering his near-death experience behind the shelving. Barrington12 seemed to clock this and, reminiscent of his tenderness with the players, placed a firm hand on Gerry's shoulder, squeezing slightly. Gerry nodded to him and I was pleased to see this moment of understanding pass between them. *It wasn't your fault.* I approached the unremarkable, anonymous door marked PRIVATE. Using Dr Pebble-Mill's Keycard on the scanner on the wall, the door swung open and we scurried inside. The room was dark, save for the illumination from a bank of monitor screens full of scrolling lines of data and code that read like complete gibberish to me.

'Right, hook yourself up, just like before,' I said to Barrington12. His large head turned with a metallic squeak and he stared at me balefully.

'BUT, KEVIN KEEGAN,' he said. 'IT WAS THIS BEHAVIOUR THAT SAW ME SENTENCED TO DEATH. IF I UNDERTAKE THIS COURSE OF ACTION ONCE AGAIN, IT WILL SURELY ONLY VALIDATE THE ACCUSATIONS CURRENTLY LEVELLED AGAINST ME AND ELIMINATE ANY SLIM PROSPECT OF A REPRIEVE.'

'No,' I said. 'This is the complete opposite. Don't you see? Now you're working for us *against* them. If you can connect to their servers and do some, I don't know, reverse polarity *Star Trek* stuff, you can try to interfere with their attack systems the way they interfered with ours, bring down their ships, anything. Damn it all, it has to be worth a try!'

Barrington12 stared at me for several long seconds. Outside, far away, came an enormous booming explosion and the sound of agonised screams. Human screams.

'Time's almost up, son,' I said. 'Do this one for old Kev.'

That seemed to swing it. With impressively deft movements, Barrington12 approached one of the monitors and the tip of one of his fingers unscrewed itself, revealing a small USB-like device within. He plugged it in and his blue eyes turned a brilliant white.

'Do you really think this'll work?' Gerry asked. Honestly, does the man have to be such a downer?

'It'd better,' I replied. 'I think it's our only hope.'

'Unless...' Gerry said, looking down at himself and trailing off.

'That's not an option, Gerry,' I said. 'So forget it.'

'But if we're all going to die anyway, I may as well let this…
thing happen to me first,' he said, his voice cracking. 'Better I die
alone than everyone together.'

'It's not happening!' I snapped. 'I'm not having your life
dictated by a fairy tale!'

At that moment there was another huge crash, this time from
right outside the library entrance.

'They may have found us,' I said. Gerry, chastened, said
nothing. 'Wait here and keep an eye on him. I'll go and see
what's what.'

The glass front of the building had been destroyed – but not
by a L'zuhl rocket. Smouldering in the entranceway was one of
their fighter shuttles, several of which had been peppering the
Compound with bombs during the assault. I might have chalked
this up to a lucky shot from one of Leigh's battalions, but then
outside I saw the shuttles suddenly begin to drop like flies all
across the smoke-blackened sky. It was working! Barrington12
had accessed their system and was zapping their ships from the
air! I peered around the charred wreck in the library entrance
and saw the L'zuhl falling back and the Compound's dwindling
military presence suddenly gaining confidence.

As though on cue, I saw something else which made my spirit
soar: there was some commotion from behind where the L'zuhl
soldiers were gathered which I initially assumed to be the arrival
of their own reinforcements – but then I heard a guttural war
cry that I had last heard from inside a cave on Great Strombago
a lifetime ago.

'Akkie!' I cried in unabashed joy.

Akplatak was flanked by a group of his fellow tribespeople,

the meagre survivors following the heavy casualties sustained during the expedition to rescue Rodway. Their spears and crude weapons were completely insufficient to pierce the L'zuhl armour of course, but their sheer force of will drove them back and clearly had them rattled. I felt humbled that the Watlaq, who had seen their land commandeered by humans without any acknowledgement, would come to our aid, even if it was more likely the case that they had come to protect Gerry. I waved across the field of battle and somehow Akkie saw me. He raised one bony arm above his head in a salute and then returned to the fray. The tide had turned at last.

But then, it turned right back.

En masse, having received an order from somewhere on high, the L'zuhl forces on the ground suddenly began to run in the same direction across the square, cutting through a side street to the south end of the Compound. For one brief, delicious moment I thought they were finally fleeing, waiting for an evacuation vessel to retrieve them – a taste of their own medicine after mankind's departure from Earth. But my relish was short-lived. The L'zuhl were approaching the Compound's electricity hub, the pylon and generators housed in a small fenced-off area. As one, they opened fire and decimated it within seconds. Before the lights above my head went out I saw one of the L'zuhl crushed to death beneath the fallen top section of the pylon; it was cold comfort.

I hurried back to the server room – it was pitch dark in there with the monitors off and I almost clattered into Gerry as he emerged through the door with Barrington12, whose eyes had returned to their regular blue.

'Power cut,' Gerry said. 'Bloody typical. I guess we'll never know whether the plan would've worked.'

'Oh, it worked all right,' I muttered. 'It worked beautifully. Barrington12 just downed a dozen L'zuhl ships in a single breath – and if we get out of this, I'll make sure everyone at The Oracle knows about it. Unfortunately, the L'zuhl are too bloody clever by half. They knew something was happening, that we had got into their system somehow, so they took evasive action. Even your old mates from out there in the wilderness can't save us now.'

'The Watlaq are here?' Gerry asked.

'See for yourself.'

Another volley of anguished cries from outside. With trepidation I approached the library entrance again. The L'zuhl ground forces had regrouped and, as though bitterly stung by our interference, fifty more warships crested the horizon beyond the falling Compound walls. Several Watlaq fighters lay dead, the rest gathering alongside the depleted Compound military force as the net closed. I spotted a bruised and battered General Leigh among them. He had made it to the end, at least. Like Akkie before him, he glanced at me – and then at Gerry.

'Please, Keegan!' he bellowed, his voice still buried beneath the tumult. 'He'll listen to you, tell him! He's our only chance!'

I looked away.

'They just keep coming,' Gerry whispered in horror.

'I don't know what else to do,' I said. 'We've tried everything and they just keep getting around it and coming back at us.'

'Not everything,' Gerry said. I tried once more to interject but he raised a hand to silence me. 'The Watlaq are here. That has to mean something. Kev, I think it's time.'

He took a step forward, out into the square.

'No, Gerry!' I reached for him and at that moment there was a deafening, rending noise from above as a L'zuhl missile smashed into the second floor of the library building.

In a haze of rubble and dust, I blinked open my eyes and found myself lying prostrate with an agonising flare of pain running through one leg. I glanced down and saw my right ankle was pinned to the ground by a large chunk of grey stone. I strained through gritted teeth as I tried to tug myself free but it was far too heavy. I saw Gerry walking out into the square, an ethereal shimmer wisping around his frame like the dust tail of a comet. It was as though he was both there and not there all at once. His feet, suddenly bare, danced lightly across the floor, his mullet fixed in place as though coated in hairspray. He seemed taller, leaner, more alive than he had ever been. It was happening.

I was powerless. I looked around for Barrington12 but he had been toppled over in the blast and, though flailing about frantically, was unable to tip himself up and back onto his feet.

A hush seemed to have fallen over the square. The guns had stopped. A murky rain had begun to fall. All eyes were now on the ghostly figure stepping forward across the battlefield, his eyes milky, his arms aloft, his time come at last.

'No, Gerry!' I screamed. 'You don't have to do this!'

I knew I was being selfish. I knew from everything I had seen on the two occasions when Gerry's other self, his apparently true self, had been unleashed, exactly what he was capable of. The destruction and the healing. It would win the battle for the Alliance, perhaps even the war. In the heat of that moment, I simply did not care. He was my friend. He was my Gerry and I could not accept that he had to die.

I spied movement in my peripheral vision – and my heart sank. A wounded and half-crazed L'zuhl soldier, his helmet blown off and his scaly skin blackened and weeping, apparently oblivious to the scene in the wider square beyond, was half-crawling, half-stumbling in my direction, spittle flecking his filthy yellow teeth.

'Not like this,' I mumbled, bashing the ground in frustration. 'Give me a break, for goodness' sake!'

With a quivering arm, he trained his gun at my forehead from barely a foot away, unable to stand up straight as his neck pumped blood from a vicious wound. What a stupid way for me to go. I felt almost embarrassed.

'Just get on with it, son,' I spat. 'I'm a pure football man, you know. We don't like timewasters.'

Just before I closed my eyes in anticipation of the end, the L'zuhl's neck burst like a piece of rotten fruit, spattering me with all kinds of sickening gunk. I blinked the effluence away and saw an angel standing there, wielding a spear which had been dropped by one of the Watlaq during the battle.

I flopped back onto the ground and covered my disbelieving eyes with my dirty forearm. I felt the rock lift from my ankle, such blessed relief, and my foot wriggled back into life. I removed my arm and just gawped.

'Gillian!' I cried. 'But how did… where are… why are you here?'

'I decided I couldn't let you go off and fight the L'zuhl all by yourself,' she said, lifting me to my feet. I grimaced sharply as I tried to put weight on my clearly broken ankle and leaned heavily on her shoulder. 'I left Laika to fly back to The Oracle for backup – not that they'd ever get here in time.'

'Blimey, Gillian,' I said, 'how on earth did you lift that rock? You really are ripped, you weren't kidding.'

'Well, I'm just glad I came along when I did,' she said, but before I could shower her with more gushing gratitude, I remembered myself and, with Gillian dragged along in tow, I limped across the square, calling out to Gerry to stop.

The L'zuhl had dropped to their knees, cowering with their gauntleted hands covering their heads. In the skies above, their ships seemed frozen in place, unable to attack or escape.

'Gerry!' I pleaded for the final time. 'You can still come back!'

He reached the centre of the square and his arms fell to his sides. He rose slowly from the ground, hovering there a foot or two in the air. In unison, every neck on both sides of the battlefield arched back to watch his slow ascent – soon his feet were level with my head and still he kept rising. He was no longer dressed in his knackered old sweater and tracksuit bottoms. He was wearing a white robe, immaculately tailored and illuminated with a light that almost obscured him. I put a hand across my face and narrowed my eyes – it was almost impossible to make out the figure in the centre but then suddenly his silhouette became clearer and I could see him at last. His head turned slowly to behold each of the expectant, fearful faces below him. The Watlaq were openly weeping, tears of unabashed joy. I almost envied them.

'The prophecy of Slasabo-tik has been fulfilled at last,' he said in a voice that was not Gerry's. *'Peace will come. Evil will fall. So it is written, so it must be.'*

Slasabo-tik raised his arms again in dramatic fashion and a burst of hot energy surrounded him. I closed my eyes, partially from the glare but mostly because I did not want to see. There was a pause and I half opened them, wondering whether I had missed it. Finally, Slasabo-tik turned and was looking down at me. Somewhere in that dazzling alien light, I saw Gerry's face, himself once again. He was smiling.

'Goodbye, Kev,' he said. It was his own voice, just for that one moment.

'Goodbye, Gerry, lad,' I croaked.

Then he exploded, a supernova firework display that bathed the entire Compound in its glory.

AND THAT WAS THAT

Weeks passed. Life in the Compound returned to normal – whatever that was. Gerry/Slasabo-tik had helped the Alliance – and the galaxy in fact – to a monumental victory. The L'zuhl who had had the misfortune to have been deployed to Palangonia that fateful day had been entirely obliterated and their remaining forces out there in the blackness of space were scattered, divided, panicked. It wasn't over, not yet – it was extra time but penalties were around the corner and the L'zuhl's heads had long gone. They were on the back foot. Victory felt not just possible, but likely. My friend's sacrifice had not been in vain.

This fact did not make his loss any easier to take.

The wounded had been healed in the prophetic blast – my ankle was as good as new and Little Dunc was back up on two legs; not only that, but he was also no longer cross-eyed, so he was absolutely made up with that. The buildings had been repaired as though a reset button had been pushed. As before, Gerry's powers did not extend to resurrecting the dead and there was much grief and mourning for those who had been lost.

The General arranged a ceremony to honour the fallen, with a special tribute for Gerry, but I declined to attend. I was too burned out from everything, not only the battle but all that had gone before. The idea of reliving everything was simply too much for me. I was pleased that it would ensure that Gerry's contribution would be acknowledged by every citizen of the Compound, that he would be hailed for the hero that he was, but they would never understand, not really. How could they? Its like would never be seen again. But I knew. And oh, I missed him terribly.

Dr Pebble-Mill was abuzz with excitement about the prospects of a super-vaccine to treat pain and even heal the previously desperately sick, and that, if it panned out, would be one heck of a legacy for my friend to leave behind. There was great excitement across all the human colonies about its recent deployment as a long-sought-after cure for approxial mylosia, the infinite malaise disease that had caused so much heartache for so many since the invasion of Earth. I tried to console myself with thoughts such as these but it was still too painful. There was no cure in the known galaxy that would bring my friend back from where he had gone.

In the immediate aftermath of the battle, which, on the face of things, now looked as though it had never even taken place, Leigh approached me. I was expecting some sort of rollocking for not having 'deployed' Gerry sooner but instead he grabbed my shoulder and squeezed it.

'We did it,' he said gruffly. I almost thought I glimpsed a tear in his eyes. 'I'll make sure he's remembered, Keegan. I'll ensure that people know.'

I nodded but couldn't bring myself to respond. I walked away.

Akkie and the Watlaq were overcome with elation at having witnessed first-hand the fulfilment of the prophecy and I was heartened to hear later on that the General made special recognition of the part they had played in the victory during the memorial ceremony. He and everyone else in the Compound assumed that the Watlaq had arrived on the scene to unite in a common purpose to prevent the destruction of Palangonia, and I was more than happy to allow that misconception to stand. Despite my personal disappointment, I was happy for them. Their lives were now complete. I spoke to the General a few days after the battle about the promise I had made to Akkie when last we had parted, when I had told him I would ensure that we helped his people rebuild after the losses they had sustained in helping rescue Rodway – in light of their intervention in the battle, Leigh agreed. I considered asking him for my football club back too, but I didn't. What would be the point without my number two? Before he and his people left, I thanked Akkie for his bravery and he chattered back happily. I didn't understand a word of it but smiled and wished him well. If I'd had Barrington12 with me, he would have been able to translate for us.

My hopes that Barrington12's crimes might be pardoned fell on deaf ears, especially as the General's obliging mood evaporated back to his usual dour form not long after.

'Absolutely not,' the General told me firmly when I spoke to him the following morning. 'Whether he intended for any of this or not is entirely beside the point. He sold us out to the L'zuhl either way. That, Keegan, is unforgivable.'

'General, how can you be so stubborn?' I demanded, feeling emotion for the first time following twenty-four hours of numb anaesthesia. 'How can you be so cold?'

'I appreciate your depth of feeling on this, Keegan, really I do, but there can be no discussion. Even if I relented, The Oracle will see that it's done. I'm sorry, but that's that.'

'I've already lost one pal,' I said, angry with myself as I heard my voice crack. I blinked away the threat of tears. I wouldn't give him that. 'Don't make me lose another.'

'I'm sorry,' he repeated, nodding towards the door. 'Unfortunately your machine did what he did and there's no getting away from that.'

Except he didn't, I thought as I trudged home. *Or, at least, he never meant to.* And had he not hacked the L'zuhl systems during the battle to bring down their ships and give us a fighting chance? Without his intervention, Gerry might never have been in a position to do his whole thing in the first place and we'd all have perished. Could that truly count for nothing? Gillian's place on the Council made her privy to information that she was surprisingly willing to share with me.

'After all you've been through together, I think you have a right,' she said one evening in Mr O's as she treated me to a sausage and egg bap. 'I'm with you on this one, of course.' She squeezed my hand across the table. 'Barrington12 didn't know what he was doing. Take comfort in that thought. He had no idea he was responsible for all of this.'

'They're going to scrap him,' I said disconsolately. 'There's no comfort to be had, Gillian. There's no hope left in this stupid universe.'

'There… might be,' she said carefully. 'For you, anyway. What are you doing tomorrow?'

I shrugged. 'I dunno. No plans, really. I feel like I've been in limbo these past few weeks.'

'Why don't you come on over to the stadium?' she asked, a smile dancing on her lips. 'The boys will need a coach, after all.'

I stared at Gillian over my roll, unsure where she was going.

'What's this?' I asked, taken aback.

'The Council voted on it this very evening. Now that the spy has been apprehended and the L'zuhl all but defeated, funding that had been reserved for military affairs can be, in part, redirected back to essential Compound services. I called a vote on reinstating the football club with you back at the helm, in recognition of your services in helping to save the Compound. I wish I could have told them about your bravery in rescuing Rodway too, but I'm afraid that will have to remain our little secret. If word gets out that we breached the lockdown, even now that all has been resolved...'

'Hang on,' I said, trying to keep up. 'You're saying... the club is back? Palangonia FC lives again?'

'I've even spoken to the secretary of Galactic League C and she has agreed that Palangonia will be restored to the league, albeit at the bottom given that we're several matches behind everyone else. But I'm sure results will pick up very soon. I saw Rodway in the gym earlier this week; he's the picture of health. This experience has changed him, you know – I don't think he'll return to his hard-drinking, party-animal ways. He's a special talent, Kevin.'

'Aye, he is that,' I agreed.

Then I shook my head.

'No,' I sighed. 'I'm grateful, don't get me wrong, but... I can't. Not without Gerry. It's not right.'

Gillian considered this and looked away out of the window. I drummed my fingers quietly on the table.

'Do you think this is what he'd want?' she asked finally. I glanced up at her and frowned.

'How do you mean?' I asked.

'Well, Gerry gave up everything so that life in the galaxy could continue and people could have a hope of peace. Do you think he also wanted you to mope around and lose the one thing that brought you the most joy? The most fulfilment? I mean, I didn't know the man as well as you did, but I'm quite sure Gerry would be dismayed that he gave you the chance to resurrect the football club you built together and you turned it down.'

She was right. Damn it all, she was right. I found myself laughing, and she reached across and patted my hand.

'Can this really be happening?' I asked disbelievingly.

'It's happening,' Gillian laughed. 'So buck up! This will be Gerry's legacy, his parting gift to you – a chance to continue the great work you did together here on Palangonia. And needless to say, we will always remember Barrington12's contribution to the club too and everything he did for us, not least over the past month or so. He will live on in our hearts and minds forever. Football is made up of comings and goings, but we'll carry on. We must.'

I felt myself welling up again, the daft old softie that I was. I was still exhausted from all that we had been through, but the news that I'd been given the one single thing I'd truly wished for – my football club – made me feel a flicker of life, of rejuvenation. I owed it to Gerry to pick myself up and carry on. I suddenly found that I couldn't wait to walk back through those gates again. To do what I was born to do. For ninety minutes on a Saturday afternoon, no intergalactic war would ever dampen my spirits.

'I am still sorry, you know,' Gillian said. 'About Gerry. For not getting to you sooner when you were pinned down. Who knows, maybe you could have reached him in time if I'd been faster.'

I shook my head.

'You can't apologise for that. If Gerry hadn't done what he did then… well, I'm a big enough man to admit that if I'd had my way, we'd probably not be sitting here right now. And anyway,' I added, 'you weren't too slow at all.'

'I wasn't?'

'No. You gave me the chance to say goodbye.'

She smiled and looked genuinely humbled by this. After a moment's ponderous silence, I wolfed down the last of my bap and stood up, explaining to Gillian that I would see her at work first thing the next morning. I had one more thing I needed to do.

'We're going to get promoted this season, you know,' I said as I put on my coat and headed for the door. 'I can feel it. Now that Rodway's back to full fitness and Andy Gill finally knows how to take a throw-in, we'll be unstoppable. That'll show the General!'

For all the thawing of the hostilities between he and I, there was no doubt he'd have been devastated to hear of the club's reinstatement. I allowed myself a grin at the thought of his face on hearing the news.

'On the contrary,' Gillian said, turning in her seat to face me. 'The Council were tied 2–2 on restoring Palangonia FC's funding and it was Leigh who held the casting vote. It was against his better judgement, no doubt about that, but he did this for you. "Tell him we're all square," he said to me at the end.'

I blinked, astonished. I had no idea what to say.

'Go on, off you go to wherever it is you need to be,' Gillian said. 'I'll see you tomorrow.'

'Gillian,' I said, halfway through the door. She looked at me expectantly. 'Thanks. For everything. I know I can get a bit arsey about this and that but… at the end of the day, I'm proud to have you running the club from upstairs.'

Before she could respond, I slipped out into the rain-soaked Compound streets. Kevin Keegan was back. Life could, as much as was possible in such uncertain times, return to normal at last.

I had one final stop to make.

LAIKA'S GIFT

'This really is highly irregular,' sniffed Lieutenant Emberley, the stuck-up guard on duty that evening. He stood irritatingly close to me in the hallway inside the Mark Aspinall Prison within Fort Emmeline, a place I had hoped I would never have to step into ever again. 'Really not the done thing at all.'

Presently, a door at the far end of the narrow corridor creaked open (I made a mental note to recommend WD-40 to the General when I next saw him) and two familiar figures entered, their disparities in height and appearance never more emphatic than under the harsh white glow of the strip lights on the ceiling.

Barrington12 walked with his head down, clanking miserably along the steel-grated floor. Laika trotted in front of him, her face a picture of seriousness. Two guards flanked them (or rather, walked just behind them as the corridor was too cramped), their hands restless on their rifles.

'Barrington12,' I said, stepping forward. What was the appropriate thing in this sort of situation? A hug? A handshake? In the end, I did nothing but stand there like a fool as he slowly came to a halt in front of me. His wrists were manacled, as were his ankles. His usually bright blue LED eyes were faded and dull. He looked an absolute wreck.

'Are you ... okay, son?' I ventured tentatively. 'Are they treating you well?'

'We're treating him the way a spy deserves to be treated!' Emberley interjected, the arse.

'That's enough, please,' Laika said sternly. Emberley gave a small wave of apology and was still.

'HELLO, KEVIN KEEGAN,' Barrington12 said in a small, barely audible voice, quite unlike his regular blaring foghorn. 'BARRINGTON12 IS PLEASED TO SEE HIS FRIEND.'

'Yeah, well, make the most of it,' sneered Emberley. 'This afternoon it'll be the junkyard for you!'

'What did I just say, Lieutenant?' Laika snapped angrily. Emberley once again waved and stepped back. I looked down to her.

'I ... really am grateful for this, Laika,' I said.

'Well, let's get on with it,' she said. The two guards squeezed awkwardly past Barrington12's bulky steel frame and opened the door opposite. Inside was the interrogation room, where Leigh had attempted to keep me imprisoned before I'd persuaded my idiot lawyer that the General's timelines didn't hold water. The room still looked plain and dingy; I really was going to have to have a word with someone about this. A lick of paint – anything!

Laika walked in first, then Barrington12, the guards prodding him with the barrels of their guns to prompt him. Then I followed and moved to close the door, bumping Lieutenant Emberley on the nose behind me.

'Watch it!' he snarled, holding it theatrically. I hadn't seen play-acting like that since Robbie Savage in his pomp.

'What are you doing?' I asked him. 'You're not sitting in on this.'

'Yes, I bloody well am!' he insisted. 'Move!'

'Lieutenant, please wait outside in the corridor.'

'But, Laika—!'

'Don't make me ask you a second time,' she glowered at him, baring her teeth just faintly. 'I am quite capable of supervising this meeting alone.'

Emberley sighed and retreated, slamming the door. There was a moment's uncomfortable silence before Laika directed Barrington12 to sit and I took a seat opposite at the table. She trotted over to the corner and lay down.

'I can give you ten minutes,' she warned me. 'Say your piece, Kevin.'

I nodded and looked at the robot sitting across from me. He was staring vacantly at the table, unwilling to meet my gaze.

'Kid, look at me,' I said gently. He didn't respond. 'It's me – it's old Kev. I'm here… because I want to say goodbye. Don't stop me from doing that, son. Please.'

After a moment's consideration, he raised his head with a metallic squeak and saw me at last.

'I'M SO SORRY, KEVIN KEEGAN,' he said in the saddest electronic voice. 'I DIDN'T WANT TO CAUSE ANY TROUBLE. I'M SORRY THAT I BETRAYED MANKIND. I DID NOT MEAN TO.'

'Now, you stop that kind of talk right now, you hear me?' I said firmly. 'I won't hear it. I don't believe all that claptrap about how you knew what you were doing – utter rot! You can't help the weaknesses in your system nor how the L'zuhl exploited them. You were used and chucked away, a scapehorse for powers greater than all of us. You must never apologise for being you.'

Barrington12 continued to stare at me but said nothing.

'I'll be brutally frank with you,' I went on. 'When Gillian first brought you in to training and said I had to show you round the stadium and integrate you into the coaching setup, I was pigged off. We were pootling along just fine, we didn't need any extra help. But I always do as I'm told, and I brought you into the fold. And as time progressed, I went from resenting you to tolerating you.'

'THANK YOU,' Barrington12 said, without a hint of sarcasm or reproach.

'Right, but I haven't finished yet,' I said, smiling in spite of myself at the unfailingly sweet nature of this tangle of wires and processors sitting across from me. 'What I was going to say is that over the past four or five weeks, I've grown from tolerating you to liking you. To caring about you. Bugger it all, man – to loving you. Not in a weird inter-technology-romance kind of way, you understand. You're family – to me, to Gillian and to all the lads. And to Gerry, too, I'm sure. None of us will ever forget the contributions you made. Least of all young Rodway – without your help on our journey to Great Strombago, we would all have copped it.'

I could see Laika twitching curiously in my peripheral vision – I kept forgetting how that mission was still supposed to be a secret. I pressed on regardless.

'I'm devastated that this has happened. I'd do anything to get you out of here – you know that, don't you?'

'YES,' Barrington12 replied quietly. 'I KNOW.'

'I tried to tell them about how you helped out during the battle but the obstinate sods just wouldn't have it. They said it still wasn't enough to cancel out your crime. We're led by idiots, we really are.'

I winced as I heard Laika growl softly. I mouthed a 'sorry!' and continued.

'I am still a bit confused about why you took Gillian's Keycard in the first place, mind you,' I said delicately. 'Was that some kind of hack job? They forced you to do that?'

'NO,' Barrington12 said in a voice so small that I had to strain to hear. 'I... TOOK IT OF MY OWN VOLITION.'

I sighed.

'You don't do that, son. That's stealing. That's not right.'

'I KNOW. I DID NOT MEAN TO CAUSE TROUBLE. IF I MAY CONFESS TO YOU NOW, I HAD BEEN DISCREETLY BORROWING THE CARD FOR OVER SIX MONTHS FOR ONE PURPOSE ONLY. I AM SORRY THAT I FORGOT TO RETURN IT THIS LAST TIME.'

'What possible use could you have for it?' I asked, baffled.

'MY FAVOURITE PLACE IN THIS COMPOUND IS THE LIBRARY. I ATTEMPTED TO JOIN, BUT WAS INFORMED THAT ROBOTS ARE NOT ELIGIBLE FOR MEMBERSHIP.'

Poor from Caroline, that. Though this did at least explain the books that had appeared on Gillian's borrowing history, which she was adamant she had never taken out.

'But I've told you, you don't need the library; your databases are chock-full of more information than the rest of us will ever know.'

'I UNDERSTAND,' he went on. 'BUT THE SELF-

DETERMINED ACQUIREMENT OF KNOWLEDGE IS MORE POTENT AND ENRICHING THAN HAVING IT AWARDED UNASKED. I WANTED TO READ THE PAGES, THE STORIES, THE PEOPLE'S LIVES FOR MYSELF. IT MAKES ME FEEL… ALMOST LIKE YOU. ALL LIFE IS THERE, KEVIN KEEGAN.'

I felt awful. The kid had only ever wanted to better himself, to feel closer to those who had created him. And it had cost him his very existence.

'I really hope that my coming here and pestering poor Laika to allow me to sit and talk to you, one final time' — my voice choked slightly at this last part — 'didn't get your hopes up that I'd be able to unravel this mess you've gone and got yourself into. Because I can't, son. I just can't. I've tried, lord knows, but the powers-that-be are bloody stubborn. Like at that quiz night last year when I accused the question master of favouring Leigh's team – I mean, they had a round called General Knowledge, for Christ's sake! How is that fair? He was bound to walk that. Unbelievable.'

What was I talking about again?

'Anyway, the sad fact of the matter is that I can't get you out of this. I wish I could.'

To my astonishment, Barrington12 reached across the desk with his two chained hands and clumsily took mine.

'I UNDERSTAND, KEVIN KEEGAN. YOU HAVE ALREADY DONE MORE FOR BARRINGTON12 THAN ANYONE. YOU GAVE ME THE GREATEST GIFT OF ALL. FRIENDSHIP.'

That nearly set me off again. I had to look away to compose

myself and my eyes briefly met Laika's, who was watching this tragic scene unfold in silence.

'I...' my voice stumbled again, so I took a breath. 'I came here to tell you one thing before you... before you go. Palangonia FC is back from the dead. And without your help over this past month, assisting us in saving Rodway's life and the General's too, that would never have been possible. You helped save our club, Barrington12.'

'I AM DELIGHTED,' he said. 'I WISH THAT I COULD BE THERE TO SAVOUR THE MOMENT WITH YOU. PERHAPS YOU MIGHT CONSIDER NAMING THE STADIUM AFTER ME. THAT WOULD BE QUITE AN HONOUR.'

'Well, steady on,' I said. 'That'd be a bit of a slap in the face for John Rudge, frankly. But maybe the shed where we keep the balls and cones overnight? The Barrington12 Memorial Equipment Shed. Has a nice ring to it.'

'IT DOES,' Barrington12 said. 'THANK YOU, KEVIN KEEGAN, FOR SHARING THIS NEWS WITH ME. IT WILL PROVIDE SUCCOUR IN THESE DARK FINAL HOURS OF MY EXISTENCE. I WISH YOU AND GILLIAN ROUTLEDGE AND RODWAY JONES AND ALL OF THE PLAYERS EVERY SUCCESS IN YOUR FUTURE ENDEAVOURS. THANK YOU FOR ALLOWING BARRINGTON12 TO BE A PART OF THIS ADVENTURE. MY ONLY WISH WAS... TO BE MORE LIKE ALL OF YOU. TO BE HUMAN, IF ONLY IN SOME SUPERFICIAL WAY. I ONLY REGRET THAT I MADE SUCH A MISTAKE IN PURSUIT OF THIS GOAL.'

There was a knock on the door.

'Time's up,' Emberley said bitterly.

Laika stood and shook herself like she'd been sprayed with water.

'I'm sorry, Kevin,' she said. 'But I think that will have to be all.'

'Aye,' I replied sadly, and met Barrington12's eyes one last time. 'That's all.'

I gently withdrew my hand from his grip – he clung on for a second longer, as though unwilling to let me go. But then he did.

I tarried in the doorway and looked back at the wretched figure still sitting at the table.

'You did make a mistake, kid, there's no denying that,' I said. 'But I've been thinking about something a bloke far wiser than me once said, which I think you should bear in mind. "To err is human." You erred, son.'

Barrington12 looked up at me. A single oily tear ran from one eye and plinked onto the table in front of him as the door closed.

Life's a funny old game. I'd lost two dear friends but had regained my beloved football club. These past weeks had left an indelible mark on me, and the wider ramifications for the Compound and for the Alliance would be felt for a long time to come. For now, we had a match to focus on – a tough encounter with the tree-elves of Aqalf-Seni.

As I walked home, I passed the library. Caroline was there, locking up at the end of another day. She had returned earlier in the week with good news – her sister (or whatnot) had been given the all-clear for infinite malaise.

'They've had some sort of breakthrough,' she told me

excitedly. 'A miracle cure, people are calling it. Isn't it amazing what science can do?'

'It really is,' I agreed, smiling warmly as she gave me a peck on the cheek and headed for home. I was just pleased she hadn't been around to witness the partial destruction of her beloved library, even if the damage had been almost instantly undone. I hadn't yet told her about what had happened with Barrington12. That could wait. I didn't mention Gerry's fate either, but I'm sure she knew. Everybody knew.

I turned the corner towards my accommodation block, and as I stepped inside the front door I picked up the post and put it on the hall table. As I headed through to the kitchen, my eyes caught the envelope on the top of the pile. It wasn't addressed, it just had my name written in elegant lettering. Instantly curious, I picked it up and pulled out a single sheet of paper. My heart pounded.

Compound Scrapyard. Lot 2ZB5.

Beneath that was another address in the Compound, from a neighbouring accommodation block, not one I recognised. There was no name provided. Then, at the bottom of the sheet, I saw something that made my heart sing. A signature that I knew well.

Without a moment's hesitation, I turned and walked straight back out of the door.

EPILOGUE

'Number 33, fifty-first floor, 7-A,' I said, checking Laika's note for the tenth time in as many minutes. This had to be the place. God only knew who lived there or why I'd been sent to see them, but they were about to get the shock of their lives at the sight on their doorstep.

I rang the doorbell. As I waited for the sound of feet shuffling from the hallway within, I grinned at Gillian. I still couldn't quite believe this was happening. Locating the Compound scrapyard had been a feat all in itself – not unlike the time my office at Fulham was relocated during renovation work and I completely lost my bearings trying to find it (the club eventually had to dispatch Paul Bracewell to collect me after I wandered out as far as East Croydon station) – and in the end I had been left with no choice but to seek some help. Gillian had been surprisingly game; even after all we'd been through together I'd expected a certain degree of stuffiness to have come into play, some slavish devotion to the rules, but when I told her that the cryptic note had been from Laika she was only too happy to help. She led me to the scrapyard, tucked away behind the post office and secured by metal fences fifteen feet high, fastened shut with several chunky padlocks. Undeterred and high on life, I scaled the fence quickly (well, it took a good thirty minutes) and immediately set about finding Lot 2ZB5 while Gillian kept watch outside the yard. The lot was a narrow compartment, wedged in the middle of a tight row with several others, all containing crates of junk that would be broken up and either disposed of or sold as scrap. But not 2ZB5. Not today.

I pulled out one such box and opened the lid. I peered inside and my heart skipped a beat at the sight of a familiar, if disembodied, head looking back at me. The blue lights of his eyes had gone out and the head rested on a nest of cables, metal plates and circuit boards. I found myself feeling a sense of profound sadness that someone I had been speaking to only that morning could have been so quickly reduced to this undignified mess. I dragged the box out of the lot and huffed and puffed my way back to the gate. I lugged it up onto my shoulder and tried to scale the gate one-handed, no doubt slipping a disc or five, before Gillian pointed out from the other side that while she'd been waiting for me to return she'd found a small unlocked exit a hundred yards along. I hadn't felt such relief since Big Sam Allardyce phoned to say he couldn't make it to my New Year's party in 2002 – I'd neglected to buy Scotch eggs and things would have turned ugly very quickly.

Now we had arrived at the mysterious address as Laika had directed. It couldn't be her own place – she had no residence on Palangonia, and in fact I had already heard that she had departed the Antioc Nebula once again to return to The Oracle. So where the heck had she sent us?

'Oh, hang on,' Gillian said, looking around, a penny dropping. 'I do know someone who lives here. But why would Laika...?'

She trailed off as a silhouette appeared behind the frosted glass of the door and peered out. I waved and, to my relief, the figure reciprocated and opened the door.

'Kevin,' Dr Pebble-Mill said, bemused though not unhappy to see me freezing my crackers off on his front doorstep late at night. 'Gillian. Is everything okay? Is there a medical emergency?'

'No, no, nothing like that,' I said.

'Okay,' he said slowly. 'So… what can I do for you?'

I went blank.

'I don't know,' I replied unhelpfully.

'We've been sent here,' Gillian said. 'But we don't know what for. I'm sorry, Andre, I know how silly that must sound.'

'Not at all,' he said patiently. Then, 'What's that in your box, there? Looks a bit heavy.'

'It is,' I replied, wheezing with the strain as I attempted to lift it again. Gillian picked it up (she made a bit of a play of showing some exertion on her face, which I was convinced was purely to make me feel better) and set the box down on the doorstep.

'Oh my,' Dr Pebble-Mill said, crouching down and peering inside with great interest. 'Is that… what I think it is? Your robot?'

'My friend,' I said. 'Barrington12. They scrapped him, Doc. I mean, you know that. And I don't blame you at all for your Council vote at the trial, I promise you. You didn't know what I knew, after all. But Laika told me where I could find him, and then, for some reason, she gave me your address.'

'This is fantastic,' Dr Pebble-Mill said, plucking a few pieces, including one of Barrington12's arms, from the box.

'I don't understand why she would send us to you,' I said, frustrated. 'You're a people doctor. This isn't your field at all.'

'Oh, but it is,' Dr Pebble-Mill said. 'Don't you remember what I told you the other week? I love tinkering with these old models. I once built myself a Barrington50 – this is a real passion of mine.'

Then, at last, I understood. I looked at Gillian, who smiled – she had got there way ahead of me.

'Can you do it, Doc?' I asked him urgently. 'Can you… rebuild Barrington12?'

He stood up and smiled.

'Bring him inside,' he said. 'This might be a long night. I'll put some coffee on.'

Dr Pebble-Mill worked into the small hours, barely pausing for breath as he pieced together tiny components and large with a dizzying speed and genuinely heart-warming enthusiasm. He was like a kid with a Lego set, a pencil tucked behind one ear, sleeves rolled up, tongue poking out slightly in concentration. Gillian and I played our part of course – she would help him to lift and hold in place some of the heavier components while I kept our spirits up by saying things like, 'Looking good so far,' and, 'Nice one.'

It was four in the morning and still dark outside as Dr Pebble-Mill finally stepped back over the jumble of discarded wires, screws and coffee mugs, and puffed out his cheeks. I glanced at Gillian, who was looking on anxiously. After a long moment's consideration, the doctor said, 'I think… it's done.'

I took a deep breath. I was almost too afraid to watch as Dr Pebble-Mill leaned round behind the back of the robot's neck and fumbled for the tiny boot-up switch. I looked at this eight-foot-tall machine with an affection I never thought possible. Dr Pebble-Mill had done an extraordinary job of piecing him together – he looked almost identical to before, though his eyes had been inserted at a slightly askew angle which left him a little cross-eyed. If this *did* work, we'd have to get Barrington12 a swift paint job to disguise his identity – no one could ever know that this was the same robot who had accidentally brought the L'zuhl to our borders. He'd never live it down.

'Here goes,' Dr Pebble-Mill said, and flicked the switch. He stepped back quickly and joined Gillian and me, the three of us standing there on the messy living room carpet, watching, waiting and hoping.

Nothing happened.

After thirty seconds of silence, I could feel Dr Pebble-Mill's shoulders sag beside me.

'Well, bugger,' he said in disappointment. 'We tried, Kevin. I guess that's just the way she goes sometimes.'

'Damn,' Gillian said disconsolately, turning to me. 'I'm so sorry.'

Come on, kid, I thought, willing Barrington12 to say something, to show any sign of life. But there was none. He was gone for good.

'We did our best,' I said, and placed my hand on his cold metal chest.

I still don't know whether this triggered something or if it was pure chance, but no sooner had I placed my palm against him, Barrington12's arms suddenly jerked up from where they had been dangling at his sides and his tiny blue eyes flickered into life.

'Doc!' I cried. 'He's alive! Barrington12 – can you hear me?
Do you recognise me?'

Dr Pebble-Mill hurried over, Gillian hot on his heels, and
stood beside me, staring up at Barrington12 in hope and wonder.
With the squeak of metal upon metal, his head moved and
he stared down at us. Was there any recognition there at all?
Would his memory banks have remained intact or would he be
Barrington12 but born anew? Dr Pebble-Mill had warned me,
in adding an extra layer of security to his system to prevent any
future infiltrations by the L'zuhl, that it could end up rebooting
Barrington12's memory to its default factory settings. It wouldn't
be ideal, sure, but it was better than nothing at all.

He didn't say anything for the longest time; he just looked
intently at the three imploring faces in front of him. And then:

'KEVIN KEEGAN. I CANNOT BEGIN TO EXPLAIN
HOW PLEASED BARRINGTON12 IS TO SEE YOU. AND
GILLIAN ROUTLEDGE, MY ADMIRED FRIEND AND
EMPLOYER. AND DR ANDRE PEBBLE-MILL, THE
FINEST MEDICAL PROFESSIONAL IN THE COMPOUND.
I NEVER DREAMED THAT I WOULD EVER BE AMONG
MY FRIENDS AGAIN.'

'Well, you are, son,' I said, blinking back tears. 'And you always
will be. I promise.'

I turned to Dr Pebble-Mill, who looked beyond thrilled that
his arduous night's work had been such a success, and embraced
him like a brother. Gillian stepped backwards to allow us the
moment but I wasn't having that – I flapped a hand at her until
she laughed and stepped forward to be pulled into the group
hug.

'Thank you, Doc,' I said. 'A hundred times over. I'll never forget what you've done for us today.'

'You're more than welcome,' he said warmly, patting me on the back. 'Really, the pleasure is all mine – I haven't built one of these in years.'

I hadn't felt such pure elation since that famous 4–3 game at Anfield in 1996. I mean, yeah, we'd lost right at the death but come on, what an absolute corker of a match that was.

'KEVIN KEEGAN,' Barrington12 said. 'WOULD I BE PERMITTED TO RETURN TO YOUR COACHING STAFF NOW THAT PALANGONIA FC IS BACK IN OPERATION?'

I stepped back and took Barrington12's hand in mine. I shook it firmly.

'I'll tell you, honestly,' I said, 'I would love it if you did, son.'

Love it.

We were all far too excited to retire for what remained of the night, so I suggested a trip out to Mr O's Place for a very early breakfast.

'My treat, of course,' I insisted. 'Though if you get something off the jumbo menu do bear in mind the price leaps up quite a bit, so let's not get daft or anything.'

Gillian was concerned about someone spotting Barrington12 and raising the alarm, so Dr Pebble-Mill screwed a metal strip over the *12-series* branding on the back of his midsection and changed his blue LED eyes for the green ones more commonly associated with Barrington50 models. In the end we needn't have worried, as the Compound streets were all but deserted, a lone road sweeper the only figure I could see as we made our way towards the dim yellow light of the café window at the edge of the square. Then suddenly my eye was drawn to something else, some movement high above our heads. I stopped in my tracks and pointed – Gillian, Dr Pebble-Mill and Barrington12 looked up as one.

A shooting star etched a path through the early morning sky infinite miles away from us, all alone out there in the darkness. A faint tail of light, almost imperceptible, followed in its wake as it made its way across the vast cosmos.

It almost looked like a mullet.

ACKNOWLEDGEMENTS

My thanks to the brilliant team at Unbound, who have looked after me so well, particularly Fiona, Georgia and Mathew. I could not have been in better hands than with my wonderful editor DeAndra Lupu, who has been such a fantastic supporter of this book and an absolute pleasure to work with. I am also indebted to Liz Garner for her wisdom, kindness and enthusiasm throughout the editing and redrafting of the novel – it became a thousand times better for her input. My thanks also to Dan Mogford for his terrific cover art and to Mark Ecob for his excellent chapter illustrations.

Huge thanks to my agent, Rory Scarfe, and to Amy Fitzgerald, who did so much to shepherd this book into reality. To Neil Blair, for giving a chance to an idiot with a daft Twitter account and without whom none of this would have happened. My thanks also to Olivia Maidment for her early editorial guidance (and zero-tolerance policy on dad jokes!).

Working on this novel has probably involved as much gnawing anxiety and self-doubt as it has actual writing, so I am extremely grateful for the encouragement throughout from Helen Barrett, James Dowthwaite, Rob Francis, John Rain, Andrew Sillett, Will Stevens and Joel Young. Sincere thanks also to Dionne Allen.

Gratitude beyond words to my wife, Laura, for her love, support, patience and everything else. To my parents, Pat and Brian, who always believed and unfailingly indulged their shy bookworm of a son in his love of reading and writing and to whom I owe so much, and to my brother, Callum, who can't stand football but is an otherwise great guy. To my in-laws, Mark and Barbara, who have been like second parents to me, and to Katherine, Dan, Sam and Meg.

To Kath, whose generosity and support I will never, ever forget.

Finally, to the followers of the @GalacticKeegan account and to everyone who pledged towards this book – thank you. It exists for you and because of you.

A NOTE ON THE AUTHOR

Scott Innes was born in Doncaster, South Yorkshire (which also happens to be the hometown of a certain Kevin Keegan), and is now based in East Sussex. He has worked for the NHS for over fifteen years. Scott has been the writer of the @GalacticKeegan Twitter account since early 2014, in which time it has accumulated more than 70,000 followers. *Galactic Keegan* is his first book.

PALANGONIA FC
HALL OF FAME

Chris Allen was Palangonia FC's record signing at a fee of 50 million kronqueks. After an excellent debut season which included 22 goals, 31 assists and 19 red cards, Allen was unexpectedly plucked from the training pitch mid-warm-down by a flock of Winged Terrors and remains missing, presumed eaten.

Paul Allen signed for Palangonia FC from Flimshwuk United, the most decorated club in the Freenk Nebula. Unfortunately, a succession of injuries meant that Allen failed to fulfil his initial promise and retired from professional football to open a bakery, which currently has a galactic hygiene rating of 'Requires Improvement'.

Tim Barber is a player who needs no introduction – four-time winner of the Galactic Golden Boot (a trophy made from aluminium but painted gold to save costs), he remains the only footballer in the Antioc Nebula to have ever scored a hat-trick while tucking into a full Sunday roast.

Andy Bignell is the longest-serving player in the history of Palangonia FC, having played there for five seasons. A dynamic midfield powerhouse, Bignell holds the record for the most bookings in one season with 76, an average of two per game.

An imposing goalkeeper with a no-nonsense disposition, **Daniel Calder** infamously killed three teammates during one ill-tempered goalmouth scramble and still went on to win the Players' Player of the Season award. Calder currently resides at Tek Rumbri, the galaxy's most impregnable prison, for undisclosed reasons.

The winner of a fan competition to play one match for Palangonia FC, **Mark Cockin** so impressed manager Kevin Keegan that he was signed on the spot and went on to captain the club to an unprecedented treble. Sadly, Cockin later had all medals stripped and was released by the club after a league official spotted a misplaced apostrophe on his original competition entry form.

While better known previously as a pop star, particularly as the singer for punk-reggae band The Gaseous Leaks, who bagged three top-ten hits on the fish-planet of Piscea, **Lex Coogans-Finch** switched career to become a reliable left-back for Palangonia FC, though he ultimately left the club under a cloud after being tapped up to return to music as the new vocalist for Fleetwood Mac (by then onto their third century of a galaxy-wide tour after pioneering robo-splice procedures prolonged their lives and careers).

Michael Follett, better known to opposition fans as 'The Troublemaker', played for two seasons as a floating midfielder. Notorious for a confrontational playing style and for punching two referees on the same day (one during a match, the other for cutting in front of him in a supermarket queue later that evening), Follett failed to report for pre-season one year and his current whereabouts are unknown.

Peter Neil Griffin Follett, aka 'Butterfingers', was the reserve goalkeeper at Palangonia FC for three seasons before being promoted to first choice after his predecessor tragically fell into a ravine while completing a cryptic crossword. Follett went on to keep a grand total of one clean sheet, an impressive club record which stands to this day.

Once described by Sir Alex Ferguson as 'I've never heard of them', **Wayne Garvie** was a jinky winger with an unerringly accurate cross. Responsible for 104 assists in two seasons but no goals, Garvie's career was cut short by a paper cut that was so distracting and irritating that it resulted in a dramatic loss of form and the eventual termination of his contract.

The youngest player in Palangonia FC's history, having made his debut up front at the age of four, **Russell P Hancock** became famous for sitting down in the centre circle and crying for a full ninety minutes, an ingenious tactic that unsettled every opponent and began Palangonia's journey to its most trophy-laden season on record. Hancock then left the club to begin a successful spell at nursery school.

Since retiring from professional football after a decorated career which yielded two league titles and free fish and chips for life from club sponsor The Happy Fryer, **Ben Hayward** returned to Palangonia FC as director of football. As no one knows what this job actually involves, Hayward currently spends each day sitting in his office and staring out of the window, waiting for the next match.

After a dazzling debut season with thirty-five clean sheets as centre-half and a nomination for young player of the season, **Jarrett Holland** tragically lost both ears in a Scrabble-related accident. Against the odds, Holland battled back into the team and, following pioneering surgery, was able to hear again. Due to a hospital administrative error, the operation also left Holland with the ability to read minds.

Now the most highly paid TV pundit in the galaxy, younger fans often forget that **Nathan Jones** was one of the deadliest goal-scorers of his generation. During a memorable season at Palangonia FC, Jones famously scored an unprecedented triple hat-trick, although as seven of the goals were bagged during half-time, some statisticians dispute the validity of this record despite the league controversially allowing the goals to stand.

After a solid-if-unremarkable career as a footballer, **Drew Keavey** is now best known for serving three terms as prime minister of the human compound on Palangonia, a period of prosperity and peace which was eventually shattered when

Keavey accidentally sat on the nuclear launch button and obliterated the neighbouring planet of Grawk. After leaving office, Keavey went on to describe the incident as 'a bit of a shame, if I'm honest'.

Geoff Lewis was one of the greatest goalkeepers in the history of Galactic League C and was such a fast sprinter that he would often double up as a striker in the same match, hoofing the ball towards goal before dashing up to the other end of the pitch to nod it in at the far post. David Seaman once described Lewis as 'the lovechild of me and Alan Shearer. Not literally – please make sure you emphasise that. There's no substance to any of those rumours.'

Rab Livingstone was signed from non-league football on the swamp-planet of Groiku VIII and went on to captain Palangonia FC to a league and cup double, though he later left the club after being exposed as a shape-shifting alien with the power to control the ball with his mind. Livingstone briefly returned to the club as manager before the board remembered why they'd got rid of him in the first place and removed him.

Better known by club's fans as 'The Midfielder', a clever nickname based on the position he played in the team, **Doug Maclellan** was a tough-tackling, never-say-die footballer who stubbornly refused to accept defeat, often refusing to allow the opposition to leave the pitch until Palangonia FC had won. Because of this, one match infamously lasted for just over six weeks before the club nicked a 1–0 win.

Originally hired by Palangonia FC as a groundskeeper, **Declan Lardybloke McEneaney** was spotted by manager Kevin Keegan completing a total of two back-to-back keepy-uppies after a training session and was offered a six-year playing contract on the spot. McEneaney went on to make a grand total of one substitute appearance for the club, after Keegan quickly realised he had made a terrible, impulsive mistake.

Liam and **Paul McEneaney** were arguably the most beloved strike partnership in Palangonia FC's history, with a combined 978 goals from 1,215 appearances, including two hat-tricks apiece in one match against Eddie Howe's Kvaanikk FC in the Galactic Cup Final. Liam said upon their retirement, 'We've always had a strong connection, although it's not as though—' '—We finish each other's sentences or anything like that,' Paul chipped in.

Andy Muckles was the first name on the team-sheet for four seasons, winning two Galactic Cups and one BAFTA (subsequently recalled by the Academy when they realised it had been awarded in error and was intended for Benedict Cumberbatch). Since retiring, Muckles opened his own bicycle shop, though it closed within two months as no one rides bikes in the future.

The first human to ever win Galactic Player of the Year, **Steve Murray** scored 47,557 goals in three seasons at Palangonia FC, a record which baffles statisticians to this day. While rumours persist that Murray is not real and that those three seasons were part of a massive computer simulation, Murray's tally still stands, even if the player himself has vanished without trace with no other record of him ever having existed.

A tough-tackling centre-half with a knack for scoring important headers, **Ross Paterson** will sadly be best remembered as perhaps the most reviled criminal in Palangonian legal history, the infamous 'Bakery Bandit' who repeatedly picked up cream buns and chocolate eclairs before putting them back on the counter and refusing to purchase them. Paterson remains on the run, with authorities offering a six-figure reward for any information leading to his capture.

A cultured playmaker once described by Teddy Sheringham as 'quite good apparently, though to be honest I haven't seen them and wouldn't know them if I passed them in the street', **David Puckridge** endeared himself to the Palangonia FC faithful by having the club crest tattooed on his face, an act of blind loyalty which later resulted in a potential transfer to a rival club falling through.

A fan favourite, **JP Rangaswami** was a striker who failed to score a single goal for the club during a four-season stay. After the club was awarded a last-minute penalty in the final match of the final season, Rangaswami stepped up only to spontaneously combust just before striking the ball. As a final indignity, Rangaswami was booked by the referee for unsportsmanlike conduct.

Described by the *Compound Chronicle* as 'basically fine', **Tom Reeve** was a regular on the left-side of the Palangonia FC defence and became renowned for his phobia of crossing the halfway line, which caused him to suffer nosebleeds, cramps and violent wind. 'People would laugh,' Reeve later lamented, 'but it was a real pain in the arse. Actually, that was one of the other symptoms.'

Beloved by fans for his loyalty to the club and for publicly stating he would never play for any other side, **Dean Rutland** was a holding midfielder during Palangonia FC's least successful period, during which they suffered three successive relegations. 'I don't care how low we fall,' Rutland said after the third demotion, 'I love this club and will never leave.' Rutland is currently a free agent.

A solid right-back, **Mathias Thu Utheim** was ever-present during Palangonia FC's promotion season to Galactic League B, scoring three goals and famously grappling with two Winged Terrors which swooped down to feed during a match. Sadly, the creatures were too powerful and Utheim was ultimately killed and eaten. The referee promptly booked Utheim for leaving the pitch without permission.

A club stalwart who both played for and managed Palangonia FC, **David Tonks** infamously failed to win a single match in either capacity. Disappointing fans for frequently forgetting the name of the club and for repeatedly stating in press conferences that football was dull and that his true passion was for ice-sculpting, Tonks currently hosts a high-brow TV arts and culture documentary series on Palangonia which regularly achieves viewing figures in the high single digits.

Marcus Townsend joined Palangonia mid-season during their dark days in Galactic League F and helped the club to successive promotions. Since retiring, Townsend moved into the film industry and has won two Oscars (one for Best Supporting Actor, the other for Best Sound Effects Editing) and is currently working on a biopic of Nottingham Forest legend Ian Woan.

Once described by Darren Huckerby as 'slightly taller than I expected', **Steve Townsend** played a key role in the push for the Galactic League A title, which was ultimately unsuccessful as the club were relegated with -10 points, the deduction a result of the league's disapproval of Townsend's 'provocative' hairstyle. Townsend later moved to Skrenkle Rovers on a free transfer, scoring once in a game that was later abandoned due to poor weather. 'It still counts,' he insisted, though league administrators continue to disagree.

Paul Walke was the most prolific striker in Galactic League C in his debut season with twenty-six goals before Christmas, before being sacked by Palangonia FC for failing a drugs test. Although it later transpired that the results had been mixed up at the lab with those of a local drug addict serial killer known as 'Hobo Frank', the club refused to re-sign Walke after he cleared his name, stating, 'The paperwork would be too much of a hassle.'

Best known today as the only player never to have had a touch of the ball during a match in a fifteen-year career, **Vahid Walker** was a reliable presence at centre-half for Palangonia FC and won two league titles. 'My only regret,' Walker said upon retiring, 'was that I never touched the ball. I mean, obviously it's going to be that. What else would it be? It's bloody embarrassing.'

Nicknamed 'The Troll' after a misleading estate agent listing for his new flat resulted in him having to live under a bridge for two seasons, **Steven White** was a true fan-favourite at Palangonia FC, despite failing to make a single appearance and only once even making the bench. Since retiring, White has attempted to buy the club but his bid of £1.79 was described by the board as 'below what we'd hoped for' and the deal ultimately fell through.

Dr Pete Williams was the Palangonia FC club physician until he was drafted in at centre-forward during one of the worst injury crises in their history, when half the squad came down with severe back injuries (which manager Kevin Keegan insisted was nothing to do with the players being enlisted to help him move house). Williams went on to score two own goals and get himself sent off for a deliberate handball. Keegan hailed his debut as 'one of the most dynamic I've ever seen' and Williams went on to play up front for a further three seasons, scoring no goals.

Jonathan Windeatt was the most prolific scorer of headers in Galactic League history, though his tactic of flying just above ground level in a hot-air balloon to outjump opponents was frequently controversial. Infamously, at the end of another high-scoring season, Windeatt's balloon was taken by a stiff breeze in the eighty-sixth minute and quickly disappeared beyond the horizon. Windeatt has never been found, though authorities later admitted that they hadn't really looked.

Phil Young holds the astonishing record of having been on the winning side in every match played for Palangonia FC. 'I'm very proud – it's something to tell the grandkids,' Young said in an interview with the *Compound Chronicle*. While some cynics have pointed out that Young only played one match for the club (as an eighty-seventh-minute substitute in a 1–0 win over the Drabalfa Colony) before being sold, it is nevertheless a record that remains unparalleled in the Galactic League to this day.

Sondre Alnes Ytterland became player-manager of Palangonia FC after Alan Curbishley's ill-fated reign came to an end following an acrimonious four-day period during which the club lost every single game it played (one). Initially a temporary measure, Ytterland's reign proved so successful that the fans demanded the job be awarded full-time. Ytterland led the club to promotion to Galactic League A before being poached by Real Grunfaal, though Ytterland's tenure there came to a premature end when its planet was completely obliterated by an asteroid.

Unbound is the world's first crowdfunding publisher, established in 2011.

We believe that wonderful things can happen when you clear a path for people who share a passion. That's why we've built a platform that brings together readers and authors to crowdfund books they believe in – and give fresh ideas that don't fit the traditional mould the chance they deserve.

This book is in your hands because readers made it possible. Everyone who pledged their support is listed below. Join them by visiting unbound.com and supporting a book today.

Best Alrewas Book Club
Alan Bews
Bill Biggles
Andy Bignell
Brian Bilston
Matt Bingham
Alex Bingle
Adrian Birchenough
Shelagh Birkett
Paul Bloomfield
Ita Bloyce
Neil Boom
John Boothroyd
Jon Bounds
Jean-Marc Bouvier
Rhiannon Bouvier
Simon Bowes
Lee Bowmar
Stewart Boyle
Gary Bradburn
Laura Bradburn
Nicky Bramley
Ole Andreas Brandal
Steve Brandreth
Tony Braqets
Gary Bristow
Alice Broadribb
Sarah Brooks
Sean Broughton
Chris Brown
David Brown
Jake Brown
Simon Brown
Steven Brown
Tom Brown
Barry Browne
Brian Browne
Ben Bruce
Kelli Bryan
Richard Bryan

Michael Bryant
Treefrog Buchan
Edmond Buckley
Neill Buckley
Mihnea Bucur
Gillian Buksh
Darren Bull
Alex Bullock
Alaine Bulmer
Rick Burin
Ryan Burnham
Josh Burnhope
Gavin Burns
Kevin Burt
Richard Burwell
Dan Bushell
David Bushell
Ruth Busse
Brian Cackett
Stephen Caines
Rich Cairns
Dominic Caisley
Daniel Calder
Darren Campbell
Graham Campbell
Mary Campbell
Anthony Candler
David Capel
Henry Carden
Steve Cargill
Scot Carrick
Dan Carter
Alex Chadwick
David Chamberlain
David Chantrey
Greg Cheesman
Brett Childs
Rory Chilton
Sean Chivers
Warren Chrismas

Joe Christian
Iain Christie
Ben Churchill
Richard Clack
Dave Clare
Jason Clark
Josh Clark
Oliver & Harry Clark
Simon Clark
Rich Clarke
Ian Clarkson
Stuart Clarkson
Neil Cleghorn
David Clitheroe
Michael Coates
Mark Cockin
Simon Cogan
Daniel Cole
Alistair Coleman
Charlie Coles
Ian Collen
Paul Collen
Andy Collin
Paul Collingwood
Joe Conlon
Lex Coogans-Finch
Daniel Cook
Richard Cook
Stuart Cook
Simon Coope
David Cooper
Lee Cooper
Michael Cooper
Liam Core
Lewis Corfield
Tom Cotterill
Dermot Cousins
Mark Cowen
Dan Cowley
Andy Cowx

Christopher Cox
Richard Coyle
Dave Cranmer
Rob Cranmer
Jonathan Cressey
Alan Curbishley
Aidan Curran
Andrew Curran
Kevin Curran
Jude Curtin
Stuart Dade
T Dams
Colin Davey
Chris Davidson
Luke Davidson
Mark Davidson
Michael Davidson
Ashley Davies
Len Davies
Shaun Davies
Tom Davies
Wayne Davies
Ian Davis
John Davis
Andy Day
Dominic Daymond
Nichola Deadman
John Dean
Maurice Deans Jnr
Hamish Deas
Adam Deller
A. Paul Denial
Alan Devine
James Diamond
John Diamond
Bruce Dickinson
Christina Didsbury
Dave Disley-Jones
Tom Dixon
Michael Docherty

Bryan Dodds
Rob Dolan
Michael Donkin
Ian Doorbar
Colin Douglas
Leo Downes
James Dowthwaite
John Dowthwaite
Stephen Duda
Michael Duffy
Kevin Dunbar
Mark Dunne
David Durose
Alex Duval
Oliver Dyson
Gary Ede
Stephen Edgar
Phil Edmonds
Duncan Edwards
Mike Edwards
Kevin Edworthy
David Eley
Chris Elliott
Rob Elliott
Tom Elson
Greg Emmerson
Debbie Enever
Ian Ericson
Adam Errington
Nigel Eustace
Kevin Evans
Graham Fabb
John Fahy
Calum Farmar
Pat Farr
Neil Feasey
Tom & Will Featherstone
Chris Findlay
Kevin Fingleton
Matt Finney

Arlene Finnigan
Amy Fitzgerald
Andrew Fletcher
Chris 'Fletch' Fletcher
Colin Fletcher
Mark Fletcher
Ollie Fletcher
Michael Follett
Peter Neil Griffin Follett
Richard Fong
Ian Ford
Mark Forrest
Thomas Fortune Bardsley
Keith Foster
Pete Foster
Gary Fothergill
Chris Fox
Neil Fox
Paul Frame
Rob Francis
Luke Freeman
Simon Freer
Peter Fry
Tony Fulford
Howard Gadsby
Mark Galsworthy
Paul Garbett
David John Gardner
Wayne Garvie
Alex Gatt
Martin Gedge
Andy Gell
Gentleman Once
Mike Gibbs
Chris Gilbert
Andy Gill
Aly Gillani
Stuart Gillespie
Mark Gillies
Adam Girling

James Glennard
Mike Glover
Susan Godfrey
Ed Goldring
Matt Goldsack
Brian Goldsmith
Mike Good
James Goodger
Mike Gore
Joyce Gosling
Tom Gower
Matt Graham
Mark Gratton
Stuart Gray
Andrew Green
Daniel C S Greenway
Chris Griffiths
Peter Grutenberg Cresswell
Jo Gurney
Steven Gyford
Neil Haddon
Kevin Hague
Gavin Haigh
Thad Hait
Ardit Haliti
Ben Hall
Benjamin Hall
Steven Hallmark
Matthew Hallsworth
Raymond Halpenny
Nathan Halsall
Nathan Hamer
Mike Hampson
Neil Hampton
Russell P Hancock
Michael Hann MBE TD
Daniel Hannon
Richard Harding
Russ Harding
Tim Hardy

Kyle Harman
Alex Harrison
Mark Harrison
David Hartrick
Josh Harvey
David Hatcher
Dan Hawcutt
Peter Hawkins
Philip Hawkins
Ben Hayes
Ben Hayward
Alex Heale
Adam Heath
David Heatley
Andrew Hebden
Thomas Hebell
William Hedley
Michael Helkvist
Jonny Henderson
Mark Henderson
Adam Henley
Simon Heptinstall
Chris Herron
Lee Herron
Damon Hesford
Phil Hey
Lynne Hibbard
Katie Higginson
Tom Higginson
Matthew Hilton
Rob Hind
Karen Hinojosa
Ray Hockley
Martin Hodgson
Stefan Hodgson
Ray Hogan
Geoff Hogg
Jarrett Holland
Nick Holmes
Andy Holt

Andrew Holtham
Sheila Hood
Scott Hopkins
Mike Horan
Fallon Horan-Swords
Andrew Horbury
Graeme Horner
Kate Horton
Ian Hosler
John "Haliborange"
  Howard
Richard Howarth
Simon Howe
Nicola Howell
Will Hugall
Dan Huggins
Gwen Humphrey
Carl Humphreys
Edd Hunt
Dave Hutchinson
Ben Ingham
Cal Innes
Marie Innes
Mary Innes
Pat & Brian Innes
Mark Isham
Katherine Jackson
Nick Jackson
Richard Jackson
Adrian "Jambo" James
Henry James
Pete Christopher James
Andy Jay
Robin Jeeps
Tim Jeffries
Huw Jenkins
Simon Jenkins
Gareth John
Brendan Johnson
Ed Johnson

Mark Johnson
Michael Johnson
William Johnson
Aled Llŷr Jones
Nathan Jones
Richard S Jones
Sara Jones
Joop
Stephen Jorgenson-Murray
Darren Kahan
Laurie KazMarchski
Drew Keavey
David Keenan
Albert Keirse
Danielle Kelly
Grant Kelly
Ryan Kelly
Tim Kelly
Tom Kelly
Stuart Kennedy
Dan Kieran
Stefan Kilarski
Ross Kilburn
Nick Killip
Iain King
Matthew Kingdon
Johnathan Kirkland
Richard Kirwan
Alan Knight
Matt Knight
Paul Knowles
Svein Frode Kvam
Paul La Planche
Evelyn Laing
John Laking
Patricia Langridge
Oliver Larkin
Kristian Laskey
Jack Latham
Laura Lavender

Kieren Laverick
W Tom Lawrie
Chris Laws
Phil Laws
Stephen Lazenby
Heather Leask
Marc Lebailly
Damian Lees
Fiona Lensvelt
Geoff Lewis
Richard Lewis
Nicola Lewton
Jacqueline Leyland
Richard Lindsay
Claire Livingstone
Rab Livingstone
Robin Llewelyn-Leach
Charlie Logan
Kari Long
Ed Losty
Peter Lucas
Phil Luker
Stephen Lund
Rebecca Lyttle
Bea Mackay
Siobhan Mackenzie
Doug Maclellan
Chris MacLennan
Dara Maguire
Michael Major
Jack Malone
Josh Mandel
Brian Manderson
Damian Manley
Ben Mark
John Marshall
Tony Martin
Andrew Martindale
Manuela Maruccia-Hirvelä
Ben Mason

Simon Mason
David Matkins
James Matkins
Andrew Mawby
Stuart Maxwell
Simon Mayhew-Archer
Antony Mays
Craig McCallum
Murray McCann
Stephen McCardle
Trevor McCarthy
Dave McCormack
Ed McCosh
Martin McCraw
David McDonald
Gerry Mcelroy
Declan Lardybloke
    McEneaney
Liam & Paul McEneaney
Steven McFarlane
Clare McGann
Mick McGonnell
Lauren McGovern
Luke McGregor
Phil Mcilwaine
Jason Mcintyre
Susan McIvor
Emma, Paul & Sam
    McKenzie
Mark Mckenzie
Lisa McLaren
Helen McLean
Liam McMahon
Rich McNab
Yvonne McNab
Dick Mcnulty
Alec Meadows
Michael Midghall
Helen Milburn
Scott Millar

David Millington
Simon Mills
Richard Milne
Duncan Milner
Jack Mitchell
Rob Mitchell
John Mitchinson
James Moran
Paul Morgan
Laurence Morris
Andrew Moss
Andy Muckles
Steve Mullins
Charles Munro
Stephen Munro
Mark Murdock
Kerry Murphy
Nick Murphy
Daniel Murray
Ollie Murray
Steve Murray
Joshua Murray-Nevill
Martin Nacey
Keshini Naidoo
Ben Nanson
Rahul Natarajan
Carlo Navato
David Neeley
Michael Neil
Christopher J Newman
Lauren Newton
Chris Newton-Smith
Simon Nicholls
Paul Nightingale
Christopher Noel
Patrick O'Brien
Tim O'Brien
Kevin O'Carroll
Paddy O'Hara
Mark O'Neill

Alex Odlin
Andrew Ormondroyd
Bridget Orr
Julian Osborne
Louis Osman
Martin Oswick
Colette Owen
Gareth Owen
Stuart Owen
Martin Oxley
James Packman
Darren Page
Jim Paine
John Palmer
Bettina Palmi
Alison Parker
John Parkin
Gavin Partridge
Penny Pash
Gary Paterson
Ross Paterson
Tom Paterson
Chris Paton
Kieron Patterson
John Pattinson
Michael Payne
James Payton
Marc Pearson
Robbie Pearson
Ian Peckett
Louis Peluso-White
John Perry
Megan Perry
David Pharoah
Sarah Phelps
Gillian Philip
Sam Pickering
Nick Pickles
Tom Pigden
Simon Pilling

Colin Pimlott
Jonathan Pinnock
Keiron Piper
Jon Plested
Justin Pollard
Steph Pomfrett
Andrew Potapa
Nicholas 'Ninety Night'
  Power
Nick Power
Simon Prentice
Barry Price
Martin Priestley
Rachael Prior
David Pritchard
Philip Proud
David Puckridge
Ann Pugh
Mike Pullen
Charlie Pybus
Gary Pyke
Margaret Pym
Kristján Ragnarsson
John Rain
Rainy
JP Rangaswami
Mike Ratford
Robert Rea
Simon Reap
Chris Redhead
David Reed
Mark Reed
Tom Reeve
Ian Revell
Andrew Richardson
Karis Richardson
Sam Richardson
Liam Riley
Connor Roberts
Jayne Roberts

Steve Roberts
Dylan Robinson
Paul Robinson
Martin Robson
Gareth Roddy
Chris Roden
Lewis Rodgers
Will Rogers
Tom Roper
Mathew Ross
Andrew Rothwell
Paul Royal
Peter Rudd
Nick Rusling
Andrew Russell
David Russell
Dean Rutland
Afraz Sajadi
Nicola Salliss
Shanine Salmon
Brian Salter
Russell Sant Cassia
Mark Saveall
Mitch Sayers
Richard Scargill
Mike Scott Thomson
Holly Seddon
Matthew Shale
Rob Shalliker
Joanne Sheppard
Paul Shields
Mark Shufflebotham
Ian Shutt
Andrew James Sillett
Gary Simpson
Paul Simpson
Andrew Simpson-Lynas
Tom Sims
Ryan Singh
Peter Skinner

Kane Slack
SleepyPete
John Slough
Darrell Smart
Stuart Smedley
Richard Smeeton
Arthur Smith
Dick Smith
Edward Smith
Ian Smith
John Smith
Martin Smith
Neil Smith
Rose-Marie Smith
Robin Smyth
Jamie Snaddon
Amanda Snowdon
Keith Somerville
Hetty Sparkles
Jamie Spears
Andy Spink
Mark Spoors
Brian Spurrell
Sam Stafford
Matthew Stanley
Jon Steed
IBW Steen
Joseph Stephens
Paul Stevens
Will Stevens
Daniel Stewart
Daniel Stokes
Graham Stokoe
David Stott
John Stott
Richard Strange
Rob Stroud
Andrew Sturtevant
Matt Stutely
Daniel Sugarman

Andrew Sutherland
Gary Sutton
Jackie Leon Sysum
Lee Taggart
Neil Tague
Simon Tait
William Tait
David Tang
Joseph Taylor
Mark Taylor
Richard Taylor
Sean Taylor
Laura Taylor-Innes
George Thain
Geoff Thickins
Mike Thompson
David Thomson
Gary Threadgold
Mark Thurkettle
Graeme Tierney
Stuart Tilston
Alastair Tomlinson
David Tonks
Marc Towers
Marcus Townsend
Steve Townsend
Chris Tracey
Lindsay Treadgold
Jonathan Tredray
Ross Tregaskis
Joe Trigg
Kev Trotter
Bob Truswell
Tim Turner
Michael Usher
Mathias Thu Utheim
Matt Valins
Jan Arne Vestbø
Steve Virgo
Dan Waddell

James Waddington
Martin Wade
Ivan Wainewright
Michael Wake
Paul Walke
Andy Walker
Don Walker
Nathan Walker
Nick Walker
Vahid Walker
Sonny Wall
Verge Walton
Chris Warnes
James Warrington
Andrew Watson
Elaine Watson
James Watson
Duncan Way
Pete Way
Matthew Webb
Christine Webster
John Welch

Neil Westgarth
Samuel Whaley
Lee Wharfe
Joe Wheeler
Ian White
Steven White
Jeffrey Whitehead
Tom Whittaker
Dan Whitton
WhovianMummah
Greg Wilcox
Nigel Wilkinson
Dr. Pete Williams
Elliott Williams
Matt Williams
Chris Willman
Willpiss
Chris Wilson
Gavin Wilson
Rob Wilson
Stuart Wilson
Jonathan Windeatt

Ben Wingate
Barry Winn
Ben Wood
Joe Wood
Ray Wood
Will Wood
Damon Woodhouse
Emma Woodrow
James Woods
Sue Yarham
Adam Yates
Ben Yolland
Stephen Yolland
David York
Rob York
Adam Young
Ben Young
Fraser Young
Joel Young
Phil Young
Sondre Alnes Ytterland
Anthony Zacharzewski